"Absorbing scenario combining recent events and fiction so seamlessly as to leave readers wondering where the line between them lies."
CBA MARKETPLACE

"A good thriller with a solid plot . . . a feeling of authenticity."
THE JERUSALEM POST

"Sends chills up my spine about how on target and current . . . . Couldn't stop reading it."
PINE BLUFF COMMERCIAL

"Combines the suspense of Tom Clancy with the drama of *Blackhawk Down,* the complexity of *Mission Impossible,* the dogged morality of *High Noon* . . . . The result is a story that causes the reader to wake up in the middle of the night wondering how much of it is true."
MOODY MAGAZINE

"Filled with action, intrigue, and events that could have been taken from the headlines. This is a must-read."
SEAN HANNITY
FOX News' "Hannity & Colmes," Author of *Let Freedom Ring*

"An exciting, solid, action-packed adventure about a Marine who, like the author, knows the meaning of *Semper Fidelis.*"
JOE FOSS, Brig. Gen. USMC (Ret.)
WWII Ace and Congressional Medal of Honor Recipient

"Superb read. . . . A primer to the hidden works and inner mechanisms of the White House and the National Security Council."
GENERAL CHARLES C. KRULAK, USMC (Ret.)
31st Commandant of the Marine Corps

THE
JERICHO
SANCTION

OLIVER NORTH

AND JOE MUSSER

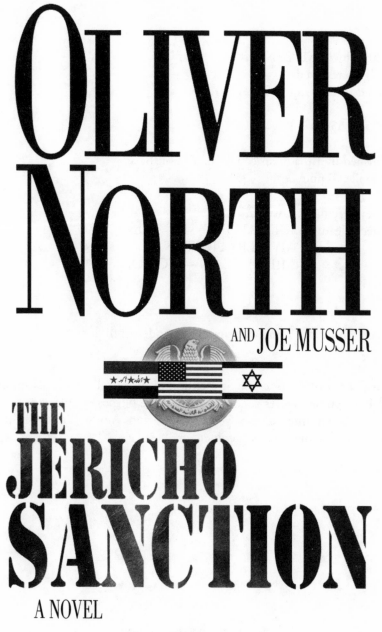

THE JERICHO SANCTION

A NOVEL

BROADMAN
&HOLMAN
PUBLISHERS

NASHVILLE, TENNESSEE

© 2003 by Oliver L. North
All rights reserved
Printed in the United States of America

0-8054-2551-9

Published by Broadman & Holman Publishers,
Nashville, Tennessee

Dewey Decimal Classification: F
Subject Heading: KIDNAPPING—FICTION
MYSTERY FICTION
MIDDLE EAST—FICTION

Jacket: AndersonThomas Design, www.andersonthomas.com

1 2 3 4 5 6 7 8 9 10 07 06 05 04 03

For Betsy,
who once again waited and prayed
while I went off to another war

IN MEMORIAM

O *peration Iraqi Freedom* began on 21 March 2003 with a night helo-borne assault against Saddam Hussein's forces in the vicinity of Basra on the Faw Peninsula. As the attack commenced, a sandstorm and smoke from oil wells set afire by Saddam's forces reduced visibility to near zero. Shortly thereafter, the third USMC CH-46E helicopter in our flight crashed, killing all the U.S. Marines and Royal Marine Commandos aboard.

This book is dedicated to the memory of the four U.S. Marines of HMM 268 and the eight members of the Royal Marine Commando contingent who were the first casualties of the war to liberate Iraq.

U.S. MARINES:

Major Jay Thomas Aubin, 36 (Waterville, Maine)

Captain Ryan Anthony Beaupre, 30 (St. Anne, Illinois)

Staff Sergeant Kendall Damon Waters-Bey, 29 (Baltimore, Maryland)

Corporal Brian Matthew Kennedy, 25 (Houston, Texas)

ROYAL MARINE COMMANDOS:

Major Jason Ward

Captain Philip Stuart Guy

Warrant Officer Mark Stratford

Color Sergeant John Cecil

Operations Mechanic 2nd Class Ian Seymour

Sergeant Les Hehir

Lance Bombadier Llewelyn Karl Evans

Marine Sholto Hedenskog

CONTENTS

ACKNOWLEDGMENTS

Tikrit, Iraq
25 April 2003

E very old soldier wants to believe that the "Best of the Best" were those warriors he served with under fire. That was my sense when I arrived here in Saddam's hometown to cover the U.S. Marines and Army in *Operation Iraqi Freedom*. I should have known better, for much of my life has been spent among heroes like these men and women serving here. They are the same kind of humble and unsung heroes of whom I make people aware through my FOX News television series, *War Stories*.

No sane person who has ever *really* been to a war ever *wants* to go to another. There is nothing glorious about war. I first saw the carnage of combat as a Rifle Platoon commander in Vietnam. And I've also been an eyewitness to the bravery and horror of war in Central America, Lebanon, Iran, Afghanistan, Israel—and now, Iraq. Thankfully, there are those willing to fight for a just cause. And when they do, they deserve to have what they are doing reported accurately. That's why I'm here on the banks of the Tigris River.

As an "embedded" war correspondent for FOX News Channel having now lived with the First Marine Expeditionary Force and the Fourth Infantry Division for the better part of the last two months, it is evident that there have never been brighter, better equipped, more thoroughly trained soldiers, sailors, airmen, guardsmen, and Marines than these. No military force has ever gone so far, so fast, and with so few casualties as this group of young Americans and our British allies. Their skill and daring, their discipline and endurance are without parallel in the world today. No other armed force could do what they have done. They put an end to Saddam Hussein's brutal tyranny and liberated a people. Being with them while they did it has been a privilege and an inspiration.

I'm grateful to Roger Ailes, my boss at FOX News, for dispatching me here to cover this war. Griff Jenkins, my cameraman/producer, lived through all of it with me—and somehow managed to hold the camera steady, even while getting shot at! And Pamela Browne, senior producer for *War Stories*, turned miles of videotape into a documentary that showed these young Americans to be as good as they really are.

Once more, Joe Musser, my friend and partner in this book effort, made it possible to finish a work. In the midst of creating our first book, *Mission Compromised*, I left him holding the pen while I ran off to cover those chasing Osama bin Laden in Afghanistan. This time, for research we went together on counter-terrorist operations with the Israeli Defense Forces. But then I left for two months in Iraq. Joe's lovely wife Nancy must be wondering what war I'll be covering when our next deadline comes due.

Because of my protracted absence in Iraq, my friend and editor, Gary Terashita, has had to read and edit this book a chapter at a time over many months. His advice and counsel have been invaluable—even when conveyed sixty-five hundred miles over a satellite telephone via my steadfast assistant, Marsha Fishbaugh.

Kim Terashita had to proof and pray her way through a belatedly delivered manuscript, and Kim Overcash found ways for Gary and me to connect—even through the "fog of war." Despite distance and delays, project editor Lisa Parnell somehow pulled all of this together in time for publication, and Mary Beth Shaw in Author Relations found ways to keep me informed.

Marketing Director John Thompson, Sales Director Susanne Anhalt, Publicity Director Heather Hulse, Senior Publicist Robin Patterson, Duane Ward of the Premiere Group, and Cathy Saypol Public Relations have all performed "above and beyond the call of duty" in promoting and selling my books—and I'm grateful. Thanks, too, for another great cover design by Greg Pope and team that "tells the story."

Of course there would be no "story" to tell without the encouragement and inspiration of my wife and our children and their mates. Once again I have left them in order to hang around with heroes in harm's way. But while I have been here in Iraq, Betsy, Tait and Tom, Stuart and Ellen, Sarah and Martin, and Dornin have all prayed for my safety—and I have seen ample evidence of their prayers being answered. In their faith and affection I am reminded of God's love in my own life—and how easy it is to appear daring when you simply know where you are going . . . and why you are going there.

Semper Fidelis,
Oliver L. North

GLOSSARY

ACS. Automated Case File System of the FBI; part of the FBI's Electronic Case File database, equivalent to a closed FBI computer intranet (also see ECF).

Ahm Al-Khass. Amn Al-Khass. Iraq's Special Security Services; also SSS.

AGM. Air to ground missile.

aka. Also known as; in describing a name and an alias.

AO. Area of operation; of Israeli counter-terrorism units, such as airports, harbors, or various national borders. Different units are assigned to each AO (also see Sayeret Matkal; S'13).

ATGM. Anti-tank guided missile.

AWACS. Airborne Warning and Control System (USA).

Bakshish. The Arabic word used to denote an expected payment or bribe.

BOLO. Acronym for "Be on Lookout"; when used as a noun, it is the term used for the picture, or artist's rendering, of a person being sought by law enforcement organizations, and refers to the photo, fax, poster, or other "hard copy" or printed version that can be placed into the hands of various agencies and their personnel.

BOQ. Base Officers Quarters.

C. The abbreviation for chief of British SIS (see MI6). A green *C* in the logo of the SIS is an allusion to its founder, the original C, Sir Mansfield Cumming. A SIS tradition is that all chiefs are known simply as C and sign their documents using green ink.

CAR15. The carbine version of the U.S. M16A1 rifle (also see M4).

CENTCOM. (Also USCENTCOM) Central Command (U.S. Central Command), one of the nine U.S. unified military command centers. CENTCOM is located at MacDill Air Force Base, Tampa, Florida, and is the unified command responsible for U.S. security interests in twenty-five nations in Central Asia, Africa, and the Gulf Region of the Middle East. CENTCOM carries out its missions through a joint service staff of nine hundred, drawn from components of the U.S. Army, Air Force, Navy, Marine Corps, and Special Command forces.

CinC. The commander in chief. The CinC of the U.S. Central Command (CENT-COM) has a rank of four-star general or admiral.

CO. Commanding officer.

COD. Carrier onboard delivery; an air "taxi" that shuttles people and equipment to and from an aircraft carrier. The usual aircraft for this is a C-2A Greyhound propeller plane.

"Cover Your Six." Military jargon; terms for direction are based on a clock dial: twelve o'clock is straight ahead, three o'clock to the right, nine to the left, and six is behind or to the rear.

CT. Counter-terror (ism).

Dead drop. A secret location where packages can be left or picked up.

DIA. Defense Intelligence Agency (U.S.); military intelligence gathering arm of the Pentagon.

DOD. Department of Defense.

Duvdevan. Israeli counter-intelligence unit (also see EU) that is responsible for operations and missions inside the country; some of these missions have included targeted killings (assassinations) of terrorists that were authorized by the government.

DZ. Drop zone.

ECF. The FBI's computerized Electronic Case File system that allows agents and any other authorized users to access classified files for intelligence, background, and cross-referencing of data. It also represents a treasure trove of information useful to spies.

ETA. Estimated time of arrival.

EU. Engagement units; those Israeli units that have counter-terrorism as a secondary specialty. Each EU is organized under an IDF command within the country, including North Command, Central Command, and South Command. The Sayeret Golany EU is based in the North Command; three EUs are based in the Central Command (Sayeret T'zanhanim, Sayeret Nahal, and Sayeret Duvdevan); and Sayeret Givaty is the EU based in the South Command.

EWO. Electronic warfare officer.

Federal Security Service. Successor to the KGB; also SVR.

FFP. Final firing position; usually refers to a position used by a sniper.

FIR. Flight information region.

Firm, The. The internal nickname for the United Kingdom's Secret Intelligence Service (also see MI6).

FM. Foreign minister.

G-1. Administrative and personnel function for a military command of brigade or higher (also see S-1).

G-2. Intelligence and counterintelligence function for a military command of brigade or higher (also see S-2).

G-3. Operations and training function for a military command of brigade or higher (also see S-3).

G-4. Logistics and supply function for a military command of brigade or higher (also see S-4).

GCHQ. British Signals and Intelligence Agency, similar to U.S. National Security Agency.

GID. General Intelligence Directorate (Syria); see IAA.

GRU. Soviet Military Intelligence Service.

Gunny. Slang for Marine gunnery sergeant.

H-hour. Military designation for time of an attack.

HAHO. High altitude, high opening parachute deployment.

HALO. High altitude, low opening parachute deployment.

Hezbollah. Party of God (also known as Islamic Jihad, Revolutionary Justice Organization, Organization of the Oppressed on Earth, and Islamic Jihad for the Liberation of Palestine). Known or suspected to have been involved in numerous terrorist attacks, especially on the U.S. and Israel.

IAF. Israeli Air Force.

IAA. *Idarat al-Amn al-'Amm.* General Intelligence Directorate, Syria; the agency responsible for gathering intelligence and dealing with covert operations for the country (similar to the U.S. FBI or CIA).

IDF. Israeli Defense Forces; the military force of the state of Israel.

IFF. Identification Friend or Foe icon; a graphics box that is displayed on a computer screen for reference, similar to that on an air traffic controller's screen that identifies the various aircraft in the vector.

IM. Instant Messaging. Wireless instant messaging differs from e-mail primarily in that its main focus is immediate end-user delivery and does not use typical computer architecture and hardware.

INC. Iraqi National Congress, the anti-Saddam opposition movement of Iraq.

In sha' Allah. Arabic, from the Quran, means "God willing."

IR. Infrared.

ISA. Intelligence Support Activity; a small, well-trained, and highly capable intelligence unit of the U.S. Army, operating across the world on special operations focused on counter-terrorism and providing intelligence on black market nuclear and bio/chemical weapons activity.

ISEG. International Sanctions Enforcement Group; a thirty-eight-man joint U.S.-UK unit.

ISET. International Sanctions Enforcement Team; each joint U.S.-UK team has seven men.

JCS. Joint Chiefs of Staff.

KY. NATO-standard encryption equipment.

LMG. Light machine gun.

LZ. Landing zone.

LRRP. Long Range Reconnaisance Patrol.

M4. Carbine version of the U.S. M16A2 rifle.

MI6. United Kingdom's Secret Intelligence Service; deals with foreign intelligence gathering (similar to U.S. CIA).

MIT. *Milli Istihbarat Teskilati* is the Turkish intelligence service (similar to the CIA).

MASINT Program. Top Secret Measurement and Signature Intelligence program of the CIA, believed to be one of the documents given to the KGB by their Russian FBI mole.

MATKAL. General staff of the Israeli Defense Forces High Command.

MEU. Marine expeditionary unit; a reinforced Infantry battalion of approximately eighteen hundred men.

Mossad. A Hebrew acronym for the Institute for Intelligence and Special Operations. It is the Israeli Foreign Intelligence Service.

MOD. Minister of Defense.

G L O S S A R Y

NCO. Noncommissioned officer in the military services.

NRO. National Reconnaissance Office. The NRO designs, builds, and operates the U.S.'s reconnaissance (spy) satellites. NRO products are provided to customers that include the CIA and the Department of Defense. NRO satellites can anticipate potential trouble spots around the world, help plan military operations, and monitor their execution.

NSA. National Security Agency. As the U.S.'s cryptologic organization, NSA coordinates, directs, and performs highly specialized activities to protect U.S. information systems and produce foreign intelligence information (intel). A high-tech organization, NSA is on the leading edge of electronic communications and data processing. NSA is also one of the most important centers of foreign language analysis and research within the U.S. government.

NSC. National Security Council.

NTDS. Naval tactical data system.

NVD. Night-vision device; an optical device for sighting targets in darkness through a scope mounted on a rifle or other weapon.

NVG. Night-vision goggles; worn by soldiers or special operators to see in the dark.

OPCON. Operational Control; a military term used to specify what headquarters unit has responsibility for another unit within its zone of action during a specific operation. At some point following an operation, OpCon would shift back to its "parent" or original headquarters.

PAL. Permissive action links are supplemented by sophisticated coded switch systems. PALs are devices that prevent the release or launch of an armed nuclear weapon by terrorists or rogue military leaders.

PAX. Military abbreviation for "passengers."

PFLP. Popular Front for the Liberation of Palestine, a terrorist organization.

PFLP-GC. The General Command of the PFLP.

PM. Prime Minister.

POTUS. President of the United States.

QRF. Quick Reaction Force (U.S. Marines).

RAF. Royal Air Force (Great Britain).

RLEM. Rifle launched entry munition; a door-breaching device that is used in counter-terrorism and hostage situations to take down a door, including steel or other reinforced entries (also see Simon).

RPG. Rocket-propelled grenade.

RTO. Radio transmitter operator. The acronym is used in military jargon for the radio operator.

S-1. Administrative and personnel function for a battalion or regiment military staff or command.

S-2. Intelligence and counter-intelligence function for a battalion or regiment military staff or command.

S-3. Operations and training function for a battalion or regiment military staff or command.

S-4. Logistics and supply function for a battalion or regiment military staff or command.

S'13. Israeli counter-terrorism unit, responsible for foreign (outside of Israel's borders) maritime operations and counter-terrorism missions.

SAM. Surface to air missile.

Sanctum space. An area where secure communications can be made, usually sound-proofed and free from electronic eavesdropping.

SATINT. Satellite intelligence; gathered through orbiting satellites offering images, telemetry, radio, and video transmissions for military and intelligence purposes.

SAR. Search and rescue.

SAS. Special Air Service; elite unit of the British Royal Army and Air Force used for special operations.

Sayeret Matkal. Israeli elite commando and counter-terrorism force, which is claimed by some to also carry out "extrajudicial" executions, assigned to foreign (outside of Israel's borders) operations and counter-terrorism missions.

SCIF. Sensitive Compartmented Information Facility.

SECDEF. Secretary of Defense (U.S.).

SF. Special Forces.

SHABACH. Israeli general security service.

SHABAS. Israel prison service.

Shin Bet. Israeli internal general security service.

SIGINT. Signal Intelligence; gathered through interceptions of telephone, radio, satellite, or other transmitted signals, as done by NSA and ECHQ.

SIM card. Subscriber Identity Module for Iridium Satellite Phone.

Simon. Door-breaching rifle grenade (see RLEM).

SMG. Submachine gun.

SOARS. Special Operations Aviation Regiment Section.

SOP. Standard operating procedure.

SSS. See Amn Al-Khass.

Stand-off Rod. The front projectile element of the Simon or RLEM that carries the explosive charge to disable and breach a door (also see Simon; RLEM).

STU-III. U.S. government encryption telephone system for classified communications.

SVR. See Federal Security Service.

SWS. Sniper Weapons System.

UNSCOM. United Nations Special Commission for weapons inspections.

UNSG. United Nations Secretary General.

USG. United States Government.

Wadi. A dry watercourse that is found in desert geography; a riverbed, dry creek, or valley.

WHSR. White House Situation Room.

WHCA. White House Communications Agency (pronounced "wha-cah").

Walk-in. A person who comes voluntarily to an intelligence-gathering organization to offer information. Since he or she may be unknown to the organization, the information and the person have to be checked, double-checked, and cross-referenced with information from other sources for truthfulness and accuracy.

War of Mitzvah. The claim of Israel that in its right of self-defense in response to terrorism and other attacks they have the justification for and the legal right of preemptive killings based on commandments from the Talmud.

XO. Executive officer.

BETRAYED
AND ABANDONED

PROLOGUE

J. Edgar Hoover Building
Washington, D.C.
Monday, 26 January 1998
1050 Hours, Local

Captain Mitch Vecchio sat in the reception area of the FBI head-quarters looking at his watch. He had worn his TWA pilot's uniform to the meeting both to impress the people he was about to meet and to save time. Vecchio had to be at Dulles for a listed flight and was hoping he hadn't scheduled his time too tightly. His appointment with FBI Special Agent Glenn Wallace wasn't until eleven o'clock, but Vecchio had hoped that by coming in a few minutes early he might get it pushed up.

"Did you tell Agent Wallace I was here?" Vecchio asked for the second time.

The receptionist nodded but offered no further information.

He had called the FBI earlier that morning after thinking it over for several months. He knew that they'd be asking why it took him so long to come forward, but he wasn't entirely sure himself.

It had begun on one of his TWA flights overseas with a layover in London. When he was changing out of his uniform in the pilots' lounge, he noticed a poster on the bulletin board near the lockers. It was an international BOLO notice, distributed by the FBI, Interpol, and various other law enforcement agencies alerting one another, all border checkpoints, transportation authorities, and local law enforcement to "be on the lookout" for fugitives wanted because of their involvement in serious crimes. In his years as an airline pilot, Mitch Vecchio had seen dozens of these bulletins hanging in briefing rooms and airport offices—and had never given them more than a cursory glance. But this time Vecchio was stunned to recognize the picture on the poster. The "criminal" being sought was someone he knew.

The caption beneath the photograph stated that the fugitive's name was Gilbert Duncan, an Irish terrorist wanted by Interpol for placing a bomb on a UN airplane in March of 1995, causing it to explode over Iraq, killing all aboard. Mitch vaguely remembered something in the news about an incident in Iraq involving the loss of a UN plane. But that wasn't what had caught his attention. Mitch Vecchio knew for certain that the "terrorist" in the photo was not Gilbert Duncan. He was Pete Newman, the husband of a former TWA flight attendant. And the reason he knew it was her husband was because he had seen the photo in her wallet—the wallet she left on the dresser on the occasions when they shared a hotel room.

Vecchio recalled when Rachel Newman came to him to break off their yearlong affair. It was right after she "got religion." He had thought she'd get over the religion thing and come back to him—at least he'd hoped she would. But Rachel disappeared shortly after that, and Vecchio hadn't seen Rachel or her husband since—almost three years now.

Mitch remembered driving by the Newmans' Falls Church, Virginia, home one Sunday, a month or two after he'd seen Rachel for the last time. He was surprised that there was a For Sale sign out front and that a realtor was holding an open house. Vecchio stopped, went in and met the realtor, and asked discreetly about the reason the couple was selling their house. The real estate agent shrugged and said, "I'm not sure what happened. I'm told that there was a death in the family and a sister from out of town is selling the house."

As he drove away from the Newman's home, Vecchio's imagination played that information over and over. At first he wondered if Pete Newman had discovered his affair with Rachel, maybe even killed his wife in a jealous rage. But no, Mitch would have read about such a thing in the papers. Then he thought maybe Rachel had killed herself because she felt such guilt and remorse about dumping him. His ego liked that theory, but even he had to admit that it wasn't anymore likely than the first idea. Mitch was troubled to think that, in either case, Rachel might be the one who was dead. He had wondered about the Newmans, off and on, for many months.

It wasn't until he saw that poster that he began to put things together.

An FBI agent interrupted the pilot's reverie. "Captain Vecchio? I'm Special Agent Glenn Wallace. Would you like to come with me into a conference room where we can talk?"

"Hi . . . Mitch Vecchio . . . glad to meet you." He stood and shook Agent Wallace's hand. Mitch followed him into a nearby room where the two chose adjoining seats at the end of a long, oval table.

"You said when you called that you had some information regarding an international fugitive who's wanted for murder and terrorist acts?"

Vecchio nodded. "But you've got the wrong name on the wanted poster. He's not Irish, he's American," he said. "And I don't believe he's a terrorist."

Agent Wallace looked up from his legal pad. "Just who are we talking about?"

"The guy you're calling Gilbert Duncan. He's not Irish—I know him. He's a U.S. Marine officer. His name is Peter Newman. He lived in Falls Church until a couple years ago. I-I was . . . uh . . . a close friend, I mean . . . a coworker, with his wife. I think her husband was a Marine major or colonel—something like that—and he worked at the White House. I do remember that. She told me a little about him but not all that much. I got the idea that her husband's work was secret or classified or whatever."

The FBI agent was giving the pilot his full attention now. "Go on."

"Well, no . . . that's it. That's all I know. Gilbert Duncan is Peter Newman. I mean Pete Newman is Duncan. Duncan's not his real name, and he's not an Irish national. I just thought you ought to know."

Agent Wallace was not content with such sketchy information. And he was savvy enough to recognize in the pilot's stammer that there was likely a good bit more to this story. When Mitch stood to leave, Wallace tugged at his uniform sleeve and pulled him back into the chair. "Just a minute, Captain Vecchio. I have a few more questions about this matter, but I need to check on something first. Can you give me a few minutes?"

"Uh, well, I've got a flight at three o'clock this afternoon out of Dulles. How long will this take?" Vecchio was beginning to regret having come.

"Not long at all. Wait here. I'll be right back." Agent Wallace spoke the words like an order and not a request; then he rose and left the conference room by a back door.

✪

Special Agent Glenn Wallace hated walk-in duty. Every junior and midgrade agent assigned to the Hoover Building had to stand a shift of this duty a couple of times a year. In addition to doing their regular jobs, the younger agents were required to spend a day responding to inquiries and taking down information brought to them by any citizen who strolled through the front door. It made for great breakroom chatter: people talking about receiving covert messages through fillings in their molars, reports of alien abductions . . . you name it, and you were likely to hear it on walk-in duty.

Outside the back door of the conference room, Agent Wallace went to a computer terminal reserved for the duty officer's use and typed the names Peter Newman and Gilbert Duncan into the Search field. There was a brief pause while the computer crunched information from a server located far off in the mountains of West Virginia. Suddenly, the borders of the display on the monitor turned red, and a box appeared in the center of the screen:

RESTRICTED DATA
ACCESS DENIED

An instant later, a phone next to the computer terminal rang.

"Special Agent Glenn Wallace."

He listened.

"No sir, it was in response to information from a walk-in."

He listened some more.

"Yes, sir."

Wallace hung up the phone, clicked Exit on the computer screen, and grimaced. *Just my luck. This nut case Vecchio has to show up on my watch. You'd think he was coming in here claiming to know the identity of the shooter on the grassy knoll. Whatever he said, the FBI head shed went nuts. Sounds like I'll be writing this one up for weeks.*

Agent Wallace walked back into the room where Mitch Vecchio sat with a sheen of sweat on his forehead. He looked as if he hadn't moved.

"Mr. Vecchio, I think you'd better make a call to whoever it is you report to because it's quite likely you aren't going to make your flight this afternoon."

"Wh-why is that?"

"We need some more information on this Peter Newman or, rather, Gilbert Duncan character. You can use the phone at the reception desk. I'll be right here, waiting."

The airline captain had a sick look on his face. He got up out of the chair and walked slowly toward the reception area. A minute or so later, he came back into the conference room. This time, he put the width of the conference table between himself and Agent Wallace.

"Why don't we start at the beginning and you tell me how it is you know this person?" Wallace turned to a fresh sheet of paper and leaned forward, staring in anticipation of Vecchio's answer.

Almost two hours and nine pages of legal tablet later, Special Agent Glenn Wallace leaned back in his chair and looked Vecchio squarely in the eye.

"Now . . . what I want to know is for how long you and Newman's wife were having this affair."

Vecchio slumped back in the chair, and his mouth dropped open. Wallace knew he had him; Mitch Vecchio was ready to tell the FBI anything they wanted to know.

Office of Foreign Missions
FBI Liaison Office
U.S. Department of State
Washington, D.C.
Thursday, 29 January 1998
1935 Hours, Local

Three days after Agent Glenn Wallace in D.C. started the file on Peter Newman following his interview with Mitch Vecchio, FBI Agent Robert Hallstrom, a twenty-one-year veteran, was surfing the computer files in the FBI data bank. Most of the other people in his section had left for the day.

The Newman file had been forwarded to the FBI's Counter-Terrorism Office in New York and on to the FBI Counter-Terrorism Liaison Office at the State Department. Wallace had poked around some more, trying to learn about Gilbert Duncan, aka Peter Newman. The young agent had done a little more digging in the Bureau's main Criminal Index files and in LexisNexis, but after running into various firewalls he gave up and submitted what he considered to be a rather cursory report to his superiors. Within a day, Wallace was busy again with his regular cases; the so-called terrorist with dual identities was forgotten.

The file languished in an overflowing electronic in-box for only twenty-four hours before an FBI computer analyst entered it, without comment, into the FBI's Counter-Terrorism database.

And now, only eighty-one hours after Mitch Vecchio had walked into the Hoover Building, FBI Senior Special Agent Robert Hallstrom was reading the file.

The reason Hallstrom was working late had nothing to do with his conscientious nature; FBI Agent Hallstrom was a Russian mole. He'd started spying for the Soviet Committee on State Security—the KGB— in 1979, when Russia was still part of the Soviet Union. At the time, Hallstrom had some serious financial problems and decided selling secrets might prove both financially lucrative and intellectually challenging. The KGB recruited Bob Hallstrom only four years after he joined the Bureau in '75.

The fledgling spy had begun his espionage career audaciously. Because he was familiar with U.S. counter-espionage techniques, Hallstrom refused to identify himself to the Russians, other than the fact that he worked for an American intelligence organization. Using the alias Julio Morales, Hallstrom had written to the home address of a Russian GRU agent operating undercover as a UN diplomat in New York. He told the Russian to deliver a sealed envelope personally to the KGB. The GRU agent's home address was covered by diplomatic immunity; his mail wouldn't be intercepted and read by FBI "flaps and seals" technicians. Also, by keeping the Russians in the dark about who he really was and where he worked, Hallstrom was confident he could effectively eliminate any risk of getting caught by his Bureau colleagues.

The KGB officer who opened Hallstrom's letter was Major Dimitri Komulakov. Hallstrom had found his name on a list of Russian diplomats that the FBI suspected of spying for the KGB. Komulakov was indeed a rising star in the Soviet intelligence apparat, having been awarded the Order of Lenin for his spycraft and overseas work, especially in the United States. In 1979, when Hallstrom first wrote to him, Komulakov was assigned to the Russian Embassy in Washington as a cultural and trade attaché.

The first package of secrets that Hallstrom delivered to Komulakov immediately caught the eye of the KGB hierarchy at Moscow Center. And over time, Komulakov earned ever-higher accolades from his Moscow superiors for the quality of intelligence that Hallstrom was sending them. Komulakov's career had spiraled ever upward after that.

Hallstrom's first package, to prove his capability and sincerity, contained volatile information. He gave the Russians the names of Soviet military officers who were double agents for the United States. Eventually, he also betrayed other American spies overseas, and the Russians, thoroughly impressed, left huge sums of U.S. currency at his designated dead drops.

In the ensuing years, Hallstrom sent the KGB hundreds of packages of national security secrets, including reams of classified documents and countless computer disks with volumes of data about U.S. weapons, military equipment, covert military plans, and details about intelligence operations—including the names of the U.S. and foreign national personnel involved. From time to time, Hallstrom would hear about agents who were killed or captured—agents he had betrayed—but the

KGB's mole never accepted personal responsibility for their deaths. "It's a mean business," he would tell himself. "They knew the risk. People are bound to get hurt."

Hallstrom was promoted several times, not so much for his proficient FBI work but simply due to his seniority with the Bureau or because some superior in his then-current position grew tired or irritated at Hallstrom's odd personality and habits and had him "promoted" to a new assignment just to get rid of him; ironically, each time the spy was moved, it was to another sensitive area. This gave Hallstrom access and opportunities to compromise more and more of his nation's most sensitive secrets—secrets ranging ever wider in scope and intelligence value.

By 1997, Hallstrom was one of the FBI's most senior counter-terrorism agents, with access to information and materials from other U.S. intelligence agencies as well. He was able to send the new Russian Foreign Intelligence Service packages of photocopied documents of CIA files, NSA intercepts and other secrets, along with highly sensitive FBI counter-intelligence documents.

In the 1980s when Komulakov "retired" from the KGB—reassigned to diplomatic service by the Soviets—Hallstrom, the most productive mole in the U.S. government, was handed off to another Russian KGB officer. Hallstrom continued to leave secrets at dead drops that he alone would select and, in return, they would leave him packages of cash and diamonds. He had made it known to his handlers that he was especially fond of diamonds—they were much harder to trace and easy to exchange for cash. And because the quality of the information he provided was so good, his normally penurious KGB go-between willingly complied with packages of money and jewels.

In the '90s, when the USSR collapsed and the Russian Federation was formed, the world was told that the KGB had been disbanded. But in fact only the name had changed, and Julio Morales, as the Russians knew him, continued as the Russians' mole for the successors to the KGB, the new Federal Security Service, or SVR.

On the night of 29 January 1998, Hallstrom was surfing through the FBI's Counter-Terrorism database computer files, looking for new information to sell to the Russians, when he came across Agent Glenn Wallace's file on Peter Newman/Gilbert Duncan. He read it quickly, not seeing anything of tremendous value, when he suddenly saw a quite familiar name: General Dimitri Komulakov. Wallace's report was based on speculation from an airline pilot named Vecchio about some kind of secret mission involving a Marine officer named Newman, who had served on the NSC staff, and his being misidentified as an IRA terrorist named Duncan. Wallace had also included Vecchio's "confession" that he'd had an affair with the Marine's extremely attractive wife, if the file pictures were any indication. The information was titillating, but hardly worth the attention of the FBI. However, in the backup material, Agent Wallace had attached a 1995 FBI interview with Dr. Simon Harrod, in which the former National Security Advisor emphatically insisted that Newman had been tragically killed on a highly sensitive UN-directed mission—and that the operation had been compromised by the Deputy Secretary General of the United Nations—Dimitri Komulakov, Hallstrom's former handler.

Fascinated by what he was reading on the computer screen, Hallstrom looked for any follow-up on the National Security Advisor's '95 allegations. He could find none.

He did a computer search in the FBI's Automated Case Support system to see if there were any files that were related to this case file submitted by Agent Wallace. The ACS search turned up three others. The first was a duplicate of the 1995 interview with Harrod that a senior Justice Department official had sent to the President in November of that year.

Hallstrom found a second file in a CIA database that was apparently a copy of a British MI6 interview with a Special Air Service officer attached to the United Nations under Komulakov. The SAS officer, Lieutenant Colonel Wilbur Ellwood, had apparently given testimony—before his untimely death—that General Komulakov had compromised a United Nations operation, but Ellwood was unable to provide proof of Komulakov's complicity, so the British had never followed up the charge. However, the report also gave additional details of a failed UN mission in Iraq in March 1995, the same one referred to in the Harrod debrief. In Ellwood's deposition, he claimed Komulakov had compromised the mission and then blamed Newman. The British officer also alleged that Komulakov had caused international arrest warrants to be issued for the Irish terrorist, Gilbert Duncan, but that Duncan was really a U.S. Marine officer—Lieutenant Colonel Peter Newman.

Hallstrom opened a third entry, an FBI file dated April 1997. A special agent in the Washington Field Office had received the file from former Marine Lieutenant Colonel Oliver North. Hallstrom read the file with renewed interest. It contained a transcript from some computer files—submitted by a retired CIA officer, William Goode. Apparently it was information taken from a laptop computer that more or less proved Komulakov's complicity in a UN-directed attempt to assassinate known international "lawbreakers," including names like

Saddam Hussein and Osama bin Laden, during an attack on Saddam's palace in Tikrit on 6 March 1995. The information provided by North and Goode also pointed to the complicity of Simon Harrod, and to a Silicon Valley defense contractor, along with Komulakov and some "freelance" Russian agents. Yet no one had yet connected the dots and gone after those mentioned in the allegations.

Hallstrom quickly realized that if others in the FBI put all this information together, there would be enough information for the FBI to arrest Komulakov if he ever returned to the United States. He also wondered what the other U.S. intelligence agencies might have done or would be doing with the new information that Agent Wallace had stumbled upon.

Hallstrom checked to see where the Wallace files had been sent. As far as he could tell, there were only five addresses. One was the Attorney General's, another copy went to the President, one each to the directors of the FBI and CIA, and a final copy to the Commander in Chief of the U.S. Central Command: Lieutenant General George Grisham, USMC.

The FBI spy saved the file to a three-and-a-half-inch floppy disk. After the information had downloaded, he closed the files, logged out, and shut down the computer. Just before the screen went black, Hallstrom removed the floppy disk with the copied files, slipping it into his attaché case.

When he got to his car in the parking garage beneath the State Department, Hallstrom removed a five-by-seven-inch manila envelope from his glove compartment and wrote on it, "Pass along to General Dimitri Komulakov—VERY URGENT—From Julio Morales." Hallstrom sealed the disk inside. Then, instead of proceeding directly to the E Street Expressway and across the Roosevelt Bridge as he normally would have on his commute to his home in Vienna, Virginia, Hallstrom traveled up Twenty-third Street to Washington Circle. There, he made a double loop of the circle to make sure he wasn't being followed, and on his second loop suddenly turned north on New Hampshire. Once again checking his rearview mirror for any sign of a tail, he made another quick left—turning north on Twenty-second Street, then a hard right on Q.

Just after crossing Twentieth Street, Hallstrom pulled his car over and parked in an open spot. He stayed there long enough to be certain that he had slipped away from anyone who might be following him, and then he put on a pair of thin leather driving gloves. Reaching under the seat, he retrieved a roll of one-inch, white adhesive tape. From the roll of tape, he tore off a foot-long strip and taped it to his shirt under his jacket. Then Hallstrom got out of his car and walked quickly, less than seventy-five feet to the intersection of Twentieth and Connecticut Avenue. There, on the north side of a utility pole, so that it could be easily seen by traffic proceeding south on Connecticut, he reached under his jacket, took the strip of adhesive tape, and placed it vertically on the pole, about seven feet above the sidewalk.

Confident that his prearranged emergency Call Out signal would be spotted by a Russian "diplomat" the following day, Hallstrom returned to his car, removed his gloves, pulled out of his parking spot, turned right on Connecticut, and proceeded south where Connecticut turned into Seventeenth Street. He pulled over once again, this time opposite the Old Executive Office Building, to make sure yet again that nobody was following him, then made a right turn onto New York Avenue, onto the E Street Expressway, across the Potomac, and into Virginia on Route 66.

Hallstrom exited the interstate as he usually did, at Nutley Street, but instead of going directly home, he made several turns in Vienna, then headed down Creek Crossing Road to the entrance of Foxstone Park. He stopped the car and opened his trunk, removing a green garbage bag. He placed the manila envelope in the bag and stuffed it inside the north-facing side of the storm drain underneath the blacktop drive into the park.

Feeling satisfied with his evening's work, Hallstrom drove home for a late supper with his wife, who would have already fed the children. The kids would all be doing their school homework—disciplined just as he had trained them to do.

Amarah Prison
Southern Iraq
Friday, 30 January 1998
0905 Hours, Local

An iron door clanged against the limestone wall of the ancient prison and awoke the prisoner with a start. He shivered in the damp cold of the cell. British Special Air Services Captain Bruno Macklin was lying on a concrete slab in the corner of the eight-foot square, windowless room, clad only in a dirty T-shirt and a pair of baggy prison dungarees. Almost three years earlier, he had been stripped of his desert camouflage uniform. He knew that even if he had it, it would no longer fit his shrunken frame.

Captain Macklin was a survivor of the mission headed by Lieutenant Colonel Peter Newman and assumed that he was the only one to make it. He often wondered if those who were dead had been the lucky ones.

Captured when his Quick Reaction/Extraction Force unit crossed into Iraq from northern Turkey to rescue any survivors of the doomed mission, he had been mercilessly beaten by his captors. His nose and left wrist were broken, and he had a number of lacerations that festered with infection and never healed properly.

A guard stood outside his cell, apparently the cause of the noise that woke him. The guard, a skinny kid about eighteen, wore an ill-fitting Iraqi Army uniform; he had rolled up his sleeves so they wouldn't hang down past his hands. Fortunately he was also able to blouse his pant legs over his boots or he'd likely trip over his cuffs. The kid called out in broken English, "Hey, you get food now. Come, eat."

Macklin looked at the tray his guard was carrying. It was a piece of cardboard box, on which the kid had balanced a tin cup of water and two small pieces of hard bread. It was the only nourishment he was likely to get today. But the delivery of this meager ration was enough to break the monotony. He would eat the bread and conserve the water. Then—if it was a good day—he would be able to go back to sleep.

Although Macklin never knew it, it was an elite unit of Hussein Kamil's fierce SSS that had captured him. Hussein Kamil, Saddam Hussein's son-in-law, had been given detailed information on the UN raid—even the exact route to be taken by the British officer and his QRF. The information had been provided by UN Deputy Secretary General Dimitri Komulakov and passed along to Kamil by Komulakov's "business partner," Leonid Dotensk, who had just sold three nuclear weapons to Kamil, stolen from the former USSR. With the detailed intelligence supplied by Dotensk, Kamil was able to ambush the QRF's vehicles just after they crossed into Iraq as they sped southward along the Tigris River toward the prearranged "Zulu" pickup coordinates just north of Lake Tharthar and east of Tikrit, the site of the failed UN-directed attack on Saddam Hussein and his terrorist associates. Macklin did not remember being thrown from the four-by-four when it was hit by the rocket-propelled grenade and being knocked unconscious by the fall.

In the firefight that followed, the small Quick Reaction/Extraction Force was outgunned twenty to one. It was a massacre. All the others were dead in minutes. At first his attackers had thought Macklin had been killed by the RPG blast; his apparently lifeless body sprawled grotesquely on the rocky ground. It wasn't until the Iraqi soldiers were searching the bodies for maps, intelligence, or just plain souvenirs that one of the soldiers noticed the SAS officer was still breathing. The Iraqi had raised his rifle, had pointed it at the British captain's face, and had been about to pull the trigger when an SSS officer ordered him to stand down.

"We will take him back as a prisoner," he had told the soldier. "Perhaps we can get him to talk."

The first thing that Macklin remembered was being dragged into a helicopter hangar and brought before Hussein Kamil, who ordered an Amn Al-Khass major to blindfold the prisoner, take him to one of the other hangars, and guard him until he could be interrogated.

Two hours later, Kamil was about to start the interrogation when Qusay Hussein, the dictator's son, arrived. "I am sorry I underestimated you," he told Kamil. "How were you able to predict the American-British attack and destroy it so effectively, dear brother-in-law?"

Kamil grinned and then lied. He wasn't about to reveal to his rival the role of Dotensk or the delivery of three "special" weapons, so he said, "You always underestimate me, my dear Qusay. I have a very secret source at the top of the United Nations and a direct link from the UN command center. We knew everything about the planned mission, and we were always one step ahead of them."

Qusay, surprised at Kamil's response, pondered how his sister's husband had been able to intercept the UN's communications. However, he decided that he would wait until later to wring more from Kamil. Instead, pointing to the prisoner, he asked, "What are you going to do with him?"

"I was about to execute him."

"No . . . not yet," Qusay said.

Macklin remembered looking into Kamil's eyes at that moment. He had no way of knowing why the commander of the Iraqi SSS did not want any witnesses left alive. But Kamil could not tell Qusay that some of it related to his plans to soon defect to the West, and so he simply asked, "Why not kill him?"

"The United States' National Security Advisor met with our ambassador to the UN and offered us a deal. He guaranteed that the Americans will not interfere with our attack on the Iraqi traitors in the North and that the U.S. will stop all military assistance to the resistance movement. But in return, they do not want us to reveal to the world the story of their attack on Tikrit. The United States would be implicated, and they are willing to concede the North to us if we keep quiet. They also gave us their veiled acquiescence to make sure there are no survivors from the UN Special Forces operators."

"Yes, I know . . . that is why I planned to execute this prisoner."

"I have other plans. My father taught me that sometimes it is better to keep some prisoners alive. The time might come one day when you need them . . . for negotiation purposes."

Neither of the Iraqis knew that Macklin understood their language and heard everything that they had just revealed to him about the role of senior U.S. and UN officials in the failed attack. Macklin had made a vow that moment that, God willing, he'd somehow get out of Iraq and tell people what really happened when their UN-sanctioned mission was compromised.

But now, rotting in this filthy prison cell for nearly three years, Captain Bruno Macklin was beginning to wonder if he would ever again see freedom. The interrogations, torture, and beatings had stopped a little more than a year ago. Now, he simply subsisted on meager rations, too little water, and the faint spark of hope that he was being held as a bargaining chip in case the Americans or the British ever had something that Saddam wanted. Meanwhile, he counted the days and tried to rebuild his strength. Getting out of here was a long shot, but it was all he had left to hope for.

TRACKED DOWN!

CHAPTER ONE

Café Al-Rabat Bayram
63 Al-Wad Street
Old City of Jerusalem
Saturday, 7 March 1998
0730 Hours, Local

Ｈow did you find me?" the startled, bearded man asked. He had just stepped out of the little Arab coffee shop onto the narrow, cobblestoned street called Al-Wad when the athletic black man emerged from the long, gray, early morning shadows. The bearded man was clearly wary and, for just an instant, the fight-or-flight reaction of his adrenal cortex was evident in his eyes.

Sensing the man's alarm, the younger black man replied in a voice barely more than a whisper, "I came here to find you and was told where to look, sir." Though a Chicago Cubs baseball cap covered his completely shaved head and shadowed his eyes in the colorless dawn, it couldn't hide his wide, white smile. He wore a black T-shirt, khaki slacks, Nike sneakers, and a lightweight gray-green jacket with no insignia of any kind on it. Now that he was closer, the bearded man could see it was a U.S. Marine-issue windbreaker.

For an awkward moment, the two men stood in the open doorway of the shop, just out of earshot of the two Arab men inside. Above their heads, *Rabat Bayram* was printed in Arabic, Hebrew, and English on a battered Coca-Cola sign. In the bearded man's right hand was a brass tray with two glasses of boiling-hot, rich, black Turkish coffee and two glasses of water, in the custom of the region. In his left hand he had hot rolls, wrapped in paper and smelling of yeast, almond paste, and anise. The coffee and bread were steaming in the early morning chill, and the aroma of both surrounded the two men.

When the man made no reply, the black man reached out with his left hand, took the coffee tray out of the bearded man's right hand, and then gripped it firmly in his own right hand, leaned forward and whispered, "It's good to see you again, Lieutenant Colonel Newman."

Newman smiled for the first time and just as quietly responded, "It's good to see you again, too, Staff Sergeant Skillings."

"Yes, sir . . . except now it's Gunnery Sergeant Skillings. You've been gone a long time, Colonel."

At this reminder, Newman stepped back as if suddenly remembering where he was, that there were photos of his clean-shaven face on Interpol BOLO posters all over the world. He quickly scanned the street, inspecting not just the sidewalk level but the windows and tiny balconies above as well; they were decorated with clothing, bed sheets, and carpets of every color and description—and he saw the ubiquitous surveillance cameras of the Israeli security service.

Had it not been the Jewish Sabbath, the narrow avenue would have been crowded with pedestrians, even at this hour. As it was, the two men were alone on the shaded byway, and Newman could see a video camera in its protective casing, mounted on an electric utility pole, pointed directly at the intersection where they stood. He suspected that somewhere within an Israeli police station a digital record was being made of this unusual meeting between two men who were obviously neither Israeli nor Arab.

"Come on, we can't talk here. I live just a block away," he whispered to Skillings, pointing up the street Arabs call Al-Wad and Jews refer to as Haggai.

"I know."

Shin Bet Sector HQ
44 Patriarchate Street
Armenian Quarter, Old City of Jerusalem
Saturday, 7 March 1998
0735 Hours, Local

Police Sergeant Ephraim Lev was bored. He had been on duty since midnight, staring at the three banks of television monitors mounted on racks above the duty officer's console. The screen of each monitor carried four different images, transmitted by security cameras mounted on buildings, utility poles, and rooftops throughout this sector of the Old City—all part of the most sophisticated integrated law enforcement, security, and intelligence system in the world.

As Sergeant Lev drank his fifth cup of coffee on this watch, more than a hundred cameras fed images into this command center. The digital signals had been multiplexed into video distribution amplifiers and sorted by subsectors within the fifteen city blocks that were his area of responsibility. With the use of a device that looked much like a TV remote, he could transfer any of the images to a thirty-six-inch Sony flat screen monitor and zoom in on any scene that he deemed in need of closer scrutiny. A few strokes on the computer keyboard in front of him would instantly record any of the images onto a DVD disc, information then sent to the Shin Bet headquarters on Helini Hamalka Street, about a kilometer outside the ancient walls of the Old City.

Sergeant Lev stood up, stretched, and glanced at the digital clock mounted on the console. The twenty-six-year-old Israeli Defense Forces veteran was looking forward to going off duty in less than half an hour. It had been a quiet night, one of the most tranquil since the Intifada had started again in February. Ever since the rock throwing, looting, and tire burning had begun, he had been wondering about his decision two years ago to join the police after six years in the IDF. He had considered making a career in the army, but his wife had convinced him that the Shin Bet offered less danger to the father of two young children.

Perhaps she was right about this job's safety, he mused. At 0700 he had made an entry in the duty officer's computerized log that the Israeli government curfew was working—at least in his sector, the Arab quarter. Shortly after dawn, when it was legal to be outdoors, he had seen a handful of Arab shopkeepers moving down the streets and alleys, but there was no sign of any angry Palestinian youth or adult organizers exhorting violence or setting up street barricades as was common in what the Arabs called the "occupied territories."

As Ephraim Lev prepared to brief the sergeant who would relieve him, an electronic *ping* came from the monitor console; he looked up to see a red border flashing on one of the four images labeled Haggai 65A, B, C, D. He grabbed the remote and pushed a button. Instantly, the image from camera Haggai B appeared on the Sony preview screen mounted beneath the banks of smaller monitors.

The Israeli police sergeant watched as two men in Western dress, one caucasian and one black, strode away together from a coffee house in the Arab quarter. He noted that the Caucasian carried a paper-wrapped package and that the black male balanced a traditional Arab coffee tray. As the two men walked out of the frame, he switched the image on the preview monitor to camera Haggai 65C, covering the intersection of Via Dolorosa and Haggai Street. In more tranquil times, this corner would be crowded with Christian pilgrims and tourists. But the new Palestinian Intifada had scared off all but the most devout. On this early Sabbath morning, the crossing was empty as the bearded man led the way toward an ornate, three-story limestone villa at 35 Via Dolorosa. The house occupied almost half a city block.

As the two walked toward the stone steps at the front of the building, the police officer noted that they were striding together in step and not conversing. "Ah . . . what do we have here?" he muttered to himself. He sat down at the computer keyboard, activated the recording program, and zoomed in on the pair as they paused outside the arched stone entrance of the structure.

A kilometer away, at Shin Bet headquarters, a spinning DVD disk quietly documented the image of the bearded man and the black man with the military bearing as they arrived at a heavy oak door. To the right of the portal was a polished brass plaque. The high-resolution camera, Haggai 65E, mounted in what looked like a water cistern on the roof of the residence across the street, dutifully zoomed in on the words engraved on the plaque: Hospice of Saint Patrick.

As the two men entered the doorway and disappeared from view, Sergeant Ephraim Lev made a computer entry that appeared on the DVD immediately over the date/time code: "Military men? Whose? What are they up to?" Then, another entry for the next watch officer: "Retrieve stored images from Haggai A, B, C, and D to determine if recognition signals are used. What is in the package being carried by the white male?"

Hospice of St. Patrick
35 Via Dolorosa
Old City of Jerusalem
Saturday, 7 March 1998
0745 Hours, Local

When the outer door closed behind them, Newman and Skillings were in an enclosed entryway, about ten feet square. The only other access was a locked heavy steel security gate. Above the gate, Skillings could see the probing eye of a fixed video camera, along with a button and speaker box mounted on the stone wall beside it. A sign in English, Arabic, and Hebrew instructed visitors to press the buzzer to announce themselves for admission. The two men had not exchanged a word since leaving the coffee shop, and now Newman pushed the button and said into the speaker box, "Isa, open the door please . . . it's me, John."

Immediately there was a loud, buzzing clatter as someone, somewhere inside the building, activated the electronic gate lock. The heavy barrier groaned on its hinges as Newman opened it, motioning for Skillings to follow. Once they were through, the gate clanged noisily back into its secure, locked position behind them.

As they climbed the dozen stone steps, polished by decades of people ascending and descending, Newman put a finger to his lips, signaling silence. Skillings nodded and looked at his surroundings. Flower boxes adorned the walls beyond sturdy, polished brass handrails. The building was obviously well maintained and meticulously cared for. Compared to the street they had just left, it was an oasis.

On the main upper floor there was a small, ornate lobby, like that of a small hotel. A young couple, apparently European by their language and dress, stood in front of a chest-high mahogany counter. On the other side of the reception desk, a young man wearing a white shirt with an open collar was speaking with them in German. As the two men walked by, Newman waved and said in English, "Thank you, Isa."

"Yes, Mr. Clancy," the receptionist replied with a smile, then returned his attention to the young couple.

The two men walked through the lobby and opened a heavy mahogany doorway that led into a grand hallway with a high ceiling. The hallway ran the entire length of the building. Early morning sunlight poured through the tall window on the east end, dappling the long Persian carpet that covered the marble floor.

When the door closed behind them, Newman led the way into a small parlor on the front side of the building.

"If you don't mind waiting here, Gunny, I'll go upstairs to our apartment and make sure Rachel's dressed; then we'll have some breakfast."

"Yes, sir. Man, oh, man, Colonel, these are nice digs! This sure isn't what I expected."

"What did you expect, Sergeant Skillings, our old barracks back at Recon Battalion?"

"No sir, not exactly. But when General Grisham told me you were living in Jerusalem at the Hospice of Saint Patrick, all I knew about a hospice was the place my Aunt Louise stayed when she was dying of cancer two years ago. But this place looks more like a hotel. A nice one."

"You're right, Gunny. I'll show you around later, but it is more like a hotel. I guess you don't know, in Europe and here, a hospice is a place to stay—like a hostel or hotel. This one is a bit different, though. It's more of a religious retreat center, where Christians—people we used to call pilgrims—can come and spend some time studying, praying, and visiting the holy sites."

Newman picked up the coffee tray and the paper-wrapped rolls.

"I'll be right back. Make yourself comfortable. I need to be sure Rachel's ready for an unexpected guest. She was feeding James when I left to get the coffee."

"James?"

"Our son. He's two years and three months old now."

"You *have* been busy, Colonel . . . congratulations."

"Yeah. It's been quite an adventure. Give me two minutes to run upstairs. This room was supposed to be the parlor, but I use it as my office. Feel free to look around, but I wouldn't go out there," he said, pointing to two double doors that opened onto a patio, furnished with potted palms and flowers, overlooking Al-Wad Street and Via Dolorosa below.

"Why not, sir?"

"The Israeli security cameras."

"Do they know who you are?"

"I don't think so. Do they know who you are?"

"I hope not." The Marine gunnery sergeant had been keeping his voice low, imitating his host, but these last words came out in the softest of whispers.

Shin Bet Sector HQ
44 Patriarchate Street
Armenian Quarter, Old City of Jerusalem
Saturday, 7 March 1998
0800 Hours, Local

"The only unusual activity all night long was an apparent meeting between two non-Arabs outside the Café al Rabat Bayram, at 0730 hours. I recorded it and entered it in the log for headquarters." Sergeant Ephraim Lev was briefing his relief, anxious to get home to his family.

"Were the images clear enough to get a facial recognition scan?" asked Sergeant Mordecai Miller. Unlike Sergeant Lev, Miller had more than a dozen years of service in the Israeli national police. He knew how things worked and how to work the system to ensure that the things that might get overlooked wouldn't be.

"I don't know. But I'm pretty sure the still frame where they stopped on the stairs should be good enough."

"The stairs? Where did they go?" the older policeman asked.

"They went into that Christian place—the Saint Patrick Hospice."

"The Hospice? That's interesting. Let me see."

Sergeant Lev reached for the remote as he had done a half hour before and cued up the feed from the DVD. As they watched, a black man wearing a baseball cap, accompanied by a white male, strode briskly along Haggai Street and up the steps of Hospice of Saint Patrick.

"I know that white man," Sergeant Miller said. "He's the director of the place or something . . . at least he works there. I've seen him in the area."

"So then you think that this meeting doesn't mean anything?"

"I didn't say that. We should still check it out."

"Well, I'll let you follow up on it. I'm through with my shift. I'll see you tomorrow," Lev said, picking up his jacket and walking out the door.

Hospice of Saint Patrick
35 Via Dolorosa
Old City of Jerusalem
Saturday, 7 March 1998
0805 Hours, Local

Instead of sitting down, Skillings looked around a room that would have been gloomy but for the light through the double French doors that his host had declared off limits. The morning sun filtered through the thick foliage of the palms and olive trees outside, giving the walls a warm, golden glow. One long wall of the room was lined with old glass-fronted bookcases. Many of the volumes had German, French, and Spanish titles; some were in English, several were Arabic, and many were Hebrew. Skillings could smell the soft mustiness of old paper, printed pages, and ancient leather covers.

There was an antique desk near the window, with a computer, circa mid-90s, and a newer laser printer. Across from the desk, balanced on an old piano bench, was a fairly recent photocopier. Otherwise, little in the room would date the place to the late twentieth century. The well-worn desk and chair were generations older than even the ancient GSA-issued wooden desk that Skillings used in his Marine Corps office in America. He ran his hand appreciatively over the smooth, dark, worn wood.

Beside the desk on the floor were toys—a large ball, a stuffed giraffe, several children's books. Apparently little James was a frequent visitor to his father's office.

Skillings looked up as Peter Newman came back into the room, carrying a small boy and followed by his wife. "She wouldn't believe me when I told her you were here," Peter said. "I had to show her."

"It's good to see you again, Mrs. Newman," Skillings said with a huge smile.

Rachel Newman rushed past her husband. She threw her arms around the big Marine and kissed him on the cheek. "Sergeant Skillings, I can't believe it! It's so good to see you. How did you find us?"

"Trade secret, ma'am." Skillings grinned. Rachel Newman hadn't changed much either. She was still pretty, trim, and radiant, Skillings thought. He could tell that her brown hair was longer now, even though she had it pulled back in a ponytail that made her look younger than her thirty-eight years. Her eyes sparkled; none of the stress and fear that formerly lined her face was present. Though she and her husband had been in hiding for three years, their time in Jerusalem had made Rachel seem even more beautiful—maybe it was the gift of motherhood and time spent with her husband.

"When did you get here?" Rachel asked him.

"I arrived last night at Ben Gurion Airport on a flight from Turkey. I napped for a few hours and then woke up all bright-eyed and bushy-tailed at three-thirty this morning. So I watched TV—everything has Hebrew and Arabic subtitles, you know—then I got up. I even already worked out in the hotel's exercise room and swam a few laps before it was light outside! So I went back to my room, showered and changed, got a taxi, and had it drop me off at the Damascus Gate. I had your address and knew that you—I mean John and Sarah Clancy—were both living here, so I was conducting my own little recon of the area when I saw your husband walk into the coffee shop. I just waited in the shadows until he came out."

"Well, I've just made some breakfast. Peter brought the coffee and rolls, right?" Her husband nodded. "Come and join us; then you and Peter can talk," Rachel said, hooking an arm in the sergeant's. "You can tell us everything that's happened since we last saw you."

"Yeah," the big Marine said. "And maybe you two will be kind enough to fill me in on how you fared after I dropped you at the airport after that awful night in Larnaca three years ago."

Rachel glanced at her husband, standing by the doorway holding their son. He shrugged and she said, "I think that's the least we can do for the man who saved our lives."

✪

The breakfast dishes had been cleared, and Rachel sat across the kitchen table from Skillings while her husband read to their son in his bedroom. Sunlight bathed the kitchen table and the cup of tea she had wrapped her hands around.

"Amos, you're the first person I've talked to about all this besides Peter. You know that, don't you?"

"If you say so, ma'am. If you want, I can talk to the colonel—"

"No, he said it was OK. I just don't want little James to hear any of this. Obviously, he's still too young to understand about his father being a fugitive; but, even as young as he is, he might sense something was wrong if he heard us talking."

"I understand, Mrs. Newman. I sure hope that someday, someone will tell that little boy what a hero his daddy really is."

"Maybe you can do that for him . . . someday."

"Maybe, but that's not going to be for awhile. There's an awful lot of stuff to sort out. For now, why don't you fill me in on how you two came to be running this bed and breakfast in the Old City of Jerusalem?"

She smiled for the first time in several minutes and said, "I will . . . but first, tell me what you found out about that man who tried to kill me in that shop in Larnaca, Cyprus . . . you know, the one near where Bill Goode's sloop *Pescador* was berthed."

"Well, ma'am, as it turns out, that guy wasn't trying to kill you. He was trying to kidnap you, to use you as leverage to get to Colonel Newman. Our boys got that much out of him before the Brits took him into custody and kept him in the British base hospital. He wouldn't talk during their questioning, but we sent his prints and photo to the FBI and Interpol and found out he had been a KGB security officer, probably working freelance, and most likely hired by the people who were after your husband. Unfortunately, nobody could prove any of that. They had local police bring assault and attempted kidnapping charges, but without you there to testify, the case never came to trial. We had no evidence that he was connected with whoever planted the bomb on the *Pescador* either, so they had to let him go. Last I heard, he'd disappeared from the island."

"How about that Russian general at the UN and the fellow at the White House who was Peter's boss, before . . ." her voice trailed off.

"Komulakov and Harrod?"

"Yes, I remember reading in the *Jerusalem Post* shortly after we arrived here that Harrod had resigned as National Security Advisor and gone back to teach at Harvard. But I never saw anything about the Russian."

"That's about all I know, ma'am," Skillings said, "except that General Komulakov still seems to be in the espionage business, even though the Russians are supposedly our new best friends."

"But isn't the Russian the one behind all that happened to Peter— and the bomb that blew up the *Pescador*? Isn't he the reason why we're still in hiding? Why isn't *he* on Wanted posters, like my husband?"

"I don't know, Mrs. Newman," Skillings said, looking her straight in the eye. "What I do know is that there are still people out there who want your husband dead, and until we deal with that, both of you— and your son—are in danger. That's one of the reasons General Grisham sent me here. He's concerned you may still be in jeopardy."

"But no one from the U.S. has contacted us directly for the three years we've been here. Even our families go out of town to mail us letters addressed to 'John and Sarah Clancy.' We never write back from here. Nobody from home has ever called us, and we don't call them. How could anyone find us? How would anyone here even know our real names?"

"I don't know how, but they do know generally where you are. And from what almost happened to you that night on the *Pescador,* you know they're capable of anything. That's partly why General Grisham sent me out here. He wanted me to make sure there was no way anyone could trace you to here from Larnaca. The general knows, and so does your husband, that no cover ever works forever."

"Is someone looking for us right now? Is that why you're here, Sergeant Skillings?"

"I don't know for sure, ma'am," he said quietly. After a pause, he continued. "I do know that about ten days ago General Grisham received an inquiry from the FBI. Somebody at the Hoover Building has been poking around, asking questions about your husband. Last week they called HQMC and asked for his military record. Then, a few days ago, we got an inquiry from someone else, curious that your bodies were never found. The general thinks they'll eventually figure out you're alive and may already be looking for you. Something—we're not sure exactly what it was—got the FBI interested in this three-year-old case. So General Grisham contacted Mr. Goode because he was the only person who knew exactly where you were. And then the general sent me here to talk to you."

"What's he expect you to do, Gunny?" Peter Newman had walked into the kitchen while Skillings had been describing his mission to Jerusalem.

"Where's James?" said Rachel.

"Taking a nap. He dozed off while I was reading him a story."

"Well, sir, first, he wants me to verify that your tracks were covered between Larnaca and here so we can buy time until we get a handle on things," Skillings said. "Kind of a 'vulnerability assessment,' you know?"

"And then?"

"And then I report back to the general and he comes up with a course of action that will keep the two of you safe until he can figure a way to have your name cleared."

"What does the general want us to do?" Newman asked.

"He told me to reconstruct your route from Larnaca to here and try to figure out how anyone might be able to connect Lieutenant Colonel Peter Newman, U.S. Marines, with Irish citizen John Clancy."

"Where do you want to start?" Rachel asked.

"Let's start with the night of 10 March 1995 and go forward from there," said Skillings, removing a small pad and a pencil from his hip pocket.

"You know," Rachel said, "it never occurred to me that I would be married to a wanted man."

"Well, unfortunately, you are. Now it's our job to make sure you don't become the widow of a wanted man. It really is important to try to figure out if anyone could track you here from Larnaca. We probably should have done this before now, but the general didn't want anyone to contact you from the States for fear of a trace."

"We understand," Rachel said, taking her husband's hand.

"General Grisham gave me a bunch of questions to ask, so let's get them out of the way first," said the Marine. He peered at his small notebook. "First, who else besides Mr. Goode knows that he gave you Irish passports as John and Sarah Clancy?"

"We haven't told anyone besides you," Peter said. "Well, actually, I assume General Grisham knows. And of course, our parents back in the States know our identities. Other than that, the only other people I can think of are Yusef Habib and some of his extended family in Iraq. He visited us here that first Christmas, shortly after James was born."

"Is it possible he may have told others?"

"I suppose it's possible, but I doubt it," Peter said. "The man and his son both risked their lives to get me out of Iraq. I trust them as fully as I trust you."

"Do you still have all of the other identity documents and pocket litter Goode gave you aboard the *Pescador?*"

"Yes, I think so," Rachel said.

"Colonel, is it possible you could have left any of the Clancy paper-work aboard the *Pescador* that might have been found floating on the water after the ship was blown up? After all, you left in a really big hurry that night."

"I don't think we left any of that stuff. But maybe—we did leave the boat in a big hurry . . . otherwise, we'd have been fish food."

"And if Sergeant Skillings hadn't been right there with the car, we still might never have made it," Rachel said.

Is it possible it's really been three years since that awful night? Rachel thought.

ESCAPE

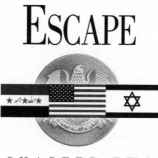

CHAPTER TWO

UK Sovereign Base
Larnaca, Cyprus
Friday, 10 March 1995
2050 Hours, Local

R achel! Grab your stuff and c'mon—we have to get off this
boat, right away!" Peter Newman shouted as he came flying
down the aft ladder into the main cabin of the blue-hulled,
sixty-two-foot sloop, *Pescador*.

"What are you talking about, honey?" Rachel said, stepping out of
the forward stateroom. She was getting dressed for a celebratory dinner
at the Royal Officer's Mess, overlooking the harbor of the British base.
Her cheerful smile turned puzzled and then to a look of fright as her
husband rushed by her and started grabbing clothing and personal

effects and stuffing them into a duffel bag on the bed they had shared little more than an hour ago.

"There's someone with air tanks in the water, Rachel. I saw the bubbles while I was up on deck waiting for you to finish getting ready. Whoever it is followed the entire length of the hull on the side away from the pier and then came back and paused right there for a good minute or two," he said, pointing aft toward the galley.

"What's there?" she asked, now joining her husband in a frenzy of packing.

"Inside the hull there's a propane tank on that side of the boat. And just below the tank are the starboard fuel tanks. If someone placed an explosive charge there, against the hull, this boat's a goner! I don't know if that's what he's doing, but I'm thinking he can't be up to any good messing with someone else's boat."

"Oh dear God." Rachel threw clothing into a bag. As she furiously gathered her things, she noticed her husband had emptied the contents of a manila envelope onto the small table along the stateroom bulkhead.

From the pile of documents on the table, he grabbed a sheaf of papers and shoved some into the pocket of the blue blazer she had purchased for him just hours earlier. "Here," he said. "Take this with you." He handed her a green-covered passport stamped "Republic of Ireland."

She paused long enough to look inside. There, beneath her picture, was the name "Sarah Clancy." She opened her mouth to ask a question, but he shook his head.

"Later, honey," he said. "We've got to get off this boat—now!"

He grabbed her bag, made a quick cursory look around the stateroom, and started pushing her toward the ladder that led onto the deck.

Newman stuck his head up first, saw the black Mercedes idling on the pier beside the boat, and prayed it was Staff Sergeant Amos Skillings' silhouette he saw through the tinted glass windows. He vaulted up the ladder and then reached back to help his wife. As he did so he felt, rather than heard, the zing of a silenced bullet rush by his head and smack into the mast ten feet beyond.

"Quick! But stay low! Move fast!" he shouted and virtually dragged his wife up into the cockpit of the vessel, where they huddled for a moment.

Guessing that the shot had come from one of the buildings across the street from the concertina wire-encircled chain link fence that protected the naval base quay, Newman shouted toward the car, "Skillings! We're taking fire! Open the door—we're headed your way! Cover us!"

The rear door of the car opened—and a second later, the driver's door did as well. The snout of a noise/flash suppressor-equipped MP-5 submachine gun appeared over the top of the door.

As Newman and his wife made a dash for the open rear door of the Mercedes, another bullet slammed into the deck boards between them—followed by a muffled burst from the MP-5. There was no more incoming fire as they threw themselves into the backseat and slammed the heavy armor-plated door.

As they piled in, Staff Sergeant Skillings slid back behind the steering wheel, closed his door almost nonchalantly, put the car in gear, and said, with Marine bravado, "Good evening, Colonel and Mrs. Newman. Where to tonight?"

"Did you see him?" asked Newman, pulling himself and his wife off the floor and onto the seat in the back of the sedan.

"Yes, sir. He was on the roof of that three-story building, directly across from the pier. I think I might have hit him," the staff sergeant replied.

"Well done—" Newman started to say when suddenly there was a bright flash and the concussion of a large explosion behind them. Even through the heavy ballistic-protective Mylar-laminate rear window, Rachel could feel the heat from the blast.

She instinctively ducked as her husband shouted, "Go! Go! Head for the gate! Let's get out of here!"

With the debris from the *Pescador* raining on and around the car, Staff Sergeant Skillings maneuvered the sleek, black, armored vehicle toward the main gate, swerving wildly to avoid the few pedestrians— who had been walking nearby but were now sprawled on the walkway, tossed like rag dolls by the force of the blast.

As the car raced toward the open gate, a uniformed military sentry came out of the guard shack and held up his arm at the Mercedes hurtling toward him. Skillings chose to ignore the warning to stop, sensing it was more prudent to get Rachel and Newman away from there than to stop and explain their actions. The sentry saw that the car wasn't going to halt so he held his rifle in the "port arms" position across his chest to make his warning more threatening. But at the last second, he jumped aside as Skillings careened past him out the gate and made a screeching left turn to get into the traffic on Victoria Street. The guard, assuming that the driver was the perpetrator of the bombing explosion and was now trying to escape, reacted as he had been trained to do—he fired. First a single shot, then a volley of semi-automatic rounds struck the back of the car.

Newman yanked his wife down below the seat back as a bullet struck the rear window, shattering but not penetrating it. Several more rounds struck the back of the car, and they could hear them slam into the armor plate behind the backseat. As the vehicle rounded the turn at the end of Victoria Street and headed for Highway G-4, Newman and his wife cautiously raised their heads.

"We've got to get off this island. Let's head for the airport," Newman said, as much to his wife as to Staff Sergeant Skillings.

"Yes, sir!" The driver replied, throwing a map into the backseat. "See if you can find a less traveled road to get you two to the airport— one where we'd be less likely to encounter a roadblock, sir."

"But can't we go back to the British base?" asked Rachel.

"No," Newman said. "General Grisham already told me we needed to lay low for awhile, until he can deal with that Wanted poster and the trumped-up terrorism charges. That's why he made arrangements with Bill Goode to take us away in the *Pescador* in the first place. We were supposed to head for Italy tomorrow. But now, with the boat gone, we'll have to improvise."

Newman unfolded the map and scanned it.

"I don't think we'll have any trouble on this road," he told Skillings. "It's lined with farms, and it seems fairly deserted right now. And it sort of parallels the four-lane highway that goes to the airport, so we won't lose much time. Just follow it until we get closer to the airport; then we can get back on the G-4 highway."

Larnaca-Nicosia International Airport
Friday, 10 March 1995
2210 Hours, Local

Skillings drove, mostly without headlights, on the remote road for nearly forty-five minutes before getting on the access road to the main highway. When he turned onto the airport entrance road, Newman said, "Pull into the parking lot instead of going directly to the terminal. That way we can look the place over and decide what to do."

"Do you know where you want to go?" Skillings asked.

"Yes, I think so—providing we can get a plane out of here tonight. If we wait until morning, the local police might start piecing things together and close the airport. It'll be awhile before they get the fire under control at the dock. Then they'll start quizzing Goode about the *Pescador.*"

"I could go inside the terminal and check the flights and buy the tickets," Skillings said. "It would be one less opportunity for them to ID you."

"No. I don't want anyone other than General Grisham or Goode to be able to connect you to us. The airport surveillance cameras would record you buying our tickets, and then you'll be dragged into this mess. We'll just go in and buy tickets like any other tourists."

"But how will you pay for the tickets? Do you have a credit card?"

"No, too easy to trace. But Bill Goode gave us plenty of cash when he gave us our identity papers. We'll be all right."

Skillings pulled the Mercedes into an available spot facing the terminal windows. It was dark outside, but the ticket counters and security stations were well lit. Skillings shut off the engine, and the three of them sat quietly for a moment.

"You guys stay here. I'll go alone—just in case," Newman said.

"No! I'm going with you!" Rachel said. "If someone remembers that Wanted poster and is looking for that guy in the picture, it'll be more confusing if we walk in as a couple."

Skillings nodded. "She's right. They're probably looking for a clean-shaven white male, traveling alone, with no luggage. If the two of you are together, and if we can find you some more luggage to carry besides that duffel bag, you'll be less likely to fit the profile."

"You guys are good," Newman said with a wide grin. "Where were you two when I was on the run in Iraq and Syria?"

"I'll go inside to the duty-free shop and see if I can find some luggage for you to use," Skillings said. "You can check on airlines and flight schedules; we can meet back here in a half hour or so."

"Let's do it."

Newman opened the car door and offered his hand to Rachel, who slid across the seat to join him. Then he handed Skillings several large bills.

"Pay cash for the bags."

Skillings nodded and pocketed the money.

Peter and Rachel Newman walked into the terminal building and strolled through the corridors, checking the airline schedules. Skillings, meanwhile, sauntered into the terminal through a different entrance and looked for the duty-free shop, hoping it wasn't on the wrong side of the security checkpoints that required a valid ticket. He was lucky—there were several shops in the middle of the concourse. He picked one and entered at a leisurely pace.

At the other end of the concourse, the newly minted "Irish" couple stopped and looked at a board listing departing flights. "The next flight out tonight is one leaving for Tel Aviv," Rachel said to her husband.

"No. We have to find a way to get to Italy. That's were Bill Goode told me he was going to take us. He planned to sail to Naples on the *Pescador* and then take us to Rome to link up with some people who would hide us. Besides, we'd never pass muster with the Israeli security people. We would have to know someone in Israel and already have a place to stay. They'd check us out and we'd be caught. We'll have to skip El Al."

While they were looking at the "Arrivals and Departures" board, they noticed a security officer posted at the entrance to the corridor leading to the airline gates. He was carefully gazing at the crowd, as he was trained to do, trying to spot anyone suspicious. As his arc of vision moved in their direction, Newman turned abruptly and placed his back to the man's view. He pretended to be talking about something involving the direction from which they had just come. He pointed that way and explained in a whisper, "Just nod your head. I need to wait until that security guy looks somewhere else."

When he felt it was safe, Newman put his arm around his wife and began looking at the other airline flight listings. Suddenly he saw what he wanted. "There! That's it. Czech Airlines flight 407. It leaves at 3:45 A.M. for Prague, with a connecting flight to Milan. We can be in Milan in time for breakfast!"

They went to the ticket counter, presented their Irish passports, and bought tickets. He paid for them with the English pound notes that Goode had included in his currency stash. Then, pocketing their boarding passes, the couple walked back to the car in the parking lot to meet Skillings, who had already returned with three pieces of luggage. The staff sergeant had also purchased several shopping bags of stuff—books, magazines, snacks, toiletries, and a couple of sweat suits—things they could put in the bags to give them some weight and credibility in case they were searched.

Back inside the Mercedes, Peter and Rachel removed the sales tags and packed into the new luggage the newly purchased clothing and personal items, along with the few things they had thrown into the duffel bag. They had just finished when Skillings said, "Uh-oh."

"What's wrong?" Peter asked.

"Over there . . . at the other end of the parking lot. It's the Military Police from the British base. They're checking out that black Mercedes parked over there. We've gotta leave the car— Now! Come on!"

Quickly Skillings grabbed a towel off the front seat of the car and began to wipe down all the surfaces in the front of the vehicle. In the backseat, Peter Newman used a recently purchased sweatshirt to do the same.

Rachel watched the two men for a moment, looked out at the two British MPs as they slowly approached, scanning the airport parking area.

"What are you two doing? We have to get out of this car," Rachel said.

"Fingerprints," Peter said.

When the two men had finished, the three of them tried to leave as surreptitiously as possible, luggage in tow.

"What are we going to do for the next four hours? They'll be looking for the driver of the Mercedes," Rachel asked. "They'll know it's the right car. It ought to be obvious with those bullet holes in the trunk and shattered rear window."

Skillings spoke in a voice just above a whisper. "I've got an idea. You two take your luggage and stroll along the curb toward the Arrivals area over there. I'll go over to the car rental counter and rent a car. I'll drive by and pick you up there, and we'll leave the airport and stay away until it's nearer the time of your flight. Let 'em find the Mercedes. I'm sure it was too dark for the guard back at the base to identify me as the driver. Plus we wiped the car down. If they find my prints, no big deal. I signed for the vehicle at the motor pool this morning. I'll report it stolen when I get back to the base. The Brits will guess that somebody stole the car and drove it to the airport to escape the country. And we know that whoever is trying to escape would take the first plane out and is probably already gone by now, right?"

"Sounds like a plan to me," Newman said.

Hotel Delle Nacioni
Via Cappellini 18
Milan, Italy
Saturday, 11 March 1995
1055 Hours, Local

The flight from Larnaca-Nicosia Airport was anticlimactic. At three o'clock in the morning, Staff Sergeant Skillings drove the rented Range Rover up to the Departures sign in front of the airport and dropped off two people who looked like dozens of other departing tourists. The couple—their Irish passports identified them as John and Sarah Clancy—mingled with a throng of young people headed home from holiday. They stood in line to check one of their bags, then made their way to the assigned gate.

With its 4:00 A.M. takeoff time, Czech Airlines flight 407 truly earned the nickname "red eye." Still, the flight was smooth, and the Newmans actually landed in Prague three minutes earlier than they were scheduled—at 6:02 A.M. local time. Their flight from Prague to Milan took off a few minutes late but still managed to arrive at

Malpensa International Airport just after nine. By the time the couple deplaned, picked up their baggage, and caught a taxi, it was only a half hour later.

They were pleased that the taxi driver spoke English. As they traveled the Autostrada Dei Laghi from the airport into the city, they asked about the best small hotel, the location of the train station, and the frequency of the scheduled trains to Rome. By the time they pulled up in front of the hotel recommended by the cab driver, they were both feeling the effects of their dramatic escape and the flights from Larnaca and Prague. Both Rachel and her husband were physically and emotionally drained.

Hotel Delle Nacioni was a perfect spot for them to recover from their night of terror. Peter looked up at the stainless steel, curved sign above the entrance. He wanted a small, inconspicuous hotel, one where they were less likely to run into other Americans. The Hotel Delle Nacioni was small, all right, but it also signaled a sense of stylish modernity. A row of international flags atop the sign was meant to welcome overseas travelers. But at this point, the two weary fugitives would've welcomed almost any room with clean sheets on the bed.

As they walked into the lobby, Rachel noticed that the attractiveness of the interior exceeded even the small hotel's pleasant exterior. Her husband, ever concerned with their security, failed to notice the charm of the place. The walls were high and as white as the ceiling. On their right, they passed an expansive glass block wall that seemed to glow with a sea-foam iridescence from the backlit corners. Rachel was so taken by the surroundings that she almost stumbled into the life-sized marble statue in her path. It was beautiful—a reproduction, no doubt, of some Italian masterpiece.

There was only one other couple in the lobby, and they had just finished checking out. Peter requested a room and presented his forged international driver's license and Irish passport.

When the manager finished registering the couple, he waved to the bell captain, who was just coming back inside. The bellman took the room key from the desk counter and grabbed their bags.

As they waited by the elevator, Rachel admired the floor-to-ceiling mirror that ran the length of the hall by the elevators. She checked her image in the reflecting glass and winced at what she saw. Her hair and makeup were a fright, and her eyes were red and puffy from sheer exhaustion.

Their room was much more simple and unpretentious than the rest of the hotel would have led Rachel to believe. There were two twin beds and a dresser, and not much else in the way of furniture. The bellman walked toward the window to pull back the drapes.

"No, thank you," Peter said. "Leave them closed, please. We're going to get some sleep. We've been traveling all night and need to rest."

The man nodded and bowed ever so slightly as he moved toward the door. Peter stuck a bill in his hand and shut the door behind him. In less than twenty minutes, both Rachel and Peter were sound asleep.

Almost four hours later, Peter woke, still feeling groggy. Despite his lingering fatigue, he knew he had to call the number in Rome that William Goode had given him.

With Rachel still asleep in the other twin bed, he began the arcane process of trying to dial the number directly but soon gave up. After a brief consultation with the hotel operator, who eventually placed the call for him, he heard a booming male voice on the other end of the line. The voice announced "Community of Saint Patrick"—first in Italian, then French, Spanish, English, and German.

Peter introduced himself as John Clancy, and to his surprise, the man in Rome said that his call had been expected. Then he asked, "Can you and your wife arrive in Rome by Monday the thirteenth?"

Peter agreed to do so, and the deep bass voice in Rome signed off with the Spanish benediction, "*Vaya con Dios.*"

Peter sat on the edge of the bed for a few moments and then got up, went into the bathroom and took a lingering shower—mentally thanking Staff Sergeant Skillings for remembering to put together a bag of essentials along with the luggage he had purchased for them. His kit included toothpaste and toothbrush, deodorant, and a comb. Skillings had also done his best to outfit Rachel with a few useful feminine items—including hairspray, brush, even a hand mirror.

Rachel was stirring as Peter finished showering. He went to the side of her bed and leaned down to kiss her. She was fully awake now and reached her arms up and pulled him down to her. The kiss was lingering and intense.

Suddenly she began to weep. "I thought I was never going to see you again," she whispered.

"Yeah . . . me too," he said, kissing her face and wiping her tears. "But now we're together. The rest is in God's hands."

Coming from Peter, they were strange words—"in God's hands"—and Rachel wasn't quite sure if he was using them as a glib comment or if he meant something deeper. She knew this much, however—each of them had developed a strong spiritual awareness because of the events leading up to the life-threatening disaster of Peter's compromised mission in Iraq.

She moved over on the narrow bed and allowed her husband to lie beside her. Before long, feelings were aroused and, hidden in a small hotel in Milan—despite being on the run from every police and intelligence service on earth—their love found expression.

✪

There were other distractions in Milan. Even though they had less than two full days in the ancient city, they played the part of tourists with enthusiasm: they took in an opera at the nearby Teatro La Scala; they stood awestruck in front of the "Last Supper" by Da Vinci; they walked hand-in-hand to the Galleria Vittorio Emanuele.

Then, early Monday morning, they arose, walked to the station, and boarded the morning train for Rome. In a second phone call to the Community of Saint Patrick, they had both been provided with an address and instructions to meet a car that would bring them to the group's central offices in the Trastevere section of the city.

✪

The couple spent nearly three months with the Community of Saint Patrick in Rome, living in a small student apartment next door to the ancient church that served as the focal point for the community. For Peter/John and Rachel/Sarah, it was a unique experience. The sixty men and women with whom they met every day were young and old, from every walk of life, and from more than two dozen different countries—and they apparently belonged to almost every Christian denomination.

The daily routine was simple. A morning prayer service—led by one of the community—was followed by a light breakfast. After the morning meal, they all participated in an intensive Bible study session and then community prayer before heading out to work as volunteers all over the city. Some went to schools, others to hospitals, and some even went to the jails.

"John Clancy" found himself on a construction crew working to restore a block of apartments along the Via del Moro. The work suited him well, and he quickly recovered his strength from the injuries he had sustained in Iraq the previous March.

"Sarah" volunteered to work in a nearby hospital where she could put her college nurses' training classes and compassionate nature to good use. She immediately became one of the most sought-after aides on the children's ward.

At the end of each day, the group would meet again in the ancient church for prayer and then join together in an evening meal. Hard physical labor five days a week meant that for most, retiring early was a welcome pleasure.

Having spent most of his adult life in the Marines, Peter Newman was fascinated by the lack of any obvious hierarchy in the community. Leadership responsibilities rotated among the members, leaders chosen each week by consensus. The other person "in charge" surprised him. It turned out not to be the man with the deep voice who had answered the phone when Peter first called. He was not a doctor, minister, professor, or scientist—though there were some of each among the members. Rather, he was a modest, blue-collar type. Everyone called him Galvani. He told Rachel one day that he was fifty-four years old and had been an electrician before becoming part of the Community of Saint Patrick.

Galvani reaffirmed what Bill Goode had told Newman about the community on the voyage from Turkey to Cyprus. The group began during the revolutionary 1960s when Italian Christians turned their backs on traditional organized religion and sought a simpler, more genuine faith. Instead of trying to shake up the West by testing and trashing establishment politics and religion, they felt that more permanent change could be accomplished in other ways.

The youthful "revolutionaries" gathered together every evening to pray and read the Scriptures. As they did so, they were transformed by the simplicity of the gospel. The teachings of Christ—love your enemies, live peacefully, pray in the name of Jesus, help the poor and sick, turn your back on greed and sin, and love God with all of your heart—were the same teachings that had convinced a poor Albanian nun to move to India and begin her work among the poorest of the poor. She became Mother Teresa, and her Sisters of Mercy had certainly demonstrated the love of Christ in the streets of Calcutta.

In two years, the single church community in Rome gave birth to nearly a hundred other cells, as these revolutionary believers founded other communities. They also began clinics, schools, homes for the poor and sick, and classes to teach immigrants the language of their new countries. Before long, the work spread to other countries and cultures, yet with essentially the same first-century qualities of the original Community of Saint Patrick. And now, some thirty years later, more than a thousand other communities had been founded, each operating in conjunction with a church in their neighborhood and each sharing a similar vision. By the time "John and Sarah Clancy" arrived in Trastevere, there were nearly a half million "members" around the world. They carried no identity cards, nor did they wear badges or symbols of rank; they simply identified themselves as "believers." And each of them carried the sign of the community: a tiny metal fish.

One rainy evening three months after they had arrived in Rome, Galvani asked "John" and "Sarah" to stay, following the evening prayer service.

"Our hospice in Jerusalem needs a couple like you to run it. Please pray about it and let me know," he said.

That night in the privacy of their little apartment, Rachel and Peter did just that. Afterward, they talked quietly in the darkness, while the rain dripped on the orange tiles outside their window. For different reasons, they both came to the same conclusion—that taking the assignment in Jerusalem was the right thing to do. And that's when Rachel announced to her husband that she was pregnant.

Hospice of Saint Patrick
35 Via Dolorosa
Old City of Jerusalem
Saturday, 7 March 1998
1130 Hours, Local

"We arrived here in Jerusalem in July," Rachel said. "And little James was born in December."

"That's quite a story." Gunnery Sergeant Skillings had by this time filled up several pages with notes, and now he was flipping back through them.

"OK, let's assume you didn't leave any traces of your new 'Clancy' identities on the *Pescador*. But is it possible you may have left something that would identify you as 'Newman' in Milan or Rome?"

The husband and wife looked at each other. Skillings could see a new kind of concern on both their faces.

LEGACY
OF DEATH

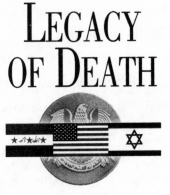

C H A P T E R   T H R E E

Al-Fajir—Project 555 Special Weapons Site
Jabal Makhul Presidential Complex
Samarra, Iraq
Saturday, 7 March 1998
1030 Hours, Local

What do you mean? You have searched everywhere and you cannot even confirm that the weapons exist? If there were records anywhere, why in Allah's name would not they be here?" Qusay Hussein, the youngest son of Saddam, the heir to the "throne" of Iraq, was angry.

To the other four men in the room, all senior officers and officials in the fascist government of Iraq, it seemed that the dictator's son was always angry. They kept quiet, studying the fine grain in the imported mahogany table. Finally, one of them spoke.

"Sir, we have looked everywhere possible—not just here in this site, but everywhere else the weapons could have been taken. If the traitor Kamil succeeded in acquiring three nuclear weapons from the Russians as you say he did, we cannot find any trace of them or any records for them." The speaker was Lieutenant General Abd al-Khadir Salman Khamis, the man who had succeeded Hussein Kamil as Minister of Defense Industries.

"Well," Qusay said, "you have had more than a month. If you haven't found them, and you haven't located any records, I will just have to tell my father that you have been unable to accomplish the simple task he has given you. Perhaps he needs to find some competent officers who are loyal enough to do as they are told."

Khamis bristled, but he had enough restraint to remember that making the son of Saddam Hussein unhappy was a dangerous thing to do. Though he was seething inside, the general spoke quietly, controlling his tone.

"My dear cousin Qusay, it is not a matter of loyalty. It is a case of not having enough information. Further, we cannot launch the kind of search we want without raising the suspicions of the UN inspectors."

"My father assures me that the UNSCOM spies will soon be gone—and that they will not return. What will you use for an excuse then?" Qusay's teeth were clenched as he spoke.

Khamis let the personal insult and the revelation about the UN inspectors pass without comment. He wanted to learn more about these three nuclear weapons. Apparently, Qusay was convinced they were hidden somewhere in this ten-square-mile nuclear weapons design facility—officially designated as a presidential palace. "Please, Qusay, tell us all you know about these nuclear weapons. The more we know about them, the better the chance we will have of finding them."

Qusay sounded like a teacher explaining a simple math problem to elementary school students. "We are still trying to untangle the web of deceit created by the traitor Kamil. Last month, I informed you how we discovered that Kamil very likely purchased three nuclear weapons from old Soviet stockpiles. I also told you of my father's decision that they be located."

"Yes, but you did not tell us what led you to this suspicion," said Lieutenant General Manee Abd al Rashid. Rashid was head of the General Intelligence Service, the Mukhabarat al-Amma.

"No, and for good reason," Qusay said. "Before I tell you more, I must remind you that if anything we say in this room becomes known to the Americans, their British lapdogs, or the Zionists, my father will deal most severely with everyone in this room."

There was little ambiguity about the meaning of this last phrase. When Saddam's own sons-in-law, Hussein Kamil and his brother, had defected to Jordan in August 1995, the Iraqi dictator had provided an object lesson in severity.

Kamil had expected to be welcomed with open arms and an open checkbook when the CIA officers met him in Amman. Unfortunately for Kamil, the Americans weren't willing to trust his intelligence about Iraq and Saddam. The CIA was convinced that Kamil, who had been Iraq's Minister of Defense Industries and head of the dreaded Amn Al-Khass, had defected as a ploy by the Iraqi regime to plant disinformation. After a few weeks, Kamil was all but ignored.

Some of those sitting around the table had been involved in the secret overtures to Kamil and his brother, aimed at convincing them it was safe to return to Iraq. Major General Khalid Salih al-Juburi, the head of Military Intelligence, had secretly traveled to Jordan to deliver Saddam's personal promise of amnesty—and a father's plea to his two daughters that if they returned to Baghdad with their husbands, all would be forgiven.

And every man sitting at the table also knew what had happened when Kamil relented and returned to Iraq on 23 February 1996. Within hours of their arrival, Kamil, his brother, and every member of their families, more than fifty men, women, and children—everyone except Saddam's two daughters—were executed. The official Iraqi news media described the killings as "a spontaneous administration of tribal justice." In addition, scores of Iraqi military officers suspected of having any allegiance to Kamil were also executed, including a number of senior Republican Guard officers, and even some in Saddam's inner circle.

No one in the room wanted to be the object of Saddam's next lesson in severity.

"I did not tell you last month, because I hoped you would be able to find the weapons," Qusay said. "Now, with my father's permission, I will tell you more, but to do so, I have asked my brother to join us."

Qusay went to the door of the conference room. When he came back in, beside him, leaning on his arm, was his older brother Uday. Qusay helped his elder sibling to the chair at the end of the table.

The four generals rose out of respect for Saddam's oldest son, but it was evident to all of them that Uday was unlikely to recover completely from last December's assassination attempt.

On 12 December 1996, Uday's champagne-colored Porsche had been ambushed in Baghdad. He had been alone, driving without his bodyguards, when two men opened fire, spraying the vehicle with automatic weapons. Eight rounds struck Uday, wounding him critically. Now, even after a year in and out of hospitals, he still needed intensive therapy and rehabilitation. Though no longer confined to a wheelchair, he still needed a cane and walked only with difficulty.

Persistent rumors named Qusay, or perhaps even Saddam, as the perpetrator of the assassination attempt. Uday's behavior, reprehensible even for the shameless Hussein regime, had embarrassed the entire clan, and some supposed someone in the family had engineered the shooting. Maybe they hadn't intended to kill him, but merely to teach him a lesson. Maybe it was significant that the ambush took place only a block from Mahabarat Prison, headquarters of the Amn Al-Khass, headed by Qusay. SSS personnel would have known when his brother left the home of his mistress, that he was alone, and where he was going.

But if those rumors had reached the ears of the wounded Uday, there was no evidence of it this morning in the conference room of the Special Weapons Facility at Jabul Makhul.

Hunched over the table, his chin cupped in his hand, his elbow on the table, Uday spoke in a thin, weak voice to his brother, though his words were aimed at the entire group. "Thank you, my brother, for inviting me here with your friends."

The four leaned forward as one, straining to hear Uday's almost whispered words.

"So, they want to know how it is that our father, you, and I are the only ones in Iraq who know about Kamil's nuclear weapons?"

Qusay nodded.

"Well, did any of them wonder why it was that after his unforgivable treachery, Kamil still felt safe to come home from Amman?"

"No one thought to ask," said Qusay.

Uday shrugged. He looked at the other men, one at a time.

"It is because he confessed it to me while I was killing him."

Uday said it like someone giving a weather report.

"But I did not believe him—so I shot him in the groin, then in each leg, then in each arm—and then in the stomach. He kept screaming about being the only person who knew where three nuclear warheads were hidden—'special weapons' he called them. While I was reloading, the coward kept pleading that he would show me where they were. I waited to hear, but unfortunately, before he could tell me, he bled to death."

The recollection seemed to strengthen Uday. His voice was sounding stronger.

"I did not think more about what Kamil had said until a few weeks later when my brother told me about a discovery in the financial accounting of the Amn Al-Khass."

Qusay picked up the story: "In 1996, shortly after I took over the SSS, I asked the Finance Ministry to conduct an audit of all Kamil's personal and office accounts. Kamil had access to tens of millions—funds mostly hidden to keep the activities they financed secret from the Americans, the British, and the Jews.

"It took almost two years for the accountants to complete their audit. When they finished, they reported to me that the books were all in order except for a single, huge debit posted in March 1995. It was for gold bullion equivalent to 150 million Swiss francs. And it was totally unaccounted for!"

"How could this be? Did he steal it?" These were the first words from the taciturn General Taha Abbas al-Ahbabi. As the head of the

General Security Service—the Al-Amn al-Amm, Iraq's secret police—
al-Ahbabi was responsible for stamping out corruption. The fact of the
theft didn't surprise him—it was the amount: 150 million in gold bullion was an impressive sum. Al-Ahbabi was a little jealous.

"Did Kamil steal the money?" Qusay allowed the question to hang
in the air. "It does not appear so from what we have learned, but we
really do not know for certain. The auditors found that the debit was
listed as 'research and development,' but could find no other paper
trail. They also discovered that the funds had been transferred to a Swiss
bank just a few months before Kamil succumbed to the temptations of
the West and went to meet the CIA in Amman. At first the accountants thought this money had gone into Kamil's accounts to finance his
new life. But during his time in Amman, he never made an attempt to
retrieve any of it. When the Swiss officials finally acknowledged that the
account had been emptied a day after Kamil made the deposit, our
auditors concluded that Kamil had indeed used the 150 million to purchase something of extraordinary value. Yet, after almost two full years
of audits, we were unable to figure out what Kamil had bought with all
that money."

"But then, a little over a month ago, a man telephoned the presidential palace in Baghdad on a number that used to be Kamil's," Uday
said. "Colonel Shiraz, who works for me at the Ministry of
Information, answered the call. The person calling asked for a meeting
with our father. He said that he wanted to discuss a matter of 'great sig-
nificance regarding a purchase that had been made by the now departed
Hussein Kamil.'

"Colonel Shiraz put the call through to me. The man said he was
calling from Damascus, a fact confirmed by our Al Hadi Project 858

technicians. The man said his name was Leonid Dotensk, and said that he was a Ukrainian businessman who had sold three 'special devices' to Kamil and asked if we wanted to buy any more."

By now the generals were hanging on Uday's every word.

"Without knowing what these 'special devices' might be, I asked Dotensk how much Kamil had paid, and he told me 'Fifty million Swiss francs . . . apiece.' I told him that I was not prepared to discuss any such arrangements over the telephone and that he would have to come to Baghdad."

Uday nodded at Qusay.

"I confirmed with our border police records that Leonid Dotensk had indeed spent considerable time here in Iraq," Qusay said. "His name is all over Kamil's appointment books and phone logs. In fact, it turns out he was with Kamil that day in March 1995 when the American and British mercenaries tried to kill our father. It also turns out that he still has an office here—at the Al Rashid Hotel—although he apparently had not been back since Kamil fled to Amman."

"Had not been back?" said General Al-Ahbabi. "Does that mean that this Dotensk person has since returned here?"

"Yes," said Qusay.

"When?" Al-Ahbabi was visibly put out that his own organization hadn't reported this to him.

"Dotensk was here last month. That is what started all this." Qusay shook his head as he looked around the room. "You all should have known these things if your intelligence services were anywhere near as good as you claim in the briefings you provide to my father."

"It turns out," Qusay said after allowing an awkward silence, "Dotensk was the recipient of Kamil's 150 million. All of it."

"Are you quite sure, Qusay?" blurted General al-Juburi, the head of Military Intelligence. "If Dotensk is telling the truth, somewhere in Iraq there are three nuclear weapons just waiting to be used. What makes you think this man Dotensk got all the money?"

"Because he told us so. He said he had been paid in full in 1995 and that the reason he wanted to see the president last month was to sell him more of the 'special equipment' like the three he sold to Kamil."

"Are you sure they were nuclear weapons?"

"Quite. The Ukrainian has no reason to claim he received 150 million Swiss francs if he did not. Think of it—for that kind of money he would have been selling military aircraft. Anything else—computers, rifles, ordnance—would fill scores of warehouses and that kind of inventory would have shown up. We would have found it by now."

"But it was not airplanes, was it?" Uday said, clearly enjoying the discomfort of the four generals sitting at the table. "The 150 million was payment for three weapons. Only three."

"Dotensk bragged to us how he and Kamil arranged to have the weapons smuggled into Iraq under the very noses of the UN inspectors at the airport," Uday said. "He told us that after taking possession of them, Kamil took precautions to have the weapons secretly hidden. Though he was not sure, he surmised that Kamil and a few of his bodyguards had taken them to one or more of the remote locations where they stored things, away from the prying eyes of the UN and anyone else who might discover them."

"When did all this happen?" asked Salman Khamis, the Minister of Defense Industries.

"I told you: March of 1995, just five months before Kamil defected."

"No . . . I mean your meeting with Dotensk. When did he tell you all of this?"

"Last month. He was here in Baghdad for just a day. Needless to say, we saw to it that he got his meeting with President Saddam. Though neither of us were there when they discussed another possible purchase, our father called us in when Dotensk left; he is the one who told us to learn where Kamil had hidden those three nuclear weapons."

"Last month? Why are we just learning all the details about these nuclear weapons now? This is something that the Al-Amn al-Amm should have been handling from the start!" General al-Ahbabi sounded like a man preparing an alibi for the courtroom.

"You were given all the information you needed to know," Qusay said, his voice rising. "I told you to search for three small nuclear weapons. Besides, the president told Uday and me to be discreet. He did not want any leaks about what we have . . . no one must find out about these nuclear weapons. But more than that, he does not want anyone to know that we have been hopelessly uninformed on the matter. Our nation has purchased three nuclear weapons, and nobody knows where they are! He fears that Dotensk could make him look like a fool."

"I suppose all of Kamil's bodyguards were executed in the purge when he returned?" said General Khamis.

"Actually, they were not," Uday said. "Apparently, Kamil had them killed himself, before he defected—right after they hid the weapons. He had another squad execute them. His record of the matter simply reports that they were 'serious security risks to the nation,' and they were executed. That would not be an unusual situation."

"No," General al-Juburi agreed. "So all of those who hid the nuclear weapons are dead? No wonder our month-long search has been fruitless."

"Yes . . . but I assure you that we do not consider that fact an acceptable excuse for failure." Qusay was once again in charge of the meeting. "The president has instructed us to find the three nuclear weapons. Perhaps we may be able to buy more from this Dotensk person, perhaps not, but it is most important that the enemies of the state do not become aware there are three missing nuclear weapons. Can you imagine what might happen if the Americans, or the Jews, or even the Kurdish resistance learn about these weapons before we can find them?"

There was an uncomfortable silence.

"What does your father wish us to do?" asked General Khamis.

"Simple. Just find the three nuclear weapons before someone else does."

"Is anyone else aware of these weapons besides Dotensk, your father, or those of us in this room?" asked General al Rashid.

Qusay looked straight at the head of the Mukhabarat but spoke to all of them. "We do not know who else might be aware. But my father told me to remind you that they must be found soon. And when they are found, he intends to celebrate by using one of them on the Jews—to punish them for what they have done to our brothers in the Occupied Territories."

THE
LETTER

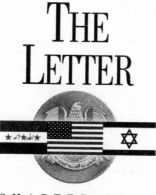

CHAPTER FOUR

Hospice of Saint Patrick
35 Via Dolorosa, Jerusalem
Saturday, 7 March 1998
1145 Hours, Local

Once again, Gunnery Sergeant Skillings flipped back through the pages of notes he had made in the small spiral notebook.

"A few moments ago I asked if it was possible that you left something in Milan or Rome that could identify you as the Newmans—and you both looked at each other but didn't say anything. If you don't mind my asking, what was that all about?"

"You haven't lost any of your powers of observation, Gunny," Newman said.

"No sir, I hope not."

"Well, it wasn't in Rome or Milan that something happened to make me a little nervous about my 'Newman' identity—it was here, just a week or so ago. I was in Tel Aviv with the hospice pickup truck. Normally I avoid the area where the U.S. Embassy is located, but the police had vectored traffic away from the scene of another bus bombing. I had no choice; I had to drive right past it. While I was stopped at the intersection across from the embassy, a man I recognized walked across in front of the truck. He looked at me, stopped, came up to the window and asked, 'Are you an American?'

"I told him, 'No, I'm Irish,' but then he said, "Well, you sure look like a fellow I once knew in Washington, an American Marine named Newman.' So I replied in my best Dublin brogue, 'Sorry, not him,' and drove off when the light changed. But I noticed in the rearview mirror that he stood on the sidewalk looking at the truck until I was out of sight. Then he went inside the front door of the embassy."

"You said you recognized him, sir—who was he?"

"His name is Jonathan Yardley. Back in '95 when I checked in at the White House, he was a U.S. Army communications specialist and one of the senior watch officers in the White House Situation Room. I can only guess that he's now assigned to the embassy."

Rachel slid her hand into her husband's.

"I'll check to verify Yardley's in Jerusalem, but it figures," said Skillings. "After Dr. Harrod resigned as National Security Advisor, they reassigned everyone over there to what amounted to duty in Siberia. They probably stuck him over here in the embassy as a communications attaché, thinking he was out of the way."

Skillings made another notation in the small notebook.

"When General Grisham sent me here, I had two missions. First—to determine just how threatened you might be. I was supposed to report back to him whatever you told me about possible threats."

"What was the second part?" Rachel said.

"Well, if he thought you were still safe here, he was going to leave you alone and I'd simply go back home. But if our evaluation indicated you were at risk of discovery, I was to give you a letter he sent with me. Now I'm thinking I should just give you the letter and let you make your own judgment."

Skillings' eyes moved back and forth from Peter to Rachel. Peter recognized the gunnery sergeant's dilemma. Like all good Marine non-commissioned officers, Skillings had been trained to think on his feet and make life-or-death decisions—especially in combat—and often without the benefit of guidance from superiors. Now, though, he was faced with more variables than he could comfortably manage.

"Gunny, why not just go ahead and contact the general and let him know what you've learned? Let *him* decide whether you're to give us the letter or not."

"I would, sir, but the only way I have of communicating with him is to send an encrypted message through the embassy. If this Yardley fellow is there as a communicator, he's liable to put two and two together and then you're in real trouble. He's probably not real happy to have gone from the White House Situation Room to the U.S. Embassy in Tel Aviv, and he might just figure that turning you in to Interpol could be his ticket out of here."

"That's probably true. Good thinking."

Skillings stood up and said, "Excuse me, ma'am." He turned away from her and pulled up the black T-shirt he was wearing, revealing a previously invisible nylon pouch wrapped around his waist with a Velcro-faced nylon strap. From the pocket in the pouch, he lifted out a thermal-sealed plastic bag containing an envelope.

"This is the letter. I don't know exactly what it says, but the general told me that if I gave you this letter, I should give the two of you time to talk it over alone."

Skillings handed the sealed envelope to Newman. "He also told me to ask you to destroy these papers as soon as you've finished reading them, sir."

"Then what?"

"Then I come back later and you give me your verbal answer. I'll take your reply back to General Grisham on the next available flight to Florida."

"Florida?"

"Yes, sir, General Grisham is now the commanding general, U.S. Central Command—at MacDill Air Force Base in Tampa."

"General Grisham's CinC at CENTCOM? That's great!"

"General Grisham was very clear that I should leave you both alone to talk over what I just gave you. I'm staying at the David Citadel Hotel, in room 623, registered as Calvin Mellis. Call me and I'll come back—or come to the hotel if you want."

There was an awkward silence. Just a moment ago, the three of them were laughing and reminiscing, but now the choice that hung over Peter and Rachel—even though they didn't yet know its exact shape—had shifted the mood. Rachel moved closer to her husband and leaned into him.

As Peter looked at the envelope, old anxieties began to surface as he remembered why he had been on the run in the first place.

Skillings walked to the door.

"I'm sorry to have intruded on you like this, sir . . . ma'am. But General Grisham said this is really important. And I know it must be because as far as anybody else is concerned, my little trip to Jerusalem never happened. He sent me over here from the States on an Air Force tanker to Incirlik, Turkey, but I flew commercial from there to here. I'll also fly back to Incirlik the same way, so there's no U.S. military record of my coming here. I'm supposed to be catching a C-141 on Monday morning from Incirlik back to Charleston. The general was very specific about making sure there was no paperwork showing up in Washington about my side trip here."

Newman nodded. "Understood. I'll call you, Gunny."

"Yes, sir. Good morning, ma'am. By the way, I meant to tell you before . . . that's a fine looking son you have."

And then Skillings was gone.

✪

Peter sat down on the sofa beside his wife. The two-page missive from his former commanding officer lay on the coffee table before them. Each of them had read it; neither of them spoke.

Several minutes went by before Peter picked it up and read it again. But the message hadn't changed. In typical Grisham fashion, the letter was addressed to both of them because the man who had written it had known that the reply would affect them both.

Dear Peter and Rachel,

    I have directed GySgt Amos Skillings to deliver this to you personally because it is the safest way to communicate.

You already know that you can trust him with your lives. Please do not feel that William Goode betrayed a confidence in giving me your location. I do not wish to jeopardize either of you or your child in any way, but I need you to consider the following information and give me a reply.

First, you need to be aware that over the course of the last 30 days, there have been several official inquiries about you both. I have told GySgt Skillings to advise you of them and trust that if you are reading this, he has done so. Though I do not know what prompted these inquiries now, three years after you were both declared dead, I am deeply troubled by the likelihood that your true identities may soon be discovered and the extraordinary jeopardy that would result for you. It is possible that the FBI and/or the CIA may already have started official investigations. If they have, given the abysmal state of our security, it is only a matter of time before hostile foreign intelligence services learn of it. That could lead those who tried so hard to kill you before to learn about it. Given these events, I believe it is time for us to find a new identity and a safer place for the three of you. Our mutual friend, William Goode, agrees.

Unfortunately, as we were developing options for relocating you, another pressing matter arose. Last week, a credible Iraqi defector told our commander of the CENT-COM training unit in Amman that at least three Soviet-made nuclear weapons were smuggled into Iraq back in

'95 by Saddam Hussein's son-in-law, Hussein Kamil. When Kamil fled Iraq in August '95 and defected, he bragged to the CIA that he had acquired some nukes for Iraq but nobody believed him. And as you probably know, Saddam had Kamil killed when he returned to Iraq in February '96.

According to the defector, Kamil had a ten-man security unit of his Amn Al-Khass Special Security Service hide the nukes and then a second special unit of the SSS was ordered to execute those who had hidden the weapons. It makes sense that Kamil would make sure he was the only one alive who knew where the nukes were hidden, but the secret apparently died with him. If the story is true, and I have to assume the worst, we must find these weapons before Saddam or others in Iraq are able to do so. But unless Kamil told someone where he hid the nukes—which is highly unlikely—nobody knows where they are.

The aforementioned defector claims to have an uncle who was one of the execution squad and thinks the uncle may know something of the whereabouts of the nukes. He also says that, a month ago, Saddam launched a major effort to find and recover those nuclear weapons himself.

I have some recent NSA intercepts that indicate key Iraqi intelligence units have been told to search for the weapons and to do so without alerting the UNSCOM inspectors. Interestingly, there are also some old CIA reports about missing Soviet warheads disappearing from the Ukraine at about the time your trouble took place. I can give you more background on this in person.

It is imperative that we locate and recover these weapons before the Iraqi regime does. Though CIA disagrees, DIA believes, and I concur, that if Saddam gets his hands on nuclear weapons, he'll use one against Israel, Iran, or some Western military base and use any others he has as a deterrent against a U.S. or Israeli counter-attack. I believe this rumor is true, and that Iraq does have nuclear weapons within reach. All they have to do is find them. I suppose it's because of what took place in Iraq in '95 and those who compromised your mission that I'm a believer. I am convinced that Kamil was telling the truth and now we have to find those nukes, but we have to keep it off the CENTCOM radar. The Pentagon goes along with the CIA on this, and they think it might be "politically unwise" to conduct a U.S. military operation to go after these weapons.

Given the increased threat to the three of you and the intelligence about these nuclear devices, I propose the following course of action:

1. We immediately find new identities and a safe place for the "Newman/Clancy" family to relocate within the next 30 days.

2. We use Bill Goode's new sailboat to make the move as soon as the new location is found.

3. In the interim, Pete, I need your help in finding out the truth about the three nuclear weapons believed to

be in Iraq. It's terrible to admit, but you have better contacts inside Iraq than anyone else in our government. I
envision you contacting those who helped you escape
from Iraq in '95; it should not entail any great risk to
them or you. Hopefully we can wrap this all up in less
than the 30 days it will take to work out the plan for relocating you, Rachel, and your son.

I don't make this request lightly. You've already sacri-
ficed more for your country than can ever be revealed—
and no one knows better than I the risks you have faced
in the past.

Pete, no one in the USG knows that I am making this
request. Except for Bill Goode, GySgt Skillings, yours and
Rachel's parents, and your sister Nancy, no one else even
knows that Lt. Col. Peter Newman is still alive. If you
want to keep it that way, I understand. If, on the other
hand, you are willing to step into the breach once more, I
believe you may well be the only one capable of saving a
lot of American, Israeli, and U.S. Marines' lives.

If I am right about those nukes, we *must* do something about it. And if we are successful, this operation
could be just what we need to make sure you all can come
back home where you belong, as the heroes you really are.

Please discuss this and then, if you are willing to consider this mission, please tell GySgt Skillings, "Yes," and
I'll figure out a way to brief you on what I know and the
plan that I have in mind. If, on the other hand, after
prayerful reflection, you both decide that you've done

enough, that the risks are too great, particularly after what you have already endured, just tell Skillings, "No," and I'll try to find some other way to eliminate this threat. Whatever you decide, I will respect your decision, and we will press ahead as fast as possible with plans to get you new identities and relocate you.

Semper Fidelis,
George Grisham
General, USMC, CinC, CENTCOM

Peter and Rachel each read the letter again, silently and slowly. Peter watched as his wife read and saw tears well up in her eyes.

Finally Rachel broke the silence. "I almost lost you the last time you took one of these assignments . . ." She didn't have to finish the sentence for Peter to know how she felt.

"Neither of us wants this, especially right now," Peter said in a quiet voice. "But if we've got to relocate from here anyway, it seems like we should at least consider it. If there really are people looking for me, I don't want to be here when they come knocking."

"But what about James and me? Are we going to be safe while you're wandering around doing whatever it is you have to do to help find three nuclear weapons buried in the sand?"

Peter put his arm around her. "It's likely I can handle all this from Turkey—I probably won't even have to go into Iraq—although from what Gunny Skillings told us and the way that letter reads, I might be safer in Iraq than I am here. There sure isn't anyone looking for me there—and you'll likely be safer with me gone."

"But things have changed!" Rachel said. "You've changed since your last mission—you're a different person. And I'm different. We have a new perspective . . . a spiritual perspective."

Peter nodded. There was a time when he might have argued with her, might have rationalized the need for his involvement in the mission. He didn't feel like arguing now. Still, something tugged at him from the inside.

"Honey, we've spent the past three years studying both Hebrew and Arabic. I can speak both well enough to get by anywhere in the Middle East. It's a lot different than last time, when I didn't know any Arabic."

"And we have a child who needs *two* parents—"

"Yes. I know that. But still . . ."

"What?"

"I don't know; I can't explain it. But somehow I have to give General Grisham's request a fair hearing. I know we don't have a clue about what this is all about. We only know that it could be . . . uh . . . difficult."

"Difficult? How about dangerous? Peter . . . he makes it sound easy, but you and I both know you're probably going to have to go into Iraq! You barely escaped with your life the last time you were there. If the government of Iraq knew you were back, they'd pull out all the stops to find you. They'll capture you for sure. And if they do . . ."

"They've forgotten all about me by now. They have more important things to think about these days. Sure . . . there's risk involved. But I've been trained to accept a certain amount of risk as long as I'm not reckless. You know me well enough to know that I don't take unnecessary chances."

"I've got a bad feeling about this, Peter."

"That's natural. But we can't rule our lives based on feelings alone. I wish I could hear all the facts first. I'd like to talk to General Grisham in person. But given what we've learned, we ought to try to give him an answer today. The more time he has to plan our relocation, the safer and smoother it'll go."

Rachel hated the idea of leaving this refuge in the heart of Jerusalem, and she liked even less the thought of her husband going back into harm's way. But strangely—though it was hard to admit, even to herself—she had an inner peace that the two of them would eventually reach agreement on what to do. She was confident that the spiritual and emotional changes and growth in their lives during the past three years were enough of a foundation; they would be guided to the right decision.

"Honey, let's leave it for awhile," Peter said. "I'm going to take a walk while you put James down for his nap. It'll give each of us some time alone—to reflect, think, and pray about it. Ask the Lord for wisdom. I promise you . . . I will not jump to any conclusions; whatever decision is made, we'll make together."

David Citadel Hotel
Ha'Aliyya Street, Jerusalem
Saturday, 7 March 1998
1815 Hours, Local

"Mr. Mellis," the voice on the telephone said, "it's me." Neither man knew the full extent of the Israeli security and intelligence operations or whether the Mossad routinely bugged the hotel rooms and phones of foreigners, so they were both careful. "We were wondering, could you come for a late dinner?"

"Yes, sir," Skillings answered, looking at his watch. It was already 1815 hours and dark outside. "What time?" he asked.

"Why don't you come in an hour or so?"

"I'll be there."

Skillings put on a clean, civilian dress shirt and his Marine windbreaker. He walked briskly to the bank of three elevators. He felt the inside pocket of the jacket to make sure he still had the city map he had torn from one of the travel brochures. He looked over the street map as he waited for the elevator and decided to walk instead of take a taxi.

A group of European tourists were noisily chatting in the lobby when he exited the elevator. Another group was at the reception desk checking in. Skillings glanced up at a lone man on the escalator. A woman called out to him at the top of the escalator, and the two walked toward the restaurant on the upper level.

Skillings walked quickly to the revolving door and went outside. "Have a nice evening, sir," the hotel bellman said to Skillings. It was the same man who had been on duty earlier that afternoon when the American had returned from his jog through the city streets. He had stopped Skillings at the entrance and assumed a different role—from that of bellman to security staff—and asked him to kindly wait a moment while he had a visiting businessman open his attaché case for inspection before entering. The rash of explosions caused by Palestinian suicide bombers made such security a matter of everyday protocol at the hotel.

The Marine waved off a waiting taxi. It was less than a thirty-minute walk from the David Citadel to the Old City, and the chilly evening air made the trek a brisk one. His watch showed 1840 hours as

Skillings reached the Damascus Gate, just a short three blocks from the Hospice of Saint Patrick. A few minutes later, he was in front of the building. The large door was still unlocked and Skillings went inside the entry area. He pushed the button and announced himself into the speaker unit as Calvin Mellis.

The security gate buzzer sounded and Skillings opened it, walked inside, and then went upstairs. Newman was waiting at the top of the stairs and motioned for him to follow him to his apartment.

Inside their comfortable living quarters, Skillings tried to sound upbeat and cheerful. "Sure smells good," he said to Rachel. She smiled and waved from the small kitchen while her husband led the tall Marine into the living room. They sat on the sofa.

James was playing on the floor and pretending to read a book. Skillings spoke to him, but the boy was shy and moved away, toward his father.

"This man is our friend, James," Newman told his son. "His name is Amos. Can you say, 'Hello, Amos?'"

The little boy stood beside his father and gained a little confidence. "Heh-wo, Amos," he said softly.

Skillings held out his giant hand to shake hands with the boy. James took his hand and shook it and smiled when the burly Marine kneeled in front of him.

"I'm pleased to meet you, James." Then Skillings sat on the floor beside the boy and asked him about his book and how old he was. Before long, they were playing together with one of the boy's toys.

After awhile, Rachel called them to dinner, and the four of them sat around the table in the small dining room off the kitchen. Rachel helped James onto a dark blue plastic booster chair. She smiled at her son.

"Would you like to say the blessing for our food, sweetheart?"

James bowed his head and folded his tiny hands and said in a barely audible voice, "Thank you, Jesus, for our food and bless us all, and Mr. Amos too. Amen."

"Wow . . . that's good, James," Skillings said with a wide smile. "You're really a grown-up boy for only two and a half."

Newman smiled proudly and passed the platter of sliced, roasted lamb to their guest. Skillings was not a great lover of lamb, but he politely took a small portion and filled his plate with vegetables and bread. They kept the conversation light and pleasant during the next hour and a half. But after dessert, with James off for the night, they settled in the tiny living room, cups of coffee in hand. The Marine gunnery sergeant finally brought them back to the topic that had brought them together.

"Well, Colonel . . . is it a yes or no, sir?"

Rachel sat beside her husband on the couch and reached for his hand.

"Gunny . . . I want you to tell General Grisham that Rachel and I have been struggling all day to come up with an answer. We've talked and talked. And we've cried. We prayed about it, and talked some more," Newman said. "Neither of us really wants to have to leave here or do what General Grisham is asking of me."

"Yes, sir . . . I don't know the details of what the general was asking in that letter. But I know he was all torn up when he gave it to me. It affected him greatly too."

There was a pause, and no one spoke.

"Uh . . . sir . . . what'll I tell him? Is it a yes or no?"

Peter looked at his wife, sighed deeply, then back at his friend. "Tell him that Rachel and I are in agreement on this. Tell him 'yes'—I'll do what I can to help him."

INTRIGUE

C H A P T E R   F I V E

Dneprovskiy Hotel

"Captain's Club," Luxury Suite 17
Dneiper River Station, Moorage 2
Kiev, Ukraine
Sunday, 8 March 1998
0830 Hours, Local

Dimitri Komulakov was awakened by loud footsteps on the wooden planks of the long walkway outside his hotel suite. He raised himself enough to lean on one elbow at the edge of his bed. The steps stopped momentarily outside. Komulakov quickly reached for the nightstand where his kept his Makarov 9mm automatic pistol. He slid the weapon beneath the covers and released the safety, all the while watching the door.

Komulakov relaxed a bit as an envelope was slid under his door. The ex-KGB officer put the safety back on and laid the gun back on the nightstand. Then he remembered leaving instructions with the front desk that he wished not to be disturbed and asked that no phone calls be sent through to his suite until he asked for them again. The envelope probably contained a message that would have otherwise been forwarded to his room phone.

The management of the luxury hotel was usually very reliable, and they bent over backward to cater to their clientele. The only disagreeable part of the present equation was the fact that the bellman's heels made so much noise on the tiles in the hall when he placed the message under his door that the front desk clerk might as well have awakened Komulakov to deliver the message by phone.

General Komulakov yawned, then looked at the heavy gold Rolex on his wrist. He decided it was time to get up anyway. He had been up late, drinking and entertaining rich and politically powerful friends from Moscow, and as a result he hadn't retired until after three o'clock in the morning, a little bit tired and a lot drunk. The events of the previous evening had started out well, but then deteriorated. Komulakov didn't want to think about that just now.

He sat on the big, rumpled bed and suddenly remembered why he felt so terrible: an empty vodka bottle sat on the nearby credenza, and he could only assume he had finished it by himself. Unsteadily, Komulakov walked over to pick up the envelope, and as he bent, the blood rushed to his already throbbing head. He groaned aloud. Then he read the message:

> *General Komulakov, there is someone in the lobby who*
> *has a package to deliver to you personally. He says that it is a*
> *matter of great urgency, and he will wait. Kindly call the*
> *front desk and advise us how you wish to respond.*

The Russian reached for the telephone and called the front desk, asking to speak with the visitor who wanted to see him. The visitor was given the phone and he introduced himself. "General, my name is Saratov. I was sent by Colonel Mikel Borodinsky from the SVR Centre in Moscow with an important package of information for you. He wants you to see it and for me to wait for your response."

"All right," Komulakov said. "Get yourself something in the coffee shop, and come up to my room in thirty minutes." And then he hung up the phone.

The retired Russian KGB officer and former UN First Deputy Secretary General had kept pretty much out of sight since resigning from his duties at the UN in June 1995. After a hasty departure from New York, he had gone immediately to Switzerland, transferred 90 million Swiss francs to another account—nearly all of his share of the 150 million received from Iraq for the delivery of three nuclear artillery rounds—and promptly set off for Stockholm with Greta Sjogren, his mistress and former Swedish military aide at the UN.

The pair had secluded themselves in Sweden until it was clear there were to be no repercussions from the UN's disastrous counter-terrorism mission in Iraq. In November of '95, Komulakov and his lover arrived in Moscow, ostensibly to pursue "new business ventures." In fact, Komulakov planned to use his ill-gotten wealth as a means of entering Russian politics. His plan was to become the president of the Russian Federation in the elections to be held in the year 2000.

Komulakov maintained a luxurious apartment in the new privatized sector of Moscow for his mistress and stayed there when he was in the Russian capital. But his greed and ambition also mandated that he be seen as a successful entrepreneur in the new "wild west" of the

Russian private sector. To that end, he also maintained a residence in Kiev, for the Ukrainian capital was alive with westerners and capitalists hoping to make a fast buck. It was also the best place to meet clients anxious to purchase weapons and other stolen military and government equipment. In Kiev, such commodities could be had at less than whole-sale prices by anyone with cash—no questions asked.

His choice for living quarters in Kiev was the Dneprovskiy Hotel, which looked more like a luxury liner than a hotel. The Dneprovskiy was new, built only a few years earlier, its site Kiev's beautiful Dneiper River. The "Captain's Club," as the floating hotel was nicknamed, was moored on the water, anchored on the western shore of the scenic river. To the south and a bit east, the city's sprawling Central Recreation Park stretched for several kilometers, following the river's bend.

The Captain's Club became popular almost from its opening. Its guests and residents included international show-business executives, pop music and entertainment stars, and business luminaries. Attractive not only for its high quality comfort and services, the facility gave priority to quiet and privacy, with unquestioned respect and attentiveness from the staff and service employees. Employees could be counted on to look discreetly the other way and allow guests privacy when they wanted it.

Each suite was furnished more opulently than most of the other hotels in the city. Every modern convenience was available, including satellite television, music entertainment center, comfortable designer furniture, a luxurious bath—Komulakov's suite boasted a Jacuzzi—and two separate sleeping quarters, each with a comfortable king-sized bed. Famous Parisian and London designers and architects had created the posh interior and atmosphere throughout the hotel, from its swank exterior to the restaurants, exercise room, sauna, and luxury suites themselves.

Komulakov had never bothered to ask the rate when he checked in as a long-term guest. It was expensive, but Komulakov simply paid the monthly invoice from his business account at the offices he leased in the Peremohy Ploshcha on Tarasa Boulevard.

Since the secret 1995 sale of "scarce" weapons to the son-in-law of Saddam Hussein through the efforts of Komulakov's agent, Leonid Dotensk, the Russian's bank accounts were always full. He had money for anything he wanted or needed. And what he wanted more than anything else was to be the leader of Russia.

Now fully awake, Komulakov went to take a shower. As he showered, his mind replayed the events of the previous evening.

✪

The visitors who had dined with Komulakov had flown to Kiev from Moscow to meet with him about the present turmoil in his native land and to discuss his political future in Russia. They were insiders, and they could tell him what he wanted to know to enhance his opportunities for political achievement. Komulakov entertained them in a private dining room at the Captain's Club.

"What's happening with Yeltsin?" Komulakov asked his friend Yuri Rykov. "It's as if he's having a purge, getting rid of almost all of his government appointees."

Rykov nodded. "It is worse than before, when he was supposedly sick most of the time. Last March, when he came back, he seemed to stay sober. That gave him the energy to start to make good on his reform promises. Yeltsin started a big housecleaning a year ago when he brought in all those young reformers."

"Yes . . . but then things got out of control," said Alexander Ilyich, the other friend. "Those reformers were just idealists. They had no pragmatism. Their ideas to save Mother Russia included more taxes and trying to shake up the bureaucrats of housing and welfare. Then these reformers attempted to restore central control, taking over the utilities and doing away with local rule. Well, as you can imagine, in light of the changes since the end of the Soviet Union, no one wants to accept such things as more taxes or a return to central control. The people began talking strikes and unions and tax boycotts. Now there is great concern about a total breakdown, chaos, perhaps even anarchy . . ."

Rykov swore and added quickly, "Hardly anyone pays taxes now, so what would happen if they *increased* taxes? No one would pay! And the government would become even more bankrupt than it already is."

Komulakov smiled. "Yes, I've heard opposition to these reforms was already happening. And we all know Yeltsin's reformers took a beating in the polls this past year. It sounds to me as if the country will *welcome* a new, strong leader." Komulakov leaned back and took a deep drag on his Cuban cigar.

"Perhaps," Rykov said. "But do not start crowing just yet. The word in the corridors of the Duma is that Yeltsin is once again taking charge. He has started to get rid of the reformers, and he will get his way—as you know. Yeltsin is gaining popularity now because he was able to settle the Chechnya war last May. And . . . rumors are flying that Yeltsin is about to replace Prime Minister Chernomyrdin with Sergei Kiriyenko."

"Kiriyenko? That nobody energy minister? Why would he do that?"

"Think about it, Dimitri. Don't you see? Yeltsin has already made up his mind that he won't run again in 2000. He is putting in Kiriyenko to front for him, simply to maintain the status quo while Yeltsin decides who will be his personal choice as successor," Ilyich said.

"Interesting. Then what are my chances of winning the election in 2000? Can you help me get Yeltsin's blessing?"

"I am afraid not." Rykov looked down a minute, as if trying to decide how to frame words Komulakov wouldn't want to hear.

Ilyich took the initiative. "What Yuri is trying to say is that your chances are not very good."

"Why? If I read the Russian people correctly, they are looking for *some* reforms, but they also miss the order and respect of the old USSR. That's why I think a reformed communist and former KGB officer like myself can convince them that I represent old order and stability, while the present government represents chaos and economic ruin. The people will respect my KGB strengths and abilities."

"You are partially right," Ilyich said. "Your KGB background will help. In fact, it could be a deciding factor. But the problem is, Dimitri, you have competition for that part of your résumé."

"What do you mean?"

"I mean that there is *another* former KGB officer who is being considered—by Yeltsin himself. His name is Vladimir Putin. The rumors say he will be Yeltsin's handpicked choice to succeed him as president of Russia. Yeltsin has already decided."

Already decided. The news was a blow to Komulakov. For more than two years, he had been working hard on his plan to become the next president of Russia. But if his friends were right, it was not to be. Unless . . .

Komulakov smiled to himself. Never mind—he still had several cards to play. The first thing that came to him—and something that he could not bring up with his friends—was his ability to raise enormous amounts of money for his political war chest.

Even if Putin did have the backing of the current Russian president, he'd still have to campaign, and these days that cost a lot of money. Like those who ran for office in the capitalist West, Russian politicos were now hiring American strategists and consultants to teach them about the power of advertising, radio and television exposure, and mass media. The retired KGB general had planned for this contingency during his post-UN sabbatical, knowing it would cost bushels of rubles.

Komulakov already had lots of money. And if he needed more, all he had to do was sell more of the nuclear weapons he had stolen from the stockpile destined for destruction in the Ukraine in 1992. He'd have more than enough cash to outspend Putin and get the exposure and media coverage needed to buy the election. He decided to keep that information to himself, forget about politics for the rest of the evening, and get drunk.

✪

After finishing his shower and reflecting over his dismal dinner meeting the night before, Komulakov sat on the edge of the bed in his silk robe. The shower had not cleared his brain; his hangover was still making his stomach churn and his head ache. He made a pot of strong, black coffee and poured himself a cup. Just as he took the first sip, there was a knock at his door.

Komulakov walked over to the door. The man standing outside in the hall wore an ill-fitting wool suit and a narrow, outdated tie. Komulakov was about to invite him inside but the man hesitated. "Sir, I am to leave this package with you and come back later . . . in case you have a reply or instructions."

"All right. Wait in the coffee shop. I'll either call you there or come down to get you." The man handed him the package and walked away.

Back in his suite, Komulakov noticed that the flap of the package had a wax SVR seal, indicating that Borodinsky had taken precautions that the contents would remain secret. As he broke the seal and opened the package, Komulakov saw there were several pages of photocopied material and a computer disk. He took the computer disk and put it into his laptop.

While he waited for the computer to boot up, he glanced through the papers. They were from Julio Morales, the most productive spy he had ever handled. Morales had been Komulakov's responsibility years ago when he was the KGB *Rezident* in Washington.

So . . . Morales is active again. What is important enough to bring him back? The written material in the package told Komulakov that the mole he had run for the KGB twenty years ago had recently discovered some files that might be of interest to his old handler.

The computer was ready. According to the directory, the disk contained only a single file. As Komulakov read the hard copy and the contents of the digital file, he soon forgot his hangover.

General Komulakov,
    Greetings from the Direktor. Please find enclosed
some material that recently arrived at the Moscow Centre

from your former agent, Julio Morales. You will note from the contents that he says the American FBI is making inquiries about a person linked with you when you were assigned to the UN in 1995. The names in the file are Lt. Col. Peter Newman, an Irish terrorist named Gilbert Duncan, and an Irish national, John Clancy. Morales suggests that these three may actually be the same person. Here at the Centre there is great concern that if Newman is still alive and ever reveals what he knows or suspects about your connection to the SVR while you were at the UN, the accusations would be a major embarrassment to our government. If your role in Newman's failed mission is uncovered, the Direktor is concerned that the UN may even ask for your extradition to the U.S. to face charges. And as you know, the Direktor is trying to convince Washington that we are their friends. He expects that you will deal with this matter expeditiously in order to avoid compromising our new relationship with the Americans.

Sincerely,
Mikel Borodinsky, Col., SVR

The cover letter from Moscow left no room for misunderstanding. It meant that Komulakov was expected to take care of any and all "loose ends." The information Morales had sent in the computer files simply confirmed to Colonel Borodinsky what Komulakov had already concluded about Newman. If the Marine really was alive, he had to be found and silenced.

But Komulakov also knew that Newman wasn't the only loose end. The former KGB spymaster knew that another American could compromise Dimitri Komulakov anytime he felt the need. Newman was a definite threat, but so was Morales.

I assumed that Newman was dead. But Morales says he might be alive. Morales is the only one in the U.S. government who knows who I am, who can tie me to the UN mission. He had no second thoughts about betraying his fellow agents to their deaths. Why wouldn't he give me up if he ever got caught?

Komulakov had an idea. True, he would have to set aside his ambitions for Russian politics for now. But perhaps there was a way to take care of both of his problems.

He quickly threw off the robe and dressed. He then sat down at his laptop and typed out a quick message to Colonel Borodinsky at Moscow Centre.

My dear Mikel,

Please ask our *Rezident* in Washington to make the following requests of Morales immediately:

1. Please send anything more you can find on Newman, Duncan, and Clancy.

2. Please inform immediately any indication that Newman is alive.

3. If there is a chance he is alive, inform immediately of any known or suspected location.

4. Is Newman's wife alive? If so, where is she?

5. Have any other agencies, U.S. or other, expressed an interest in the Newman matter?

Mikel, please ask Moscow Centre to transmit this request to our *Rezident* in Washington as expeditiously as possible. I need everything Morales can get on this matter. Pay whatever Morales wants. If Moscow Centre balks at his price, let me know, and I will pay it personally. I especially need to know if Newman is alive and if his wife survived the explosion in Larnaca. Then, I want to know where I can find them. And by the way, please also ask Centre to inquire of our *Rezident* in Washington whether they have ever figured out who Morales is and where he works.

Sincerely,
Dimitri Komulakov, Lt. General
Committee on State Security (Rtd.)

Komulakov read over what he had written, encrypted it with the system built into his laptop, and then copied it onto a disk. He went downstairs to the coffee shop and found the messenger from Moscow Centre. He handed him the computer disk.

"When you've finished eating, I want you to leave right away for Moscow with this response for your superior," Komulakov said. "Give the disk to Colonel Borodinsky only. Do you understand?"

"Yes, sir."

Komulakov turned and walked away. Instead of going back to his room, the retired KGB officer decided he would go for a brisk walk along the banks of the Dneiper. He felt suddenly electrified by the prospect of once again hunting the most dangerous prey of all. As he walked in the cold air, he turned his plan over in his mind. Soon, he began to smile. It was so simple—yet so elegant. It would work, and his two great problems would be eliminated . . . forever.

SAILORS, SOLDIERS, AND SPIES

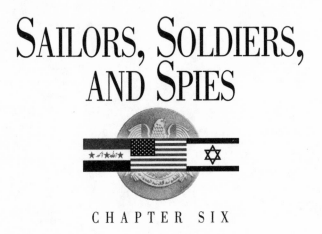

C H A P T E R   S I X

Aboard *Pescador II*

Jaffa Harbor, Tel Aviv, Israel
Saturday, 14 March 1998
1015 Hours, Local

The white-haired skipper eased the seventy-seven-foot *Pescador II* into the calm waters of the Mediterranean Sea just off Tel Aviv. Jaffa Harbor was beautiful, one of his favorite ports of call. He had furled the mainsail of the Solas Kelsall sloop while still in the deeper water and now used the diesel engine to guide the huge vessel toward the breakwater protecting the shallow waters near the berths for pleasure craft.

William Goode—former Marine, former CIA clandestine services officer, and now master of the sailing vessel *Pescador II*—watched carefully to starboard as he approached the kilometer-long breakwater, making sure the bottom of his keel, seven feet below the water line, avoided the rocks nearby. He occasionally stole a glance to port, viewing the imposing cityscape of high-rise office buildings, hotels, and apartments. It seemed to him that every time he stopped in Jaffa, the skyline had changed. He saw construction cranes in every part of the city. As the *Pescador II* passed the first of the six larger docking berths, Goode slowed the sailboat to a scant three knots to make the turn into the third row of berths. The first four of the six major rows were reserved for larger boats, and the *Pescador II* was among the largest.

The skyline on the port side changed as he passed the first rows of ships anchored in the harbor. Coming around ninety degrees to the left, he could see the Old City of Jaffa dead ahead through the pilothouse windows. He appreciated most of the centuries-old buildings of native stone, the color of a hundred shades of sand. This time of day, the morning sun was already high enough to reflect off the sides of the buildings, giving the entire view a brilliance he rarely encountered anywhere else. The light in Israel was different from any other place on earth, Goode thought. The scenery was always an agreeable pleasure, but today it was especially exhilarating.

As his sailboat neared its berth, Goode put the engine in neutral and let the craft coast for another twenty meters before shifting the transmission into reverse and bringing the sailboat to a full stop. A dockhand gave signals to Goode from the floating pier and waited for him to cast the lines. After cutting the engine, Goode walked to the bow of his new boat and tossed the lines to the waiting harborhand. He had so skillfully brought her into berth that the man on the dock hardly had to pull on the braided nylon lines to bring the blue hull up against the fenders along the floating pier. The harborhand grinned and gave the captain of the *Pescador II* a thumbs-up sign.

The entire process took only five minutes, and Goode was just getting his land legs on the dock when he saw a familiar form about a hundred meters down the quay. Goode waved at the man, motioned for him to join him, and then reboarded the boat after checking to make sure all the lines had been made secure. The bearded man approached the gangway that had been placed from the pier to the gunwale of the *Pescador II* and said in a voice just loud enough to carry to the cockpit, "Hey, Captain Goode! Permission for an old Marine to come aboard?"

"Permission granted! Come aboard, my friend," Goode said with a wide smile. The bearded man, wearing jeans and an open-collared dress shirt, jumped onto the deck, saluted the strange ensign hanging from the stern, and walked toward the pilothouse. The captain, standing in the cockpit, reached out his hand and said, "It's good to see you again, Pete. How are you?"

Peter Newman grabbed the older man and hugged him vigorously.

"I'm fine. It's great to see you again, too, Bill. I see you've got yourself another sailboat. But what's with the strange ensign?" Newman pointed to the flag hanging from the fantail.

Goode nodded. "Well, this boat was made in South Africa. She's built for single-handed sailing in the Southern Ocean—but the ensign, that's the Dutch flag. I've just come from Saint Maarten. That was my last port of call in the Caribbean, and I thought a Dutch flag was less likely to attract attention than Old Glory."

"And the name?" asked Newman.

"Yep, *Pescador II*," said Goode with a great big smile. "So far, she's lived up to her namesake."

"Yeah, well, let's hope she doesn't meet with the same fate."

"Amen to that. Let me show you around, and then we'll have an early lunch."

Goode put his hand on the younger man's shoulder and steered him toward the captain's cabin. "I always start here because that's the best feature." He led Newman inside. The room was magnificent, mainly mahogany, resembling an old English drawing room. On one bulkhead was a large bookcase, filled deck to overhead with hundreds of volumes. Newman let his hand browse along the rows of books, stowed with a wooden bar midway across each shelf, to keep them secure when the boat rolled in heavy weather. The titles ranged from classical literature to inspirational reading—along with a good selection of fiction, biographies, and travelogues. "This is great, Bill. You must feel very much at home here."

Near the bookcase was Goode's navigation table. It doubled as his desk, but it was as neat as something in a furniture store. Not a scrap of paper cluttered its polished mahogany top. Besides a harbor chart, the only object on it was a small brass lamp, bolted to the tabletop, with a white oyster shade. Matching lamps were mounted on the bulkhead opposite the bookcase, and between the lamps was a large bed. Newman noted that, like everything else aboard this boat, a floor lamp in the corner was also fastened to the deck.

A narrow passageway between the bookcase and a tall wooden locker led to the salon, located amidships. Newman walked through the hatch on the ribbed teakwood deck and whistled softly. "Nice."

The space in the salon was bright, lit from large portholes on three sides, and overlooked the deck. There were couches and several captain's chairs, a square coffee table, and another table for eating or working on charts. The forward bulkhead had a built-in sound system, and Newman recognized the mellow saxophone of Grover Washington playing in the background.

Goode smiled. "We'll finish the tour of the boat later, after we get underway. I'd like to set sail by 1800 hours. Oh, by the way . . . that hatch across the salon, just below the porthole line, leads below deck to your cabin. You can stow your stuff there and get comfortable. We'll have lunch in about a half hour."

Dneprovskiy Hotel
Dneiper River Station, Moorage 2
Kiev, Ukraine
Saturday, 14 March 1998
1230 Hours, Local

Komulakov hadn't touched his lunch. He was still engrossed in the material just delivered to him by a former KGB associate now working for the GRU in the Russian Federation. Yuri Ancheckov had made a special trip to Kiev just to meet with Komulakov regarding some additional Russian intelligence—at least that's what he told his former boss. The truth was, Yuri just wanted to have a spring weekend in Kiev at the expense of Moscow taxpayers. It was seldom that anyone ever learned anything new from Komulakov.

Ancheckov sat across from Komulakov at the opulent dinner table and showed no reluctance in eating the meal laid out before them. He felt a little sheepish when he was nearly done wolfing down his own plate, so he offered a little encouragement to the man across from him. "General, your food is getting cold. Aren't you going to eat?"

Komulakov grunted and kept reading the photocopied material from classified FBI and CIA documents. Much of it was the same as that delivered to him in a sealed envelope from the SVR headquarters in Dzerzhinsky Square a week before. Moscow Centre was the same building that had been KGB headquarters when the USSR existed, the building where Komulakov had served part of his career. Ancheckov had brought a similar package from GRU, and the retired KGB general was engrossed in perusing the files stolen from his former American adversary—all of which contained his name and the name of Peter Newman. There were also numerous files pertaining to the fugitive Irish terrorist Gilbert Duncan—along with photographs, BOLO notices, and Wanted posters of the terrorist that had been circulated all over the world.

"Yuri, you know, I just figured out what the Americans' biggest problem is."

"What's that, General?"

"They have too much information. They have so many intelligence sources, so many police agencies, so many security services, that no two of them ever talk to one another. Look at this," said the KGB general, holding up a photograph of Peter Newman in a Marine uniform and an Interpol BOLO notice of Gilbert Duncan, wanted IRA terrorist. "Wouldn't you think that somewhere in the vast U.S. government, somebody would have figured out by now that Newman and Duncan were the same person?"

"Well, it hass been three years since you did that, General. Three years since you created Duncan and Newman disappeared. That is what you wanted. What difference does it make if Newman died as Duncan or if Newman died as Newman aboard some sailboat in Cyprus, as long as he is dead?"

"It doesn't—as long as he's really dead. But according to these files, he may not be dead. And if he's not—I have a problem."

Ancheckov returned to his food, and the KGB general resumed perusing the files that the mole Morales had placed in a dead drop in Virginia, just days prior. "This file is interesting," Komulakov said, pointing to a classified FBI file that had explained William Goode's report on Peter Newman. "I'm trying to contact Morales and see if there's anything more on this case—anything fresh. This fellow, Goode, the former CIA man, reports on Peter Newman's mission and gives details that he could only have gotten from talking with Newman. It could have been that he got this information during the time he brought Newman from Turkey to Cyprus on his sailboat. But I doubt he had enough time for that. These things that Goode mentions in his debriefing sound like the result of extensive conversations and review."

"Does it matter how he came into possession of the information?"

"Yes . . . If my impression is correct, it means Peter Newman did not die in the explosion aboard Goode's sailboat in Larnaca. Goode would have gotten this information from Newman after the attempt on his life. No . . . I think Newman is still alive."

Ancheckov put down his fork and met Komulakov's eyes. "Well, if Newman is still alive, we have a problem, General . . . you and me. I do not know if he actually saw me on the train coming out of Syria three years ago or not, but I do not want this guy showing up again. I do not see how he could have survived the explosion on that sailboat, but if he did, we had better find him and get rid of him."

"Yes, Yuri, that's true. I've already put some things in motion and will apprise you as soon as I learn more. In the meantime, there's something very important you can do for me."

"What is that, General?"

"I want you to quietly see if you can find out just who Julio Morales really is. You know, during all the years I was his controller in Washington, I never knew his real identity."

"I will try, General. But you know better than I how closely held that kind of information is at the Centre. May I ask why, after all these years, the identity of Morales is so important now?"

Komulakov looked over his reading glasses at the younger man.

"No, you may not."

Office of Commander in Chief

U.S. Central Command
MacDill Air Force Base, Florida
Friday, 13 March 1998
2140 Hours, Local

General George Grisham went over his checklist one more time and then deleted the list from his laptop. Everything was done, and he was ready for his midnight flight from MacDill to Incirlik, Turkey. The fifty-six-year-old Marine ran a hand through his short-cropped gray hair and drank the last swallow of cold coffee from the mug on his desk. As he stood to put his laptop in his attaché case, there was a knock on his office door.

He turned as the door opened and Gunnery Sergeant Amos Skillings came in.

"Excuse me, sir. Anything else that you'll be needing for the trip tonight?"

"I think I have everything. That classified file you brought me this afternoon—is that the latest we have on Colonel Newman's case?"

"Yes, sir. I checked with the various other agencies, and they told me they have nothing new. The NSA never called me back. But I didn't expect we'd hear anything from the White House on this. Some deputy something-or-other called me right after I called the NSA and wanted to know what we were doing with this case. I told them it was just routine housecleaning; I was just making sure there wasn't anything new before we closed the books on it."

"Then as far as all of the other U.S. agencies are concerned, Lieutenant Colonel Newman is still officially dead?"

Skillings nodded. "Yes, sir. Everything's quiet on his file now. I just hope I didn't stir up any interest by making that one last check."

"I doubt it. The entire case was built on politics. His chief antagonists, Harrod and Komulakov, are both out of the picture. I think people have pretty well forgotten about the late Peter Newman."

Skillings grinned. "Well, sir . . . for a dead man, he sure looked mighty good when I saw him last week."

"I'm looking forward to our meeting in Larnaca on Monday. Did you get those clothes and things I requested for him?"

"Yes, sir. They're in that package over there beside your carry-on bag."

"Well, what's in that other package—that long one by the couch?"

"That's for you."

"What is it?"

"Happy birthday, General. It's a gift from your office staff. We hope you'll have a chance to enjoy it on your trip next week."

General Grisham smiled and said, "How thoughtful, Gunny. Be sure and thank the staff for me."

"I don't think that'll be necessary, sir." Skillings opened the door to the outer office a little wider.

The entire CENTCOM CinC staff, from every service branch, stood in the outer office and began to sing "Happy Birthday"—mostly off-key—to their boss. He laughed and shook his head.

"I can't believe you guys are still here on a Friday night. Gunny I can believe—he's married to the Corps—but the rest of you able-bodied soldiers, sailors, airmen, and Marines. What's the matter with you people—don't you have lives?"

They all laughed. A few offered fake excuses about all the exotic places that they'd be right now if Gunny hadn't "ordered" them to show up tonight. Staff Sergeant Marianne Kimmel came forward with a cake.

"Sorry, General Grisham, but we couldn't afford all of the candles. That many would've drained our wallets and set fire to the cake."

"Oh, watch it, Staff Sergeant. I'm not so old that I can't order you to do a couple dozen laps around the admin building for your disrespect." Sergeant Kimmel laughed.

Grisham picked up the long box and opened the colorfully wrapped package. He pulled the wrapping away from the contents and smiled when he saw a deep-sea fishing rod and reel.

"Hey, this is great! I just hope I have enough time to spend a few minutes with it in the Mediterranean. Thanks, all of you. I appreciate it very much."

By 2300 hours, General Grisham excused himself and went back inside his office. Ten minutes later, Skillings came in to get his luggage and take it to the Gulfstream V that was presently undergoing its preflight procedures for the trip that the two of them would be taking within the hour.

Habirah Prison
Near Salman Pak, Iraq
Saturday, 14 March 1998
1735 Hours, Local

Bruno Macklin had been traveling most of the daylight hours, blindfolded, in the back of a military four-by-four. He was handcuffed with his arms in front of him and shackled with leg irons and waist restraints that tied him securely to the rollover bar of the vehicle.

This procedure had become routine to him by now. Every few months, Macklin was transferred from one Iraqi prison to another. At first when it happened, he was afraid they were taking him to be executed, and the guards reinforced this impression by their actions—since that's what the guards had been told by their superiors.

Macklin figured the frequent transfers were his captors' way of making sure, if word ever leaked that Macklin was still alive, that Western intelligence agencies would have an impossible task in finding and rescuing him. And so, every six to eight weeks, he was moved to another prison.

There was perhaps another reason: the Iraqis wanted to make sure he was never at a prison long enough for his guards to become friendly with him. More than once, Macklin knew, guards had bonded with prisoners sufficiently to help them escape, and sometimes the guards themselves would flee as well. It was a strange phenomenon, but it could happen.

The most difficult part for Macklin was the uncertainty. Every time he was moved, he lost track of the time. He always tried to mark the days off on a makeshift calendar, but he wasn't always able to check it when they came to get him for another move. He felt certain he had been in their captivity for three years, but perhaps it was only two and a half, possibly even as many as four.

But today, he almost enjoyed the transfer. The fresh air that blew across his blindfolded face felt good; it erased the stench of his filthy cell. And unlike the brutal jailers at the other prisons that he had been taken to over the past three years, the Iraqis on this transport detail were almost humane: they had halted for regular rest stops to allow him to take care of toilet necessities; they had even let him eat during one of the breaks; they offered him bottles of water when he was thirsty; and, on one occasion, they even gave him water *before* he asked.

One of the three transport guards spoke some English and tried to converse with Macklin. Though the British officer was blindfolded, he still was able to detect the differences in voice tonality. The one speaking to him now had a maimed hand, he recalled. "How did you lose your hand?" he asked, to test whether he was right.

"Ah, yes . . . my hand," the guard said. "I was wounded in 1991, in the 'War with the West.'"

"I'm sorry," Macklin told him honestly. "I know what it's like to be wounded."

"That was long ago," the man answered in a matter-of-fact tone. "I hardly miss it anymore."

"But you're still in the Iraqi Army. In the West, if a soldier loses a hand, he is honorably discharged from the service and goes back home."

"Yes, I have heard that," the Iraqi said. "I probably could have gone home after that too. But I would not be able to work. My family would have starved. The military let me stay and transferred me to lighter duty. It's a good job."

"Tell me about this new prison," Macklin said.

"It is like any other Iraqi prison. They are all alike."

"Yeah, I suppose so."

"Except that you may meet some of your friends at Habirah Prison. It is a new prison, and no one knows that it exists, except those of us who work there. The government built it for special political prisoners."

"Political prisoners?"

"Yes. Many of the Kurdish resistance leaders are kept there before they are executed. There are several senior Iranian officers there and some other prisoners of war. You may meet the Americans," the guard said.

Americans! He wondered if any of them were survivors of the compromised mission. *Even if they aren't,* he thought, *we might be able to work together and find a way to escape.* Though his face was a grim mask covered with the rags that blindfolded him, inwardly Macklin was smiling. It was a slim hope, but it was the most he'd had in a very long time.

TRAITORS
AND HOSTAGES

CHAPTER SEVEN

Russian Embassy

8 Kutuzova vul.
Kiev, Ukraine
Monday, 16 March 1998
1130 Hours, Local

Your package from America has come through for you, General Komulakov. I have the information that you are expecting."

Komulakov smiled as he took the sealed package from the attractive young woman, a GRU officer assigned to the Russian embassy staff in Kiev as an economic attaché. His hand brushed hers, and he winked at her. The young woman blushed and smiled before escorting him to the embassy's *Rezidentura*—the space inside the embassy set aside for classified intelligence work. These rooms were theoretically free from the threat of foreign penetration, intercepts, or electronic monitoring. Every Russian embassy had these "sanctum spaces," where communications specialists encrypted and decrypted intelligence service messages on Kappelle devices, encoding machines used for transmitting and receiving sensitive traffic. Such a device had been used to decipher the message Komulakov now held in his hand as he sat down at a desk in one of the small, windowless rooms of the *Rezidentura*.

The GRU major had to squeeze past Komulakov in the narrow hallway that led to the tiny room. He yielded no space and made sure their bodies touched as she slid past him, her perfume lingering in his nostrils. Komulakov's eyes followed her as the door closed behind her. But when she was gone, the Russian was once again all business.

The former KGB officer was impressed at how quickly his mole had responded to his questions. The computer disk that Morales had left at the dead drop in Foxstone Park on 29 January had reached Komulakov via the Russian diplomatic pouch on 3 March—quick by the usual standards. An SVR courier had delivered it in a sealed briefcase straight from Dzerzhinsky Square. After reviewing the contents of the disk, Komulakov had drafted an encrypted message to the SVR *Rezident* at the Russian embassy in Washington, containing a list of questions for Morales. By Thursday night, 5 March, the overseas *Rezident* in Washington had already placed a handwritten note with Komulakov's questions in a ZipLoc plastic bag at the Foxstone Park dead drop.

The next morning, the *Washington Post* carried a Help Wanted ad, placed by the Washington *Rezident* as a prearranged signal to the mole. It read: "Mortician's Assistant, Board Cert. Rqd. 6 yrs exp. pref." The

Maryland phone number listed was bogus, but the phony ad informed the spy that it was an emergency, that he was to look for a delivery on the sixth.

Now, a mere ten days after he had received the list of questions, Morales had delivered answers.

✪

It was easier than Hallstrom had expected. He had anticipated that Komulakov would pay handsomely for any and all information he could find on the Newman matter. Since Komulakov's name had appeared in several of the files, Hallstrom had started searching every entry pertaining to Newman in the computerized ACS database, even before he heard back from his SVR handler at the Russian embassy in Washington by way of the March 5 classified ad. He had chuckled at the irony of the ad: though there was no way his Russian handlers could know it, inside the Bureau, his nickname was "The Undertaker."

Hallstrom had been extremely careful that neither Komulakov nor any of his other handlers had ever learned the true identity of the mole who identified himself as "Julio Morales." Still, Hallstrom knew it had long been evident to the Russians that whoever he was, he was highly placed within the U.S. government's national security apparatus. The former KGB general couldn't know it, but Hallstrom's current assignment as the FBI's liaison at the State Department's Office of Foreign Missions gave him access to a virtual treasure trove of secrets—including ongoing CIA operations and all overseas FBI investigations and counter-espionage activities. Also included in Hallstrom's purview were highly sensitive matters pertaining to U.S. military units and operations overseas. That's how he had discovered that Lieutenant

General George Grisham, USMC, the Commander in Chief of the U.S. Central Command, had received the FBI interview report prepared by Special Agent Glenn Wallace, in which a TWA pilot named Mitch Vecchio claimed that the IRA terrorist Gilbert Duncan was actually a Marine officer named Peter Newman.

By digging deeper in the ACS database, Hallstrom had discovered a computerized red flag dating all the way back to 1995, requiring any and all reports on "Peter Newman" or "Gilbert Duncan" to be forwarded by Flash precedence, eyes only, to General George Grisham, first at the Marine headquarters in Washington and then to Central Command, after the Marine general had become the CENTCOM CinC in April of '96. By searching back through the old records, Hallstrom had noticed that Grisham had also directed he be given immediate notice of any reports pertaining to a John or Sarah Clancy.

It was while he was musing over the possible connection between Newman, the terrorist Duncan, and the Clancys that Hallstrom had stumbled onto a piece of information that seemed to tie it all together. As he was sorting through a stack of message traffic on the afternoon of March 8, searching for more classified nuggets to send to Komulakov, the spy found a brief back channel message from the DIA communications chief at the U.S. embassy in Tel Aviv to a colleague at DIA HQ at Bolling Air Force Base:

```
SECRET/NOFORN
ROUTINE/PERSONAL
DTG: 281830ZFEB98
FM:   COMMO, DIA STATION, AMEMB TEL AVIV
TO:   COMM CHF DIA HQ, BOLLING
```

SAM, HOPE ALL IS WELL WITH YOU. I'M DOING ABOUT AS WELL AS CAN BE EXPECTED IN THIS HELL HOLE. THERE SEEMS TO BE AT LEAST ONE PALESTINIAN BOMBING EVERY FEW DAYS NOW. WE'VE ALL BEEN TOLD TO AVOID NIGHT SPOTS, PUBLIC TRANSPORTATION, ETC. IT'S QUITE A COMEDOWN SINCE OUR DAYS IN THE WHSR AND WHCA.

IT MUST BE GETTING TO ME BECAUSE I'M BEGINNING TO SEE GHOSTS. YESTERDAY, WHILE I WAS WALKING ACROSS THE INTERSECTION IN FRONT OF THE EMBASSY, I THOUGHT I SAW THE GUY WHO CAUSED US ALL TO GET TRANSFERRED: THAT MARINE TROUBLEMAKER, PETER NEWMAN.

THIS GUY WAS A DEAD RINGER FOR NEWMAN EXCEPT FOR LONG HAIR AND A BEARD, AND THE FACT THAT HE WAS DRIVING A PICKUP WITH ISRAELI PLATES. I WENT UP TO THE WINDOW AND ASKED HIM IF HE WAS AMERICAN, BUT HE SAID HE WAS IRISH. I EVEN JOTTED DOWN HIS LICENSE NUMBER AND HAD IT CHECKED OUT BY THE ISRAELI POLICE BUT THEY CONFIRMED THAT THE TRUCK WAS REGISTERED TO A JOHN CLANCY IN JERUSALEM. JUST GOES TO SHOW YOU THAT OLD WIVES' TALE THAT EVERYONE HAS A DOUBLE.

ANYWAY, STAY IN TOUCH. LET ME KNOW IF ANYTHING OPENS UP THERE OR AT THE PENTAGON. I'VE BEEN OVERSEAS EVER SINCE THAT FIASCO WITH HARROD AND NEWMAN BACK IN '95 AND AM REALLY LOOKING FORWARD TO GETTING BACK TO SOME STATESIDE DUTY.

WARMEST REGARDS, JONATHAN YARDLEY

BT

Hallstrom's pulse quickened as he read the message. He knew that, although these unauthorized personal communications through official channels were prohibited, they were commonplace among professionals. He also knew it would be highly unlikely for such a message to be widely circulated. Had he not been in the State Department's Foreign Missions Office, Hallstrom would never have known of its existence. Now, his investigative instincts, well honed from two decades in the FBI and almost fifteen years of surviving as a spy, told him that

Newman, Duncan, and Clancy were all one and the same person. It might not be the kind of proof that would stand up in court, but "Morales" knew it would be more than enough for Komulakov.

✪

After reading the twelve pages of documentation, along with the cover letter from Morales, Komulakov chuckled.

"Brilliant! Of course . . . where's the last place in the world you'd expect a terrorist to hide? The one country with such tight security that it would be impossible for him to hide there—Israel. Newman is in Israel!"

Morales had even gone the extra mile: following the discovery of Jonathan Yardley's personal back channel missive, he had called the embassy in Tel Aviv and asked to speak to the communications specialist. After identifying himself as the FBI liaison at the State Department and putting the fear of God into Yardley for using official channels for personal communications, Hallstrom asked the young man if he still had the license number for the pickup truck he'd mentioned in his cable. After getting the tag number from Yardley—and warning him again about transmitting personal messages over government circuits—he called the Israeli police. The Israeli officer who took the call, anxious to satisfy an American FBI inquiry, supplied Hallstrom with the name and address of the vehicle's owner.

In his response to Komulakov, Morales had thoughtfully provided the information to his Russian controller: "John Clancy, aka Gilbert Duncan, aka Peter Newman, resides at the Hospice of Saint Patrick, 35 Via Dolorosa, Jerusalem."

Hospice of Saint Patrick

35 Via Dolorosa, Jerusalem
Tuesday, 17 March 1998
0930 Hours, Local

Rachel Newman didn't know quite how to answer her friend. Then she simply settled on a response that was generic and truthful as far as it went. "John's away on a business trip—to Tel Aviv," she told Dyan Rotem.

"That's odd," Dyan said. "In the two years I've known you, I never knew your husband ever to travel on business. In fact, I don't think either of you have ever taken a trip anywhere, and I always see your husband working here at the hospice."

Rachel shrugged and tried to change the subject. "What did you find out from your doctor? Did you get some good news?"

"Oh yes! I almost forgot why I came to see you. Yes, it's good news. I'm pregnant! Can you believe it? I'm so happy."

"Is Ze'ev excited too?"

"Yes, he very much wants a son. He's very happy."

The two women talked for another half hour about children, husbands, and the little details shared by friends with one another. Yet, as close as these two friends were, each of them had secrets they had never shared.

Dyan was an Israeli, married two years to Ze'ev. She was originally from Canada and, as a teenager, immigrated with her parents to Israel in the mid-1980s. In 1993, Dyan met Ze'ev Rotem at Hebrew University in Jerusalem, where they were both engineering students. They dated off and on during that time, but lost track of each other when Ze'ev left school and enlisted in the Israel Defense Force. It wasn't until the spring of 1995 that they met again, when Dyan had transferred to the Yellin

Teachers Seminary in Jerusalem, where Ze'ev was posted for guard duty. They began to date once more, and some months later, on January 22, 1996, the two were married and moved to an apartment near Ziyyon Square, close to City Center.

It was Ze'ev who had learned that John and Sarah Clancy were working at the Hospice of Saint Patrick. He suggested to Dyan that she should try and meet with Sarah and get to know her, that they might find they have some common interests. He was right. The two women with different backgrounds became fast friends and enjoyed spending time together. The pair did their shopping together, taking leisurely trips to the Ha'Bucharim or Me'a She'arim markets. Sometimes they would spend several hours strolling through Gar Ha'Alzmaut (Independence Park) or Ha' Shalom Park (Peace Forest) to enjoy the sun, flowers, and tranquility, as well as each other's company.

They had made arrangements for another such excursion to the park. Rachel had asked Ay Lienne, the wife of Isa, the hospice manager, to watch James while they were gone. Ay Lienne was a convert to Christianity from South Asia and had met Isa at a church planted by the Saint Patrick community in Phnom Penh, Cambodia, where they were both students before coming to study in Israel. The petite woman with two children of her own was glad to baby-sit for her friend, whom she knew as Sarah Clancy. Rachel's little boy, James, enjoyed playing with Ay Lienne's children, and Rachel often watched Ay Lienne's two toddlers when Ay Lienne had to run errands.

After making sure that James had his favorite toys and that Ay Lienne remembered what time to put him down for his nap, Rachel and Dyan were finally ready to go.

"Sarah, let's take my car," Dyan said. "I'm parked just across the street by the Othman Taghmor."

The two women walked down the marble steps of the front entrance of the Hospice of Saint Patrick and let themselves out through the iron security gate, then out the big wooden door into the street.

They were laughing and joking about Dyan's pregnancy and the weight she was liable to gain when, as they approached the Al Ahran Hotel and the minaret adjacent to it, a Mercedes sedan moved beside them on the narrow street, forcing them to walk close to the stone wall on the left. At the same time, a van pulled up behind them and stopped. Her mouth went dry as Rachel realized they were trapped between the two vehicles.

The van door slid open beside them and four men jumped out. Then a fifth leapt from the passenger side of the front seat, carrying an Uzi automatic machine pistol. Before the two women could react, the four men grabbed them; hard hands clamped over their mouths, wrists, and legs. Rachel's eyes widened in fear, and she tried to scream. But the men holding her were too strong, and they dragged her into the van, pushing her down on the floor. Her face smashed into the hard surface.

Dyan was shoved in on top of Rachel. The men's moves were quick and practiced; the women had no chance to escape. Within seconds, the van door slid shut and the driver began to pull away. The four men in the back wrapped the women's mouths with duct tape, pulled cloth bags over their heads, and tied their hands behind them with narrow nylon straps. The driver turned up the radio in the van, effectively drowning out the women's frantic efforts to cry out. Rachel and Dyan were only just able to breathe through noses that were smashed and bleeding. Realizing that with her mouth taped shut she could easily suffocate, Rachel went limp, feigning unconsciousness, hoping simply to suck in enough breath through her bloody nostrils to stay marginally alert. Once she appeared to be unconscious, the man who had been kneeling on her back got off her, and Rachel was able to catch her breath.

The whole thing had taken less than twenty seconds. Rachel was certain there were no witnesses to the abduction.

✪

But she was wrong. The operation, swift and well-planned as it was, had been seen by someone else. Mordecai Miller, the duty officer in front of his video security system in the police station less than a kilometer away, watched helplessly. He quickly called Officer Nat Binyamin at Shin Bet headquarters to look at the dramatic scene on the preview monitor. Binyamin grabbed a microphone and immediately relayed a description of the car and van carrying the terrorist suspects and the two women.

Binyamin then went to other cameras in the command center and rewound the tapes to watch the event from other angles to see if he could get a license number or a better description of the kidnappers or their captives. He knew time was critical and that they had to capture these criminals before they had a chance to escape or harm the captives.

✪

Rachel assessed her injuries. Her nose had stopped bleeding beneath the hood, and she could breathe more easily, although she felt sure her nose was broken. Her left knee hurt, throbbing from its scrape against the doorway of the van. And from the way her left wrist was throbbing, she was sure it had been sprained when her captor twisted her arm to tie her hands together. As she tried to roll over to become more comfortable, one of the men again pressed his knee into the small of her back, pinning her back to the floor of the van. Once more she felt a wave of panic as she tried to breathe through the thick fabric of the bag.

She could feel Dyan lying beside her and heard her crying. Rachel was afraid too. She had no idea who had snatched them or where they were being taken.

Rachel heard one of the captors speaking in Arabic on a cell phone or radio. She couldn't understand all of what he was saying, but she guessed he was speaking to his superior. She could make out the Arabic words for "one woman" and "two women." Rachel guessed they had only intended to abduct one of them.

He listened for a moment, then responded with a word that Rachel understood: "OK."

The driver asked a question and the man with the phone answered. And the van drove on, apparently unchallenged.

✪

The van drove to a place just outside the walls of the Old City, only twelve blocks away from the place the women were taken. There, it pulled into a garage with an overhead door that raised just as the van approached and lowered quickly after it pulled inside. The Mercedes continued down the narrow street, pulling into another garage. By now the police were looking for both vehicles, so the kidnappers knew that they had to switch to something the police wouldn't be looking for.

The building was in an industrial area, and a large tractor-trailer truck was parked outside in an alley. The trailer was packed high with what appeared to be twelve-foot-long sections of eight-inch water pipe. There were two stacks of them, end to end, piled fifteen high and eight across on the flatbed trailer. In the center of the load of pipes was a rectangular wooden box, seven feet wide, seven feet long, and eight feet high. The frame of the box had shipping labels and stenciled markings identifying its contents as "Valves" and "Fittings" in English, German, Arabic, and Hebrew. If a highway check or customs inspection required the box to be opened, all that would be seen when the top or a side panel were pried off would be rows of neatly packed valves, joints, and couplings for a water main. And because the valves weighed hundreds of pounds, it could be expected that few inspectors would be zealous enough to lift them out. The box was chained down in the center of the load, between the two stacks of steel pipe.

The only way to access this steel-encased box was from the underside of the flatbed trailer.

Once the van pulled inside the garage, the four men pulled the women out of the vehicle and forced them to stand upright. A couple of the men steadied them, and the other two wrapped more duct tape about the women's ankles. They were picked up like rolls of carpet, carried outside to the tractor trailer, and stuffed upward through the opening in the bottom of the trailer until they were both shoved into a seated position on either side of the trap door. The metal door beneath the trailer clanged shut.

✪

Even through the cloth bag, Rachel could tell it was dark. She smelled diesel fuel and heard the idling of the engine.

The engine roared louder, and she heard the sound of air brakes being released. The tractor-trailer rig began to move.

Rachel and Dyan were cramped together with little room to move. After a few minutes of lying still in the darkness, Rachel realized the tape covering her mouth had begun to lose some of its adhesion. She pushed at it with her tongue and tried to open her mouth to loosen it some more. Finally it came loose and she could speak.

"Dyan, are you all right? Can you hear me?"

Dyan moaned softly as she tried to answer. "Mmmm . . . mmmm." A moment later, Rachel heard Dyan moving about.

"Aaugh! Mine came off too," Dyan said. "I think the blood from my lip must have softened it. I—I guess I'm all right. Are you OK?"

"More or less. Do you have any idea where we are or where they're taking us?" Rachel was amazed at the steadiness of her own voice.

"I don't know. The men are Arabs, but I don't think they're Palestinians. I understood just enough of the conversation when the one man was talking on his cell phone to figure out they weren't planning to take both of us . . ."

Rachel felt her throat closing with fear. Did this have something to do with what happened in Larnaca three years ago?

"I'm sorry I got you into this, Sarah," Dyan said. "Ze'ev told me that we had to be careful; he was probably targeted because of his military work. Sometimes they take the wife as a means of getting to the husband."

"You mean you think you're the one they were looking for?"

"Yes . . . they probably want to get my husband. That's why they took me, and you were simply with me, and they didn't know us apart."

Rachel wasn't so sure Dyan's analysis was right, but she decided not to say anything about Peter, his past, or the fact that she and Peter weren't the John and Sarah Clancy whom Dyan thought she knew.

The truck began to move again, jostling the two women against the sides of their confined space. For several minutes, it seemed to be in city traffic—stopping and starting as though at intersections. Rachel could hear the sounds of cars, commercial vehicles, horns, and even occasionally what sounded like muffled voices. She wondered if these were from pedestrians on the sidewalk—just a few feet from where they were hidden.

"Dyan, can you stand up?"

"I don't know. I can try . . . but I can't see anything, and I don't know if this thing is tall enough for a person to stand. I'll see what I can do . . ."

Rachel felt and heard Dyan moving around.

"I'm kneeling," Dyan said, panting with exertion. "I tried to stand, but it wasn't high enough. I'm braced in the corner. What do you want me to do?"

"Just wait there for a minute or so if you can. I'm going to try and move my arms around to the front."

Rachel scrunched her knees up and stretched her arms as best she could and then pulled her bound wrists down over her buttocks and thighs. Then, by rolling onto her back and drawing her knees up to her chest, Rachel pulled and pushed until she got her hands forward of her feet, and at last, above her knees.

"I did it! I have my hands in front of me now. I'm going to try and take this thing off of my head." Despite the numbness in her fingers from lack of circulation, she was able to find the end of the tape that held the cloth sack around her neck and after a few more minutes of tugging, she lifted the sack off her head.

A dim light from narrow slits in the floor filtered into their cell. It was enough to allow Rachel to peel off the tape that held the sack over Dyan's head.

Her friend's face was a mess. Her lip was swollen, she had broken a tooth, and dried blood from her broken nose was caked all over her face.

"Aren't we a couple of beauties," Dyan said. "Can you tell what direction we're going?"

Rachel knelt down and put her eye to one of the narrow slits in the floor. She could see pavement flashing by below her, and by moving back and looking forward, she could see the dual rear wheels of the truck pulling their prison. And then she noticed that the tires were making a shadow on the pavement—and that the shadow was directly behind the tires. She twisted her wrist to cast some light on her watch. It was 10:35. "The sun is directly in front of us. We must be headed east," she said.

Rachel stood as best she could and asked her friend to turn around so that she could try and undo the nylon cable ties binding her wrists. But, like her own, she found them impossible to get off. They would have to find some way of cutting them.

After ten minutes or so of trying to find something sharp enough to cut the ties on their wrists, the women were thrown to the floor as the truck made a hard left turn onto a smoother road. Rachel knew that it must be a highway, since the truck picked up speed, and she could hear the sounds of traffic passing in two directions. She put her eye to the slit in the floor and could see that the sun was now on their right-hand side. "We're going north," she guessed aloud. "Do you have any idea where they might be taking us?"

"Probably to Palestinian-controlled territory. Then, who knows? Jordan, maybe Lebanon . . . perhaps even Syria. They'll probably demand a ransom, then offer to trade me for my husband," Dyan said.

Rachel had a sense of déjà vu. That was exactly what Gunnery Sergeant Skillings had said when she was almost kidnapped in Larnaca three years ago. She wondered which of the two women the kidnappers were supposed to take.

And now she wished she hadn't agreed that Peter should go and meet with General Grisham in Cyprus. He was meeting Bill Goode in Jaffa, but the two of them would then sail to Larnaca harbor. Rachel wondered if her kidnapping had something to do with Peter's mission. It would be a week before her husband was scheduled to return. How she wished he had been at home when she was taken. Pete would surely know what to do. But she felt absolutely helpless. *What about James? Will they take him next?*

Aboard *Pescador II*
Larnaca Harbor, Cyprus
Tuesday, 17 March 1998
1015 Hours, Local

Bill Goode had taken precautions this time. Instead of berthing his sailboat at the docks in Larnaca harbor, he advised the harbormaster that he would anchor some distance from the docks. That limited the access to the boat and might have prevented the explosion that destroyed his first vessel. They would be able to detect any attempts to get to the boat, and it wasn't much of an inconvenience to use the *Pescador II*'s motorized Zodiac dinghy to shuttle back and forth.

General George Grisham and Gunnery Sergeant Amos Skillings were to be picked up at ten-thirty on the dock. They arrived with a full security detachment. Two dark blue Range Rovers, fore and aft, escorted General Grisham's staff car from the British Sovereign Air Base to the dock. Goode lowered the dinghy with the aid of an electric-powered winch, climbed over the side of the *Pescador II,* and started the engine on the back of the Zodiac.

"I don't expect any trouble this time," he told Newman as he headed for shore, "but just in case, there's a Sig 9mm with a full magazine in the pilothouse chart table drawer. If anyone approaches . . . well, you know what to do."

Newman nodded and waved him off. He watched as the small powerboat cut through the waters toward the dock. The *Pescador II* was almost a quarter-mile from the dock, and it would take Goode several minutes to make the trip. Newman walked back to the pilothouse, scanning the harbor basin for unusual traffic or anything that might seem out of the ordinary.

✪

A half hour later, General George Grisham and Gunnery Sergeant Amos Skillings, both dressed in casual civilian clothes, boarded the *Pescador II.* Bill Goode came up the ladder last. The general ordered Skillings to remain on lookout in the pilothouse while he, Goode, and Newman retired to the salon to discuss the matters that brought them all together in Cyprus.

General Grisham wasted no time getting down to business: "When the CIA interviewed Hussein Kamil in Amman right after his defection from Iraq, he told them he had acquired three nuclear weapons and brought them into Iraq under the very noses of the UN inspectors. In fact, he claimed to have taken delivery of them the same week you and your UN Sanctions Enforcement Group were assembling for the attack on Saddam and Osama bin Laden in Tikrit."

"Did the CIA follow up on this information?" asked Goode.

"No, they didn't believe him. Apparently, our station chief in Amman was convinced the whole defection business was fabricated to disseminate disinformation. One CIA guy I know pretty well told me, 'The whole defection thing was too pat. Kamil came over and was willing to spill his guts about the nukes, and then six months later, he goes back home when we don't take his bait.'"

"But he was killed when he went back, along with his entire family," Newman said. "And why would he bring over fifty family members with him if he was planning to go back to Iraq in six months? Doesn't his assassination give some credibility to the idea that he was telling the truth?"

"It would give me second thoughts if I was part of that CIA debriefing team," added Goode. "In fact, I'm guessing Kamil believed that since he was the only one who knew where the nukes were hidden, that was his insurance policy against Saddam's wrath."

Grisham nodded. "Yeah, everybody had perfect vision after the fact. But at the time, there were too many doubts and questions about Kamil's agenda."

"But what about now? Do the FBI and CIA think he was telling the truth?" Newman asked.

"No one in Washington is ever willing to admit a mistake. The CIA's sticking to its assessment that Iraq won't be able to acquire a nuclear weapon for the next two to three years," Grisham said. "If these guys have changed their minds about Iraq having nuclear weapons, they aren't putting it down in writing. I even went to NSA and DIA but didn't get any help there either. No one wants to admit the unspeakable—"

"—that Saddam has nukes," Newman said. "And when I worked for Harrod at NSC, I heard quite a bit about what Saddam would do if he *did* have nuclear capability. One leading theory is that the first thing he'd do is level Tel Aviv or Haifa. He thinks by attacking Israel he'd be an instant hero to the other Islamic nations."

"But that's sheer stupidity," said Goode. "Israel would use their own nukes to level Baghdad and turn the rest of Iraq into molten glass. Surely Saddam isn't *that* insane."

"He might be," Grisham said. "I've seen some FBI psychiatric profiles on this character. That's Saddam's style. Remember, Adolf Hitler is his idol. He's patterned his entire government after the Third Reich. Saddam doesn't get the respect he thinks he deserves from the rest of the Islamic world. *And* he knows his days are numbered—by the United States, Israel, or one of his own people. These profilers think he might be the world's most anxious suicide bomber. If he can create the world's greatest and most horrible suicide bomb, the profilers think he's fanatical enough to do it. Up until now, he's always had others take the bullet for *him*, but now, in his crazy mind, he could become the martyr of all martyrs by exploding a nuclear bomb in Israel."

"But why Tel Aviv or Haifa?" asked Newman. "Why not Jerusalem?"

"Jerusalem is a holy city to Muslims too. Saddam's idea is to eliminate as many Jews as he can so that one day Jerusalem can be strictly a place for Muslims."

"OK, but if he only has three bombs, why would he gamble with Israel?" Newman asked. "As Bill just said, Israel has hundreds of nuclear weapons. Their Jericho-2 missiles can reach Baghdad in less than an hour. Saddam would start Armageddon if he ever exploded a nuke in Israel."

"You may be right, of course. It's entirely possible Saddam will simply make it known he has the weapons and is prepared to use them, then demand some kind of fealty from all the rest of his neighbors. Either way, the danger is too great if Kamil really did take delivery of three weapons. If they are inside Iraq, we've got to find them before Saddam or someone else does," Grisham said.

"But why doesn't the CIA pick up on this? Or—"

"Or the United Nations? Yeah, they're supposed to be the world's peacekeepers now. But their win-loss record isn't all that great—especially on nuclear weapons inspections in Iraq. The State Department is sticking to the CIA reports of two, three years ago. They're discounting the idea that Saddam has really gotten his hands on some of these weapons—they're betting he hasn't. But that's wishful thinking. We have to assume *he does.*"

"And since Iraq is part of CENTCOM's responsibility, you've had to take it on," Goode said.

"I'm not the Lone Ranger in this," Grisham said. "I've been to the Pentagon and met with the Joint Chiefs. I've talked with men I trust who know the history and players well. Almost everyone I've talked to in uniform agrees the threat has to be taken seriously. However, because of the politics involved . . ."

Goode looked at Newman knowingly. "Yes, politics. Wasn't that the gasoline that somebody threw on the fire when Pete and his UN-sponsored ISEG guys were supposed to deal with this threat last time? With this President, and the United Nations, State Department . . . Congress . . . the Senate." Goode shook his head. "Is there anyone I left out? Every one of them has a personal agenda. That's *politics!*" Goode made the final word sound like an expletive.

Newman nodded. "Bill's right. Politics compromised my last mission. I used up eight of my nine lives on that one. What makes this mission any different?"

"Well, for starters, *I'm* running the show. I hope you know you can trust me—with your life, if necessary. This will be nothing like last time. I won't be compromised by . . . uh . . . politics." Grisham looked at Pete and Goode, and all three of them were seeing the faces behind the names Grisham had just avoided mentioning.

"And besides, Pete," he said, "I'm not going to share our secrets with those who pretend to be our allies, but then turn on us when they get the first chance."

"So you're going to do an end run around the White House?" Newman asked, then answered his own question. "Yeah, you're right to do it that way. It was Harrod who sold me out. But he had to have the approval of the President to do what he did. Just like when he did his behind-the-scenes dance with Iraq—as soon as my mission went south. Harrod told Saddam the White House would look the other way when Iraq invaded the north and went after the Iraqi Resistance Movement if the Iraqis kept quiet about the aborted attack on Tikrit."

Newman looked at Grisham. "General, you know I trust you implicitly. But how do I know the White House, or State Department—even the Pentagon—won't do something like that again if I become a political liability?"

"Because you won't even be on their radar screens," Grisham replied. "This assignment falls within *my* job description. I'm not going to go to them except to report on a successful mission. I have the assets in theater to accomplish the mission—a Delta Squadron, Night Stalkers from the 160th SOARs, Air Force and Navy strike aircraft—everything I need to get the job done. This isn't going to be some half-baked operation run out of the UN."

"Will the UN even be involved in any of this?" Newman asked.

"Not on your life."

For a moment, the three men sat without speaking, just soaking up what had been expressed so far. It was Newman who broke the silence.

"All right, General," he said, "what do I have to do to help you find these three nuclear weapons?"

"Hopefully, you won't even have to go into Iraq," Grisham said. "I'm hoping you can simply contact those who helped you escape three years ago and put them on the scent. If they can dig up anything that can help us locate the devices, I've got the people and equipment to get them out."

"I don't know if that will work. Even if Eli Yusef Habib and his family knew *where* to look, I'm pretty sure they wouldn't know *what* to look for."

"Look," said Grisham, "I'm not trying to minimize the difficulty in finding these things, but if Hussein Kamil hid them, then there must be *someone* alive today in Iraq who can lead us to them. And according to NSA intercepts, Saddam is looking for them as we speak—but even he doesn't know where they are. Yet, he has the best chance of stumbling onto them, so we've got to act quickly.

"I've put together a file of intel—some good, some not so good—that'll bring you up to speed. We know at least twenty-eight places in Iraq where they're *not* hidden."

"That's great." Goode chuckled. "Only a million places to look, *minus* twenty-eight."

"Well, almost," Grisham said, smiling reluctantly. "But our guys, working with the NRO satellite people, have eliminated another couple of thousand where it would be highly unlikely to find them. In fact, they've offered their top ten or so ideas as to where Kamil is likely to have hidden them."

"Yeah, well, once Newman's team starts searching for them, they may trigger a response from Iraq's Special Security Service. There's likely to be a national mobilization of Iraqi troops if a U.S. Special Forces operation starts turning over rocks," Goode said.

"Except Newman won't be leading a Special Forces team this time."

"What do you mean?" Goode asked. "You're sending him on this operation *alone?* That's insane!"

Newman didn't seem flustered. "Explain what you have in mind, sir."

Highway 90, Northbound

Near Tiberius, Israel
Tuesday, 17 March 1998
1410 Hours, Local

Rachel and Dyan were stiff, sore, cold, and dehydrated. Their injuries, the cramped quarters, and the frosty spring air had taken a toll.

But more than that, they were frightened. During the several hours they had been in captivity they had talked, cried, and prayed.

Dyan was certain she was the cause of it all. The Arab kidnappers surely wanted her husband, and this was a way to get to him. Rachel wasn't so sure but said nothing.

"Where do you think we are?" Dyan asked.

"I don't have the vaguest idea. But I have noticed that, except for the first twenty minutes to a half hour when we started out, we've been traveling north." She looked at her watch, grateful for its back-lit face. "It's almost fifteen minutes after two. We've been traveling a little over four hours. We must be more than a hundred miles from Jerusalem."

Dyan thought for a moment. "There are really only two stretches of highway out of Jerusalem where you can travel that long without turning east or west. We must be on either Highway 60 or Highway 90. And when we first started, we were going east until we got on the highway going north. Highway 60 goes straight north from the city, and Highway 90 goes north along the border, so you have to drive east on Highway 1 to Jericho in order to pick up 90. I'm thinking that we *must* be going north on Highway 90.

"If they hadn't taken our purses, I'd call my husband and tell him. My cell phone's in my purse," Dyan added.

"Yeah, mine too," Rachel said, but then felt in her jacket pocket. "Dyan! It's here! I forgot to put my cell phone in my purse this morning. I still have it!"

She struggled with her hands, still tied, to reach the phone. It was in the zippered pocket inside the left breast pocket of the jacket. After a little fumbling, she retrieved it. Nervous and excited, Rachel flipped it open and scrolled to the speed dial number of her husband's cell phone. As the call began to ring at the other end, she prayed Peter would hear it and answer right away.

She heard a voice.

"Peter!"

But the voice was a recording, announcing that the number she was trying to reach was out of the calling area, and to please try the call again later.

"Oh, no!" She remembered Peter had sailed to Cyprus with Bill Goode. She had the telephone number for Goode's satellite phone, but it was on the counter beside the phone at home.

"Here," Dyan said, "let me try and call my husband." But her hands were still tied behind her, and so she gave the number to Rachel, who punched it in to the keypad.

When the call began to ring, she held the phone to Dyan's ear. She watched as Dyan's expression was first hopeful, then gloomy.

"Voice mail. Push one."

Rachel pushed the button and held the phone back to Dyan's ear.

"Ze'ev, it's me!" Dyan said. "I've been kidnapped! Sarah Clancy and I were taken alongside my car this morning. It's just after two o'clock. We're bound and locked inside a box on the back of a large truck. I think our captors are Arabs. But they may not be Palestinians. There are at least six of them. They had guns. Sarah and I think we're at least a hundred miles north of Jerusalem, possibly on Highway 90. They may be taking us to Lebanon or the Golan Heights. Please help us. I love you, my darling. I love you with all my heart. Good-bye."

Rachel pushed the button to end the call.

"Do you think we'll ever see our husbands again?" Dyan asked, her voice breaking with emotion.

"Of course we will, Dyan. Count on it."

Rachel wished her confidence matched her words.

BLOWN COVER

CHAPTER EIGHT

Aboard *Pescador II*
Larnaca Harbor, Cyprus
Tuesday, 17 March 1998
1545 Hours, Local

The salon's hatch swung open.

"Excuse me, gentlemen," Gunnery Sergeant Skillings said.

Newman, Goode, and Grisham had a sheaf of papers and maps of various Middle Eastern countries spread out on the broad table in the center of the salon. They looked up at Skillings.

"Yes, Gunny," General Grisham said. "What is it?"

"I think it's something of an emergency, sir. There's a call on the satellite phone . . ."

"For me, Gunny?"

"No, Mr. Goode . . . it's a call from some woman with a foreign accent . . . calling for Mr. John Clancy."

The men looked at each other. Who would be trying to call John Clancy here aboard the *Pescador II?*

"What do you make of it, Pete?" General Grisham asked.

"The only person who knows I'm here is Rachel. She wouldn't call unless—" He bolted up from his chair.

"Take the call in my cabin," Goode called after him.

Newman reached the master's cabin in seconds and grabbed for the phone, mounted in a heavy weather bracket on the starboard bulkhead.

"Hello? Who is this?"

"This is Ay Lienne, Mr. Clancy. I am calling you from your apartment."

"What is it, Ay Lienne?"

"Mrs. Clancy telephoned me just awhile ago. She explained where I could find the telephone number and told me to call you. I—I am afraid that she is in trouble."

The Marine felt the rush of adrenaline in his gut, and his pulse quickened almost immediately. "Go on."

"She said that she has been kidnapped by some men with guns! Mrs. Rotem was with her. She says that Arabs took them both!"

"Did she say she was all right? Or where they took her? Did they force her to telephone with the information?"

The questions were coming faster than the young woman could respond in her imperfect English. Newman forced himself to wait for the reply.

"She said that she was calling with her mobile telephone, and that they were locked inside a big container that was being transported on a truck. Mrs. Clancy said that she had called home to leave a more detailed message on the answering machine there. She also said that so far they are all right, and the kidnappers do not know they have a telephone. They are still traveling on the truck. She told me to take care of your little James and to call you. She said you would know what to do."

There was a pause. Ay Lienne was probably hoping "Mr. Clancy" would tell *her* what to do. But Newman was grappling with his emotions, feeling more helpless than he had in a long, long time.

Got to keep it together!

"Ay Lienne, thank you. I am so grateful that Rach—uh, Sarah—was able to reach you. You did the right thing. I appreciate it. But the number you called here is not in Jerusalem. I am out of town, and it is likely to take me some time to get back."

"Shall I call the police?"

Newman paused to think before answering. He knew there was great risk in contacting the police. It wouldn't take them long to figure out who he was and discover his international terrorist status. For a moment, he thought if he could get back to Israel right away and immediately start looking for Rachel, he still might be able to keep his identity from the police. But two things bothered him about that idea: first, he knew that time was of the essence in any kidnapping, and precious hours had already passed; second, he had to think not just of his wife and himself, but also of the woman captured with Rachel. For Dyan's sake, the police should be notified right away, even if it meant his cover would be blown.

"Ay Lienne, I'd like to have you call Mr. Rotem. I think I recall his wife saying he works for the Israeli government. He may have some ideas. Their phone number is in the blue address book beside the phone in our kitchen. His name is Rotem—R-O-T-E-M. When you talk to him, you can give him *this* number and have him call me. Then I'll have *him* call the police. But if you *can't reach him* in an hour or less, *you* should call the police and report the kidnapping."

"I understand. And please don't worry about your son. James is safe with Isa and me. Is there anything else I can do for you, Mr. Clancy?"

"No . . . thank you. Not now, Ay Lienne. Just call Mr. Rotem right now and tell him what you told me, and then have him call me at this number as soon as he can."

"Yes . . . and, Mr. Clancy? I want you to know I am sorry for what has happened. Isa and I will pray for you all. I hope nothing happens to them . . ."

"Yeah, me too. Thank you, Ay Lienne."

Newman hung up the phone and leaned against the wall, his face in his hands.

Dear God, please . . . please . . .

After a few seconds, he stood up straight, took a deep breath, and went back to the salon. He needed to tell General Grisham that plans had just changed.

Hezbollah Safe House
Vicinity of Or Tal, Golan Heights
Tuesday, 17 March 1998
1630 Hours, Local

For nearly another hour after Rachel's phone calls, the truck had rumbled north along Highway 90. But then the vehicle had changed direction and traveled on a rougher road in a generally northeastern direction. Now the heavy truck had stopped, after meandering east on bumpy, unpaved roads for the past twenty minutes or so.

Dust stirred up by the tires filled their nostrils, and the women could taste it in their parched mouths. They could also tell the sun was beginning to set in the west behind them; the shadows of the wheels, viewed through the narrow slit in the floor, were much longer.

As the truck idled, Rachel called home again. This might be her last opportunity to share information. She left a brief message on the answering machine. "We've stopped. I have no idea where we are, but I think it might be in a village or some rural area. I can't hear any sounds of other traffic, but I can hear children's voices, dogs barking, and some livestock. I hope I'll be able to call back . . . but I'm not sure." She turned off the mobile phone and shoved it into her inside jacket pocket.

The women sat huddled against the metal walls of their container and waited. Dyan could hear men talking outside and figured out they were stopped at a Hezbollah safe house to get directions for the remainder of their trip. Then the voices faded.

After ten minutes, Rachel and Dyan heard voices and footsteps approaching the truck. There was scuffling in the gravel beneath the flatbed trailer. The men's voices were the same ones they had heard in the van when they were first captured—so their captors were still with them. There was the clank of a tool directly beneath them—bolts being unscrewed and removed.

Then a small plate, about sixteen inches square, was removed from the floor of their cell, and a hand appeared. It held a liter-sized plastic bottle that contained a colored liquid. The hand opened, and the bottle rolled across the floor, coming to rest against Rachel's leg. A moment later, a paper bag was handed up as well. Finally, the hand placed something small and shiny on the edge of the opening.

A male voice said in heavily accented English, "Here, you may use this to free your hands. Then you may remove the hoods over your heads so that you may eat and drink. You may also remove the tape from around your feet. If you make any noise, I will kill you and no one will *ever* find your bodies. Do you understand?"

Rachel could only nod, staring helplessly at the opening. Dyan said, "Yes."

The metal plate was reinserted in its aperture and screwed back into place. They heard the diesel engine of the truck rev and the grinding of gears. As the vehicle began to move, they smelled—or rather tasted—the truck's exhaust. In the dim light, Rachel could see what the shiny object was: a fingernail clipper.

It took Rachel almost fifteen minutes, working with the fingernail clipper in the near darkness, to cut through the tough nylon cable ties on Dyan's wrists. Rachel's fingers were numb; she dropped the clipper several times and had to grope for it as the truck lurched along a bumpy rural path. When she finally got Dyan's bonds cut, Dyan sat for a few minutes and worked her fingers, trying to restore circulation. Then, Dyan went to work on Rachel's wrists.

By the time they had both cut through their ankle restraints, an hour had passed, and they were exhausted.

Rachel reached for the paper bag. It contained two apples and four pieces of pita bread. The plastic bottle had been filled with a kind of tea.

They hadn't had any food or beverage since morning. Normally fastidious about her food, Rachel would have eaten the apples and bread even if they had been sliding around on the floor of the cell instead of in the paper bag. Dyan was hungry, too, so they finished the scant nourishment quickly.

"Did that tea taste strange to you?" Dyan asked.

"A little, yes," Rachel replied. "Let's save the rest of it for later. Who knows when we will stop again?"

The truck came to a particularly bad stretch of road, and the women were thrown back and forth inside their portable dungeon.

✪

Three large Arab men squeezed together inside the cab of the truck, nearly as uncomfortable as their captives. In the gathering dusk, the driver maneuvered the heavy rig onto Highway 91 where it intersected Highway 90, just north of the Sea of Galilee.

Less than half an hour after they had stopped and given food and drink to the women, the driver maneuvered the truck to within twelve kilometers of the place the UN had labeled the "Separation of Forces Line," a demarcation indicating the disputed boundaries between Israel and Syria. Israel had captured the Golan Heights from Syria in one of the last battles of the Six-Day War of 1967 and still occupied the commanding terrain. From the top of the Golan, it was possible to see all the way to the Mediterranean. And though Israel held the territory, Arabs who had lived in the area before the war still comprised the primary population.

Border guards flagged down the truck as it approached the final checkpoint. An Israeli customs official, accompanied by two UN guards, inspected the driver's identity papers and travel permit. Then they did the same check of his two companions, sitting beside him in the bench seat of the cab.

When the guards went to the rear of the trailer, the driver and his companions looked at each other. If the women made any noise, there would be trouble. The driver shot a questioning look at the man seated next to the passenger's window.

"Did you drug the food?" he asked in a half-whisper.

The other man nodded and made a placating motion with his hand. "Do not worry. They are out cold by now."

The driver nodded and looked in his rearview mirror.

The guards came forward, and one of them signaled for the driver to pull forward, across the border.

The truck went forward a short distance, and the ritual was repeated by the bored border police on the Syrian side of the demarcation line. The officials made a big show of checking entry documents and the truck's cargo manifest. Then a customs official looked carefully at the cargo itself, peering down each long water pipe with a flashlight and then checking the integrity of the large wooden box in the center of the truck's trailer bed.

✪

Inside their tiny prison, the two women were asleep, worn down by fear and tension, not to mention the triazolam in the tea. When the border guards opened the doors of the trailer, Rachel and Dyan were oblivious.

✪

The Syrian border guards waved the truck through, and the gate was lifted for the truck as it inched forward past the checkpoint. The men inside the cab breathed easier now. They were in Arab-controlled Syria. And they were now only an hour from their destination.

✪

The truck started climbing a steep grade and, inside the container box, the women rolled to the back of their cell, bumping into the back wall. The shaking and jostling roused them from their drugged sleep. As they became groggily aware, they both realized how uncomfortable they were; they hadn't had access to toilet facilities since that morning. The shaking of the truck made matters worse. They were buffeted from side to side and fell into each other clumsily and often with some force.

"We must be going into the mountains," Dyan said. "I'm guessing that they took us to the Golan Heights and crossed the border. We must now be in either Lebanon or Syria."

"Crossed the border—we slept through it! We could have alerted the guards," Rachel said.

Dyan rubbed her face and blinked her eyes. "I guess they drugged us—the food . . ." She looked at Rachel; her chin was trembling. "I . . . I'm afraid, Sarah. If they've taken us across the border, I'm not sure we'll be rescued."

"If we could only stop and get out for awhile," Rachel said. "If we could see where we are, maybe I could call home and leave another message."

"Yes, I wish we could stop too. But if we do, it might be so they can kill us and send evidence back to—"

"No! Don't think like that! We can't lose hope. We have to be strong."

The truck slowed and pulled to a stop. The two women looked at each other. A moment later, they heard someone beneath the truck bed again. Rachel looked down at the place where their cage had been opened before, expecting another bottle of tea or some food. Instead, she heard the fasteners being loosened for the larger metal plate that had sealed them inside. They were going to be let out—but for what?

Aboard *Pescador II*
Larnaca Harbor, Cyprus
Tuesday, 17 March 1998
1645 Hours, Local

Newman, Goode, and General Grisham were huddled in the main cabin of the sloop, staring at the scraps of paper arranged in neat stacks on the table in front of them. While waiting for the return call from Dyan's husband, Ze'ev, Newman called back to his apartment at the Hospice of Saint Patrick and carefully jotted down the snippets of information Rachel had been leaving on their answering machine. He had to form a plan.

"I've summoned you back into service, Pete, and that makes me responsible for you," General Grisham said. "That also makes it my responsibility to help you get your wife back. I have to assume the two matters are somehow related. And that makes it appropriate for me to use whatever assets are at my disposal as CinC.

"Now, the first thing we do is wait for the call from the other woman's husband. If he's somebody in the Israeli government, it could be that *his* wife was the reason for the kidnapping, and Rachel just happened to be in the wrong place at the wrong time. But we can't take that chance. We have to learn where Rachel is, develop a plan, and—if necessary—cooperate with the Israelis to get the job done."

Newman nodded.

"I can't believe that it's Rachel they're looking for," Goode said. "Most of the people who know she's alive are right here."

"I sure hope that's still true," Grisham said. "But things have changed now. If we have to work with the Israelis in order to get Rachel back, then you'll have to tell them the truth, Pete. You'll have to compromise your cover."

Newman didn't say anything for a moment. "I know . . . but . . . whatever it takes, I'll . . ."

He felt his throat constricting. He took several deep breaths.

"We have no choice but to tell the Israelis, General. And I think we have to assume that once they know who I really am, the rest of the world will find out pretty fast. Israel is a democracy. They have a free press. It's sure to leak."

"I may be able to help with that. My contacts in the IDF through CENTCOM can be trusted. I'll talk with them, tell them the whole story, ask for their help, and ask them to keep a lid on it. They may be a democracy, but they're also surrounded by enemies—and for that reason they seem to be better than we are at keeping secrets," Grisham said.

Goode shook his head. "The CIA and Mossad don't always see eye-to-eye. I know their military might be working with you, but they're sure to wonder why Pete was in Jerusalem for the past three years without checking in with the authorities. With all the flap over the Pollard spy case, they might want to exact a little face-saving by putting Pete through the wringer, if you get my drift."

There was a thoughtful silence, then Newman spoke.

"We don't have any other choice. We have to work with the Israelis since the women were kidnapped in Jerusalem. Whether they're still in the country, it's hard to say. From Rachel's cell phone messages, it sounds like they've either been taken into Jordan from Jericho, or north to Lebanon or Syria. From her descriptions, it doesn't seem like they went south."

"No, they're not in Egypt," Goode said. "Jordan, maybe. But the border crossings there are a lot hotter than those in the Golan Heights."

Newman shrugged. "If only we had somebody who saw them . . ."

"I need to issue you new paperwork and documents to prove that you are who *I* say you are, and that you're working for CENTCOM," Grisham said. "I'll get Gunny on that right away. Meanwhile, you guys work on a way to get Pete back to Jerusalem ASAP. I'd take you over in my Gulfstream, but that would tip off Washington, and I don't want to have to answer too many questions from the Potomac until we get your status ironed out. Probably the best thing would be to see if the Brits can lend us an aircraft to get you back to Tel Aviv before the evening gets much older."

As he was getting up to ask Gunnery Sergeant Skillings to join them, the satellite phone rang. Goode jumped up and grabbed it before the second ring.

"Hello . . . ?"

Goode's eyes flew open in surprise.

"Just a moment, please."

He covered the mouthpiece and leaned toward Peter. He spoke in a whisper.

"It's Ze'ev Rotem—calling for Peter Newman. He knows who you are!"

Nawa Highway
Near al-Shaykh, Syria
Tuesday, 17 March 1998
1645 Hours, Local

Rachel and Dyan were finally out of their steel dungeon. As the women slid to the ground beneath the flatbed trailer, they were grabbed by two men each. The men all but dragged them from beneath the dust-coated tractor trailer and stood them against the side. Although the sunlight was fading fast, there was still enough light that the women had to squint; they'd been riding in the dark all day. The stiff breeze chilled them after being confined for nearly seven hours in the metal box. As they stood shivering, a man came up behind them; he fastened a handcuff around Rachel's right ankle and fastened the other cuff to Dyan's left ankle.

"You may go over in those bushes to relieve yourselves," one of the men said first in Hebrew, then in broken English. The women hobbled awkwardly together to a nearby patch of scrub vegetation that would give them meager cover. It was humiliating, but they did as they were told.

One of the men waved an automatic rifle and said, "Do not try to run away, or I will shoot you." Then he and his partner walked back to the truck to wait. From what the women could discern in the gathering gloom, the truck had stopped just off what appeared to be a major east-west highway and just before the intersection with another road that seemed to run north and south. There did not appear to be any other traffic on either thoroughfare.

Relieving their painfully full bladders helped, but they needed more to eat and drink.

Watching carefully for any sign of her captors' approach, Rachel used Dyan as a screen and reached inside her jacket for her cell phone. She punched in her home number. Nothing happened. She looked at the display: no signal.

A confirmation they were no longer in Israel, Rachel guessed. There, the cell phone coverage was nearly universal. The absence of a signal might mean that they were across the border somewhere. *But where?*

Rachel looked toward the setting sun. It was falling behind some high mountains. However, they were much bigger than anything the truck had climbed on its way here.

Dyan spoke to Rachel in a soft voice. "Those large mountains over there must be Lebanon, by the Bekaa Valley. We've been traveling east for a long time. I think we're in Syria. Does your phone work at all?"

Rachel shook her head, but then noticed the "in service" icon on her screen; the signal was weak, but it was definitely there. She tried her home number again. A recording told her she needed to check the number and dial again. She tried again, using the country code for Israel, and this time the call went through. Quickly, as soon as the answering machine picked up, Rachel recited all that she thought would be helpful about where she thought they were, what direction they were heading, and the time. Then she closed the phone and hid it back inside her jacket.

Their captors were coming to get them and escort them back to the container on the truck. This time, however, they left their hands unbound and didn't replace the blindfold cloth bags. One of the men handed them some water, candy bars, and more apples. "Make this last," he said. "You are being transferred to a train in a half hour. It will take you to where we are going, but will take a long time. You will have no more food, water, or rest stops until we get to our destination, about midnight."

The women took the nourishment and began to eat and drink while the heavy metal trap door was once again screwed into place.

Within minutes, the truck was once again on its way. In another twenty minutes, it pulled into a railroad freight yard. A forklift truck came to hoist the box onto a flatcar where it was strapped down. An hour later, the train began to move.

An hour after that, both women were asleep.

THE WOLF

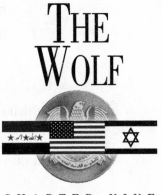

C H A P T E R N I N E

Ben Gurion International Airport
Tel Aviv, Israel
Tuesday, 17 March 1998
2330 Hours, Local

N
ewman awoke as the tires beneath the belly of the Royal Air
Force C-130 screeched against the tarmac of Israel's largest
civil and military airfield. Despite the anxiety that he was feeling about the desperate plight of his wife, he was practicing what he had
so often preached to his troops: *If you're not driving it or piloting it, sleep
on it, because you don't know when you'll get to sleep again.*

Now he could feel the rapid deceleration as the pilot reversed the
pitch of the four giant propellers and turned off the runway to the taxi-
way that would take this old workhorse of military aviation to the large,
yellow, Israeli Air Force hangar at the west end of the field. As the air-

craft came to a halt in the pool of orange light cast by the sodium vapor lamp mounted atop the hangar, Newman checked his watch. The two-hundred-mile flight from Cyprus had taken a little more than an hour and a half, less than the time that it took him to ride in an armored Land Rover from Larnaca to the airfield at the British Sovereign Base at Akrotiri. On the opposite side of the aircraft cargo bay, Gunnery Sergeant Amos Skillings was stretched out on the red nylon web seat. He sat up and nodded to Newman.

The commander of the RAF Transport detachment on Cyprus had been only too willing to oblige General Grisham's request for an aircraft to make a "no-notice courier sortie for two U.S. PAX" to Israel. And the Israeli Air Force had quickly facilitated the mission by granting the necessary diplomatic clearance for the flight—while assuring the Commander in Chief of U.S. Central Command that it would be unnecessary for members of the CENTCOM staff to pass through Israeli Immigrations or Customs. It had all gone, Newman reflected, extremely well thus far.

But now that the RAF crew chief, in his gray-green Nomex flight suit, was lowering the ramp at the rear of the aircraft, the Marine's anxieties returned. As he stood and grabbed the duffel bag that had been his pillow during the flight, Newman could feel the tightness in his gut and a pounding in his temples as he thought of what his wife and her friend, Dyan, might be enduring at that very moment. He worried, too, that their captors might grow unsure of their worth as hostages. And then, as it had earlier, the thought occurred to him: *what will happen if their kidnappers decide they have to get rid of the women, who could testify against them, in the event of their capture?* He knew the answer to that question and did not want to entertain it in his thoughts.

His mind raced with various options for rescuing the kidnapped women and bringing them home without any further harm or complications. His brain tried to organize the various plans swirling around in his mind and to give them priorities—while bathing all the options in fervent prayer.

Newman returned a salute to the crew chief as he and Skillings exited the rear of the aircraft. A feeling of awful sadness touched the Marine at the fleeting thought of losing Rachel; since they had first come to Israel three years ago and begun to remake their lives, he and Rachel had grown closer and more in love than ever before. Their love was made even more complete by the arrival of their baby son, James. To think of her now, in harm's way, was almost more than he could handle. *This isn't helping. Lord, help me stay focused on what I have to do, instead of what might happen. Please grant me clarity and wisdom.*

Pete forced himself to list his tasks in some kind of order. First, he had to find the husband of his wife's cocaptive. Ze'ev Rotem had told Newman he would meet him here, in front of the big Israeli Air Force Transport hangar.

Newman was surprised when Rotem told him on the telephone that he was, in fact, Major Rotem of the Israeli Defense Force. That information actually brought the Marine a sense of relief; this man was likely a kindred spirit, someone he should be able to trust on a mission to rescue their wives. Ironically, Newman guessed, both men had much more in common now. Each surely felt the same dread and cold anger toward those who had taken the women hostage.

As Newman walked toward the small group of men standing in the shadows beside the large Israeli Air Force hangar, he patted the breast pocket of the battered old leather flight jacket that William Goode had loaned him aboard the *Pescador II*. Inside the pocket were the three black-covered diplomatic passports that General Grisham had handed him as he boarded the C-130 in Larnaca—one for himself, another for Rachel, even one for little James. During the flight, he had stared at the pictures of his wife and son. It was the first time he had seen his young son identified by his real name: James Atkinson Newman.

A trio of Israeli officers—accompanied by six armed soldiers carrying Uzi submachine guns—greeted Newman and Skillings and escorted the two Americans inside the hangar through a small door beside the large aircraft portal.

Inside, they found themselves in a well-lit office where an Israeli Army brigadier general was waiting. He dismissed the others, and they went into the hangar bay. With his hand outstretched, he said, "Good evening, Lieutenant Colonel Newman and Gunnery Sergeant Skillings, I am General Yem Burach. Welcome back to Israel. I am sorry about what has happened to your wife. May I see your passports, please?"

The two Marines reached in their pockets and handed the Israeli officer their passports. He looked at each and handed them back. "I have had several lengthy discussions with General Grisham today. We have known each other a long time. We were classmates at your Amphibious Warfare School many years ago. I trust him totally. He told me that I could trust you the same way, Colonel Newman. Is that true?'

"Yes, sir—absolutely," replied Newman, uncertain where this line of reasoning was heading. "Is there any more news about my wife? Do you know if my son is all right? General Grisham told me that James would be brought here."

"Slow down, Colonel, first things first," replied the general. "We have some intelligence about that, and you will be fully briefed in a few moments. Your son is on his way here with the wife of your *chef d'hotel*. However, before we proceed, I must have your word that you will keep us informed on all your movements within the country, and I insist that you coordinate all of your activities with Major Rotem. Is that acceptable to you?"

"Yes, sir," said Newman, knowing that there was no other answer.

"Very well," General Burach said. Then he pointed to another office across the expansive hangar structure. "Major Rotem is waiting for you in that room over there."

"Gunnery Sergeant Skillings, it is my understanding from General Grisham that you are flying back to Cyprus on the British C-130. Is that correct?"

"Yes, sir. I'm to take Colonel Newman's son back with me."

"Good," said Burach. "If you wish to join Colonel Newman as he meets with Major Rotem, I will inform you when our vehicle arrives with his son and the young woman who has been watching after the boy. Oh, I almost forgot. Here's a mobile phone, Colonel Newman, courtesy of the Israeli Defense Forces. You may use it while you are here. It also has international capability, so you can dial overseas directly."

Newman took the small phone and nodded. "Thank you, General." He stuck the phone into his pocket, guessing it was probably carefully monitored; any conversations carried over that particular phone would likely have every word recorded in an Israeli intelligence facility. In his duffel bag, Newman had an encrypted Motorola Iridium satellite phone that General Grisham had given him before leaving Cyprus.

Newman and Skillings walked across the hangar to the office that had been pointed out to them. Newman knocked on the door and opened it. A muscular man with close-cropped hair sat on the edge of a wooden desk, an IMI Galil suppressed sniper rifle slung over his shoulder. He was in civilian clothes, but two armed, uniformed IDF soldiers were seated nearby, loading ammunition into magazines for their own automatic weapons.

"Major Rotem?"

"That's me," said the man in civilian clothes. "Please come in."

The two soldiers stood up and left the room to guard the door.

Ze'ev Rotem was feeling guilty about what had happened to the wife of the man standing in front of him. The Israeli major was, in fact, certain that his own wife was the target and that "Sarah Clancy" was simply an innocent victim of the terrorists. The Israeli major had good reason to believe this, since Ze'ev Rotem had secrets of his own.

Newman extended his hand and Rotem shook it. "So, we get a chance to meet at last," Major Rotem said with a smile. "Our wives are good friends, but we have not had the opportunity to meet before this. Unfortunately, under these circumstances, the pleasure is lacking."

"Any word about our wives?"

Rotem shook his head. "Only the messages your wife was able to leave on your answering machine at home. Thankfully, she had such presence of mind and composure to think of calling and trying to leave helpful information. Did you hear the messages?"

"Yes, I called home from the British airbase and played them back. I tried to piece together Rachel's accounts of the trip, and I think she's right. From her descriptions, the time it took, and so forth, I'd bet they were taken north on Highway 90, then on 91 into the Golan Heights, and from there into Syria. But after that . . . I'm not sure."

"I agree. It's the only route that works. From her last call, I think they were near Izra, Syria. That's probably the major highway intersection that she mentioned. At Izra, there's a freight train connection that goes north. She said that they were locked in a large container of some sort. If this is the Hezbollah cell I think it is, they are working with the PFLP and probably put them on a train that would take them to a place north of Damascus. That's a route the Iranians and Hezbollah use a lot, and they don't think we know about it yet. If it's that one, they probably transported the women to the city of Hims—up here." Major Rotem pointed to the map on the office wall.

"That's quite a distance north of Damascus. Why do you think they went there?"

"It's safer for them in this more remote area. Word gets around faster in the city . . . so if they were to stay in Damascus for any length of time, we'd hear right away from our agents. We haven't heard anything so far, and that's why I think they'll have them in Hims."

"Do you know exactly where to look in Hims? And do you think they'll keep them alive?"

"The answer is 'yes' to both of your questions. The reason we haven't bothered the PFLP or Hezbollah in Hims is because we've wanted to see where that intelligence leads. But I know exactly where their compound is—where they'd be holding them. This place is about seventy-five kilometers from the coast, just northeast of Lebanon. We can get there fairly easily from the sea and move in without being detected.

"I'm guessing that whoever is holding them will probably get word to us, to tell us whatever it is that they want from us. I think they only took both women because they weren't sure which was the one that they wanted—no doubt to get at one of us. But the question is, which one of *us* do they want, Colonel Newman? You . . . or me?"

"Look, I'm not here to play 'you show me yours and I'll show you mine.' I'm here to tell you why they might want *me*. But I'm guessing you've already figured that out; otherwise you wouldn't know my real identity. However, if we're going to work together and trust each other, I have to know what *you* know—and why it could just as easily be you that they're after."

"Fair enough. And since, as you say, I already know quite a bit about you, Colonel Newman, I'll tell you about myself.

"I am a major in the Israeli Defense Force. I serve in the Sayeret T'zanhanim under the control of Sayeret Duvdevan."

"My Hebrew is pretty rudimentary," Newman said, "but doesn't 'Sayeret T'zanhanim' mean you're a paratrooper, and that you deal with counter-terrorism outside of Israel?"

"Yes, I'm a paratrooper with Israeli foreign CT ops."

"But I'm not sure about the Sayeret Duvdevan."

"Sayeret Duvdevan is the name of the Center Command in the middle of our nation, where I am assigned," Rotem said. "My work is in counter-terrorism, but with a specialty. I am one of a small cadre of those who are responsible for 'extrajudicial action' outside of Israel."

"I think I take your meaning, sir. Clearly, you're no regular IDF soldier. 'Extrajudicial action' could be understood as 'execution,' 'assassination,' 'removal,' 'liquidation,' or 'termination.' It all means pretty much the same thing—correct?"

"Does it bother you, Colonel Newman, that I am an assassin for my government?"

"Bother *me*, Major Rotem? I'm not sure if that's the right word," said Newman. "I don't know how much you know about me, and I don't know that it matters, but I've had some experience in . . . uh . . . that line of work, and that experience taught me that that kind of thing doesn't work very well."

"I understand why you would feel this way," said Rotem. "But the way the United Nations was trying to carry out assassinations when your mission was compromised is entirely different from the way we would handle it here. We get our orders from a small, secret council made up of an official from the Ministry of Defense, another from the Internal Security Service or *Shituakh,* the IDF Chief of General Staff, and a member of the Israeli judiciary. This council reviews requests for actions of termination, and the decisions have to be unanimous. What happened to you, Colonel Newman, could never happen to us."

"So this council decides who lives and who dies. How does a terrorist make the list?"

Rotem was feeling a little fidgety at the idea of revealing state secrets, but General Burach had told him that the American Marine had full clearance to this information. "Our intelligence services keep a list of known 'targets' and updates it regularly. It's a list of about a hundred names. When some are taken care of, they add others."

"But many people—even here in Israel—say that assassinations are a violation of the Geneva Convention," Newman said.

"No . . . that is not true. When a person is selected for extrajudi-
ciary removal, it's because that person is an enemy terrorist, making war
against us. The Geneva Convention forbids killing of innocent *civilians*. It doesn't cover someone who is a party to the conflict. We have
chosen this way because we found it necessary to protect ourselves."

Newman waited.

"Yes, we kill terrorists," Rotem said, "but our goal is to do so before
they have a chance to blow themselves up on a school bus, or among
Israeli women shopping in the marketplace."

Rotem saw the look on Newman's face. "This is not a new idea,
Colonel Newman. I didn't invent my job. Nor was it invented by any
of the other Duvdevan units. You see, our country has been forced to
live by this credo for more than thirty years. As you know, there are
countless numbers of terrorists from many different countries who
make it their goal and mission to destroy Israel. It is my job to make
sure they are not successful. Instead of waiting for them to attack us and
then respond, we learn of their plans and make certain they cannot be
implemented. We must kill them first.

"If I don't kill them first, they might come and board one of our
buses and blow up a dozen schoolchildren. If I don't kill them, they
might put a bomb in a crowded marketplace and take out scores of
innocent people.

"Our government has debated this in every political and religious
forum in our nation. One of our chief rabbis cites justification for what
we do, based on a twelfth-century doctrine from the Talmud. Israel is
fighting a war of *mitzvah,* and it means we have a right to self-defense.
We might have to kill a hundred terrorists in order to save a thousand

innocent men, women, and children from being killed or maimed. It is justified."

"So . . . based on what you know about this cell that's holed up in Syria with our wives," Newman said, "are any of these guys on your 'hit list?'"

"Yes. They are now."

PFLP Safe House
Hims, Syria
Tuesday, 17 March 1998
2330 Hours, Local

Although it was nearly midnight, Rachel was still awake. Her mind was reeling from all that had happened since she and Dyan had been seized just after nine that morning. It seemed to her that the timeline had to be wrong—that the kidnapping had happened several days ago. She lay on the floor atop a filthy mattress, still dressed in the clothes she had been wearing when she was grabbed. Dyan was sleeping fitfully across the small room, also on the floor. A pile of old newspapers formed a pillow for her head.

The women had not been treated as harshly as they had feared. Their captors gave them something to eat and drink when they got to this old limestone building, about three hours ago. True, the men were rougher than they needed to be when they searched them: one of the men slapped Rachel when he found her cell phone inside her jacket pocket. He took it and threw it violently across the room, smashing it against the rock wall. The blow across Rachel's face made her nose bleed again, and the cut inside her lip stung enough to distract her from some of the other aches and pains she was feeling.

They had tried to question her about the phone, wanting to know if she had contacted anyone. But the terrorist who spoke the best English, the one who seemed to be the leader, was not there, so Rachel had told them that her husband was out of town and could not be reached, and that there was no one else at home to take her call. She also told them, convincingly, that she did not call the police—only her babysitter, to ask her to keep her child until she returned.

The captors locked the women in the cramped room and gave them no lamp, furniture, or bedding, other than the two thin, dirty mattresses.

Dyan was sick, either from her pregnancy or from the rough handling and confinement in the hot, airless metal cage that had detained them during the long trip to the terrorists' safe house.

Rachel tried to recall everything she could about pregnancy from the nursing classes she had taken in college. She prayed Dyan wouldn't have any complications brought on by their ordeal.

Just before exhaustion overwhelmed her, Rachel began to think about her own child. She had been able to reach Ay Lienne and ask her to watch James until Peter returned. She knew her two-year-old son was in good hands—at least for the time being. As she pictured her little boy, asleep in his crib, she began to cry softly. The tears were still wet on her cheeks when she fell into a fitful, restless sleep.

Ben Gurion International Airport
Tel Aviv, Israel
Wednesday, 18 March 1998
0030 Hours, Local

"So how did you know my real name was Peter Newman? How long have you known that I wasn't really John Clancy?"

The two men had been sitting at a conference table in the hangar office for more than an hour, waiting for Newman's son to arrive and for an intelligence officer from IDF to bring them the latest on the kidnapping.

"I couldn't share all the details even if I knew them, and I don't," said Rotem. "But I do know that in early February, both Shin Bet and Mossad received a new 'BOLO' notice from your FBI that there was another alert for an IRA terrorist named Duncan. We know the IRA has worked very closely with the Libyans, the PFLP, and even Hezbollah, so we ran the photo through the facial recognition software, and even with your beard, your face came up as a match.

"It took less than forty-eight hours to figure out where you lived and what your alias was. That's when I was assigned to keep an eye on you, to learn what you were up to, and to keep track of anyone you met. You may recall, that's when my wife and your wife first met. I asked her to do that, to befriend Sarah—I mean, Rachel—so that she would get close, and we could start to build a profile on you."

"Swell."

"The trouble was, Dyan really liked your wife. They—how do you say it?—'hit it off' right away. And every night when I was home, she would berate me that the intelligence services had it all wrong, that 'John and Sarah Clancy are just nice Christians sent to run the Hospice of Saint Patrick.' It was getting so that even I believed her.

"But then, just a week or so ago, our signals intelligence people intercepted something—I don't know what—from the Russian Intelligence Service communications channels that linked 'Clancy,' 'Duncan,' and 'Newman' together. We went back further in our records and found a very nice photo of Major Peter Newman in Israel in 1993, here with a group of Marine officers for the Desert Storm Tactical Symposium. Do you remember that trip?"

"Of course. We were here for three days."

"Well, you made quite an impression. That's why, when we figured out who you really were, the decision was made simply to keep an eye on you. Everyone up my chain of command knew that a man with your credentials couldn't be a traitor or a terrorist. We were about to make some quiet inquiries when our wives were kidnapped."

Newman sat quietly for a few moments, thinking about what he had just been told.

"I'm concerned about two things, Major Rotem. First, what prompted the FBI to issue the BOLO in February? And second—but of greater concern—how is the Russian intelligence service involved in all this?"

"I don't know the answers to either of those questions, but I shall inquire."

As Rotem spoke, there was a knock at the door. Rotem opened it to admit another IDF officer, carrying a cloth briefcase.

"Colonel Newman, this is Captain Zakheim. He is one of our intelligence officers, and he has the most recent information."

The captain entered without any formalities, took a videotape and a DVD out of his briefcase, plugged them into a combination VCR/DVD player, and then turned to Newman.

"Colonel Newman, I want you to see if you recognize any of these people."

Newman stared at the screen, horrified as he watched the abduction of his wife and her friend. The entire operation lasted less than fifteen seconds. Then an enhanced version came across the screen. The image of each of the men's faces froze on the screen. But on one view, the frame froze as one of the men held Rachel by the hair while another man pinned her legs as they tried to throw her into the van. The terror on Rachel's face made Newman want to turn away.

"Do you recognize any of them?"

"No. Do you?"

"Two of them are PFLP. At least one appears to be a well-known Hezbollah operative," said the captain. "It's unusual for them to operate together, but not unprecedented. What is most unusual is for an operation of this kind to take place in Jerusalem—particularly inside the walls of the Old City."

"Do we know where they are now?" asked Newman, still staring at the fear-filled image of his wife.

"They are probably in Hims. Inside Syria. Out of our reach."

"Thank you, Captain. That will be all," Rotem said. "You may leave the material. I'll see that it is returned to you."

"Are they really out of reach?"

"Well, not necessarily," said Rotem. "I've undertaken some planning. A rescue mission might be possible, but risky. Six of my men have volunteered to help get them back. I have permission and have been promised IDF assets—within reason."

"Are six men enough?"

"I hope so, because that's all the Ministry of Defense is going to allow us to take into Syria. Besides, we don't want to take a chance on too many of us, in case of a problem or capture."

"Are these guys experienced in counter-terrorism?"

"I'd put them up against your SEALs, Rangers, or Delta Force any day."

"They're that good, huh? And that's why you're only taking six men?"

"Actually, we'll only take four—plus the two of us. We'll follow the coastline, below aircraft radar, and land on the beach in Syria. Once there, we'll rendezvous with four additional people from inside. That'll give us a force of ten."

"Good . . . that sounds about right," Newman said. "Can you fix me up with a weapon and some other gear?"

"Over there in that locker by the door. We can get you some boots when we know your size."

As Newman was going through the gear and checking the automatic Uzi, there was another knock at the door. This time Skillings opened it. A figure outside motioned to him, and Skillings stepped out of the hangar bay, closing the door behind him. A moment later Skillings was back. He poked his head inside. "Sir . . . your neighbor has arrived with James."

Newman dropped the gear on a map table and hurried out the door. Across the inside of the hangar, a police car had pulled up nearby and the police officer from the passenger side got out and opened the rear door.

The first face he saw was the wife of the hospice manager. "Ay Lienne, I'm so sorry to put you through all of this."

Then he saw his son, lying across the backseat, asleep with his head in Ay Lienne's lap.

"He was asking for his mommy and daddy after dinner," she said, "but he hasn't been cranky. He was just wondering where the two of you were. Any word . . . ?"

"Not yet, but the kidnappers will probably contact us later this morning, most likely with a ransom demand. Can I impose on you to help me—will you go back to our apartment with these policemen and wait? If Rachel . . . I mean Sarah, or the kidnappers call, I need you there to reassure my wife that James is safe and that I am taking care of things. Can you do that?"

"Of course," Ay Lienne replied. "Is there anything that you want me to tell the kidnappers if they ask why you are not available to take the call?"

"Tell them the truth—that I was in Cyprus when it happened and am not yet back in Jerusalem. That's all you need to say. Then take a message. The police and one of Major Rotem's men will be there with you. They'll know what to do."

Newman reached into the back of the police car and picked up his little boy. James wriggled as Newman lifted him, then snuggled against his father's chest.

After watching for a moment, Gunnery Sergeant Skillings leaned over to whisper in Newman's ear. "Sir, I really ought to be moving along with your son. Your sister's Aero-Med flight is due to land at 0600 on Cyprus."

Newman looked at the sergeant, then at his son, sleeping in his arms.

"Don't worry, sir. You know your sister will take good care of James . . . until his mommy and daddy come to get him."

"Thanks, Gunny."

Newman's eyes had misted. James roused from his sleep.

"Daddy?"

Newman looked at his son, then bent down and stood him up on the floor of the hanger. The sleepy little boy looked around at all the colorful activity and lights, and blinked several times.

"Daddy." He hugged Newman's leg.

Newman wiped his eyes, then squatted down, face-to-face with his son.

"How's my boy? Did you come to see Daddy?"

The little boy nodded and looked up at Skillings.

"Do you remember our friend Amos?"

Again the boy nodded.

Skillings reached down with his big hand and let the boy grab his forefinger to "shake hands."

"Hey, pal . . . Daddy's going to go get Mommy. It's far away, so you can't come with me. You get to go with Amos on the airplane. You'll stay with him and your Aunt Nancy until Mommy and Daddy come to get you. OK?"

James clung to Newman.

"Daddy. Stay wif Daddy."

Swallowing hard, Newman had to peel the boy's hands from his neck and hand him over to Skillings, who took James gently in his big hands. He talked softly into the boy's ear as he walked away, toward the C-130. "You're gonna see your Mommy and Daddy again, real soon," Newman heard Skillings saying. "But first, we're gonna go for an airplane ride . . ."

Newman could hear James start to whimper as the gunnery sergeant walked with him up the ramp of the big transport craft. He had to turn away.

A few minutes later, the tail ramp closed and the big turboprop engines began to whine and then roar. Without pausing, the big craft lumbered toward the runway for takeoff. Newman watched it climb quickly into the black, moonless sky.

The boy's father felt a comforting hand on his shoulder.

Major Rotem said softly, "He'll be fine, Colonel Newman. He's in good hands. I know you've had a difficult day, but we're running out of night. We need to go over the plan once more with our whole team, and then we must go. Our aircraft is almost ready."

"I'm OK," Newman said. "I'll get my gear and get dressed. I'll be ready to go in five minutes."

Lovebirds Gentleman's Club
Low Street at Orleans
Baltimore, Maryland
Tuesday, 17 March 1998
1930 Hours, Local

Bob Hallstrom had looked furtively around as he dropped the package into the Out of Town mail chute at the old U.S. Post Office on Fayette Street in Baltimore, some thirty-two miles from his FBI office at the State Department in Washington. This out-of-the-way mail drop was only one of the many elaborate steps Hallstrom took to avoid detection by his FBI colleagues.

For this package, he had carefully weighed the reinforced envelope the night before at home. On his way to work this morning, he bought stamps at the Mailboxes, Etc. shop at Tyson's Corner, then put them on the parcel in his car in the parking lot. Later, after work, he had driven all the way to Baltimore to drop the package into the mailbox. His Russian handlers—and FBI or CIA investigators—would have a difficult time tracing the package to him. Of course, the return address was fake, including his cover name—Julio Morales.

The FBI mole didn't like to use the U.S. mail to ship his stolen secrets to the Russians, and he only did it when he couldn't wait the forty-eight or more hours it might take for a Russian intelligence officer to see and respond to his "Emergency Call Out Signal," a chalk mark on a mailbox down the street from the Russian embassy. In the package Hallstrom had just mailed were two computer disks and a coded cover letter, setting up a new series of dead drops and visual codes.

But Bob Hallstrom had other reasons for coming to Baltimore— reasons that had little to do with tradecraft. He also liked to frequent a seedy joint where the drinks were bad and the girls were worse. The Lovebirds Gentleman's Club was terribly misnamed. A degenerate dive and locale for all kinds of illicit and illegal activity, it was a place where teenagers could score liquor with a phony ID and where the bar was headquarters for drug dealers and petty thieves fencing stolen goods. Hallstrom knew that it was also a place to buy a fake ID, a bogus driver's license, or even a passport. It was the kind of place where a guy like him, in a suit and tie, was noticed as soon as he walked in.

All the windows in the place were painted black; Hallstrom had to stand alongside the bar for awhile until his eyes adjusted. The place really assaulted all his senses, and he once again ran through his reasons for being here. He only drank an occasional glass of wine, so it wasn't for the alcohol. He was a militant nonsmoker, so he certainly didn't crave the thick haze of tobacco stench that hung in the air. And it wasn't the loud, grating noise billed as music that drew him here.

Actually, it was one reason alone—the nasty, edgy thrill that he got from watching the topless dancers.

Hallstrom's better instincts continually informed him that his was a sick pleasure, and he had no business being there. But somehow he was drawn there, time and time again. The bartender and dancers knew him, but not by name. One of the dancers, Susie Paley, had worked there for almost nine years. Bob had met her after she first started dancing at Lovebirds, and he had taken a strange liking to her. It wasn't a prurient attraction, at first. He initially came to watch her dance; then he talked to her and got to know her, he left her generous tips, and he began to buy her lavish gifts with money he got from the Russians.

Susie was stunned one day, after she had previously told him a bad luck story about her car breaking down, when Bob handed her the keys to a car parked outside. They had walked outside to see it, and Susie was amazed and ecstatic to see that Bob was giving her a large, almost-new Mercedes.

Hallstrom knew the car would be a dead giveaway if anyone in the Bureau knew about it. That was the challenge—and facing challenges like this was part of the thrill of his game. Coming to this sleazy club was a challenge. Seeing Suzie was a challenge. Once, just to show himself how much smarter he was than the rest of the sleuths in the FBI, he had even taken Susie overseas on an FBI trip. They took separate flights, of course, and he booked her in her own room at the hotel, but if anyone had found out about their trip together, it would have been the end of the line for the spy.

But Susie wasn't working tonight. Hallstrom had forgotten; she only came in on weekends now. Bob laid down a five-dollar bill on the table, beside his unfinished glass of Chablis, and walked out.

The FBI mole drove west on Orleans until it fanned into Franklin Street. He drove without any particular destination in mind. His wife had made plans to go shopping with a friend, so he was in no hurry to get home. Hallstrom cruised aimlessly through Baltimore's old streets. Seeing the sign for the Cathedral Street intersection ahead, he remembered the old basilica just one street over, across from the library.

Hallstrom always made it a point to go to confession at least once a week, and he recalled that he had missed his usual time the previous week when he was out of town on Bureau business. He thumbed his left-turn signal and swung his car sharply onto Cathedral Street.

As Hallstrom walked up the steps and inside the church, he looked for "his" confessional booth along the left side of the sanctuary. He knelt in a pew a few feet away; when an older woman came out of the booth, he strode toward it, his shoes clicking loudly against the marble floor.

Hallstrom shut the door behind him and took a deep breath as he knelt on the padded cushion inside. "Forgive me, Father, for I have sinned." His voice was just above a whisper.

On the other side of the partition, an aging priest invited him to confess and seek forgiveness. Hallstrom began with a recitation of where he had just been, and the carnal urgings that had led him to go there.

The FBI agent even told the priest about other indiscretions he had not shared with his own parish priest: details of infidelity and betrayal of his wife. He hoped these sins might be forgiven. He felt enormous guilt, and not just for those illicit urges and liaisons; he had secret sins he *couldn't* share. Hallstrom didn't confess that for more than fifteen years he had been compromising the most sensitive secrets his country had—nor did he mention that he had betrayed at least a dozen brave men, every one of whom had been executed by the KGB for spying against the Soviet Union. These people were dead at his hand, as surely as if he himself had pulled the trigger. He didn't tell the priest that he had sold classified secrets and taken money for betraying military secrets. Which of the Ten Commandments had he *not* broken?

Hallstrom thought of his most recent betrayal—providing information that would allow the Russians to track down and eliminate someone who posed a serious threat to his original Russian handler—Dimitri Komulakov. It was his superior intellect, Hallstrom realized, that enabled him to deduce that Marine Lieutenant Colonel Peter Newman, the Irish "terrorist" Gilbert Duncan, and John Clancy were all one and the same—and that this Newman/Duncan/Clancy character was probably a threat to Komulakov. And now, if Komulakov was at risk, Hallstrom reasoned, so was *he!*

Kneeling in this confessional, Hallstrom knew what would happen to this Newman character when the Russians caught up to him. For an instant, Hallstrom felt a twinge of something—*was it guilt?*

The spy thought seriously about getting these anxieties off his chest. He told the priest that he believed in God, and he hoped God might be able to forgive him. Even as he promised not to repeat the sins he had committed, he knew better—he had no intention of stopping what he was doing. It was too challenging. Besides, while he said that he believed in God, he believed entirely on his own terms. He knew the difference between right and wrong, but he had nevertheless conditioned himself to continue doing evil.

When Hallstrom finished, the old priest absolved him and ordered him to pray daily for forgiveness and for the strength to overcome temptation from the world, the flesh, and the devil.

As the old priest on the other side of the partition was talking, Hallstrom considered again the possibility that he should confess his other sins and really get right with God. He knew of the sanctity of the confessional—everything said to the priest would be confidential. He could tell the priest everything, and the cleric would be duty-bound to keep it to himself. Besides, it was getting harder and harder for Hallstrom to keep his secrets inside. There were times when he wanted to scream out to someone what he was doing. Perhaps he *should* tell his priest.

Still, he knew that he couldn't take that chance.

MAKING PLANS
WHILE MARKING TIME

C H A P T E R   T E N

Sayeret T'zanhanim Headquarters
Tel-Nof Air Force Base, Israel
Wednesday, 18 March 1998
0230 Hours, Local

N ewman looked out his side of the Anafa B-212 helicopter as it banked into the early morning fog, obscuring the lights of the Israeli Air Force base below them. It had been a short flight from Ben Gurion Airport to Tel-Nof. As the helicopter penetrated the fog, he could see the runways, hangars, and a few buildings. But unlike a U.S. air base, not a single aircraft was visible. Newman realized the craft were all in the hardened concrete hangars and revetments built against the low hills less than a hundred meters south of the main east-west runway. As the helicopter slowed its airspeed and began to transition into a hover, Newman noticed several arrays of satellite communications dishes.

Just before the helicopter landed, landing lights came on, illuminating a fifty-by-fifty-foot square alongside one of the arched concrete hangars. The lights cast shadows throughout the interior of the helicopter, making Newman, Major Ze'ev Rotem, and the two IDF Special Ops soldiers who had accompanied them squint while their eyes adjusted to the glare. As the bird touched down, the Israeli major jumped out and motioned for Newman and the two soldiers to follow him.

Major Rotem escorted Newman past a two-man guard post and to the door of an earth-covered concrete building next to the hangar. They waited, bathed in invisible infrared light from the high-intensity bulbs mounted above and on either side of the door. A speaker beside the door announced something in Hebrew that Newman couldn't understand. Rotem said something toward the speaker and held up his IDF identity badge to the lens of a wall-mounted camera.

Rotem turned to Newman. "They knew we were coming, but we're not used to having visitors here. In fact, you're probably the first non-Israeli ever to see this place."

"And what is this place?"

"This revetment covers the Duvdevan operations center. It's also the headquarters for Sayeret T'zanhanim, the unit to which I am assigned. As you'll see when we finally get inside, very little of it is above ground. Most of it is buried deep inside this hill."

There was the *whoosh* of escaping air and then what sounded to Newman like hydraulics as the steel door in front of them slid open, revealing a five-foot-by-five-foot enclosure and another steel door on the opposite wall.

As they stepped inside the red-lighted room, the outer door closed behind them. "The whole bunker is a 'citadel' space," Rotem said. "This small room is what you would call in English an 'air lock.' The interior of the operations center is maintained at several PSI above the outside atmospheric pressure so that the interior is protected against the effects of a biological or chemical weapon. It also protects those inside against radiation from a nuclear device as long as the structure is not breached."

As the interior door slid open, Newman felt his ears pop with the increased pressure. Rotem led the way down a concrete corridor, also lit with red lights to protect the night vision of anyone leaving the space during the hours of darkness. They walked down the passageway, their rubber-soled boots treading in step.

"We operate like this 365 days and nights a year, Colonel Newman. The red lights come on every night at sunset, and the white lights come on automatically at dawn. That's one of the differences between this place and your Delta Force Headquarters at Fort Bragg."

"When were you at Bragg, Major?"

"Two years ago, several of us were invited to visit your Special Operations Command and exchange ideas for dealing with terrorism," Rotem said as they arrived at another steel doorway. Once again, Rotem held up his ID badge and once more the door opened at the command of an unseen hand.

When the door closed behind them, Newman realized they were standing on the mezzanine level of a highly sophisticated command and control center. Banks of monitors relayed video pictures of locations throughout the nation. In a hushed voice, Rotem pointed out that most of the feeds were from the hot zones in the central part of the nation. Another bank of monitors covered sites in the West Bank and still others, key border locations.

There was little action taking place tonight, and the facility was on a reduced alert status, except for the outpost and lookout tower at Ralah in the Gaza Strip. When Newman asked what had happened there, Rotem explained, "Last night, just after sunset, three terrorists were shot and killed trying to plant explosives near the outpost. It's right at the border where Israel, Egypt, and Gaza meet—and we have a platoon of soldiers there. Yesterday a sniper killed their company commander. We've had three attacks there in the past two weeks."

Newman was reassured, not only by the business-like atmosphere, but by the sophistication of the equipment. It was clear to him that the optics and other sensors monitoring the various sites across the country were as up-to-date as any he had seen in American installations.

Rotem proceeded to introduce Newman to the duty section and allowed him to observe as the senior watch officer gave orders by encrypted radio-video link to an intelligence unit colocated with an IDF armor detachment, positioned outside the PLO compound in Ramallah. The Israelis were using barrier-penetrating optics to view activities inside, behind the walls of the building. The images were quite clear, and those watching could not only distinguish how many people were in the room but also if any of them had weapons.

"Isn't it amazing," Major Rotem said quietly, "that we now have the ability to see through walls? We've come a long ways since Joshua had to send spies to find out what was going on behind the walls of Jericho."

Newman nodded appreciatively.

"The technology helps us avoid killing innocent civilians," Rotem said. "As you can see, the personnel in these other rooms are non-combatants. They do not have any weapons. But those," Rotem said, pointing to the location that now appeared on the monitor, "are armed. They are all carrying AK-47s. These are the ones we need to take out, the ones who attacked a café in Hebron last month. Today we intercepted their plans to attack another site sometime this week. We are going to eliminate them—before they can carry out their attack."

There was now a hush throughout the command center. Newman watched as the sophisticated device continued to scan all the floors in the building in Ramallah, reconfirming the disposition of the occupants. Once the personnel in the operations center were certain that the room on the northeast corner of the second floor of the PLO compound held only armed combatants, the senior watch officer made a telephone call on a phone, Newman noted, remarkably similar to the U.S. STU-III. The phone call lasted less than three minutes and, when the senior watch officer hung up the phone, he turned to a radio operator and said something in Hebrew.

There was a momentary delay while the two radio operators conferred, validating the instructions. And while he could not understand the entire conversation in Hebrew, Newman could tell from the tension in the room what the orders were. Every eye in the center was now fixed on the monitor with the video feed labeled "Ramallah 3W."

As they watched, a Mirkiva tank fired a single round from its turret cannon. The green glow on the screen flashed white as an explosion ripped a huge hole in the room they were monitoring on the screen. As the dust cleared, an infrared sensor mounted in a truck beside the tank slowly recalibrated. There was no sign of life. But the on-scene commander apparently wasn't satisfied. As Newman and the others in the command center watched, another IDF tank crew opened fire with a .50-caliber machine gun at the gaping hole in the side of the building. And then, as quickly as it started, the attack ended. It had all taken just forty-five seconds from the time the order was given.

There was no jubilation or cheering inside the Tel-Nof Operations Center. There was no backslapping, no "atta-boys" offered. The senior watch officer simply went to a DVD recorder and removed the disk that had recorded all the audio-visual signals leading up to and during the attack, wrote a notation on it with an indelible marker, slipped the silvery disk into a cardboard sleeve, and handed it to a courier.

"What happens to that?" asked Newman.

"It will be delivered to the Prime Minister tonight. Tomorrow morning, the international press corps will accuse us of killing innocent children. The Prime Minister will have proof that they were not children, but terrorists," Rotem said in a matter-of-fact tone.

"But will he release that DVD to the press so they know better?"

"I doubt it. We never have. They wouldn't believe us anyway. We're now the bad guys in all of this. Or hadn't you noticed? Come, now we must decide what's to be done about our wives."

The Israeli bent over and waved to get the attention of one of the young female soldiers at a communications console. She pulled out a red folder with Hebrew words stamped across the cover and handed it to Rotem. He glanced at the contents, nodded, and motioned to Newman. Then he led the way out of the Operations Center, across the corridor, and into a small conference room.

✪

Rotem sat down and motioned for Newman to do the same. The major spent a few moments reading the three pages inside the folder. He looked directly at Newman.

"First, the Israeli intelligence services have initiated full coverage over our respective apartments and the telephones in both. If anyone calls—your wife, my wife, or the kidnappers—they will be able to trace the call and will notify us immediately. Second, I have been given the authorization that we need to launch the operation to rescue our wives."

Newman merely nodded, though he felt again, despite his fatigue, a jolt of adrenaline.

"And third, after conferring with General Grisham, the Defense Minister has agreed that you may remain here and monitor the operation . . . or, if you agree to certain conditions, you may accompany our rescue unit."

"What are the conditions?" Newman asked.

"First: I am the commander of the operation, and my executive officer is second in command. You must follow our orders or you may not come along."

"I agree. Now, when do we leave?"

"I made plans to move my team into Syria tonight. We still have almost three hours of darkness. The terrorists will not expect us to react this quickly. And we know from experience that kidnappings rarely get better with time."

Newman, whose experience in the U.S. military was one of lengthy planning and analysis before any operation, listened carefully. Somehow he was reassured by this man's experience. When Rotem finished, he nodded.

"Good. Let's get going."

Mediterranean Sea

Aboard USS *Theodore Roosevelt*, CVN 71
105 Nautical Miles NW of Beirut
Wednesday, 18 March 1998
0340 Hours, Local

The U.S. Navy flight deck crew scurried to tie down the SH-60B Sea Hawk helicopter next to the island of "The Big Stick," their nickname for the USS *Theodore Roosevelt*. The crew of the little Sea Hawk, ASW/Special Ops chopper had already put in a full day of flying—and the sun wasn't even up yet.

At 2200, the Sea Hawk had launched from its mother ship, the USS *Mobile Bay*, and headed over the dark waters of the Mediterranean to the British Sovereign Base at Larnaca. There it took on fuel, Lieutenant General George Grisham, and four of his CENT-COM staff. Then, without breaking radio silence, it had launched for the prearranged rendezvous with the carrier, in the vicinity of 34° N and 35° W.

General Grisham was now huddled over the table in the *Roosevelt*'s flag quarters. His host, friend, and Naval Academy classmate, Rear Admiral Henry Hennessey, was staring at the Marine general with red-rimmed eyes. At Grisham's request, Hennessey and his Battle Group staff had spent the last four days hastily putting together a plan to recover three loose nukes somewhere in Iraq; and now he was being told that the operation was on indefinite hold.

"Run this by me again, George." The admiral leaned over a mug of hot, black coffee. "You're telling me that the guy who was supposed to find these things—this formerly AWOL Marine named Newman—has lost his wife?"

"Kidnapped, Hank. She's been kidnapped."

"So now I'm to stand down the SEALs and the Marines from the MEU who were the back-up for this Op until the Israelis can find his wife?" The Admiral ran his hand through his close-cropped gray crew cut.

"That's what I'm saying, Hank. We can't locate the nukes without him, and after what he's been through, I can certainly understand him wanting to get his wife back before he goes off on this new mission."

Admiral Hennessey arched his neck to relieve the headache he'd been nursing for more than an hour. Then he looked at the general and asked, "George, do we have any idea where this woman is?"

"No. The Israelis think they know, and they're launching a mission tonight to try to get them back."

"Them?" said the Admiral. "More than one hostage?"

"Yes, them. Apparently an IDF officer's wife was kidnapped at the same time."

"Well, let's ask the Israelis where they think they're being held," said Hennessey. "How about we go get these gals and then get on with the more important business of getting these loose nukes rounded up? By the way, do the Israelis know about the nukes?"

"I don't think so," said Grisham, "though at this point I'm not absolutely sure who knows what."

"And we have to stand down on this mission until this one Marine lieutenant colonel finds his wife?"

Grisham grinned through his fatigue and frustration. "Well, most of the toughest missions only need one good Marine, Hank. This boy's all we need to get the job done."

The admiral rolled his eyes.

"Seriously, Hank, we have to wait," Grisham said. "We have no other way of finding the weapons. The White House reined in the CIA five years ago, and we haven't had any decent intel from Iraq since then. Oh, from time to time we get radio and telephone intercepts, some stuff from defectors, things like that. But everyone, including Saddam, seems to be in the dark about where these things are."

"Did you really clear this plan with the Sec Def?" Admiral Hennessey asked. "I can't believe this no-guts crowd would approve this mission."

"The people who need to know, know what I'm doing. But we've got a serious intelligence leak, and I suspect that it might be coming from the FBI or CIA."

"Does anyone at either agency know?"

"Yeah, I called the Director of the FBI and filled him in. He'll keep the details quiet and wait until our work is over to add it to the FBI files, just in case . . . ."

"Well, I'll put the lid on things here, George. And if the Israelis run into trouble with this wife recovery thing, let me know how we can help."

"I'll keep that in mind, Hank."

The admiral leaned back in his chair. "George, what makes you so sure you can believe that defector—what's his name again?"

"Hussein Kamil. He was Saddam's son-in-law . . . Saddam killed him."

"Yeah, Kamil. Anyway, what makes this Kamil guy so credible? How do we know he wasn't just giving the CIA a snow job?"

"We don't know—for sure—but I believe he was telling the truth. What we *do* know is that Saddam's trying to acquire some more nuclear weapons and has launched a massive search for the three that his dead son-in-law supposedly acquired in '95."

"So . . . how long before we turn this thing back on?"

"Well, it's a little early for me to know."

"Man, this situation gets crazier by the minute." Admiral Hennessey chuckled and shook his head. "So—who took the women, and why? Ransom or revenge? It's usually one or the other."

"Nobody knows yet. Newman called me by sat phone and said they were taking a couple of Israeli helicopters and some IDF special ops guys and infiltrating Syria north of Lebanon. He gave me the coordinates where he expects to find the women. That reminds me, Hank . . . how about seeing if your boys can download some overhead imagery of the area of interest in Syria? I'd like to see the most recent satellite passes—and the ones again early tomorrow morning. Maybe make it look like an NTDS drill so the boys at NRO don't get in a lather."

"And what will you do with the imagery if we can get it, George?"

"Well, if it shows anything worthwhile, I might want to pass it on to the Israelis."

The admiral looked at his old friend, shook his head and said, "Man, you're going to get me fired yet!"

Mediterranean Sea

27 Nautical Miles West of Beirut
Wednesday, 18 March 1998
0340 Hours, Local

As General Grisham and Rear Admiral Hennessey discussed the delayed nuclear weapon recovery mission aboard the USS *Theodore Roosevelt*, Newman was aboard a Sikorsky "Yusur" CH-53 helicopter over the Mediterranean Sea, headed north along the Lebanese coast. Major Ze'ev Rotem and four other IDF special ops troopers were spread out inside the spacious fuselage of the chopper. Not more than a hundred meters to the aircraft's port side and slightly behind them was an identical CH-53 carrying their ground transportation, a prototype, six-by-six AIL Desert Raider.

Because of its long-range transport capability, the Israelis used Sikorsky CH-53s for missions all across the Middle East, where it was especially effective on Scud hunts, intelligence operations, and special missions like this one. During the 1990–91 Gulf War, Israeli Special Operations units had gone all the way into Iraq on these aircraft without detection by anything other than U.S. AWACS.

Both of the CH-53s were flying with their engines muffled, only fifteen meters above the whitecaps of the Mediterranean, to evade audio detection and radar exposure. Newman was grateful the night seas were calm, or they could fly into the crest of a wave.

As they roared up the Lebanese coast at two hundred knots, Newman peered out into the darkness on the left side of the aircraft. It was, he knew from long experience, a perfect night for this kind of operation—overcast, a high ceiling, and very little ambient light from the quarter moon filtering through the clouds. As he looked out over the dark water, he wondered if any of the E-2 Trackers from the *Teddy*

Roosevelt had painted them on their airborne radars. He knew the carrier was supposed to be out there—somewhere— between Cyprus and the Syrian coastline. She had been getting into position to support the recovery of three nuclear weapons hidden somewhere inside Iraq. Newman hadn't even thought about that mission since he had learned of his wife's kidnapping. Now, he wondered if that operation would ever be reactivated.

The crew chief interrupted his thoughts when he signaled that the two helicopters were twenty minutes from their destination and the soldiers should start making last-minute checks of their weapons, ammo, and equipment, making sure everything was squared away and ready— if and when it was needed. Rotem climbed up into the cockpit, GPS in hand, to confirm that its location checked out with the one mounted on the pilot's instrument panel. Newman used the time to check his weapons again. He had picked out a Colt M16 carbine as his weapon of choice and had strapped a Sig Sauer P228 to his hip. All the rifles had muzzle suppressors and laser-assisted targeting. Newman's sidearm used a thirteen-round magazine, and he carried six magazines in his vest.

The carbine and automatic pistol that Newman carried were also the most popular weapons among the IDF troops—except for Major Rotem, who favored a suppressed IMI Galil, patterned after the AK-47. He also carried a Sig Sauer P226, a heftier, older model pistol that carried fifteen rounds instead of thirteen, a slight advantage in a firefight.

The prototype all-terrain vehicle in the other helicopter was a surprise for Newman. He had looked it over carefully as it was loaded into the CH-53. It was smaller than a U.S. Humvee but larger than a Jeep, and it had six drive wheels instead of four. Newman asked Major Rotem about the vehicle.

"An Israeli firm developed this AIL prototype for us. It's proven so successful for Special Operations work that it's going into full production for the whole IDF. Four years from now, all our units will have them."

"What's the advantage of this thing?"

"Well, it's nicknamed 'The Desert Raider' because it's ideal for Middle East desert terrain. The Jeep and the Hummer are well-proven and highly maneuverable, but the AIL six-by-six is even better. Because of the all-wheel drive and independent suspension, this thing can go places you'd think were impossible."

"Yeah?"

Major Rotem nodded. "It can climb a seventy-degree slope full of rocks. You ought to see it. It can move even if only *one* wheel is touching the ground. Let's see a Jeep try to do that."

"How fast can it go?"

"I've had it up to 110 klicks per hour—but that's on a pretty good road. Yet even in sandy terrain, it can really tear up the dunes. I've used it twice, and I love it. Can't wait for the production models to come out."

"What's that firepower mounted on it?"

"Three IMI Negev 5.56mm light machine guns are standard. With the three LMGs and the six of us, we're practically invincible."

Newman grinned. "I just hope it gets us where we're going and back. What about the guys we're meeting? What kind of wheels do they have?"

"They'll be driving an old beat-up Toyota four-by-four. And no LMGs. But they have a few other surprises you may not have seen used before."

"Yeah, like what?"

"Like the Helopoint Snipco, for one."

"The what?" Newman asked.

"It's part of our SOP for intervention tactics against terrorists. In circumstances where we have to use minimum force, like the hostage barricade situation we're likely to have in Syria, we have a portable system we can set up that ensures synchronized fire from an entire team of snipers. The team deploys in an arc around the target. Each sniper rifle is fitted with a 20-power electronic day/night scope that transmits what each sniper sees back to the team leader and is displayed on a screen. That way he can judge the attack angle and perspective from every rifle—even the .50 cal weapons. And because he has a radio link to every man in his team, he can "call the shots" for all of them—even order a simultaneous engagement from all locations—to achieve maximum effectiveness and surprise."

"Sounds great, but how does the lead sniper coordinate it all? Does it have a tie-in back to Central Command?"

"He has a wireless PDA that receives each rifle's video signal, and he can also have that transmitted directly back to headquarters—much like the event at Ramallah that we saw earlier."

The helicopter crew chief came aft and signaled two minutes from touchdown. Newman, Rotem, and the others lowered their night-vision goggles and made a final equipment check. The gunners manning the 7.62 Vulcan miniguns mounted in the port and starboard portals and on the tail ramp charged their weapons and flicked off their

safeties. As Newman and the other five special ops men began to prepare their rappelling equipment, the crew chief once again signaled
them. They wouldn't have to lower themselves on the braided nylon
climbing lines; the pilot had spotted an LZ where he could set the bird
down.

The pilots brought the birds in low and fast, straight across the
beach about six kilometers south of Al Hamidiyah, a remote village
overlooking the sea. They rose over a low cliff a few hundred meters
inland, and then the pilot pulled the nose up sharply to bleed off airspeed. With the transmissions screeching at the abrupt maneuver,
both aircraft settled quickly on the ground. Rotem's team disembarked in less than five seconds, and the enormous CH-53 lifted off
the ground and disappeared to the west, invisible, even with the aid of
Pete's night-vision goggles, in seconds. Seventy-five yards south, the
other CH-53 settled down, and the five men watched as its ramp
came down and it disgorged the Desert Raider, as though the helicopter were giving birth.

Then, the second CH-53 popped up and chased the first bird west,
out to sea.

The silence after the birds departed was startling to the men. Even
though they had removed the earplugs they had worn to protect their
eardrums from the high frequency noise of the helicopters, it still took
five minutes or more for them to begin hearing the night sounds from
the orchard around them.

Satisfied they hadn't chosen a Syrian Army encampment for a landing zone, Major Rotem signaled to the team that it was time to move
out. The men quickly dispersed around the area, trying to obliterate
any sign that they had been there. The tracks from the helicopter tires

and the wheel marks of the Desert Raider were swept out of the sandy soil with pine branches. Gear was checked, a quick headcount taken. Then Rotem gave the signal to board the six-wheeled vehicle. Once all were aboard and in their assigned stations, the major whispered into his helmet microphone.

"OK, guys . . . let's make things happen."

PFLP/Hezbollah Compound
Hamah, Syria
Wednesday, 18 March 1998
0700 Hours, Local

Rachel Newman awoke with a start. She had been dozing fitfully most of the night, only dropping off for real just before daybreak. A noise from the other end of the darkened room had awakened her and, for a brief moment, she was frightened and disoriented. Then she remembered, but that didn't lighten the fear.

At one in the morning, there had been a loud commotion when the kidnappers rushed into the small room where Dyan and she were being kept. The men again put the blindfolds on the women and tied their wrists, while herding them into an old VW van to drive them to another site. The women were almost frantic at being awakened and rushed so quickly into the vehicle, not knowing that they were only being moved—of course, they had no idea what was going to happen to them. The van had been driven for nearly forty-five minutes on rough roads.

Rachel had no idea where they were being taken, or even what direction. At their destination, they were taken from the van and hustled into this new compound, still blindfolded. They were taken to another back room and untied. When the blindfolds were taken off,

Rachel could see that this room, unlike the previous one, at least had a window—but no lights. And the window appeared to be painted over.

The kidnappers used flashlights to illumine their new accommodations and ordered the women to rest there until morning. As before, they were provided with two dirty mattresses and two filthy, threadbare wool blankets.

Now it was morning, and Rachel sat up on the floor where she had slept and dreamed so fitfully. Her bones ached, and her muscles felt sore and cramped. As she stood up, her friend Dyan also woke up; like Rachel, she had slept little during the long and difficult night. As they both recalled where they were and how they got there, they looked at each other for support and courage.

"I wonder where we are," Dyan said quietly. "Wherever it is, no one will be able to find us. Not even after you left that information on the answering machine. Once we crossed into another country, it became hopeless. And I wonder why they even bothered moving us from that one house to this one in the middle of the night."

"I don't know, but we can't give up. They haven't hurt us badly yet, so they must think we're worth something to them. Maybe they want to trade us for something—or someone."

"Oh, Sarah . . . I'm scared. I'm really scared."

Rachel felt a twinge of guilt as her friend called her by her alias. After enduring together an ordeal like this . . . but Rachel still said nothing. It was better if Dyan didn't know, especially if the kidnappers interrogated them, or if they suspected who Rachel really was.

"I'm frightened, too, Dyan."

"What do you suppose they plan to do with us?" Dyan asked.

"I have no idea. It's probably better if we don't think about it too much."

"I get morning sickness if I don't have something to eat when I wake up."

Rachel reached into her pocket. "Here . . . I saved this pita bread from last night . . . just in case." She handed the small piece of bread to Dyan.

The painted-over window admitted some light, enough for the women to see the bars outside. They could tell only that the window faced east; the morning sun warmed the opaque glass, and it in turn warmed them a little. As she stood by the window soaking up the warmth, Rachel began to think about her husband and little boy. Though it made her feel like crying, she struggled to control her emotions. Rachel was determined not to let the kidnappers intimidate her and frighten her more than she already was.

I should pray. That's one thing they can't keep me from doing.

She closed her eyes and leaned against the windowsill, praying for more than ten minutes—for Peter, for James, for Dyan and her husband and unborn child, and for their safety and rescue.

She could hear the sound of a vehicle outside, its tires crunching in gravel. She put her eye to a tiny spot where the paint had flaked off the outside of the glass.

Right outside the window she could see a black Mercedes sedan, a big one.

Rachel watched as an Arab jumped from the front seat passenger side and hurried to open the door to the backseat. A moment later, a tall, light-haired man, dressed in an expensive gray suit and carrying a soft leather attaché case, got out of the car. He also sported a light tan camelhair topcoat slung over his left arm. At the last instant, he decided to toss the coat back onto the car seat.

Rachel stared at the man. He looked out of place somehow. She wasn't sure if he was European or American, perhaps Canadian—but he surely wasn't Arab. And yet, he seemed very much at ease with the men who were her captors. Rachel watched as he and the two Arabs who had arrived with him walked to the left and out of her line of sight. A moment later, somewhere else in the house, she could hear voices welcoming the man—then laughter—and then the sound of a heavy door—*the front door?*—closing with a slam. Rachel checked her watch. It was precisely seven-thirty.

"What is it?" Dyan asked.

"I don't know. Someone just arrived. He looks European—maybe even American. He's very well dressed."

"Oh, Rachel, was that him laughing just now?" Dyan appeared to be on the verge of tears. "I don't feel good about this."

Rachel moved closer to her pregnant friend, put an arm around her, and said, "Don't worry, Dyan; it's going to be all right." But even as she said the words, something about the sight of this mysterious stranger made her shiver.

X-Ray Rendezvous
12 km South of Juwaykhat, Syria
Wednesday, 18 March 1998
0745 Hours, Local

Rotem, Newman, and the other Sayeret team members had arrived twenty minutes ahead of schedule at the rendezvous point and were concealed in heavy shrubbery alongside the dirt road that ran east and connected to the Hims highway. Here they were to meet four

Duvdevan operators who had been inside Syria, collecting intelligence when the kidnappings occurred. "Don't be surprised when you see them," Rotem had said.

"Why, what's wrong with them?" Newman whispered.

"Nothing. They're just different. You'll see."

When they arrived, precisely on time, Newman couldn't believe they were Israelis. They were in a beat-up Toyota van, dressed in tattered civilian garb, and appeared to be a group of Arab or even African laborers. Rotem came out of his concealment and embraced their leader. He called him 'captain,' although he didn't look like an officer to Newman. As far as the American was concerned, all four of them looked like emaciated refugees.

Rotem brought the captain and one of the sergeants into the brush, while the other two babysat the van with the engine compartment open, pretending to have a mechanical problem. Given the appearance of their vehicle, it certainly appeared plausible.

Rotem introduced the captain and the sergeant to Newman, but Pete missed their names. It hardly mattered; the captain's news was all bad.

"We have to call off the operation. The women are not there."

"What do you mean?" Rotem asked.

"We went in as close as twenty meters, and the place was empty. We used NVDs to check it out. There was only one man, probably a watchman, and nobody else was there."

"Do you think that they might have been there earlier, but left?"

"Hard to say. We got there at 0200 and no one was there. We waited until dawn to see if they were just late in getting there, but no one showed up. By then, it was too late to call off your coming here."

Newman was peering from Rotem to the other man. "I thought you said you knew where they'd be."

"They were there," Rotem said. "I know their ways . . . they took the women there from the train. It's always the way they work."

Major Rotem was silent. Newman knew the instructions from Rotem's superiors were very clear: if the women were dead or could not be located, they had to withdraw. The Israeli MOD wasn't about to risk having one of its special operations units hunted down inside Syria.

Major Rotem turned to the undercover commander. "It's not your fault, Captain Naruch. I thought our intelligence was good. Either we had a leak . . . or they're just being extra cautious. In either event, we could be chasing all over the Syrian desert looking for them and still never locate them."

He turned to Peter. "I'm sorry, Colonel Newman, but my orders are clear. We must return to Israel until we either hear from the kidnappers, or we get better intel."

Newman nodded reluctantly.

"Captain Naruch, you and your trackers return to your tasks. We'll signal you when we know more. If you see or hear anything about the two women, report it immediately and we'll come back."

The captain merely nodded and then he and his sergeant rejoined their comrades at the van. After checking the road in both directions, they slammed the engine compartment closed, jumped back into the vehicle, and roared off down the dirt track as if the devil himself was on their tail.

After they had been gone for about ten minutes, Rotem, Newman, and the other men got back into the Desert Raider and headed cross-country to the southeast, in the general direction of Tall Kalakh.

"We must get to a different extract point for pick up," Rotem told Newman. "We'll pull into the forest and hope the Syrians don't have any patrols along the Lebanese border today."

As they drove their strange new six-by-six vehicle toward the hills to their south, Major Rotem used his encrypted RF radio to call Tel-Nof and tell them to send the helicopters back to get them. When he finished, he called to the driver, "Slow down. We have plenty of time before sunset, and I don't want to be sitting around too long in one place while we wait. Let's try to find some concealment where we can wait without being seen." The driver nodded and slowed down, looking for scrub vegetation that he could drive the vehicle into if they saw anyone or heard any Syrian aircraft overhead.

Late in the afternoon, when they arrived at their harbor site, a few hundred yards from the extraction LZ, Rotem ordered them to cut branches and shrubbery to camouflage and conceal the vehicle. When they were finished, he told the men to rest at 50-percent watch. "If anyone sees anything—military, police, or civilian—do not engage unless you are spotted . . . and do not kill unless the person tries to escape or fires on you."

Once his men were posted, Rotem turned to Newman and said, "You should rest, my friend; I must monitor the radio for instructions."

"I will, in a bit. Tell me, Major, those four men in the van—they don't appear to be Israelis. Are they Syrian agents of the Mossad?"

"No." Rotem paused for a moment before continuing. "They are from one of our 'Tracker' units. Captain Naruch is an Ethiopian Jew. So is the sergeant who was with him. The other two men are Israeli

Bedouins. They are all members of the IDF; and they have been operating in Syria for more than four months."

"Do you think they'll find our wives?"

"We will find our wives. And I will kill those who did this to them."

RELUCTANT ACCOMPLICE

C H A P T E R   E L E V E N

PFLP/Hezbollah Compound
Hamah, Syria
Wednesday, 18 March 1998
0800 Hours, Local

Yalla! Yalla! Get up—now!" One of the kidnappers burst into the dimly lit room and was standing, silhouetted in the doorway, pointing an AK-47 at Rachel and Dyan. Hungry, thirsty, sore, and dirty, the women had dozed off, trying to conserve energy. Now one of their captors was screaming at them in a mix of Arabic and English to get up and come with him.

The two women were pushed roughly, half-stumbling, toward the large room at the front of the building. Rachel could see there were several more terrorists now than there were before. In the dim light she counted seven, including the one who came to get them. They seemed to be simply hanging around, some leaning against the packing crates and boxes that lined the walls, one standing smoking by the only window, occasionally peering out the filthy panes as though he might be on lookout or watch. The room smelled of stale cigarette smoke and the odor of unwashed bodies. As she was shoved forward, Rachel looked for the man who had arrived in the Mercedes, but she could not see him.

The two women were pushed toward the only furniture in the room, a battered table and four wooden chairs. The remnants of someone's crude breakfast, scraps of pita bread, date pits, a half-eaten apple, and empty plastic water bottles, remained. The man behind Rachel jabbed the barrel of his assault rifle into her ribs and commanded them to sit. He gave the order in Arabic, but both Rachel and Dyan understood him and stopped.

Three other terrorists came forward. One grabbed Rachel by the hair, jerked her head forward toward his face, while another pinned her hands behind her. She could smell the terrorist's foul breath.

Is he going to rape me?

Rachel writhed violently as she tried to resist. Suddenly the kidnapper behind her pushed one of the wooden chairs into the back of her knees, and she collapsed into its frame. Two other terrorists grabbed Dyan by the shoulders and slammed her into another chair.

One of the men said something Rachel couldn't understand, and two coarse ropes were produced. The man roughly yanked the rope across her arms as he prepared to tie her up. The rope burned, leaving painful red traces of its path, but she did not cry out. The four men took their time tying the women to the chairs, their hands wandering freely as they did so. As the rough rope cut painfully into her skin,

Rachel noted that their hands were rough, unwashed, their nails broken and encrusted with grime.

Rachel and Dyan were both tied in the same manner—legs pulled to the side of each chair and their ankles lashed to the back legs, wrists bound behind their backs. Rachel felt exposed, vulnerable, and helpless. While the four men worked at ensuring that there was no way either woman could flee or fight back, the other three terrorists smirked and made lewd gestures.

Rachel heard an English voice with an accent she couldn't recognize.

"Please, gentlemen," the voice said, "show some respect. These are women, not cattle. You don't have to be so rough with them. They are, after all, our guests."

The four who had been tying the women to the chairs stepped aside, giving Rachel a view of the person who had spoken. As she had suspected, it was the man she had seen getting out of the Mercedes.

"Who are you? You sound almost like an American. What do you want with us?"

"Well, actually it's *you* that I want, Mrs. Newman. And no, I am not an American," the tall man in the suit said, smiling.

"My name is Sarah Clancy. You've got the wrong person."

"No," the man said, his smile gone as he sat down on one of the chairs on the opposite side of the table, placing a small camera and newspaper in front of him. "Your name is Rachel Newman. I know you well, although I have not seen you in years. But you are looking quite well. Are you all right?

Rachel did not answer. *Who is this man? And how can he possibly know my true identity?*

The man reached into his coat pocket and withdrew a photograph. Reaching across the table and shoving the breakfast detritus aside, he showed it to Rachel. It was a picture of her, with Peter, taken with a telephoto lens. "One of my . . . uh . . . associates took this picture. Do you remember?"

Rachel shook her head. She was becoming more and more confused and frightened.

"That's you, Mrs. Newman. And your husband. You had just reunited with him after he had been gone for some time. You don't remember it? It was taken on March 10, 1995, in Larnaca, Cyprus. It was taken just before the two of you were, ah, 'killed' in a terrible explosion. Now do you remember?"

Dyan let out a faint moan as Rachel's eyes widened in fear. Rachel still didn't know who the man was who had gone to such extremes to capture her, but she guessed that he was somehow responsible for trying to kill them before.

"What do you want?" she asked him, her voice faint and revealing a slight tremor.

"I only want to talk to your husband, Mrs. Newman, and ask him for a favor. In return for that favor, I will agree to return you to him."

"You're insane! I need to get back to my child. You took me away from my son! You've put my friend and her unborn baby through a terrible ordeal. What kind of person does terrible things like that?"

"Mrs. Newman, it's too bad you were taken away from your child, and I'm sorry about your friend here," he said, nodding toward Dyan, "but it can't be helped. I'm sure there are people your husband can call upon to take care of your boy while he does this little favor for me. Please don't worry about your son. If your husband does exactly what I ask him to do, you'll see your little one sooner than you think. But in the meantime, I want to take your photograph once again. Here . . . let me place this newspaper in front of you so the headline shows. It will tell your husband you are alive and well as of today."

He picked up the camera and placed the latest edition of the *International Herald Tribune* on her lap, leaning the paper against her chest. As he did so, Rachel noticed his hands. They were soft and smooth, carefully manicured, in contrast to the hands that had been pawing over the two women earlier. As the man carefully adjusted the collar of her blouse, she detected the faintest hint of cologne. Satisfied with her appearance, the man in the suit stepped back and took a picture of each woman. The miniature flash made Rachel blink.

"Aren't these new digital cameras wonderful, Mrs. Newman? I can take your picture and send it right away to your husband. If you'll just give me his e-mail address, I'll send it to him along with my instructions."

What should she do? The man obviously already knew a great deal about her and Peter. Would they be jeopardized any further by his knowing Peter's e-mail address? She was tired; she wasn't thinking straight. The letters and numbers of Peter's e-mail address ran across her mind. Was she thinking it, or had she just said it aloud, in her fatigue and confusion?

"Thank you, Mrs. Newman," the man said.

I said it aloud. Oh, Peter, I'm sorry . . .

"I can only hope your husband is as cooperative as you have been."

The man gestured at one of the kidnappers, telling him in a mixture of English and Arabic to give the women something to eat and lock them back inside the room in the rear of the building.

When they were taken back to their confinement, Dyan asked in a whisper, "Is that true? Are you really this other person?"

"Yes."

As they ate, she told Dyan the real story of the past three years.

Hospice of Saint Patrick

Old City, Jerusalem
Wednesday, 18 March 1998
2100 Hours, Local

"Mr. Clancy, I am grateful to God to be able to see you again!"

Isa Boyian had come running down the stairs to open the front door of the hospice as soon as he heard Newman's voice over the intercom. If he was surprised to see his boss in military clothes, accompanied by an Israeli military officer, he didn't show it.

Though he was practically breathless, Isa still managed a running commentary and a string of questions as he, Newman, and Rotem walked up the stairs to the main reception desk.

"Have you received any word about Mrs. Clancy? My dear wife, Ay Lienne, has cried every hour since she brought little James to you at the airport. Do you know that we have Israeli policemen staying *here?* I told them they could not be here because this is a religious site, but they said you approved."

Newman put his hand on the younger man's shoulder. "You did everything right, Isa. Please tell Ay Lienne how grateful I am for the care she has given to James. He's now with my sister on Cyprus. Has . . . uh . . . Sarah called again?"

"I do not know, Mr. Clancy. The policemen have been answering the phones. They only allow me to talk if it is something to do with one of our guests or a call pertaining to the hospice. They have even set up recording devices at the switchboard."

Newman reassured Isa, repeating again that he had done everything properly. Then he led Rotem off to the apartment he and Rachel shared. As he approached the door, he was once again overwhelmed with emotion. This was the place where he and Rachel had resurrected their marriage, where they had laughed and cried, made love, and lived life as it was meant to be. Here they had played with their infant son and prayed together as they watched him grow. It was here they had finally become a family. Here had been their home. And as he put the key in the door, he suddenly realized it never would be home again— no matter what happened.

Rotem put his hand on the Marine's arm. "Wait a moment, Peter."

Newman stopped and looked at the Israeli soldier. The wives of both men had been kidnapped. The two husbands had flown together into Syria on a rescue mission. Less than three hours ago, just after sunset, they had been snatched out of a small clearing along the Lebanese-Syrian border by an Israeli CH-53 helicopter. And though the operation had been flawless, it had also been a failure; neither man was any closer to seeing his wife than he had been the night before.

"I know that this is very difficult," Rotem said. "You have been through a lot, and it's not yet over. Inside you will find several policemen. They've been through everything in your home, looking for clues to help find your wife. The same thing is happening at my apartment. But here, the police may ask you about your true identity. If they do, it will help if you are honest with them. I will stay as long as you want;

then I will go to my apartment and pick up some uniforms and personal things."

"I understand."

Newman opened the door. There were three men in the small living room, all wearing civilian clothes. The tallest of the three rose from the chair where he was making notes on a small tablet.

"Good evening, Colonel Newman, Major Rotem. I am Detective Aaron Marks." He pulled out a badge that identified him, in Hebrew and English, as a detective lieutenant in the Israeli National Police—the IP. "I have been assigned to this case."

The three men shook hands and were introduced to the other two men, technicians who had been monitoring the recording devices they had hooked to all the telephones and extensions in the entire hospice.

After Rotem left to return to his apartment, Marks said, "When I was downstairs in your office, I noticed you have a fax machine. I checked it in case the kidnappers tried to contact you in that way, but there were no messages. But I also noticed your computer there. It's possible they tried to e-mail you. Have you checked your e-mail messages lately from some other location?"

The idea caught Newman by surprise. He had not thought of e-mail at all. "C'mon," he said, "let's see." The two men hurried down the marble stairs to Newman's office. He went to his desk, turned on the computer, and logged on to the Internet. He clicked on the "mail" icon and glanced through the list of new e-mails.

There!—from an unknown sender, but the subject box said, "Letter from Rachel." Newman opened the e-mail, and the message came up on the screen:

Peter Newman:
   This message is being sent to you to prove that your wife
enjoys good health and safety in my house. A photo file is
attached to this message that will confirm my protection and
hospitality.
   Your wife wishes to be reunited with you as quickly as possible, and I can arrange this immediately. However, in return for
this, I shall expect you to do me a favor. I will explain all to you
when we are together.
   As soon as you receive this message, reply to the "OK" and
no message text. I will then telephone you at your home with
further instructions. Do not contact U.S. or Israeli authorities or
your wife will be executed.

The return address of the sender was a random combination of letters and numbers that Newman hardly noticed as he opened the JPEG
photo file attached to the e-mail. He could feel his heart begin to race
as the image appeared on the screen: his wife, bound to a chair with a
newspaper propped in her lap.

He zoomed in on the image, looking for signs of injury. He could
see what appeared to be blood on Rachel's collar, some swelling
around her nose, and a cut on her lower lip. But her eyes drew his
attention: they were not turned down or away from the photographer,
no sign of dejection or fear. When the photo was taken, Rachel was
staring straight into the lens. And in her eyes, Newman could see only
defiance.

Lieutenant Marks was reading a printout of the e-mail.

"Smart fellow, this one. He was careful not to use any of the 'red
flag' words that would alert GCHQ or other monitoring agencies. He
was either lucky, or he knows his way around security."

After several seconds of staring at the image on the screen, with
Lieutenant Marks looking over his shoulder, Newman clicked the

mouse to print the photo. As the color printer on the table next to him began to warm up, he keyed his computer to respond to the kidnappers' e-mail.

"Don't reply just yet," Lieutenant Marks said. "Our guys will want to check out this e-mail and try to trace it. He pulled out his mobile telephone and punched in a preset number on the speed dial. "Ben, it's me. Listen, I need you to come to the Hospice of Saint Patrick in the Old City as soon as possible. Bring your computer. I need you to do a trace." He ended the call and returned the phone to his pocket.

"I don't expect them to make things that easy for us," Newman said. "I'm guessing they hijacked someone's account and sent the message through a series of hacked computers. There's no telling where they are, or even where my reply will go."

"Yes, you're probably right. But we need to try. Maybe the kidnapper is careless or isn't all that familiar with computers. If he's sending this through a server in a country friendly to his cause, it wouldn't matter because they'd never cooperate with us and give us access to him anyway."

Newman picked up the cell phone that the IDF man had given him the day before in the hangar at Ben Gurion Airport. He dialed the preprogrammed number for Major Ze'ev Rotem's mobile phone.

"It's Peter Newman, Ze'ev . . . I just got an e-mail message from the kidnappers. I thought you might want to check and see if you also received one."

"I received a message too. It says: 'We regret taking your wife. It was a mistake. She will be returned to you by Peter Newman after he meets with us. Do not try to come with him, and do not involve the authorities. If you disregard this warning and involve them, the police, or your own service branch, your wife will not be returned alive. We will notify you when and where you will be able to get her back.'"

"There is an attached photo file of her," Rotem said. "What did your message say?"

Newman read him the message.

"So . . . all along it was *you* they wanted," Major Rotem noted. "Who are these kidnappers? And why do they want you?"

"I have no idea. We're waiting for an IP computer expert to come and try and trace the e-mail. Maybe you should have them do the same with your message."

"My Duvdevan unit has already taken care of that. Our software is probably more advanced than that of the IP. I'll have my man come over there too."

"Has your guy had time to track your message and see where it originated?"

"Yes. Theoretically, it was sent from a computer café in Belgium, after being routed or forwarded from France to Switzerland to Italy to Lebanon. At each switching point, it was encrypted and decrypted using a total of four different codes. The original message was probably faxed to the guy in Belgium, using coded language, and re-sent from there. We're still working on tracing the reply address, but that's probably going to end up at some dummy e-mail account somewhere. By the time the Internet providers track it down, he will have already gotten the reply message and skipped. There'll be no way to find him."

"Well, so much for that idea," Newman said. "So, is there any reason to wait to reply to my message? I'd like to get the ball rolling. Today is almost over, and I want to get whatever instructions they are going to give right away. As you yourself said, 'Kidnappings don't age well.'"

"Tell the IP officer what I told you, and then go ahead and answer them. It's more important that you make contact with them as soon as possible to let them know you'll be waiting for their instructions. You're right. We don't want our wives stuck with those animals any longer than necessary."

Newman hung up the phone, turned back to the computer, and clicked the "reply" icon.

Lieutenant Marks started to protest, and Newman's explanation about what Major Rotem had just told him did little to appease him. "Colonel, you cannot just do as you want. The IP is in charge here, and if you want to get your wife back, you're going to have to work with us."

Peter typed "OK" in the subject box and sent it on its way, just as instructed. He turned and looked at Lieutenant Marks.

"Well, with all due respect, Lieutenant, I'm doing what I believe needs to be done to save my wife. I'm not going to sit here waiting all night for you guys before getting back to the kidnappers. I want to go get her and bring her home as soon as possible."

"Why do the kidnappers want to meet with you? How can you do them a favor? What are you holding back from us?"

"Listen, I know you guys are trying to help me to get Rachel back. But since I don't know who the kidnappers are or what they want, I have absolutely no idea what that favor is. In fact, I can't even speculate."

The Israeli detective shrugged and sat down to wait with Newman. Seven minutes after Newman sent the e-mail, the phone extension in his office began to ring.

Newman was reaching for the phone when Lieutenant Marks said, "Wait. Let me make sure that they have the tape machine running to record the call."

Newman nodded and waited for Marks to pull a radio from his belt clip and speak into it. The phone rang three more times. Marks signaled with a "thumbs up," and Newman picked up the phone.

"Hello . . . this is John—uh . . . Peter Newman," he said in the most emotionless voice he could muster.

The voice on the other end, filtered through a modulating device that changed the caller's pitch and timbre, began immediately. "I will not give you time to trace this call, so listen carefully. Tomorrow morning go to the Tel Aviv airport and take Turkish Air flight 46, to Istanbul, Turkey. In Istanbul, you will take Gulf Air flight 5633 to Damascus.

"There are two reservations made for each flight. One reservation is in the name 'Peter Newman,' and the other is in the name 'John Clancy.' We do not care which name you use, but once you have the boarding pass for your flight to Istanbul, go to a courtesy phone and page 'Mr. Kline,' and tell them to have Mr. Kline go to the gate from which you will be departing. Don't bother to look for anyone—no one will meet you there. It is our way of knowing you will be on the flight. When you land at the Damascus airport, go to the International First Class lounge on the second level and wait there for a telephone call for you, in the name of 'Mr. Edwards.' The call should come within thirty minutes of your flight's arrival. It is then that you will receive your next instructions."

"Why don't I just give you my cell phone number, so that you—" Newman started to say, trying to buy more time for the IP listeners to trace the call.

But all he heard was a click and dial tone as the line disconnected. As he hung up, he told Lieutenant Marks, "I hope your guys were able to get a trace on the call."

Marks shook his head. "Not enough time . . . especially if it was an international call. Your caller knew that, and that's why he kept it so short."

Newman was upset with himself for not thinking to check his e-mail as soon as he arrived back home—if he had, perhaps he could have gotten a flight that day and flown to Syria a day earlier to get to Rachel.

Oh, God . . . please protect my wife . . .

PFLP/Hezbollah Compound
Hamah, Syria
Wednesday, 18 March 1998
2130 Hours, Local

"Are you all right?"

Rachel looked up and nodded. Dyan was standing by one of the chairs in the locked room. She had been pacing the floor for what seemed like hours. Rachel had been sitting on the floor on one of the filthy mattresses, thinking and praying, eyes closed.

"What do you think is going to happen?"

"I think things will work out all right. The European guy"—their code for the well-dressed man with the manicured nails—"said he sent e-mails to our husbands and he was waiting for an answer. I think the European is the one who planned this whole thing, and he's making Peter come to meet with him."

"It's so confusing," Dyan said. "He told me I was taken by mistake—that they really meant to kidnap you, Sar . . . uh . . . Rachel. And he knew you and your husband have different names and identities." Now there was hurt and anger in Dyan's voice. "You were living a lie. How could you do that to me? I'm your friend."

Rachel was silent for a few moments.

"It hasn't been easy, Dyan. You're right, though; I guess it *was* living a lie."

"How do you rationalize that with your faith?" asked Dyan. "Aren't Christians supposed to abide by the Ten Commandments just like Jews?"

"Yes," said Rachel, and then added gently, "but you, as a Jew, should understand that sometimes circumstances force us to do such things . . . like when Christians hid Jews during World War II and lied to the Nazis. There are some who would understand what we did, and I'm sure that some Christians would condemn us for using false identities to save our lives. But those who point the finger of blame must live incredibly easy lives, where the only decisions they have to make have very clear distinctions between good and bad, you know, easy decisions. As Peter says, 'It's a lot tougher to know what to do when the only choices are *bad* and *worse*.' That's why we pray for God's guidance . . . to know—even when we make wrong choices while trying to do right—that we're forgiven."

Dyan was quiet for awhile and then came and sat down on the floor next to her friend.

"And now . . . do you hear God telling you we are going to get out of this safely? You don't even seem to be afraid of what might happen to us. Are you?"

"Of course I'm afraid," Rachel said. "Anyone in her right mind would be scared. I don't want to die. I want to see my little boy again. I want to be with my husband again. But I'm not *afraid* of *dying*, if that's what you mean."

"Why not?"

"Because I know where I'm going, and I know why I'm going there," Rachel said. "I may or may not survive what those men do to me, but I know God has forgiven my faults and failures, and I know that when I finally die I'm going to be with my Lord and Savior. But I'm human, Dyan, and I pray that when I die, it will be later and not sooner."

Dyan sat and stared at Rachel, then said quietly, "Are you praying that we *both* get out of here?"

"Absolutely, and I'm praying that—" Rachel's response was interrupted by the sound of the padlock on the outside of the door being unlocked, and then—a knock—something that hadn't happened before.

The heavy wooden portal swung open, and there in the doorway was the European, silhouetted by the bare bulb in the hallway behind him. To his left and right stood two of the young Arab men who had kidnapped the women. They were holding AK-47s.

The European stood there for a moment and surveyed the gloomy room and the two women sitting on the mattresses. "Excuse me, ladies," he said in English. "You will be pleased to know that your husbands have acknowledged our e-mail. Mrs. Newman, I just wanted you to know—your husband will be here tomorrow."

Sayeret T'zanhanim HQ
Duvdevan Command Center
Tel-Nof Air Force Base, Israel
Wednesday, 18 March 1998
2235 Hours, Local

Newman and Rotem were seated at the conference table inside the Tel-Nof AFB operations center, surrounded by the command cell of Rotem's counter-terrorism unit—the XO, S-2, and S-3. Twenty minutes after responding to the kidnappers' e-mails and Newman's receipt of instructions to go to Damascus, both Newman and Rotem had been picked up by an IDF helicopter at the Bikur Holim Hospital helipad and flown directly to Tel-Nof.

"Are you sure you could tell nothing from the voice?" asked the Intelligence officer. He had before him on the table a digital audio tape recorder. They had replayed the tape several times already.

"No, I don't recognize the voice," Newman said, rubbing his eyes.

"Well, it almost has to be someone who knew you before you became 'John Clancy' three years ago," Rotem said.

"Could it have to do with the mission you were on in 1995?" asked the Operations officer. "Perhaps one of the major players . . ."

"I suppose so, but I can't imagine how," said Newman. "The UN officials are all gone—Harrod, the guy in Washington, is now a college professor and Hussein Kamil, the Iraqi, is dead."

"Who else in your government knew your real identity besides General Grisham?" asked Rotem.

Newman pondered the question for a moment before replying, "Other than my immediate family, and other ones I know and would trust with my life—like Skillings and Goode—I just don't know."

But that very question had been nagging at his mind. He couldn't tell the Israelis about the mission he was supposed to be on right now, hunting for missing nuclear weapons in Iraq. But the fact that Rachel's kidnapping happened right after he gave his commitment to General Grisham to help find the missing nukes seemed like too much of a coincidence. Had someone inside the U.S. government, perhaps even someone close to the general, found out about him and his secret identity? Did he still have enemies within his own government, perhaps even within the Corps? That idea was too much of a stretch for his mind to grasp. It just didn't make any sense.

Yet there was no escaping the thought that maybe the kidnappers, or someone close to them, had access to General Grisham's top secret, classified information. Any other explanation defied the odds of probability and logic. Newman came to the conclusion that someone—either inside Grisham's command or linked to CENTCOM in some way—had access to secrets that were putting his life, and his wife's, at terrible risk.

★

Newman wasn't the only one in the room in a quandary. Rotem was deeply concerned about his own wife and her safety. The e-mail he had received indicated that his wife would be released unharmed; yet he was a veteran in dealing with terrorists and knew that this was highly unlikely if she really was in the hands of the Hezbollah, the PFLP, or any of a half-dozen Middle Eastern terrorist groups—particularly if they had somehow learned he was a Sayeret officer. From long experience, Rotem knew that if Dyan was being held by any of these terrorist organizations, about the best he could hope for was that she might be traded in exchange for the release of a bunch of Palestinian prisoners held in Israeli prisons.

Nothing they had learned from the e-mails or the voice-altered phone call to Newman had changed Rotem's original assessment that their wives were being held in Syria. And, as if by way of confirming his intuition, Newman had been given instructions to go to Damascus. The IDF officer had been certain the women were being held at a known PFLP safe house—which had proved a blind lead. Yet Rotem's instincts told him there must be another location not far from the safe house where they *were* being kept. He knew the terrorists' methods and procedures too well. Major Rotem believed since the PFLP didn't know that the Duvdevan had discovered their escape route and safe house, there would be no reason to arbitrarily abandon it. *So . . . they probably have another place nearby,* Rotem thought, *another safe house or some place that the Duvdevan hasn't discovered yet, a place they use as insurance. They probably alternate back and forth between them.*

Now, with less than seven hours before Newman had to be at the airport to board the first leg of the flights that would take him to Damascus, Ze'ev Rotem had come to the conclusion that they could take no chances. Even though the kidnappers had warned both him and Newman against contacting U.S. or Israeli authorities, and had warned Rotem specifically against coming with Newman to Damascus, the IDF officer had made up his mind—he would take his team back into Syria to back up the Marine.

"In case they decide to capture you and keep or kill our wives, we need to have a backup plan," Rotem said.

"Go on," Newman said.

"My men and I will go back into Syria to the place we rendezvoused with the other team yesterday. We will meet the team again and find cover in that desolate area just northwest of Hims. I am convinced the kidnappers are hiding someplace near there."

"But how can you still be so sure? I mean, by now they could even be out of Syria. When I get to Damascus tomorrow morning, they could give me a message to go somewhere else. We have no idea where these guys are keeping our wives."

"That is possible, but unlikely. There are too many logistics in transporting their prisoners. It was enough for them to get the women out of Israel and into Syria. My guess is that they have another place— another safe house—probably near the one we know about in Hims. Furthermore, it is unlikely that they will take them very far because they want to get closure on this matter as much as we do. It would not make sense to send you on a wild goose chase to come and meet them or look for our wives. Unless they simply want to kill you and not force you to do this favor, I think they will take you to the women so you can verify they are alive and well. That is why I want to take my men back to the Juwaykhat area and wait. You will find the women for us."

"Great," said Newman, his fatigue and frustration showing. "Then what do I do, pick up the phone and tell you where I am, supposing I even know? Or maybe you want me to wear a wire. I'm sure the terrorists wouldn't think of looking for one." Newman rolled his eyes.

"Have a little more faith in us, my friend," said Rotem kindly. "We can't have you do anything as conventional as wear a wire. Naturally, the first thing they will do is check you for a wire, and if they found one, they'd obviously execute you on the spot and leave before we could find the place. I'm thinking of something a little more sophisticated— and safer for you."

"I'm listening."

"We have had some good results using this with our undercover people," the major said. He held up a tiny pellet, smaller than a pea. "This epoxy capsule contains a battery-powered microchip transmitting device that is virtually undetectable by radio-frequency scanners or metal detectors. When implanted beneath the skin, it has about one hundred hours of life, and it can be detected by satellite even if one is inside a building or vehicle. We've even tested them in bunkers and, as long as it's not covered by more than a foot of earth or six inches of concrete, the signal can reach the satellite and give us a GPS geolocation confirmation, accurate to within about two meters. The Operations Center here at Duvdevan will be able to pick up the signal from the satellite and feed the GPS coordinates to us in the field. So we'll be able to find you quickly."

Intrigued, Newman asked, "How often does it transmit? How is it powered?"

Rotem smiled. "It sends out a microburst on a discrete frequency every thirty seconds for three minutes when commanded to do so by an encrypted signal from the satellite. That's why it's so hard to detect with a scanner. And it's powered by a tiny nuclear battery."

Newman arched his eyebrows. "Nuclear? And you want to implant this in me? How? Wait . . . no . . . that's crazy. They'd see evidence of surgery if they strip-searched me."

"No, it has never happened—so far . . . and we've used this dozens of times. Come with me . . . I'll show you how we do it."

Newman walked behind the major down the narrow corridor to a small infirmary where Rotem introduced him to the Israeli doctor, a woman. She had laid out one of the devices on a sterile towel alongside a scalpel and other surgical tools.

Dr. Eliat asked him to take off his shoes and socks. The Marine did as instructed and sat on the gurney, placing his left foot out in front of him. "What's the plan, Dr. Eliat?" he asked.

"It's simple and rather painless," she answered. "I open the skin in the web between your third and fourth toes, insert the transmitting device, and close you up again. It's as simple as that. We place it there because we've determined that's the safest spot to avoid discomfort and any interference with your metatarsal arch. And it's hard to detect, even in a strip-search. That's all there is to it."

"What about the radiation?" asked Newman, noticing uneasily that Dr. Eliat was already swabbing his foot with alcohol.

"Well, we haven't had anyone go sterile yet," she answered with a wry smile.

Newman made one last try as she sprayed the area with a topical anesthetic. "But won't it be obvious if you cut a hole in my foot? Won't you have to suture it closed? How can they miss seeing the stitches?"

Dr. Eliat smiled. "Don't worry, they won't see anything. The web between the toes is a natural concealment." She proceeded to spread his toes apart to make sure that the anesthetic reached the area on which she was about to work. As the physician waited for the topical anesthetic to take effect, she rolled a small portable table over next to where she was working and adjusted the flexible overhead light above her.

"This will probably sting a little—like getting a shot with a needle."

Dr. Eliat wedged a large piece of tightly-rolled cotton packing to help spread his toes apart, and then she massaged the skin where it formed the web. Finally she took the scalpel and cut a tiny incision between the toes. Blood oozed from the cut and ran into the towel under his foot.

"She's opening the skin to accommodate the transmitter," Rotem explained.

Quickly the doctor took the small pellet and inserted it into the incision. Then she held cotton against it to stop the bleeding.

"And once it is inside your foot, she'll close the incision, but not with sutures. She's using special surgical glue. It seals the incision and promotes faster healing. By morning, you'll feel some soreness, but the incision will be almost impossible to detect," Rotem said.

"Looks and smells like Super Glue," Newman said.

"Yes," Dr. Eliat replied with a smile, "and there have been times in an emergency when we have used ordinary Super Glue."

Newman grinned. He felt a little discomfort but no serious pain. The doctor cleaned around the incision with some alcohol then told him, "You can put your shoes and socks back on now."

As he finished and stood up, the doctor asked, "Any discomfort?"

"No, it's fine," replied Newman. Then, as an idea came to him, he asked, "Do you have more of these devices?"

"Yes, but not many."

"Does each one have its own frequency?"

"Yes, it operates like the IFF beacon on an aircraft. Each one shows up on the satellite display with a separate identifier code."

"Can you get two more of them tonight and sew them into some clothing?"

"Why?"

"Insurance. If I get to wherever it is I'm supposed to go, and they separate me from the women, I want a chance to give our wives something they can wear so you can track them."

Newman and Rotem shared an understanding glance. If the kidnapper had a score to settle with Newman, the American might not leave the meeting alive.

"Even the terrorists would understand me bringing the women some clean clothing," Newman said. "If these things are as good as you say they are, you should be able to track them wherever they are."

Dr. Eliat said, "Sew them into brassieres. If it's placed right where the underwire comes together, no man would ever notice."

"Yeah . . . I brought Rachel a change of underwear and some clean clothes already, even before this was an idea. What about you?" he asked Rotem.

"Yes . . . I have also brought some clean clothes for Dyan. But where do you suggest we locate a seamstress to sew brassieres at this hour of the night?"

Dr. Eliat grinned and shook her head. "Ahh, you men. Get me the two transmitters. Record which is which, and I'll sew them in for you. You owe me for this one, Rotem."

The IDF major smiled and said, "Yes, Doctor. Now all we have to worry about is making sure Colonel Newman gives the correct clothing to the right wife." Rotem grinned at Newman.

But once they were back in the Operations Center conference room with the other men who would be going back into Syria with Rotem, the gravity and danger of the mission came back to all of them. The red operational lights were on now because Rotem and his team would be departing shortly, well before Newman left for Ben Gurion Airport and the first leg of his trip to Damascus.

The team was busy checking weapons, ammunition, grenades, breaching charges, radios, night-vision devices, and other equipment. The plan they had worked out called for them to move into position after dark the following night, to take advantage of their superior night-fighting gear.

"If all goes as planned, thirty hours from now we should all be on a helicopter headed back here," Newman said to Rotem. "I know how dangerous this is for all of you, but it's even more so for the two women we're trying to rescue. Please don't get spotted on your approach because if they see any sign of you, our wives are dead."

Rotem looked at Newman for several seconds. Then he nodded, and began checking his combat equipment.

Mediterranean Sea

Aboard the USS *Theodore Roosevelt*
112 Nautical Miles West of Beirut
Thursday, 19 March 1998
0215 Hours, Local

General George Grisham opened the hatch and re-entered the warm, red-lit interior of Rear Admiral Hank Hennessey's flag bridge. He had been out on the wing of the bridge, talking to Lieutenant Colonel Peter Newman on a satellite phone for ten minutes. He was chilled to the bone by the 25-knot wind rushing by as the carrier cut through the sea, headed toward Turkey. As the general walked up to the big leather chair on which his friend, the Carrier Battle Group commander, was seated, Hennessey said, "How's your missing Marine doing, George?"

"Well, the Israeli team launched for Syria about an hour ago. And Newman's going to fly to Damascus tomorrow morning."

"Damascus! How's he going to do that? There aren't any flights between Israel and Damascus."

"He's flying to Istanbul, then back to Damascus."

"Then what?"

"Then he supposedly gets taken to where his wife and the wife of the Israeli team leader are being held. The Israelis are using some kind of miniature transponders for him and the two women so they can keep track of everyone."

"Do we have the frequencies for these things?" asked Hennessey.

"Unfortunately, we don't."

"Well . . . it would be nice if we had them, and I could track where your boy is from one of our RF emission detectors."

General Grisham nodded but said nothing. Finally the admiral spoke again. "So . . . looks like the 'nuke recovery mission' is on indefinite hold, my friend."

"I'm afraid so. And in an hour, I've got to leave here in that awful COD of yours to go to Incirlik. The ostensible reason for me to be out here is to review CENTCOM's newest Middle East contingency plans. That was scheduled to take three days. After that, I'm supposed to return to MacDill." Grisham shook his head, a worried look on his face. "I sure hope Newman's back in Israel before I have to leave Turkey, Hank."

"That's not all that's bugging you, George. I've known you too long," Hennessey said, peering through the dim, red light at his former classmate and good friend. "There's something else eating at you."

The Marine general peered out across the long, broad flight deck where the crew was preparing to launch the twin turbo-prop, S-2 COD for his trip to the Incirlik Air Base near Adana, Turkey.

"What's eating at me, Hank, is that there is a terrible security leak somewhere back in the States. Newman's identity and location were known only to a handful of people, and yet somebody, very well connected in our government, is providing sensitive information to our adversaries. There can be no other explanation."

"Who, George? Where?"

"I don't know. It seems as if all of the usual suspects have already been arrested, killed, fired, transferred, or otherwise dealt with. Even those who escaped the harshest consequences, like Harrod, are outside any sphere of influence that could give them the power and resources to go after Newman again. And I can't think of anyone in our government who has contacts with the PFLP, Hezbollah, or other terrorists."

"Then . . . there's no connection whatsoever to the compromise of this young fellow's mission for the UN back in '95?"

"Not that I can see, Hank. When I get back to MacDill, I'll launch a quiet review of our security protocols, but other than that, I don't know where to begin." Grisham checked his watch. "I've got to get going. Don't want to keep your pilots waiting."

"Be careful, George. If I can help, let me know. But be careful. You're too valuable to fall on your sword for this one Marine."

Grisham shook hands with his friend, went down one level to the VIP stateroom where he had stowed his gear, and sat down at his laptop computer. It took him less than fifteen minutes to draft an encrypted e-mail to Bill Goode, bringing the old CIA Clandestine

Services officer up to speed on both Newman's situation and his own plans.

At precisely 0300, there was a knock on his door and a Marine sergeant, part of the ship's company, announced, "Sir, your aircraft is ready on the flight deck."

"Very well, let's go," replied Grisham as the younger Marine grabbed the general's duffel bag and headed toward the ladder that would take them to the flight deck.

As he walked out of the island onto the broad expanse of steel, a voice blared over the IMC: *"Now hear this: Flight Quarters. Stand by to launch aircraft."*

The night was clear and moonless, and the sky was brilliant with stars. General Grisham sighed, saluted the officers on deck, then strode up the tail ramp of the C-2, nodding to the rest of his staff already aboard and strapped in their rear-facing seats.

Moments later, with engines screaming at maximum RPM, the aircraft was hurled off the deck and into the air by the carrier's number one catapult. The Navy plane gained altitude quickly. Its radar never detected the two Israeli CH-53 helicopters, skimming the tops of the cedar trees one hundred and fifty miles to the northeast, preparing to drop an IDF commando team into Syria.

A MEETING
OF ADVERSARIES

CHAPTER TWELVE

PFLP/Hezbollah Compound

Hamah, Syria
Thursday, 19 March 1998
1200 Hours, Local

H as the plane from Turkey landed?" Komulakov said into the telephone. He waited for his answer. "Good. I want you to follow him. Make sure he goes directly to the International First Class lounge and waits there for my call. If he stops to talk to anyone, call me immediately. Did he clear customs as a regular visitor, or did he go through the diplomatic line? Not the diplomatic line? That's good too. Then he probably hasn't come with government help, and he's doing this on his own. He's probably nervous about bringing any attention to himself because of that outstanding terrorism warrant. All right, good work." Komulakov ended the call and placed the sat phone in his inside breast pocket.

He motioned to the leader of the Arab hostage team.

"Alert all of your men to keep a close eye on the women. The man we seek is in Damascus. I'm about to bring him here. I don't believe he would be foolish enough to bring a radio or transmitter with him, nor do I think it possible for him to have made any arrangements with the American or Jewish Special Forces. But just to make sure, if we find a device on him, execute the women, and I will personally take care of our arriving guest. Do you understand?"

The chief terrorist nodded his head.

"Just to be safe, I will not bring him directly here," Komulakov said. "I'll have him first brought to a place where we can thoroughly search him. Once we determine he isn't wired and has no one with him or following him, then we can decide what to do and where to go from there."

✪

Rachel and Dyan knew nothing about Peter Newman's arrival except that he was "on his way." That was more than twelve hours ago, and the anticipation they had both felt at first had worn thin. For breakfast, the women had been given some dates, hardboiled eggs, some pita bread, and two bottles of water each. Other than that, they were left alone, for which Rachel at least was grateful.

She wondered where James was right now. Rachel missed her child terribly and nearly began to cry every time she thought of him. This was her third day as a hostage, and Rachel began to feel more and more of the emotional weight of the ordeal. She noticed Dyan also seemed depressed and quiet. Rachel had heard her crying quietly during the night.

For the past twenty-four hours, Rachel had been trying to figure out the identity of the tall, well-dressed Westerner who seemed to know so much about her and Peter. He never introduced himself, but somehow she felt he expected her to know who he was. Whoever he was, he was definitely in charge. She had listened through the door to his orders to the kidnappers and others who entered and left the compound during the day.

The women never saw all of their captors. Locked as they were in the small room at the back of the building, the only activity they could see through the tiny hole in the paint-covered window told them next to nothing about where they were or who these terrorists were.

Rachel was peering through the little hole in the window when she heard the rattle of the padlock on their door. Dyan was napping on the floor, and Rachel quickly lay down on her own mattress and feigned sleep. The noise of the door flying open startled Dyan awake, and both women sat up to see one of their Arab captors enter, followed by a woman in traditional Syrian dress. It was the first time during their three-day captivity that Rachel or Dyan had seen another woman.

She was carrying a shopping bag filled with garments. As the guard left and locked the door behind him, the woman gave them orders in broken English.

"Take off clothes."

Dyan, still groggy from her nap, said, "What's going on?"

The Syrian woman repeated her command. "Take off clothes. You be moving to other place. Wear these." She pointed at the clothing in the bag.

Slowly but obediently, the two captives did as they were told. Rachel stripped to her underwear and was given a long, flowing, black Arab dress to wear. Dyan undressed as well, folding her garments neatly and placing them on her mattress. Rachel did the same with her own shirt, slacks, and jacket, even though she wanted desperately to keep her own clothes; putting on these garments seemed like taking another step away from her husband and son.

"Where are they taking us?" Rachel asked the Syrian woman, who did not answer.

Dyan said something in Arabic.

"I tell you—you being moved!" The woman scowled at Dyan as she answered.

Rachel tried another approach. "Well then, do you know whether we will come back here, or should we take our clothes with us?"

The woman shrugged. "Don't know. They not tell where you go, if you come back. Here." She grabbed the bag she had brought in and shoved it toward Rachel. "Put in here. You take with you."

When the women were dressed in the black robes, they looked at each other. They would never pass for Arabs. Dyan was Jewish, but her roots appeared more Slavic than Semitic, and Rachel's fair skin and light blue eyes betrayed a heritage that was not at all Middle Eastern. However, the Arab woman gave them each a black headdress that could also be used as a veil. She showed them how to put it on and cover their faces.

"It is good." She nodded, looking at them. "Now we wait."

"Wait?" said Rachel. "What are we waiting for?"

"Wait for American to come. Your husband."

X-Ray Rendezvous
12 km South of Juwaykhat, Syria
Thursday, 19 March 1998
1330 Hours, Local

Major Rotem's five-man Sayeret team assembled at a new rendezvous point near Juwaykhat. They pulled their vehicle within the ruins of an old building, long abandoned to the elements. The place would provide them with some concealment while they waited to find out where Peter Newman was being taken.

About a half hour later, Captain Naruch's four-man team arrived and pulled his beat-up old Toyota van into the decrepit building, next to the AIL Desert Raider. Rotem set up security in the building and in the underbrush surrounding it. Then he established his mobile command post to receive messages from Tel-Nof regarding the satellite tracking of the transmitters Newman was carrying.

Rotem watched as the captain typed information into his laptop computer. A map of the nearby terrain came up on the screen. The captain then taped a tiny umbrella-shaped satellite antenna to one of the broken windows and, using his compass and consulting some entries on a PDA, he carefully aimed the antenna at a predetermined point in the sky.

Next, he hooked the antenna cable to a miniature RF receiver and began to download data from a satellite in geosynchronous orbit, 32° north of the equator. With another click on the keyboard, a blinking icon showed up on the map.

"There is Colonel Newman's signal. The satellite has not yet activated the two other transponders," Captain Naruch said. "It is quite clear. He is moving north from the airport, but not on the highway. If he's not in a car or truck and is traveling off-road, perhaps he's in a four-by-four vehicle. Or maybe a horse or camel?"

Rotem and Naruch stared intently at the computer screen.

"He's moving even faster than a car or truck. Maybe he's on another aircraft. A helicopter maybe?" Rotem said.

The captain shook his head. "It's faster than a car, but slower than a plane or helicopter. And look . . . he's traveling in a straight line across the desert."

"He's on the train!" they both said at once.

"Of course," said Rotem. "That's part of the Hezbollah route that the Iranians use. We should have guessed they'd use the train—just like they did with the women."

Rotem retrieved a 1:100,000-scale military map of Syria from his case in the back of the Desert Raider. He spread it out on the hood of the vehicle. After poring over the map for a few moments, he said, "Perhaps we should anticipate they will stop at either Hims, or farther north . . . up here, by this old bridge across the river south of Hamah at Ar Rastan."

"If they aren't in Hims, they must have a place near Hamah," the captain guessed.

"Let's get out of here and head up to intersect with them. If they take him to another safe house, we'll have a head start and can set up in the general area until we find exactly where they take him," Rotem said.

"We'll need a place to hide out during daylight hours. There's an abandoned mine just a few kilometers from Ar Rastan," said Captain Naruch. "The train stops at both Hims and Hamah, and this old mine is alongside the train tracks between the two cities. Once we get a fix on where they take Colonel Newman, we'll do a recon and see just how heavily guarded it is, and then we can mount a rescue operation."

"What about this ravine area that runs from here to the old mine?" Rotem asked. "Can we safely go that way without being discovered?"

"Yes, your Desert Raider can handle that terrain. But we'll have to take our van on the highway. Since we're not as conspicuous as your six-wheeled vehicle, we can take the regular road without any trouble. We'll plan to meet you here," Captain Naruch said, pointing to a spot on the map. "You can ford the river at this spot, and go about seven or eight kilometers north. The village of Birin is just northwest, and it's the only place in the entire area where you need to be careful. We can stay in radio contact, and I can alert you to anything that you will need to watch out for."

"What time do you think they'll move Newman from the train to local transportation?" Rotem asked.

"I'm guessing that this is a passenger train and not freight. He'll probably make Hims in another hour or so . . . then, if the train follows the scheduled stops, it'll be in Hims for awhile, and then it's another hour before it gets to Hamah, where it makes another scheduled stop," Naruch said.

"And if they have other plans—like having him stay on the train all the way to Aleppo?"

"Then," the captain said, "I'm afraid Colonel Newman will be on his own."

Aboard Northbound Train

77 km North of Damascus, Syria
Thursday, 19 March 1998
1330 Hours, Local

Peter Newman sat on a bench seat in the Third Class coach between two young Arab men. He guessed them to be in their late twenties or early thirties. They had stuck to him like glue ever since meeting him in the International First Class lounge at the airport just outside of Damascus.

The rocking of the train, the clicking of the wheels over the rails, reminded him of his last Syrian train ride. Three years ago, aboard the Taurus Express, successor to the old Orient Express, he had taken the train from the Euphrates Valley across northern Syria to Aleppo. From there, he'd taken another train into Turkey. That trip had been a success: he had safely met Bill Goode in Iskenderun, Turkey, and Goode had smuggled him aboard the *Pescador*—only to have the sloop blown to bits in Cyprus.

Newman's two escorts for this trip were far from pleasant. Both were armed, and neither of them spoke so much as a word as the train traveled north. Newman had no idea where they were taking him: he expected it might be Hims, the initial place where he and Major Rotem had suspected the women were being held; the other possibility was Hamah, a city just forty-eight kilometers further north. If he remembered correctly, those were the only stops until the train arrived at Aleppo.

Newman held two small, dark-blue knapsacks on his lap containing the changes of clothing for each of the two women that Rotem and he had gathered for their respective wives.

In the car on the way from the airport, one of the two gunmen had taken the two knapsacks and meticulously searched the bags and their contents for any contraband, carefully checking each article of clothing. Newman held his breath while the man felt along the seams for anything that might have been sewn into them. He didn't feel the small epoxy pellets that had been sewn into each of the two brassieres, and Newman had released a silent sigh of relief. Now he held the knapsacks protectively on his lap.

Newman also carried Rachel's diplomatic passport that would enable her to cross any border checkpoint, board a commercial flight, or depart any port without being subject to too much scrutiny from immigrations or customs officials. For the same reason, Newman also carried the black diplomatic passport General Grisham had given him. Though the Marine had no idea what his status was with the United States government and its various agencies, this was no time to take chances. For all he knew, he might still be a wanted fugitive, and he hoped this new passport was his guaranteed ticket out of Syria or any other countries whose borders they crossed.

Sitting between the two thugs, Newman feigned sleep while he tried to focus on the matters at hand. What concerned him at the moment was Major Rotem's Sayeret Duvdevan team. They would be primed for action and, Newman assumed, close by. Despite his fears that the Israelis might act prematurely, Newman had to trust that Rotem would be the professional he claimed to be. After all, his own wife's life was at stake as well.

As he thought about the meeting with the kidnappers, Newman decided his best course of action was to go along, to not aggravate any situation. His only real objective was to get the women rescued without injury. Once they were free, then he could think about saving his own skin.

MI6 New HQ Construction Site

85 Albert Embankment, Vauxhall Cross
London, England
Thursday, 19 March 1998
1030 Hours, Local

Sir David Spelling, chief of the British Secret Intelligence Service, known as "C" inside "The Firm," was at the construction site of the new SIS office complex under construction on the south bank of the Thames River. He was standing outside, on the first-level rooftop of the nearly completed, multistoried building, making notes for his meeting with the construction superintendent when MI6 Officer Ian Downs approached him.

C liked Downs. Like himself, Downs was an authority on the Middle East and had served with him since the 1980s. Downs had ridden here with C in the armored Land Rover sedan from the aging SIS HQ at Century House in Lambeth. It was only during such rides that Downs could get his boss alone for a few minutes of uninterrupted conversation. But as the pair arrived at the construction site, Downs had received an urgent call on his mobile telephone and had stayed inside the unfinished building to take it.

As C waited for Downs to catch up, he watched as a crane manipulated a heavy steel beam through a tight opening. Though C seemed engrossed in the construction going on around him, his mind was really on his budget meeting with the Prime Minister two hours from now.

Since the fall of the Soviet empire, the SIS budget had been cut to the bone. Along with the budget cuts had come drastic personnel reductions; and today, even though he was down to fewer than three thousand intelligence officers and support employees, C knew his budget was about to be trimmed again.

Downs reappeared while C was contemplating how the SIS could possibly do the job that had to be done with the measly one hundred and fifty million pounds Parliament had appropriated.

"Sir David," Downs said, "do you have time to discuss another matter before we head back to Century House? Blackman and Thomas are downstairs in one of the conference rooms. Even though the wing isn't finished, they tell me this particular room has been Tempest-certified. We can speak securely there."

"What do Thomas and Blackman want?" the Chief asked.

"They'd like your opinion regarding a Middle East anomaly they uncovered yesterday. Do you have time before your meeting with the PM?"

C glanced at his watch, then nodded and strode toward the construction elevator. "You know," he said to Downs as they walked, "this is a magnificent view of the Thames and the city, and all of MI6 will be delighted to move here from that drafty old loft in Lambeth. But I have some concerns about this location. Take a look—down there, on the river. Some terrorist group could take a boat and cruise right by, aim one of those Matra Eryx anti-armor missiles that the French are selling all over the place, fire it through any of these windows, and we'd have one bloody, messy massacre. Has the architect thought about that? What's being done about the glass in the windows? What kind of resistance will it have?"

"I'll inquire of the architect as soon as we arrive back at Century House, Sir David. One would hope all of that has already been taken into consideration."

C grunted. "What floor do we want?"

"Six."

Moments later, C and Officer Downs walked into the unfinished conference room where two other men were waiting for them. One of the men had spread out some computer printouts of aerial photos and the other had opened his laptop computer atop a makeshift table—a four-foot-square sheet of pressed wood supported on two sawhorses.

"Blackman, Thomas, good day. What have you there?"

"Well, sir . . . we found something a bit queer when one of our analysts took a closer look at last week's NRO overhead imagery from the Americans," Thomas said. "These nine shots are from routine day and night passes over Iraq. As you know, Saddam Hussein is giving the UN weapons inspectors a hard time. Well, even though the Americans don't make much of it, Watts down in the Imagery Unit has noticed Saddam has started a regular building boom in the construction of mosques. The Americans say 'so what?' but Watts doesn't think they're really mosques. Here, let me show you the pictures."

C bent over the makeshift table and perused the printed photos. They consisted of shots of several construction sites, apparently taken from various angles during several different satellite passes over the course of twenty-one days. "Is this one of them?" C asked, pointing to one of the images.

"Yes, sir. That's one that Watts has labeled suspicious. So we went back and interviewed that Republican Guard officer who defected to us in Jordan last month . . . the one you were briefed on?"

"Yes, yes . . . what about him?"

"Well sir, he says this particular structure is not used for religious purposes at all, but instead it's a laboratory for weapons of mass destruction . . . and a prison."

"A *prison?* Why would he have a prison together with biological weapons?"

"Our guess is the prisoners might be guinea pigs."

"I see. . . . Have we notified the UN inspectors about this?"

"Not yet," Blackman said. "You see, we discovered something else when we were making the high resolution pictures of the prisoners as they were exercising in the courtyard. We thought we ought to get your thoughts on this before we involve the UN—or anyone else for that matter."

"Go on."

"These are photos of a group of six prisoners taken at highest magnification, where they were leaning against the interior prison wall," Thomas said, pointing to the photo. "We compared it to this group of prisoners about fifteen feet away from them."

"Hmm . . . I see," said C. "These men are clearly Arabs, probably Iraqis, maybe even some of the Kuwaiti POWs that were never repatriated . . . while these men here, these six, certainly seem to be Westerners."

"Yes, sir, precisely. When we saw this, Blackman remembered a new computer program that came into MI6 from the Canadians. Seems they've developed a new facial recognition software program in collaboration with the Americans. Blackman decided to try it out on this group of faces—the ones that look like Westerners—and see if it turned up anything."

"And . . . ?"

Blackman went to the computer. "Look at this, Sir David. We started with this man . . . isolated his head, fed his photo into the computer, and mucked about with it some; then the computer looked for a match in our database of thirty-seven million faces. It came up with this." Blackman clicked *enter* and the screen filled with a UK Armed Forces file photo of a man in a British Army uniform. The caption read, "Macklin, Bruno. Captain, SAS" and listed a brief resumé of his military service. Below were the words, in a larger font, "MISSING, PRESUMED DEAD. SEE FILE ACTOR 95322/9945 UK EYES BRAVO."

"And you checked the ACTOR file?"

"He was assigned by the PM as part of a special SAS contingent that went out on a rogue UN mission in '95 . . . perhaps you remember it, the one that was set up as a joint UK, U.S.A., and UN assassination mission to Iraq," Blackman said. "Everyone thought Macklin was killed in action."

"And the others in the photo?"

"We can only ID three more of the six Westerners in the picture. This one is one of ours. He's a pilot shot down while patrolling the 'no fly' zone three years ago. The other two are Americans, one a U.S. Navy pilot shot down in the Gulf War and the other a U.S. Air Force pilot— same situation. They've all three been in Iraqi prisons since 1991."

"I see." C pushed his glasses up on his nose as he stood upright. "Did you try to ID any of the Middle Eastern prisoners?"

"Uh . . . no, we didn't, sir. Should we?" Thomas asked.

"Yes . . . let's see if that turns up anything. Let's see if they're political prisoners or common crooks."

"And then . . . ?" asked Blackman.

"And then we'll discuss it some more. Meanwhile, see if you can find anything else on this Macklin fellow. Now that we know he's alive, I'm sure the PM will want to get him back—as well as any other Brits being held. We may have to plan some kind of operation," Sir David said. Then he added, almost as an afterthought, "What did the Americans say about all this? I should think they'd like to get their pilot back."

Thomas and Blackman looked at each other and then to Downs for guidance.

"When Thomas took the matter to Liaison, as we're supposed to do, their station chief in London was initially very interested indeed," Downs said carefully. "But two days later, he came back and said the CIA disagreed with our analysis, and they were not going to pursue the matter."

C said nothing for a moment.

"You've done a good job on this, Thomas . . . Blackman. Put together a brief for the PM, and I shall take it to him personally."

Then he looked at his watch and straightened his tie. "Well, if that's all, I have to run."

Blackman shuffled the photos and documents into his attaché case and shut down the computer. "Thank you for your time, sir," he said.

"Oh, there's one other thing, Sir David," Thomas said. "Our people at the GCHQ site in Cyprus reported that the brass at the Sovereign Air Base gave some sort of assistance to the American CENTCOM Commander in Chief. He's now in Incirlik, by the way." Thomas consulted a three-by-five-inch card that he had withdrawn from his shirt pocket. "Our post in Turkey also picked up some intel about something going on in Syria, by way of the Israelis. Two nights ago, the Cyprus GCHQ site picked up encrypted Israeli aircraft chatter that coincided with overhead imagery showing two blacked-out helicopters—perhaps CH-53s—transiting the Beirut FIR, then making a 'rough field' landing inside Syria. The birds were on the ground for only two and a half minutes, and then they went back to Israel. Curiously, the same thing happened last night . . . or actually early this morning, before daybreak. We assumed it was some kind of agent drop or an IDF special ops insertion and extraction because five hours ago, two helicopters landed in Syria again. Do you want us to query the Israelis on this?"

C put his hand to his chin. "I think not. Probably just intelligence gathering on some suicide bomber."

"That's what we thought yesterday. But when it happened again today, well . . . we're not so sure. As you know, the Israelis make it a matter of policy not to repeat an insertion/extraction using the same coordinates twice in a row. But for whatever reason, they felt it was important enough to break SOP and make an almost identical run a second day. That makes me think they may be up to something more serious."

"Could be, Jerry. But instead of asking the Israelis, just keep an eye on it. Call me if you find that it's anything out of the ordinary. And now, please excuse me. Can't keep the Prime Minister waiting."

Tango Rendezvous
9 km South of Birin Village, Syria
Thursday, 19 March 1998
1445 Hours, Local

Rotem watched as Captain Naruch's vehicle came into view. He was a kilometer east of where he had left his men and the Desert Raider vehicle. Rotem and his team had arrived at the rendezvous first and found cover quickly. Naruch's instincts were good; no matter which of the two cities they were taking Newman to, the Israeli commandos were less than forty minutes from either location. Rotem's men had spread a camouflage net over the vehicle and established a defensive perimeter while their commander took a look around.

A half hour earlier, Rotem had endured a fascinating—but frustrating—experience. From the Israeli observation post, he could just see the train tracks two kilometers to the east. As he watched, a train approached from the south, and he turned to the team's communicator and said, "Rafi, where does the satellite say Newman is?"

After checking, in a matter of seconds, the communicator called out, "Major, he's right there!" Rotem looked and saw the trooper pointing to the train.

Rotem moved quickly to look at the laptop, set up on the hood of the Desert Raider. There on the screen's map display was Newman's "tattle-tale," the blip of his tiny satellite transponder, moving across the screen as well as on the railway tracks in the valley below.

"Well, at least we know . . . that means they didn't take him off the train in Hims," said Rotem. "Let's hope they take him off in Hamah and not all the way at Aleppo."

Shortly after the train passed out of sight, Captain Naruch and his four-man undercover team arrived at the rendezvous. They parked their vehicle alongside the ancient bridge over the Nahr Al Asi, or what little was left of the shallow river that the Desert Raider had crossed about twenty minutes earlier. One of Naruch's men put the hood up on their decrepit-looking vehicle, while another poured a half-quart of oil on the ground beneath the crankcase to make it appear as if the vehicle had broken down. After checking up and down the road to ensure that no one saw them, they removed their weapons and equipment from the secret compartment built into the floor plates of the vehicle and walked, one at a time, over the ridge to rendezvous with Rotem's team.

Just as Rotem was about to brief Naruch and his men, one of the soldiers bumped the cord connecting the tiny satellite antenna to the computer, and the little "umbrella" fell off the top of the Desert Raider, breaking the signal-lock with the satellite. When the laptop screen went blank, the soldier operating the system jumped up to reset the antenna, carefully aiming it to the point in the sky where the satellite was parked, but by the time he tried to re-establish the signal, the blinking green icon that represented the American was not visible on the map of the area. The soldier operating the system began trying various adjustments.

After nearly thirty minutes of trying, someone suggested that they reboot the system and re-enter the coordinates. To Rotem's great relief, this plan worked; Newman's position came up immediately.

"Oh, man . . . look where he is," Rotem said.

"They evidently took him off the train at Hamah . . . but now it looks as if they're taking him by car or truck somewhere east of here," Naruch said. "They've got a real head start. It will take us an hour to get to where they are now, and they're still driving east—away from us."

"Where are they taking him—and why? What's over there?" Rotem said.

The computer operator zoomed out on the map, and the answer became more apparent.

"They're heading toward Salamiyah, sir. That's thirty-five kilometers, cross-country, line of sight, from here."

"This is bad," Rotem said. "They're still on the move." The major turned to his Ethiopian tracker. "Captain Naruch, have you or your men been into Salamiyah? If they take him there, can we go into the city to get him?"

"No, sir. There's a Syrian Army garrison guarding the city. The Army and the Interior Ministry police routinely set up roadblocks and checkpoints."

"Well, why are they taking him there? Do the Hezbollah or the PFLP have offices there?"

"Not that we know of, sir. But these guys are smart. They're doing it to make sure that their prisoner is not being followed. I think we'd better just sit this out for awhile and see where they end up, sir."

Rotem ran a hand through his short-cropped hair. "Yes, you're right." For the first time since taking off from Israel, Ze'ev Rotem was feeling something like despair; he was getting no closer to rescuing his wife, and he might never again see his American friend alive.

Centre Market Square
Salamiyah, Syria
Thursday, 19 March 1998
1605 Hours, Local

Newman was wedged in the backseat of an old Land Cruiser between his two bodyguards, trying to stay awake. He noticed that sometimes his two escorts had the same problem. But they knew he wasn't going to try to escape; they were taking him to see his wife.

The Marine hoped he was on the final leg of this odyssey. The driver had been waiting for them when they disembarked from the train in Hamah, and up until they entered the city limits of Salamiyah, they had made reasonably good time. But now they were stuck in the Syrian version of evening rush hour.

At four o'clock in the afternoon, the marketplace lacked the swarming hustle and bustle of the early morning hours; still, there were hundreds of shoppers lingering among the crowded stalls and produce stands. The narrow streets were congested with traffic of all kinds—people, beasts of burden, cars and trucks, bicycles, scooters—and more people.

After slowly grinding along for ten minutes through the crowd in the waning light, one of the two guards said something to the driver in Arabic. The car pulled over to the side of the narrow street, and Newman's guards motioned for him to get out of the car.

As they got out, Newman could sense people looking at him. He felt out of place, the only Westerner visible on the street. There were others who wore jeans and T-shirts, but their features were Arabic; fortunately, his tanned skin, beard, and long, dark hair made it a little easier for him to blend in.

His two guards walked on either side of him, as they had all day. They escorted him for several blocks through the bazaar to a shop at its edge, one of the many permanent structures with windows, doors, and a sign. Newman had a little trouble with the Arabic script, but he thought he could make out "Mahediran Jewelry." His guess was confirmed when his guards took him inside and he saw display cases of rings, bracelets, watches, and other jewelry.

Once inside, one of the guards pulled down the shades on the front windows and the door and then turned the lock. The other guard posted the sign that said "closed" in Arabic. A man behind the counter, whom Newman guessed to be the proprietor, looked up and, when he saw who had come in, immediately picked up his coat and left by a rear door.

"Sit," one of his guards ordered. Newman sat on a nearby stool, placing the two knapsacks that he had brought with him on the floor beside his feet.

They waited silently nearly twenty minutes. Newman heard activity in the back and the sounds of someone entering the shop. He turned to look, hoping to see his wife, but instead saw a tall man in an expensive European suit. Two other men, carrying automatic weapons, flanked the well-dressed man. The tall man paused a moment, silhouetted by the dim light behind him, then walked out of the shadows and into the well-lighted shop.

"Komulakov!"

"My dear Colonel Newman, you are truly like a cat with nine lives. I see that you took Simon Harrod's advice to lose that military haircut. Your hair is quite long now, isn't it?"

"Where are Rachel and her friend?"

"They are safe—for now. It was you I needed, you see."

"I want to see my wife."

"Oh, there will be time enough for all that later. First, I need to make sure you aren't being followed."

"What do you want?"

"Patience, please, Colonel Newman. May I request that you take off your clothes and let my men search you for a transmitter?"

Newman stood slowly and began pulling off his shirt.

"Oh, and . . . what do you have in the knapsacks?" Komulakov said.

"A change of clothing for the women. Any problem with that?"

Komulakov gestured, and one of the armed men grabbed the knapsacks.

As Newman undressed, one of the guards pulled out a pair of latex surgical gloves while the other watched, weapon at the ready. The terrorist with the gloves forced open the American's mouth. Then he inspected under Newman's arms and the bottoms of his feet. The terrorist shoved Newman over a jewelry counter to probe his rectum and groin for a hidden transmitter. Finally, he reached into a case and took out what looked to Newman like a hand-held metal detector, similar to the kind used at airports, and ran it over Newman's abdomen.

While Newman was being subjected to this personal indignity, Komulakov had another of his thugs carefully go through the Marine's shoes and clothing while a third searcher did the same with the garments Newman had brought for the women. He used a sharp penknife to cut the straps on the knapsacks and opened up several seams in the bags and some of the clothes. By the time he finished, the bags were virtually useless, and at least one blouse was destroyed.

Eventually, all three men were satisfied that Newman was not wired—neither his clothing nor those items he had brought for the women.

"Get dressed," said Komulakov. "You have five minutes with your wife before we leave."

"Leave? For where?"

Komulakov left the room without answering.

As he was dressing, Newman heard a door slam in the back of the shop. He was tying his shoes under the supervision of three armed men when the rear door slammed again. Then, just as he stood upright, he heard "Peter!"

Rachel was in his arms. His face was buried in her hair, her arms around his neck, her breath on his face, his arms pulling her body close. She was crying, "Peter . . . Peter," laughing and sobbing at the same time.

"Rachel . . . oh dear God, thank you . . . thank you!" He soaked in the love and energy of her being while he clung to her.

When he finally opened his eyes, Newman looked up to see Komulakov standing in the doorway at the rear of the shop.

"We will leave you alone for five minutes."

The two guards who had escorted him here exited the front door to stand outside, barring escape. The third man followed Komulakov into the back room while the Newmans had their reunion. It was only then that Peter noticed Rachel was garbed in black like an Arab widow.

"Are you all right, honey?" he asked, looking into her eyes, seeing the swelling from her broken nose, the cut on her lip.

She nodded. "Yes, and so is Dyan. But what about James? Where is he—is he all right?"

"He's fine . . . and safe—with my sister Nancy," he whispered, so no one else could hear. "I put him on a plane with Gunnery Sergeant Skillings, who took him to Cyprus. She flew over to take him back to the States. He'll stay with her—safe, honey—until all of this is over."

"Thank God," Rachel said, tears welling in her eyes. "I've been so worried about you both."

"Yeah, I've been a bit concerned about you as well, Mrs. Newman," Peter said as lightly as he could. "Is Dyan handling things all right?"

"Yes, she's in the van behind the shop. They wouldn't let her come in. She's OK, but she'd just learned she was pregnant when she came to see me on Tuesday. She's been having a little morning sickness, but other than that, she's fine. Peter . . . are they going to let us go now?"

"I doubt it, honey. Not yet, anyway. Whatever it is Komulakov wants with me, he'll probably keep you as a hostage to make sure that I do what he wants."

He leaned close and whispered so that he couldn't be overheard.

"Rachel, make sure you and Dyan wear the change of clothes I brought for each of you. It's important that you both wear those things. You'll recognize whose clothes are whose when you open the bags. But it's absolutely important that you both *wear* those clothes. Do you understand?"

"I—I guess so," she said softly.

"I can't tell you what's going on, but things are not as out of control as they seem. We'll be getting help. . . ."

He kissed her gently on the lips because of the cut, but his kiss was long and tender, reassuring her of his love and protection. They held each other in a tight embrace until Komulakov came back into the room.

"I'm sorry, Mrs. Newman," the Russian said, "but it's time for you to go. I'm afraid you'll have to say good-bye to your husband for awhile. Your permanent reunion will have to wait until he finishes an assignment I have for him. And please be patient; it may take a few weeks before he can complete everything." At this, Komulakov made a gesture, and the Syrian woman stepped past the Russian and took Rachel by the arm.

Newman's emotions ran the gamut from sadness to anger in seconds at the words of the former KGB officer. *Keep it together, Pete. For Rachel.*

Rachel looked back at him. "I love you, Peter . . . always."

Newman bent over, placed the two bags of clothing in her arms, and squeezed her hand.

"Trust me. And remember what I said. I love you." Then he watched his wife being taken out through the back of the shop and heard the door slam. He looked at the Russian.

"You miserable excuse for a human being. Someday I'm going to tear out your heart."

"I doubt that very much," said Komulakov. "I can break you like a twig."

Newman lunged for the Russian but was immediately grabbed by the two Palestinians who had re-entered the front door behind him. One of them clubbed Newman viciously on the head with the butt of his gun, and the American dropped to the floor in a crumpled heap.

★

Rachel held her tears until she was out the back door of the shop and inside the van. The Arab woman sat on one side of her, an armed terrorist on the other. Dyan sat mute behind them, armed men flanking her as well.

As the van pulled away from the shop and back down the alley, the shadows lengthened, and the driver turned on the headlights. Rachel began to sob so uncontrollably that Dyan reached forward and squeezed her friend's shoulder.

"Shut up!" someone ordered in accented English. "You stop—or I will shut your mouth for good!"

Frightened, Rachel realized she needed to hold in her emotions. She forced herself to pay attention to her surroundings. As the vehicle pulled out onto the main street, she checked her watch—ten minutes after five.

She noticed it was beginning to get dark; the crowds had thinned considerably from what they had been earlier. But there was something else different. In the gathering gloom, she tried to figure out what it was.

There . . . the faint scent of cologne. She knew it wasn't any of the men or the woman who had been guarding them. They all smelled— but not of cologne.

She caught it again. And then she noticed—the man sitting in the front passenger seat was different. On the way into the city, the seat had been occupied by one of the young thugs who had kidnapped them in Jerusalem. This was an older man, shorter and heavier. And he was wearing a European style sport coat.

"Who are you?" Rachel asked.

"Ah, that is better. You see, you cannot let your emotions rule over you," the man said. It was the same voice that had just threatened her. But now, it sounded controlled, almost friendly.

"Who are you?"

"I am Leonid Dotensk, a business associate of General Komulakov. He has asked me to watch over you for awhile."

Komulakov. That was a name she remembered hearing from Peter. She struggled to remember what her husband had said—then it all came rushing back: Komulakov was a renegade KGB general; he had caused the death of Peter's men in Iraq three years ago; he had been behind the explosion on the *Pescador* that had almost killed them both. Komulakov was the reason they had to live under aliases in Jerusalem. Now she had good reason to fear "the European."

"Where are we going?" she asked.

"It does not matter," said Dotensk. "It is enough for you to know that we will stay in Syria, but far, far away from here—far from prying eyes and ears."

Tango Rendezvous
9 km South of Birin Village, Syria
Thursday, 19 March 1998
1710 Hours, Local

Rotem was growing more desperate by the moment. Uncertain about Newman's final destination and with the two women's whereabouts unknown, Rotem had taken Captain Naruch's advice; they had been waiting in their harbor site for signs of further movement.

For more than an hour, Newman's tracking signal had been stationary in Salamiyah. They had activated the signals for the two transponders sewn into the women's brassieres, and they came up on the screen stationary—like Newman's signal.

Rotem was preparing to tell his men to post a 50-percent watch around their small perimeter so they could eat in shifts prior to setting out listening posts for the night, when the sergeant watching the laptop motioned him over.

"Sir, we have movement on the screen."

Rotem jumped up and looked at the display. Newman's icon hadn't moved. But the other two, the women's, were moving away from Salamiyah at fairly high speed.

"Captain Naruch, look at this."

As the Ethiopian tracker came to look, Newman's signal began to move as well.

"The women are moving east, and Newman is moving west toward Hamah," Naruch said.

"What do you make of that?" Major Rotem asked.

"I'm not sure. There isn't much to the east, besides the Euphrates Basin and a lot of desert. But it appears as if Colonel Newman is being brought back west, toward Hamah—or maybe even to Hims."

This entire operation is a disaster in the making, Rotem thought. "Their geographic separation makes a simultaneous rescue of all three impossible with this few men," he said quietly.

"Yes, sir. And unless the vehicle with the women stops relatively soon or they release the women quickly, we have no chance of catching up to them before dawn."

The Israeli commander knew it was true. He desperately wanted to rescue his wife, but his hope for that—at least for this night—was fading fast, as the icons sewn into the women's clothing moved farther away by the minute.

"We have no choice." Rotem said quietly. "If we're going after anyone tonight, we can only reach Newman. Alert the men to be ready to move as soon as it gets dark."

The computer operator zoomed in on the map they were watching, and the men could see more details. It was obvious now that Newman's signal was following the highway from Salamiyah back to Hamah.

"It's too bad they aren't taking him to Hims," said Naruch. "We know where that safe house is. But my men and I have only been to Hamah once. We're going to have to wait until they stop for the night before we can close up on them."

✪

After an hour, as darkness closed around the small Israeli commando unit, Rotem said, "All right, let's shut it down and get ready to move." But just as Naruch and his men prepared to go back down to the highway to board their "disabled" vehicle, the computer operator called to the two officers.

"Look at this, Major." He pointed to the zoomed-out view on the computer screen.

"The two signals for the women have stopped moving."

Rotem called to the men to wait a moment before continuing their preparations to move out. As the two senior officers intently watched the screen, there was no movement for several minutes. Still they waited.

Naruch said, "Major, we must act now. They haven't moved in ten minutes. I don't think they're going any further east."

"Or . . ." Major Rotem swallowed, then forced the words from his throat. "Or they may have killed the women and left their bodies in the desert."

"We can't think of that as an option just now, sir. Come on, Major, let's go to Hamah first, and then we'll see about the other signals. If we move quickly, we may be able to rescue all three of them before dawn."

Rotem tried to add the clues up some other way, but he simply couldn't escape the dread that was engulfing him. *The terrorists have Newman. That's what they wanted. The women are no longer of any use to them. The reason they were headed east was to take them out into the desert and kill them.*

DEALING WITH THE DEVIL

CHAPTER THIRTEEN

PFLP/Hezbollah Compound
Hamah, Syria
Thursday, 19 March 1998
1930 Hours, Local

Newman was first aware of the throbbing of his head. His second feeling was of motion—he thought he was in an automobile, though he couldn't be sure because of the blindfold. Looking down, beneath the rag that covered his eyes, he could see blood on his shirt. *Probably from my scalp where they whacked me.* He remembered the jewelry shop, going for Komulakov, then being struck from behind.

Stupid time to try and jump Komulakov, with his goons all around me. At least the bleeding seems to have stopped. Now, if I could just lose this headache . . .

But the headache wouldn't go away. He tried to brace his back against the door or sidewall of the vehicle—he couldn't tell which because his hands were tied behind him, and it was hard to sit in any one position very long without shifting his weight. Newman tried to sleep, his usual way of dealing with headaches. But it was impossible to sleep, between his awkward position and the bouncing of the vehicle.

The vehicle eventually stopped. Newman listened as the engine was cut. He heard a grunted command and another voice acknowledge what was said, then the sound of a door opening. Two pairs of hands grabbed his arms, dragged him out of the vehicle, and stood him upright on the ground. By now, Newman surmised that he had been in the back of a van and, judging by the chill in the air, it must be getting close to dark.

The cooling air cleared his mind, making him instantly alert. He was standing somewhat clumsily—his hands were still tied—when another hand grabbed the front of his belt and pulled him forward. *There must be three of them, one on each side, another in front.*

Newman heard a door open, and they marched him into a building with a concrete floor, from the feel of it. After only a few steps inside, he heard a heavy, wooden door slammed closed, and he was jerked to a halt by the hands that gripped his arms. Then he heard a voice he recognized.

Komulakov said, "Cut him loose. Put him there."

Newman felt his hands being cut free, but the men who held his arms didn't release him. Instead, they pushed him down into what felt like a wooden captain's chair, and his arms were tied to each of the arms of the chair. Likewise, his ankles were tied to the chair's front legs.

"Uncover his eyes."

The blindfold was removed, and he tried to look around, but the sudden exposure to the light of even the single incandescent bulb lighting the room made his eyes water. After a few moments, the room came into focus and he could see the tall Russian standing in front of him, a Makarov 9mm pistol in the former KGB officer's hand.

"How did you find me?" Newman asked Komulakov. The instant he spoke the words he felt a strange sense of déjà vu. He remembered asking the same question to Gunnery Sergeant Skillings—was it only twelve days ago? "You must have found a way to get into the U.S. government classified files."

"You are very perceptive, Colonel Newman. Yes . . . that is precisely how I found you. And my discovery has given me a problem that only you can help me solve."

"Me, help you? You're out of your mind."

"No, I'm not, Colonel. You see . . . this problem began long before I met you, but you made so much trouble for me three years ago that I am no longer in a position to deal with this problem myself. Now you must help me make this problem go away because I have a most important undertaking ahead of me."

✪

Komulakov knew he had to be very careful about what he told the American. Newman didn't need to know about his political aspirations. But Newman did need to know that Komulakov's problem had a name: Julio Morales. Morales could divulge Komulakov as a KGB spymaster, could document his years of espionage in the United States. Komulakov reasoned that he could weather that storm, as long as he didn't get handed over to the Americans for prosecution. What really worried the former KGB general was the prospect of Morales trying to save his own skin by telling about his arrangement with the Soviets and, later, the Russian government. If that happened, Komulakov knew, it would only be a matter of time before Moscow figured out that for every $100,000 that Centre had sent to Morales, only half of it ever actually arrived to the spy. The balance had ended up in Komulakov's numbered bank account in Aruba.

Komulakov knew of KGB officers who had ended up kneeling on the floor of a death cell in the basement of Moscow's Lefortovo Prison, waiting to be shot in the back of the head for embezzling far less than he had. Komulakov had no intention of leaving this world that way. Handled carefully, Newman would make sure it didn't come to that.

"Let me tell you this much, Colonel Newman. Helping me is to your benefit as well, and I don't mean simply the safe return of your wife—although that should be reason enough. I'm sure that you must have learned that, in my earlier days, I was a KGB officer stationed in the United States. Well, one of the spies I recruited inside your government some twenty years ago, as it turns out, is still working for the Russian Foreign Intelligence Service. Can you believe it—after all these years?"

"I have my own reasons for wishing him silenced," Komulakov said. "I don't want him to be caught, but I also want to keep him from revealing all that he knows. I can tell you this much, Colonel Newman. This man has betrayed your country's most important and most serious classified secrets. He is also personally responsible for giving us the names of at least a dozen double agents, whom we have liquidated."

"What are you talking about? What double agents?"

"Colonel Newman, we needn't play games with each other. Do the names Polykov, Yuzhin, Motorin, and Martynov mean anything to you? Or, on your side, Miller and Howard, Barnett, Peltin, and the Chinese guy, Wu-Tai Chin? This man gave them all to us."

"Are you talking about Ames? Is that your spy?"

"No. Ames, as you know, has already been discovered, and he is talking. He's spilling his guts to save his skin from the gas chamber or a lethal injection—or however you Americans eliminate your traitors. No, it isn't Ames. This mole is someone your people haven't found yet. He has been far more productive for us than Ames. Ames gave up three of the same double agents—people inside our government spying for yours, but this guy has given us many more—and he is much more ruthless. He gave up three of his countrymen overseas simply because they *might* have achieved a penetration inside the KGB that *could've* led to his discovery and shut down his spying. No . . . this fellow told us about spies inside the Soviet Union who had been spying for your government for years . . . knowing that when he gave us their names they would be executed. And I think he turned in some of them just for sport. Can you imagine that?

"And as to the kinds of secrets that he brought to us . . . well, they were worth their weight in gold. Not just the Top Secret U.S. Double Agent Program, the MASINT Program, a number of KGB assessments, and even your government's nuclear programs. He revealed a number of sophisticated U.S. and British technical programs, and best of all, he gave us the details on your Continuity of Government program—the means by which your country expected to survive a Soviet nuclear first strike. It was quite a treasure trove—unprecedented really.

"Now . . . while I regret closing that door to our Russian intelligence bureaus, I have some, ah, personal interests to protect."

"At some point, I gather you're going to tell me why I should care?"

Komulakov smiled. "Because I want you to find this mole and kill him for me."

"You've got to be kidding."

"Not at all. This man has served his purposes, and while he is a liability to your country, he is even more of a liability and a threat to me personally."

"But I still don't see why you're telling me all this. You have enough contacts and money to do this on your own. Why are you asking me to do your dirty work?"

"There is one simple reason: I don't know who he is."

Newman stared at the Russian, uncomprehending.

"Actually, this man came to us and wanted money for secrets. I just happened to be the officer in Washington at the time. I responded to his overture and was credited with recruiting him, but he really was a 'walk-in,' as we say in the espionage business. And because he has always used a fictitious name and almost always used dead drops for contacting us, I never was able to find out who he is."

"Gee, I'm really sorry. You must have been so disappointed."

"Sometimes he mails things to us," Komulakov said, "from New York, Chicago, Baltimore—Baltimore was the most recent one. You see, he has been somewhat inactive lately, so he had to contact me by name when he found a file that had your name in it, as well as mine. That's how I learned you were alive. After that, I contacted him to try and find out where you were. He's very well placed—and very smart—

because he deduced you were in Israel, and apparently learned your pseudonym. And . . . here we are."

Newman shook his head. "If you don't know who he is, how do you expect *me* to find him? That could take years."

"We don't have years, my dear Colonel. In fact, we have very little time. It must be done quickly. I will assist in every way I can, but I cannot go back into the United States to find someone to do the job. You must do it. In return, I shall give you your life and that of your wife. I think that is a generous offer, don't you?"

Newman was very quiet for several seconds. "Well, who does this guy work for? FBI, CIA, NSA, military? If you don't know *who* he is, do you at least know *where* he is?"

"I told you, I don't know. I don't know his real name, I don't know where he lives, or what agency he works for. You'll have to dig him out based on the files he provided to us," Komulakov said. "You'll probably need someone highly placed in the U.S. government to help you. Now . . . we will have something to eat, and then I will brief you on information you'll need."

25 Piers Dock
Iskenderun, Turkey
Thursday, 19 March 1998
2000 Hours, Local

"It was a good dessert, Samir; thank you for bringing it. How about another piece?" William Goode held out the plate toward his guests. "I've tasted baklava everywhere in the Middle East, but this has to be the best I've ever eaten."

"I am glad you like it," said the young man seated across from Goode. "My father selected it from a local bakery owned by a

Palestinian friend. He and his family are Christians too. The Palestinians make the best baklava."

Samir held out his plate for another helping of the dessert. "My father felt bad that he could not come. He sent the baklava as a gift, when I came here in his place."

Goode placed a small piece of the honey- and pistachio-filled pastry on Samir's plate and held out another piece to the third man. "Golz?"

Golz Kadri, Deputy Director of Operations of the *Milli Istihbarat Teskilati,* the Turkish Intelligence Service, waved his hand. "No, my friend; it is indeed very tasty, but I have already eaten more than I intended." He daubed his lips with a napkin and looked at Goode. "What you have told us here tonight is very disturbing."

Goode took another small piece and put the plate back down on the table.

"You're right—it *is* disturbing. That's why I'm here."

"May I ask," said Samir, "how you two gentlemen came to know each other?"

Kadri and Goode looked at each other and, after a moment's silence, Kadri shrugged and gestured to the retired CIA Clandestine Service officer.

"We met when I was in Ankara on government service, back in the '80s," Goode said.

"Golz was then a junior police officer." *No need to add the "secret" in front of "police,"* Goode thought, *or mention that I was the CIA station chief at the time.*

"Interestingly, we met in church, one affiliated with the same community of believers with which your father is associated."

Goode withdrew a small metal fish from his pocket and held it up. "So, Mr. Goode, you are one of the Believers!"

"The Believers, yes." Goode smiled at Samir's enthusiasm. "That's one name, but the fellowship has many different names. In Rome, they call themselves *Il Regno*—'The Kingdom.' Sometimes they're called the Community of Saint Patrick, as they are in the Christian sections of Israel. Here in Turkey, and in Syria, you call yourselves The Believers." Goode shook his head. "An amazing vision: to live out the practices and beliefs of Jesus Christ in the modern world—feeding the hungry, clothing the naked, caring for the poor, praying for one another, and working for justice and peace."

"And what had led *you* there, Mr. William Goode?" Samir's phrasing clearly reflected the very formal English his father had taught him.

"My wife and children were murdered in the Congo," Goode said. "I spent years searching for some meaning to that evil and ugliness, and never came up with any decent answers. But I ultimately found my answers in Christ, who gave my life meaning and purpose. I found Christ in this community of believers that includes people like you, and your father . . . and my friend, Golz. I can go nearly any place in the world and find such a community of people. I'm always amazed at that."

"How did you come to know about my father?" asked the young man.

"You know, actually, I've never met him. But after he rescued Peter Newman in Iraq, I learned from Peter that your father was a Christian too. I stayed in touch with him through the church here and through the Newmans, while they were in Jerusalem."

"You mean the Clancys in Jerusalem," Samir said, smiling.

"Yes, of course, the Clancys."

"And so," said Samir, turning to Kadri, "that is why you called my father last week and asked him to come and meet you here?"

The MIT officer nodded. "Lieutenant Colonel Newman had just been asked to undertake a difficult mission for his government, but we knew he would need help. Then his wife was kidnapped three days ago, and that mission was put on hold. But before that happened, I sent that e-mail to your father, Yusef."

"I see . . . and how did *you* come to know my father?"

"I met him with The Believers in Istanbul. That was about five years ago. If I remember correctly, Yusef had come to the city to pick up a load of microwave ovens." Kadri smiled. "I have never met a man with so much energy and business success, yet also a man of so much devotion to his faith."

"Yes, he has great faith," the son agreed. "And he would have been here himself, but for the flu that he contracted on his last business trip. And even his faith was not enough to overcome my mother's objections to his getting out of bed before his temperature returned to normal!"

"Well, I'm praying he recovers quickly. There's some very important work that must be done," said Goode.

"How can my family help?" asked the young man.

"We can't delay much longer on the original mission Colonel Newman was to have conducted before the kidnapping. That mission may be the most important thing any of us will have to confront in our lives."

"Surely you are not saying that you want my father and me to help find the nuclear weapons in Iraq?" Samir's face was pale, his eyes large as he looked at Goode.

Goode looked from Samir to Kadri. "We have no choice. And neither does Peter Newman. Despite his concern for his wife, those terrible weapons must be found—regardless of what happens to her."

Sayeret Harbor Site
1 km SE of Hamah, Syria
Thursday, 19 March 1998
2000 Hours, Local

Major Rotem and his commandos were well hidden among the large rocks just east of Assad Highway, Syria's major north-south thoroughfare. The four-lane road ran from the Jordanian border in the south, through Damascus, Hims, and Hamah, all the way to Aleppo in the far north of the country. From their vantage point, a kilometer southeast of Hamah, the Israelis could see their objective: a large farmhouse, a barn, and several outbuildings, all surrounded by a masonry wall about seven feet high.

When they had arrived at this place a half hour earlier, Rotem had again established his command post on the hood of the well-concealed and camouflaged Desert Raider. By the time he returned from checking the fields of fire over the approaches to their position, his RTO was checking the satellite-fed computer for the icons from the two miniature transmitters sewn into the women's clothing. The computer also verified that the transmitter implanted in Newman's foot was stationary at the terrorists' compound, and had been since 1725 hours. It was still not moving.

Rotem noted that the two icons from the women's transponders were also stationary, colocated about fifteen kilometers east of Salamiyah. The Sayeret Duvdevan operators watched for several minutes, but the two flickering icons did not move at all; they were as still as corpses.

Rotem pulled himself away from staring at the blinking icons. "We'll get Colonel Newman first, then see if we can get to where the women are. Captain Naruch, I'll take my men and the thermal imaging devices, move in close, and check out what's inside. Meanwhile, I want you to take the SWS and set up four final firing positions for snipers, each FFP aimed at a different side of the building. At my command, eliminate any guards outside the building. Have all the men use noise suppressors and take head shots so those inside won't be alerted. I'll have Sergeant Rosen use 'Simon' on the front door."

"Simon" was a great improvement over the old procedure, using explosives to break locks and hinges for a quick entry. Breaching charges put two commandos in great peril, since they had to be right at the door to place the explosives, often costing the element of surprise or placing the hostages at risk. But "Simon"—constructed with a shaped explosive charge at the back, similar to an ordinary rifle grenade, and a "stand-off rod" on the front of the projectile—solved those problems. Simon could be fired from just a few meters from the targeted door. When it struck above the middle of the door, it exploded with such force that its shock wave caused the door to be blown in and down, toward the floor, giving a clear and unobstructed entry. But it was important that no hostages be near the door; if terrorists were just inside the portal—so much the better.

"When we get in place, we need to find out where Newman is being kept. Once we know where he is, we'll take down the main entry and neutralize the terrorists," Major Rotem said. "Any questions?"

There were no questions. The group had rehearsed this scenario; each man knew his role and that of every other man in the team.

It took them a half hour to move quietly to within two hundred meters of the building where the computer said Newman was being held. Using his night-vision goggles, Major Rotem did a quick recon of the place. He could see two armed men standing guard outside at opposite corners of the building. As Rotem made his way to the SWS system, he could see his snipers already in position, one on each side of the building, each between one hundred and one hundred fifty yards from the structure.

"I spotted two guards," Rotem whispered into the handset of his Motorola radio. "One on the northeast corner and one on the southwest corner."

"Yeah, we got 'em," said a sniper's whisper in Rotem's headset. "The infrared also shows two more on the roof. There's an LMG up there with sandbags all around."

"I didn't see them or the machine gun," Rotem said. "Can you get a clear shot with all those sandbags?"

"Yes . . . no problem. Give us about three minutes, and we'll be ready."

Major Rotem whispered quick commands to the rest of his men. Sergeant Rosen was instructed when to deploy "Simon," then join the two-man assault team as they rushed the blown door. Rosen would rescue Newman while the others took care of any surviving terrorists.

The IDF major turned to the soldier carrying the thermal scanner and whispered, "See if you can get a fix on where Newman is being held inside the structure."

The operator crept forward through the underbrush until he was within fifty meters of the building. Once in position, he aimed the thermal imaging device at its walls. At the SWS platform, the plasma monitor clearly showed eight people inside and four others outside. Those within the structure were all well armed. Four of the terrorists were sitting at a table in what appeared to be the kitchen, apparently eating with their weapons slung over their shoulders. In the large room just beyond the entry door, there were four others. One of them was standing beside a table on the far side of the room. One person was sitting in a chair, positioned in such a way that he appeared to be tied up. Two other men holding automatic weapons stood near the man in the chair as if guarding him.

"That must be Newman in the chair," Major Rotem whispered.

Captain Naruch agreed.

The soldier operating the thermal imaging device now scanned the rest of the compound to make sure no one else was in the area, either inside or outside.

While the final check was underway, Captain Naruch began to move his other men into position for the charge. When Naruch's men were ready, Rotem would give the order for the assault.

"I have visual," Rotem heard Naruch say. Each sniper's weapon was equipped with an infrared video camera and gave Naruch a clear view of the snipers' targets. Each target was fixed, and each man was ready. "On my command, take aim . . . ready . . . fire."

There was no sound, but four bullets found their marks simultaneously. Four clean headshots insured that the dead men dropped noiselessly. The two on the roof slumped over the sandbags while the two terrorists guarding the front door of the building simply fell in their tracks. There was now no one outside to impede an assault. Captain Naruch had each of his snipers continue to aim at the dead men while the video cameras verified that they were truly all incapacitated. It took only a moment to get that assurance.

Rotem prepared to give the "go."

PFLP/Hezbollah Compound
Hamah, Syria
Thursday, 19 March 1998
2115 Hours, Local

"And so, Colonel Newman, do you understand my generous offer? All you have to do is locate my very devoted spy inside the American intelligence community and kill him. When you bring me proof of his death, I will return your wife and her friend," Komulakov said.

Newman stared at the tabletop. The assignment was impossible. Even if he could locate such a spy, the effort would make ripples in the U.S. intelligence community. They'd want to know who was making the inquiries, and they'd want to question that person to learn for themselves the extent of the damage.

"Well, let's see if I have this straight. You want me to waltz into the FBI, CIA, NSA, the Pentagon, the White House, and whatever else I may have left out, and ask them to help me locate—and kill—a Russian spy in their midst? And, oh yeah . . . I have no idea who this guy *is*." He gave Komulakov an angry stare. "This is nuts. To keep this kind of operation secret would take months of planning, tons of resources—and I'm supposed to tie it all up with a bow for you and come back here for my wife in a few weeks? Komulakov, you're about as crazy as—"

The entry door exploded off its hinges and came flying into the room. The concussion rocked Newman's chair, nearly toppling him to the floor. Three "flash-bang" concussion grenades came through the open doorway. Newman turned his face away and leaned over the table-top just as the grenades detonated in near-instantaneous succession.

An instant later, the lights went out; the room was in total darkness. Newman tried to tip his chair over to stay out of the crossfire, but it was too late. The staccato of an AK-47 burst flashed like a strobe light just off to Newman's left, until a red dot appeared on the shooter's forehead. A second later, Newman heard the AK-47 clatter to the floor, followed by the sound of a body collapsing.

Newman cringed as another terrorist opened fire right above his head. The muzzle flashes of the AK-47 practically singed his hair; the noise was deafening. Two more red dots appeared—one on the shooter's forehead and another on his chest. Newman's neck was splattered with warm fluids as the man collapsed in a heap beside the chair to which Newman was tied.

Now there was the quiet sound of rubber-soled shoes rushing into the room. The red dots of the laser sights made dancing, erratic trajectories, looking for targets, as the commandos swept into the room.

Then explosions, more AK-47 fire, and screams from the other room behind him. Newman strained in his bonds, twisting around to see as two men came rushing toward him from the room he guessed was the kitchen. Through ringing ears, he heard the voice of one of the men who had accompanied him from Damascus. The terrorist shouted something in Arabic, and the men again opened fire with their AK-47s through the doorway.

Newman saw in the stuttering glare of their muzzle flashes that Komulakov had crouched by the window and was pointing what looked like a machine pistol directly at him. Newman bent forward as far as his bonds would allow and then abruptly jerked his torso as hard as he could against the back of the chair, pushing with his feet.

The chair tipped over backward and Newman toppled to the floor, banging his head as he fell, but breaking one of the arms off the chair as it hit the floor. Lying on the floor, his eyes adjusted to the darkness and, in the flashes of gunfire, he could make out several figures coming through the doorframe. Their weapons were suppressed and gave neither muzzle flash nor sounds of gunfire. He saw the laser lights mounted on their weapons find the two men with the AK-47s. Each man was targeted briefly with two or three red dots—then they were dead.

There was a sudden silence. Newman shouted, "There's another one—by the window!" He heard the sound of a magazine being changed. *Komulakov must have run out of ammunition.*

Komulakov had reloaded and was taking aim at Newman. Several red dots converged on the chest of the Russian crouched by the window, then—*thk, thk, thk.* Newman heard the rustle of a body crumpling onto the floor, then nothing.

"Clear!" shouted someone in Hebrew.

"Clear in here!" another voice called from the kitchen area where, just forty-five seconds ago, four terrorists had been eating their last meal.

"Use your infrared lights and check the area. No white lights. Preserve your night vision." It was Major Rotem's voice.

Suddenly, all around the room, Newman could see the red gleam of Sure Fire halogen lights with infrared lenses probing the corners, checking the bodies. The results of the melee were horrific. Nearly every terrorist had been hit by at least two bullets. Blood covered the floor from the two terrorists who had been killed right next to Newman. Amazingly, not one of the Israelis had even been scratched.

Sergeant Rosen was cutting Newman's bonds and checking him for injuries when Major Rotem approached. The Sayeret Duvdevan commander helped Newman out of the chair and pulled him to his feet, then noticed the blood on Newman's cheek and neck.

"I'm all right," Newman said, "it's not my blood." As he wiped his neck with his sleeve, he asked, "Did you get a fix on where they took the women? They didn't bring them back here."

"Yes . . . I know," Major Rotem said quietly. "We'll go there as soon as we finish up here. My men will look for documents and intelligence to take back with us, and then we will go to the place east of here where the women's signals are coming from. But I have to tell you, Colonel Newman, I . . ." Rotem looked away for a moment, swallowing. "Their signals have been stationary—for a long time."

Newman felt an icy chill inside, but maybe Rotem's analysis was wrong. He put a hand on the major's arm. "I don't think it's as bad as that. Komulakov is the one who sent us the e-mails after our wives were kidnapped—"

"Komulakov—a Russian? What's a Russian doing mixed up in this?"

How much can I afford to tell him? "He wanted me to . . . do something for him. He knew I wouldn't even begin to cooperate if I suspected something had happened to Rachel. No . . . he probably ordered them to another safe house, but I . . . I'm sure they're alive."

"Is he dead? If not, maybe he can tell us something."

They turned toward the window where the Russian had been shot. But Komulakov was gone.

His pistol lay on the floor where he had dropped it, but the Russian was nowhere to be seen.

The two men hurried to the spot. In the faint light coming in the open window, Rotem, wearing his NVGs, could see fragments on the floor. The IDF major got down on his hands and knees, picked up what he had seen, and held it out for Newman to examine in the starlight: three flattened 9mm slugs from one or more of the silenced Uzis—and the shards of ceramic material.

"He was wearing a vest," said the Israeli.

"What?"

"An armored ballistic protective vest—with a ceramic plate. The plate shattered on one of the shots—that's what these shards are from," said the Israeli with certainty.

"Komulakov has survived?"

The Israeli looked at Newman. "Yes . . . and what's worse, he's escaped. Somehow he must have gotten past my men."

"The women!"

Rotem spun on his heel. "We must leave immediately!"

The team members finished what they were doing. Rotem whispered in his headset and received confirmation from the snipers that the area was still secure. He nodded to his men and Newman, and they moved quickly through the door into the night, to where their vehicles were concealed.

Settling the score with Komulakov would have to wait for another day, Newman realized. Right now, they had to get to Rachel and Dyan before the Russian did.

MI6 Headquarters
Century House, Lambeth
London, England
Thursday, 19 March 1998
1930 Hours, Local

Sir David Spelling hated days like this. His supposedly brief luncheon meeting with the Prime Minister had turned into a full-blown budget battle with the Foreign Office. Not only had the Secret Intelligence Service been asked to find another £18 million to trim from their annual operating budget, but he had then been summoned to a "working dinner"—an absolutely horrid term, borrowed from the Americans—to go over the numbers with the Cabinet Secretary.

As he walked back into his office, his executive secretary met him with a tray of hot tea and a sandwich. "Hello, C," she said.

Sylvia Wren was an efficient and attractive woman. Sir David had heard that some of the staff called her "Moneypenny" behind her back.

"Why is it you always bring me tea and a sandwich right after I come back from a luncheon appointment or one of these awful working dinners?" he asked.

"Because when you go to those soirées, you never eat, sir. It's usually something official, and you always talk and never touch your food."

"Well . . . thank you, Ms. Wren. Can I finish this before my next appointment?"

"If you gulp it down with your usual haste, sir. Mr. Thomas and Mr. Blackman want to squeeze in a few moments to follow up on a matter they apparently discussed with you this morning at yet another *unscheduled* meeting." She arched an eyebrow. "Shall I push back your meeting with the bookkeeping people?"

"You can push that back as far as you want. I don't want to talk to them about trimming budgets until they come up with some more even-handed, across-the-board cuts. Tell Mr. Winters to begin thinking along those lines. I can't spend time arguing which is the highest priority—they're all necessary. If I have to cut costs, it'll have to be across the board."

"Yes, sir," Ms. Wren said. She motioned for the two men outside to come into the office, then left, shutting the door behind her.

"Sorry, Chief," said Thomas as they entered. "Are we catching you at a bad time?"

"Never mind that. Pour yourself some tea. I'll eat while you talk."

"Very good, sir. Well, we have some more information on the matter we discussed this morning. We ran the pictures of those Arab prisoners through the facial recognition computer program as you suggested, and found that we *do* have some of them in our database. It seems that most of them are political prisoners—Kurds, Basra Shiites, northern tribal people from the Iraqi Resistance. We identified seven of the twelve that were in the photographs. There don't seem to be any—how did you put it this morning?—any 'common crooks.'"

"I see . . . anything else?"

"Yes, something quite serious, I'd say. One of our fellows in IT seems to have found a way to hack into the U.S. DARPA computer files."

"DARPA?"

"Defense Advanced Research Projects Agency. They do a lot of spooky R and D for the Pentagon."

Bit of a breach of protocol, that. Oh, well . . . "And . . . ?"

"Well, sir. It's quite odd. The Americans have apparently been test-ing a new type of overhead system that couples laser, infrared, ground-penetrating radar and some kind of thermal imaging to look inside caves, tunnels, and the like. And while they were running one of their tests, they did a pass over this building that we know to be a prison but Saddam says is a mosque. It turns out, according to the DARPA R and D project engineers, the walls and ceilings of that building seem to be heavily lined or layered in lead."

C scowled. "If they were trying to shield the place from electronic eavesdropping, they would've used copper. But lead . . ." C looked at his men. "That's for nuclear radiation detection. Do the Americans have anything to suggest the Iraqis are storing anything radioactive there?"

Thomas shook his head. "The American reports are unclear—though they obviously suspect the Iraqis are concealing actual nuclear weapons or are getting ready to bring some to that site."

C shook his head. "Did your hacker find out if the American R and D folks shared any of their suspicions with their intelligence counter-parts? Did the Americans report their suspicions to the UN?"

"There was nothing in the files along that line, sir."

"Who do we have in the neighborhood who can make a few dis-creet inquiries about what's going on in that site? I, for one, would very much like to know if there are indeed nuclear weapons being housed at that location. . . . What about the men in that prison photo? It may be that one or two of them will know something."

"It's possible, sir," Thomas said.

"What about some kind of prison break? Do we have the resources to manage it?"

"We can work on it, sir," Blackman said.

"Very good. Work something up, and let me see it as soon as possible."

"Yes, sir," Thomas and Blackman said simultaneously.

As soon as the door closed behind them, "C" poured himself another cup of tea. He stared out his window and worried.

Northeast Highway
6 km West of As Sa'ar, Syria
Thursday, 19 March 1998
2300 Hours, Local

The Sayeret Duvdevan special ops teams took a risk in driving together on the remote northeast highway to As Sa'ar. They split up when they came to Salamiyah; the Desert Raider stayed off-road and bypassed the city. Captain Naruch's team, in the van, merely kept a low profile and stuck to the highway.

They stopped just after they passed Salamiyah to check the computer one more time, to make sure that the tracking images had not moved since they last looked at them. Then the team sped as quickly as possible toward the GPS coordinates of the homing devices, assuming that since Komulakov had gotten away he might be trying to warn the kidnappers about the assault on the compound and his narrow escape—or worse, to give them the order to kill their hostages.

It had taken them over an hour to get here, where the satellite told them the signals were originating. Now Rotem, Naruch, and the team found themselves in a remote piece of the Syrian desert, three kilometers west of the village of Sa'ar.

"I make the spot to be less than fifty meters over there," Major Rotem said, looking first at the computer display then off to the right side of the highway with his NVGs.

"But there's no building." Newman said. *Please, God* . . .

"Shall I go take a look?" asked Captain Naruch.

"No . . . I'll go," Newman said.

"I'll go with you," Major Rotem added quickly.

Naruch walked behind the two men, covering them from behind as Newman and Rotem started toward the spot the computer display showed as their wives' location. Even in the darkness, the desert floor was flat and even, and Newman was relieved he could see no evidence of either a grave or the women's remains.

"Colonel, Major . . . over here!" Captain Naruch called out softly from twenty meters to their left.

Newman and Rotem both spun and jogged to where the tracker was standing.

"What is it?" Newman asked.

"There . . . ." Naruch pointed. Newman's gaze followed and, in the darkness, he saw a familiar blue knapsack.

"I see it," Newman said, running over to it. "And there's the other one, over there to your left."

The three men inspected the two knapsacks and their contents. The women had not been given their clothing. The brassieres, with the transponders sewn into them, were still inside the knapsacks.

Newman, Rotem, and Naruch looked carefully around them to make certain that Rachel and Dyan were not also lying nearby. Finding nothing, the Israeli major ordered Sergeant Rosen to bring up the thermal imaging device and sweep the area while the rest of the men used their night-vision goggles to search, just to make certain the women were not there. After a half hour, Captain Naruch walked up to Rotem.

"I've been looking at the area here, and it appears from the tracks on the shoulder of the highway that this is where the kidnappers changed vehicles. The tires of the van that came from Hamah had this kind of tread . . . here." He pointed to the tracks in the sandy soil. "And here, as if parked and waiting for them, is this other vehicle. See the different set of tire tread marks? I walked across the highway and saw that this other vehicle came from the opposite direction. It pulled off onto the shoulder over there to make a U-turn, and they parked here, waiting for the van with the women in it."

"I think he's right," Newman said to Rotem. "Komulakov handed them over to someone else. I'm guessing they've been taken to one of his places rather than another PFLP or Hezbollah location."

"Yeah, you're probably right," said Major Rotem. "From what you told me, this Komulakov character had an axe to grind with you, and probably doesn't want to muddy things up by having too many others in the mix—PFLP, Israelis, Syrians. For Komulakov, it's come down to just the two of you. Except for one thing . . . ."

"What's that?" Newman asked.

"He still has my wife. So it's personal for me too."

REGROUPING

CHAPTER FOURTEEN

Hospice of Saint Patrick
Old City of Jerusalem, Israel
Saturday, 21 March 1998
0715 Hours, Local

T he ringing of the telephone awakened Newman. For a moment, he couldn't remember where he was, and then he realized he was in his own bed in his Jerusalem apartment. He fumbled for the phone on the nightstand.

"Mr. Clancy, this is Isa. I am sorry to bother you, but there is an American gentleman on the phone calling from overseas who says he must talk to you. He did not have your direct line number and called for you on the hospice line. I told him that you got back here very late last night, but he insisted. He says that it is urgent."

"Uh . . . all right, Isa." Newman checked his watch. He'd only gotten three hours of sleep after returning from Syria. He rubbed his face and tried to rouse himself. "Please, Isa . . . go ahead and connect us."

There was a *click* and then the unmistakable voice of Lieutenant General George Grisham.

"Good morning, Mr. Clancy. How are you? Are you all right?"

"Yes, sir." *He's calling me "Clancy," so he knows we're on an unsecured line.*

"I hadn't heard from you, and I was concerned. Doesn't the phone I gave you work?"

"Yes, sir, it does, but I didn't want to take it with me on the last trip." Newman knew the Israeli police were recording calls to the hospice; he had to assume others might be, as well.

"And how *was* your last business trip?"

"The, ah, merchandise that we went to get was not at the place we were supposed to take delivery. My partners got very angry, and they . . . severely prejudiced any further relationship with the vendor and his associates. We won't be dealing with these vendors ever again."

"I see," said Grisham. "Sounds like a lot of people got their feelings hurt."

"Yes . . . and then our return flight was cancelled due to weather. We had to wait another twenty-four hours for the weather to clear in order to get a flight back here." A late winter storm had closed in on the eastern Mediterranean and delayed the team's extraction from Syria until 2300 last night; Newman hoped the oblique reference would explain to Grisham his delayed return.

"And what about the man who sent you the contract—was he at the meeting?"

"Yes, the—contractor was at the meeting, but he left right in the middle of the negotiations, just when things were getting exciting."

"And how about him, were his feelings hurt?"

"No. We thought so at first. But then we learned that . . . there was more to him than meets the eye. He's got a pretty tough shell—he'll survive."

There was silence on Grisham's end of the line for a moment. "Yeah, I see what you mean," Grisham said, finally. "Well, maybe I can help you pick up the merchandise you and your friend went to buy."

"No, I don't think so. First we have to find out where it went, instead of where it was supposed to go. But my partner's still hopeful. He seems to think the contractor will be back in touch even though things went so badly at our last meeting. My partner's constantly reminding me that the merchandise is only worth something as long as it's in good condition; he's optimistic, since we're the only buyer."

"You said your partner's hopeful. What about you?"

Newman took a deep breath. "Yes . . . I am too . . . I suppose."

"Now listen to me, young man. You have to remain hopeful . . . and I want you to follow my formula for success. Pray, and expect God to answer. Act, and expect positive results. Do you understand? You have to do both."

"Yes, sir."

"Good. Because while you were off on your business trip, I had my people start doing some research on how all this got started. You remember, when you called me before your flight back to Jerusalem, how the contractor wanted you to fire his associate here in the U.S.— but we didn't know how to reach him?"

Newman had called the general on the sat phone, while they were waiting for the weather to let up. He'd slipped away from the team because he didn't want the Israelis to know about the mole Komulakov had told him about; it would just complicate matters.

"Yes," said Newman.

"Well, I put your old friend Chris Jenkins to work on the problem. You remember Chris?"

"Yes, sir. We worked together a few years back." *And I heard Chris is now the CENTCOM G-2.*

"Chris figured out that the only way that the contractor could know all about you and the merchandise was through his representative over here—the one you're supposed to fire. He thinks the fellow we're looking for is either a sophisticated hacker, or a person pretty high up on our . . . corporate ladder who has access to our most sensitive business data."

"Yeah . . . that's what I was thinking too."

"OK, here's what I think we need to do," Grisham said. "We're going to look around here to see if we can figure out who has accessed your company files here. I've asked our friend on the boat to think about the problem also, and he's agreed to stay in the area. Meanwhile, I think you should stay put to see if the contractor contacts you to reopen negotiations—as I think he will."

"Do you want me to take up any of this with my partner?" Newman was uncertain how much of this he should share with the Israelis.

"Use your best judgment, but I'd give them only what's necessary," said Grisham. "And remember, as soon as we deal with this immediate problem, we still have our original issue to solve."

After hanging up the phone, Newman sat alone in his apartment on the top floor of the hospice, staring blankly out the windows, across the Old City to the eastern sky. The sun was up, splashing the buildings with pink and orange. *She's out there someplace . . . past those mountains and across the desert, hundreds of miles east of here . . . and she's waiting for me. God, please keep her safe until I can locate her and get there.*

He showered and dressed; sleep was out of the question with everything on his mind. As he was walking into the kitchen to prepare a pot of coffee, the phone rang again. He picked up the extension on the counter. "Hello."

"Good morning, Colonel Newman, I trust you slept well."

Newman stiffened. "Komulakov."

"Yes. I seem to have acquired some of your nine lives, eh Colonel?"

"Yeah . . . apparently."

"Well, in any event, I'll be brief since I must assume you may be trying to trace this call."

"Actually, no. I want my wife back, and I don't want anything or anyone else to complicate that. That attack on your place in Syria was somebody else's idea, not mine."

"Yes, yes . . . I'm sure. Just listen. I don't know if you were responsible for that assault on Thursday or not. It doesn't matter. Just make certain nothing foolish like that ever happens again. If you want your wife to be returned to you, you must do exactly as I say. Otherwise . . . you will never even find her body. I'm calling to remind you that your assignment has not changed. I will call you soon with instructions."

Newman heard a click and the dial tone as Komulakov hung up.

He's desperate. Otherwise he wouldn't bother to call me after nearly getting himself killed. He still wants his spy uncovered and liquidated. That might work to our advantage.

Offices of Amn Al-Khass
Special Security Service Headquarters
Palestine Street, Baghdad, Iraq
Saturday, 21 March 1998
0945 Hours, Local

Qusay Hussein had been putting in many more hours than usual, and he was feeling some of the strain. The massive search all across Iraq was an exhausting effort, even though he was using the most sophisticated detection equipment money could buy.

He was getting increasing pressure from his father to find those weapons, but so far had been drawing blanks. Qusay was growing fearful of Saddam's wrath if he failed.

It galled Qusay that his father held him to a higher standard than his older brother, Uday. True, Saddam had given Qusay more responsibility because he was good at following through, whereas his older brother was much less a leader. Still, it irked Qusay that his brother did so little and had so much. He was essentially given the same perks as Qusay, but he never had to earn them.

But if he could find the nuclear weapons, Qusay thought, he would clearly retain the greater stature in his father's eyes. It might prove his superior worth, ultimately permitting him to inherit supreme power in Iraq.

Qusay dialed the sat phone number that Dotensk had left and was surprised when the arms merchant answered on the first ring.

"Mr. Dotensk, this is Qusay Hussein, Minister of Defense Industries in Baghdad. I believe that you spoke with my father and my older brother, Uday, when you were here in Iraq recently."

"Yes, I did, but before you continue, Mr. Hussein, please let me remind you that certain unfriendly powers are very likely monitoring this satellite circuit and may misunderstand the purpose of this conversation."

"Yes, yes . . . of course, I understand completely, Mr. Dotensk. There is nothing to worry about. I simply want to talk to you about the costs and procedures if we were forced to replace our earlier inventory that seems to have been . . . uh . . . misplaced."

"Ah, yes, Mr. Hussein. It appears your late brother-in-law did not tell anyone about his purchase. That is most unfortunate."

Qusay had to smile at Dotensk's irony. "Yes, *very* unfortunate. But can you help us?"

"Oh, yes. We have six more in stock that we can get for you relatively soon. It might even be possible to get more, but I must admit they are getting scarcer every day."

"I see. . . . How much? And how quickly can you deliver the six?"

There was a pause on the other end of the line. "Well, Mr. Hussein, as you know, this . . . transaction presents certain difficulties. My associate, of course, has not approved this matter, and it will be awhile before I can consult with him, since he has certain, ah, pressing matters to attend to just now. I will need to think carefully—"

"Excuse me, Mr. Dotensk, but I thought you called yourself a merchant? I assume the profit motive still appeals to you? We are prepared to pay a premium, if that would help your deliberations."

There was another long pause. "Very well, Mr. Hussein. You are most persuasive. It will be, shall we say . . . seven hundred million Swiss francs for the six? Delivery can be made in six months or less."

Qusay thought about negotiating. *Still, if I agree to his price, we can probably insist on quicker delivery.* "That is too much money, but I will consider your offer if we are not successful very soon in replacing our mislaid inventory. But you will have to deliver in weeks, not months. I will get back to you."

International Scientific Trading, Ltd.
Jabal At Tanf, Syria
Saturday, 21 March 1995
1005 Hours, Local

Dotensk pushed the End Call button on the sat phone, a little perplexed. Did Qusay Hussein want some more nukes or not? It was obvious the Iraqis still had not found the three missing weapons. No doubt Qusay wanted to continue searching, to see if they could find them before having to come up with more money.

Oh, well . . . the delay would give him time to run the proposition past Komulakov, this time making sure his commission was better than last time. *After all, I am the one with the buyers.*

What if *he* could find where the three missing weapons were hidden? After all, Dotensk reasoned, he'd gotten to know the murdered head of the Iraqi SSS quite well when he sold him the original nuclear weapons three years ago. Perhaps he might be able to figure out where Kamil hid them.

Of course, Kamil would have hidden them where no one else would think to look; Qusay and his brother had probably already checked all the likely locations. Dotensk recalled two out-of-the-way places Kamil had taken him. One was a site under construction in southern Iraq, and Dotensk remembered how Kamil had once remarked casually that the place could one day be a home for his three nephews—Kamil's euphemism for the three nuclear artillery rounds. But Kamil had never talked specifically about that location, perhaps because it had not yet been completed.

Still, on the day of his visit to that place while it was still under construction, Dotensk had accidentally seen the lead shielding and discovered what they were doing. He had deduced Kamil planned to house the nuclear devices at that place.

Ah, yes . . . but what was the name of that place? Dotensk couldn't recall the name, but he'd kept a log of all of his meetings with Kamil. He opened a desk drawer and pulled out the small, black notebook. Leaning back in his costly leather chair, he swiveled slowly back and forth as he browsed through the pages on which he had recorded his visits to Kamil. Then he found the name of the place he hadn't been able to recall—it was Habirah Mosque.

Dotensk chuckled to himself at the Iraqi regime's attempt at subtlety. The place was anything but a mosque. It was going to be some kind of laboratory to make chemical or biological weapons, and a place to store the nuclear weapons. Once, when they were both drinking heavily, Kamil's tongue loosened and he had also talked about using the site at Habirah for a prison, a place to put certain political prisoners. Though Kamil had never said so, Dotensk suspected that the prisoners housed there were to be used for medical tests of the weapons manufactured or stored at the site. The Ukrainian wondered if they ever completed the construction of the "mosque," or if the site had been abandoned after Kamil's death.

As he leafed through the small notebook, he recalled other visits he had had with Kamil three years ago. Two of the meetings in particular stood out, and Dotensk still felt a twinge of fear as he recalled them. It was right after he had met Kamil, and also the occasion when they first began discussing the purchase of nuclear weapons. Both incidents had taken place at the same location, a desolate area northeast of Baghdad.

Kamil had chosen the spot not only for its remoteness, but to prove to Dotensk his ruthlessness. He had executed his own trusted chauffeur with Dotensk's pistol in an attempt to intimidate and blackmail the Ukrainian. The vicious performance had worked—Dotensk gave Hussein Kamil the same respect and trepidation he would give a poisonous viper.

He remembered that the second time he had gone to that same remote area, Kamil had executed two more people, once again showing no hesitation or remorse. He had definitely proven to Dotensk he was the most ruthless person the Ukrainian had ever encountered. But of course, in the end, Kamil wasn't the worst—Saddam or either of his two oldest sons could claim that title now, unchallenged.

As Dotensk turned another page in his logbook, he stopped reading and looked away into space. His eyes widened as if he had a sudden revelation. He turned back the pages to the account of the place he had visited twice with Kamil.

Of course! What a perfect hiding place. Not even Kamil's own bodyguards went with us to that place!

Dotensk jumped up and called for one of his assistants. A middle-aged man, more than six feet tall and barrel-chested, entered the room in answer to his call.

"Kharkiv, get the car ready; I want to go within the hour. Do we have contact with our office and men in Baghdad on the weekend?"

"Yes . . . of course. Why?"

"I want you to call them and make arrangements for a truck and a small forklift. And I will need four men. But I want *our* men—no Iraqis or Palestinians for this job. Tell them to meet me at our offices at the Al Rashid Hotel at eight o'clock tonight—and have Vanya check the computer files for the manifest we used when we went to Chernobyl in March '95. Have her make me a new set of documents. List the cargo on the manifest as computer mainframes or something like that. If I can find what I am looking for, I will want to bring the shipment back here from Baghdad on a truck. So get me fifty thousand in U.S. dollars to take with me. I might have to buy some silence and smooth border crossings."

"Do you know where they are hidden?" Kharkiv asked with a wide, hopeful grin.

Dotensk shrugged. "I am not sure. But I know a likely spot—and a site that the Iraqis have probably overlooked. There is also another site . . . so I am going to look at both places."

If he was quite lucky at the first site, Dotensk could take them away and sell them again. But if it turned out they were being stored at the so-called "mosque," then he would only get credit for locating them. Still, it would buy him some goodwill and trust for another sale. And if that was where they were, Dotensk was quite sure that Mr. Qusay Hussein would pay handsomely for the information.

"I will see to everything you need right away," Kharkiv said. "But what shall I do about the two women you brought here?"

"Nothing special. Just guard them . . . give them food and water . . . and wait until General Komulakov comes on Monday. If I have not returned by the time he comes on Monday, you can tell him where I went and what I am doing. Tell him I will get back here as quickly as I can."

Thirty minutes later, Dotensk had thrown some clothes into a garment bag and reviewed the phony shipping manifest his aides had prepared. He put the papers and cash into an attaché case and tossed it, along with the garment bag, into the back of the car that had just been washed and fueled for the ten-hour trip across the Syrian and Iraqi deserts to Baghdad. He drove out of the compound atop Jabal At Tanf; one of the guards opened the big, iron gate only to close it moments later behind the silver Mercedes. In another twenty minutes, Dotensk was already on the Damascus-to-Baghdad highway, speeding to his first destination some 350 miles away.

Habirah Prison
Near Salman Pak, Iraq
Saturday, 21 March 1998
1645 Hours, Local

Bruno Macklin strolled across the courtyard of Habirah Prison, grateful for the hour or so of fresh air and sunlight he was able to enjoy once a day. Although he was a new inmate at this prison, he had been moved enough times over the last three years to know what he had to do. First, he exercised and walked whenever he could, using these occasions to make acquaintances. Even though communications with other prisoners were forbidden, he talked with them whenever he could, either at these outdoor exercises or when the guards took them for their weekly showers. That's how he knew he was not the only Westerner confined in this prison; he had seen another Westerner once when the viewing portal had been inadvertently left open in his metal cell door and again this morning, as they were being taken in groups of ten to the shower room.

Now, across the prison yard in another exercise cage, he saw the man for a third time. Macklin moved over against the fence separating the two exercise pens. The British SAS officer sat down in the dirt near the fence and took off his shoe, making a big show of removing a stone inside it. As he did so, he scanned the watchtowers and windows high above the yard. He could see no one paying any particular attention, so he hissed to get the attention of the lanky man with the thinning, light brown hair.

The prisoner approached the fence and bent over as though he was picking something off the ground.

"I'm Bruno Macklin, SAS. What's your name? How long have you been a POW?"

"Robbie Blake, RAF. I was shot down four years ago, hit by a SAM patrolling the exclusion zone. How long have you been here?"

"Just got here. Are there any more of us here?"

"Yes, four of us and two Americans. Some of them have been Saddam's guests since the Gulf War."

"How have you been treated?"

"Bloody awful," Blake said, "just well enough to be kept alive, although I can't quite figure out why they bother. I'm sure everyone back home assumes I was killed in my plane crash. The Red Cross isn't permitted here, so I hadn't heard from anyone at home since I was shot down—until yesterday."

"Yesterday?"

"Yeah. Yesterday I was handed a note from the chief of the guards. That's how I knew there was a fourth member of Her Majesty's Armed Forces in here. The guard chief slipped me a note on my way out of the showers, telling me I should be ready to be moved, along with three of my countrymen and two Americans, sometime in the next few days. We're supposed to be—how did he put it?—'leaving the country together.'"

"What's in it for the guard?" Macklin said.

"The way I figure it, this guy wants us for a meal ticket when he defects. I get the idea he's selling us to our people."

Macklin's head was spinning; things were happening too fast. "How do you know he's for real?"

"He had the right authentication code on the note. That means someone back home finally knows we're here and is making some kind of arrangements," said the pilot.

"When is all this supposed to happen?"

"Tomorrow night."

"And you believe him?"

"I don't know. I do know I'd prefer not to die here. For all I know, you could be SSS. But I'm willing to take that risk if there's a chance of getting out of here."

Macklin squinted at the setting sun and then looked at Blake. "What if it's a trick and they use the scam to kill us, trying to escape?"

"Yeah, I thought of that too. But the authentication was correct, and besides—the Iraqis don't need to bother with elaborate hoaxes to rationalize killing us."

Macklin nodded. That was certainly true enough. He'd seen Iraqi officers execute prisoners without any apparent cause or excuse. "What about the Americans?" Macklin asked.

"I've only been able to talk to one of them this morning when I was emptying out the trash," Blake said. "The Yank I talked to said he'd go for it and said he'd let me know about the other fellow if he can."

"I see," said Macklin. "Do we know how we're going to be transported?"

"Apparently the man in charge here has faked a set of orders to have us transferred tomorrow night. He's going to escort us personally, as though we're being taken to another prison. He's scared to death because he knows if his superiors find out about this, they'll shoot him. He apparently thinks he's going to get a lot of money for delivering us out of the country," said the RAF officer. "The plan is for him to put us in a truck. He says the prison transfer documents he has will get us out the door with no problems. Then he and another guard will take us to Jordan or Saudi Arabia, where a helicopter transport will be waiting."

"And you think that this guy can pull it off?" asked Macklin, his hopes for freedom rising, despite himself, for the first time in years.

"Yeah . . . he's the chief here. His men do as he tells them, and it's sort of routine to transfer prisoners like us every few months anyway."

"How far is it to the border?"

"The guard chief says it's no more than two hundred kilometers. He says by the time anyone figures out what happened, we'll already be across."

Macklin thought for a moment, then said, "Well, count me in. Just tell me what I'm supposed to do."

"I'll get the word from the Iraqi guard and keep everyone posted," Blake said. "And I'll tell you this . . . I'll sure be glad to get out of this cesspool of a country."

MI6 Assembly Point
Rafha, Saudi Arabia
Saturday, 21 March 1998
1815 Hours, Local

MI6 Agents Thomas and Blackman had taken an RAF flight from London to Incirlik, then hopped a commercial flight to Riyadh, Saudi Arabia. There, at the British embassy, they were provided with the keys to a Land Rover located in the car park between the British and the Netherlands embassies. One of the MI6 staff from Riyadh acted as their driver, and the three men began the long drive across the desert from Riyadh to Rafha. Ordinarily, it was a rule that any trips through the desert were to be made with at least two vehicles, in the event one of them broke down. But in this case, they had plenty of fuel, water, and rations with them, and the highway was reliable enough to take a chance. Two vehicles simply would have attracted more attention.

It took them until just before six o'clock that evening to get to Rafha, the small Saudi city on Iraq's southern border that had once belonged to an AramCo geologist. The two bone-weary MI6 officers were ushered into a nondescript stucco house on the outskirts of the city; there they met the rest of the team that would be handling the extraction operation.

After introductions and a hurried meal of American MRE combat rations, the men spread maps on a large table and Thomas led the discussion. He had brought with him the background on the plan, sent via encrypted message to the MI6 station in Riyadh. MI6 HQ suggested these British and American prisoners were being held at Habirah Prison for a reason—to prevent the Israelis or Coalition powers from bombing the "mosque." According to London's thinking, the Iraqis were probably hoping the prison and its hidden stores of chemical and bio weapons were safe from Allied bombers and cruise missiles as long as Western prisoners were housed there. So not only would this mission be a way to get the six allied prisoners back; it also would eliminate the human shield that prevented destruction of the site.

"You already know most of the plan," Thomas told them. "I assume you've made contact with someone inside the prison and were able to convince him to help."

"Yeah, for a price," said Dwayne Wardell, the station chief in charge of the operation. "He had to have thirty thousand pounds and help in getting out of the country. He figured asking us for five thousand per man was reasonable."

"It probably is," Thomas said, "but although that kind of money can buy his retirement in Iraq, once he gets to the West it may not be enough. Just be prepared to have some more money on hand . . . these guys have a way of upping the price at the last minute, when there's no time to dicker."

"Yeah, that's what I figured too. I have another thirty if we need it."

"So how much time do we have?" This time it was Blackman who spoke. He had hardly said a word since the discussion began, but it was clear he was engaged in the process.

Wardell looked at his watch. "The break will begin just about twenty-four hours from now. The prisoners are returned to their cells from exercise at 1800 hours, give or take a few minutes. That's also the time the new guard shift comes on duty. Our man on the scene will use this event to get the prisoners into a truck. We've been told it's an old military deuce-and-a-half used for hauling supplies back and forth from the prison. They tried to schedule the use of a fifteen-passenger van, but it fell through at the last minute."

"Is the truck reliable?" asked Thomas.

Wardell nodded. "Probably as good as any. But just in case, we've asked for three satellite passes to track the truck after it leaves the prison. It'll be dark by then, but our liaison types at the NRO say they'll be able to watch it."

"What's the backup plan in case the truck does break down?" Blackman asked.

"Well, that's where things get ticklish," Wardell said. "We've got a company of Royal Marines from Four-Two Commando undergoing training with a contingent of the 24th Marine Expeditionary Unit about thirty kilometers south of here. They have a section of two AH-1 Cobra helicopters, two CH-53s and four CH-46s. It just happens they'll be doing some night operations not far from here about the time the break is scheduled to take place. The exercise has all been cleared in Riyadh, so it wouldn't be a bolt from the blue for the Saudis. If something goes wrong, the choppers'll fly in at low level, under radar, and go get them. The plan would be for a quick pick-up and get out of there before the Iraqis can tell their airspace was violated."

"Yeah . . . ticklish," Thomas muttered. "I wouldn't count too much on the Iraqi radar not picking them up. That desert's pretty flat there, and anything higher than ten or fifteen feet might be seen. Let's just hope the truck doesn't break down."

Incirlik Air Base
Adana, Turkey
Saturday, 21 March 1998
1825 Hours, Local

"I'm sorry we seem to be sitting on our thumbs on this one," General Grisham said, "but until we know where Komulakov is holding the women, there's not much we can do."

The CENTCOM commander was standing at a desk in the Command Suite at the sprawling Turkish Air Force Base that NATO and the U.S. Air Force had been using for decades, first to monitor the Soviet Union and now for keeping tabs on Saddam Hussein. Grisham turned to the map of the Middle East, mounted on the wall behind him, and spoke into the encrypted Iridium sat phone. "I want you to know we're doing all we can to track that phone call Komulakov made to you."

Newman's voice crackled in the earpiece. "I understand, General. I've told Komulakov I'm willing to do anything to get Rachel back, but it's hard for me to be sitting here trying to figure out a plan for giving him what he wants. Do you have any thoughts on just who this spy might be? Or where he works?"

"Komulakov didn't give us much to go on. It's incredible to me that the Russians don't know who he is," Grisham said. He consulted some notes he had made from Newman's earlier conversation. "I want to be sure about something Komulakov said to you before the Israeli raid. Did he tell you this mole they call Morales had handed over copies of classified documents from the CIA . . . some from the FBI . . . some from the NSA . . . and some even from the Pentagon?"

"Yes, sir, that's what he said."

"Well, if that's the case, this guy has access to our country's greatest secrets. It may be Komulakov is doing us a favor."

"Sure . . . a regular good guy."

"Well, I wouldn't go as far as that," General Grisham said, "but let's hope we can locate this mole before he does any more damage."

"Frankly, General, I don't know where to start. If this guy has that kind of access to secrets, he might be in the kind of place where he can also head off any attempts to catch him. I mean, whom can we trust in the intel community to get involved with us on this? The spy might be the very one we talk to about catching him."

"Yeah, I'm concerned about that too," the general said. "That's why I'm inclined to play this hand pretty close to the vest. Let me make some very quiet inquiries . . . and get Bill Goode's input. But let's try and keep a lid on this for now."

"I agree. Uh, General?"

"Yes, Pete?"

"I'm having some serious thoughts about just how far I can carry this thing with Komulakov."

"What do you mean?"

"Well, he wants this spy killed. That wouldn't be the way our side plays things. We'd want him alive to tell us how much damage he's done, what secrets he's given away, and why. And to be very honest, General, I'm bothered by the moral implications of taking on the role of judge, jury, and executioner, based on nothing more than Komulakov's word and for the sake of expediency, or . . . even my own personal reasons.

"I mean, sir . . . suppose we *do* find out who this guy is. Do the ends justify the means? Am I supposed to play God? I mean, this isn't combat, where the rules seem clearer to me. Am I supposed to just off this guy? Major Rotem doesn't seem bothered by such distinctions. He says Israel even has a religious argument for it . . . that sometimes the greater good warrants actions like this. But the last time I checked, that's not the way it works in our country, sir."

Grisham thought for a few seconds before answering.

"Well, you're right, Pete. Our system of law rejects personal revenge and places prosecutors, judges, and juries in that role, not individuals. And of course you're right about this not being combat, where a soldier has the moral right of self-defense. What Komulakov wants you to do is commit murder to serve his purposes, with the promise of achieving a noble goal of your own: the safe return of your wife. It is, I admit, a terrible choice. Most people, given similar circumstances, wouldn't hesitate to go after the spy and kill him."

"So what do I do, General? How do I get my wife back? There don't appear to be any good options here."

"I agree. This isn't a matter of choosing between right and wrong. The only choices you have are 'bad' and 'worse'—and only you can decide."

Grisham heard Newman's heavy sigh. He had heard that axiom before.

"Pete . . . listen to me. I know what you're thinking, but you've got to get hold of your emotions here. You're a Marine. The *right* way to deal with this is to find this Julio Morales, or whatever his real name is, and deal with him the right way—in our courts."

"And then Komulakov kills Rachel because I failed to kill the mole."

"Well, that's not necessarily what Komulakov has to hear," Grisham said. "Assuming we can find Morales, maybe we can deceive Komulakov about what really happens to the spy—long enough for us to get Rachel back. I don't know . . . maybe that transponder in your foot can help us find Komulakov somehow. But whatever . . . you've got to do this by the book. Otherwise, you're just Komulakov's hired gun carrying out a cold-blooded murder. Don't let it come down to that. I'm going to be praying that the good Lord will give you the wisdom you need to find the right path on this.

"You and I both know, Pete, Komulakov is not a man of his word," Grisham added. "He's evil. Even if we find this spy and you kill him, why are you assuming Komulakov's going to let you and Rachel live? He's already tried to kill you both—and that was on Cyprus, where you were supposedly protected. It's certainly not going to change in Syria, or Lebanon, or wherever he's holding Rachel right now. Think like the Russian, my friend. What would he do when you return to get Rachel after successfully killing the spy? Do you honestly think he'd let you live, given what you know about him?"

"So what do I do?"

Newman's voice sounded like a man who was already whipped. The general paused for a moment before answering.

"Here's how I think we should handle it, Pete. Give me ten days to see what I can turn up about this mole Morales. Tomorrow I'm going to have another sat phone delivered to you from our embassy in Tel Aviv. If Komulakov gets back in touch with you, give him the number on that phone. Tell him you need to use that phone for all communications because you need to stay out of sight while you search for Morales. This phone is specially equipped to help NSA track where an incoming call originates and an outgoing call terminates. That may help us to locate where Rachel is being held. You with me so far?"

"Yes, sir."

"Good. For all other communications, with me or anyone else on our side, use the Iridium sat phone you're using right now. Its encryption algorithm isn't great, but it's better than nothing. And it will at least give us some privacy. You still with me?"

"Yes, sir."

"As soon as you can, I want you to get to Turkey and link up with Bill Goode. While I'm tracking down Julio Morales and doing what we can with the Israelis to find Rachel and the other woman, I need you to spend some time doing what you can to help us find those three missing nukes—the mission we started to work on before Rachel was kidnapped. Can you handle that while I take care of these other things?"

There was a long pause on the line. Grisham waited. He knew Pete was weighing his ability to concentrate on such a sensitive mission while Rachel's life was still in danger.

"Yes, sir, I can handle it."

"Good," said Grisham, "good man. Now . . . changing the subject a bit, I originally didn't think you'd have to go into Iraq. But it looks as though you will. When you get to Turkey, you'll find Bill Goode has tracked down some other old friends to help you get in and out safely and quickly."

"Old friends?"

"Samir and his father, Yusef Habib."

"But they're civilians, General," Newman said. "We can't ask them to take part in this mission. They're not trained for this sort of thing . . . and besides, Yusef—he has to be at least sixty years old."

"No. He's seventy-four. He worked with the British in World War II. But he's in better shape than a lot of men half his age. Don't worry; we're not going to place them in harm's way. Bill Goode has met with them, and they've talked about what we want you guys to do. They're simply going to act as your guides to get you to where the nukes might be."

"That sounds like harm's way to me," Newman said.

"Let's let them, and Goode, make that decision. Nobody is making them do anything they don't want to. The fact is . . . these Christian Arabs often escort tourists and other people around who want to see a certain country. They're even licensed as tour guides in several countries. As you know from your last experience with them, they're plenty savvy in situations like this . . . you won't have to worry about them. Bill Goode says they'll be just fine. Pete . . . am I giving you too much?"

"No, sir. I'll handle it." The Marine paused for a moment and then spoke as though he was thinking out loud. "I don't have much choice, really. There isn't anything I can do here to help Rachel. James is safe with my sister. And you have a far better chance of tracking down who the mole is than I do by myself. Let's get on with it. Where do I meet Mr. Goode?"

"I'll send you instructions tomorrow in the package with the sat phone. You'll also find included ten thousand dollars in cash. Use that to pay for tickets and other expenses. If the Israelis ask where you're going, tell them you're coming here to meet with me. Don't mention anything about the nuclear weapons. Got all that?"

"Yes, sir. Seems like you've got it all covered."

"I'm not so sure about that, but I try. And, Pete . . . you know I think the world of you and Rachel."

"I've never doubted that, sir, and I appreciate it more than I can express. When you get home, please do all you can to reassure our parents."

"Count on it. Oh, Pete, one last thing. The terrorists that escorted you from Damascus to the meeting with Komulakov, those that guarded you at the site that the Israelis hit, and the ones who came with Rachel—did you notice if they had any cell phones or radios for communications?"

After a pause, Newman said, "Yes, they did. I remember being impressed by the fact that they all had Marconi DM-3 Long Range UHF radios. Why?"

"Well, I've been thinking of how we can find where the women are being held without the transponders that were sewn into the clothing they were supposed to get. And I think you've just helped me solve that riddle."

HEATING UP

C H A P T E R   F I F T E E N

Hospice of Saint Patrick
Old City of Jerusalem, Israel
Sunday, 22 March 1998
0415 Hours, Local

J ust after eleven P.M., Isa Boyian buzzed Newman's apartment to inform him that an insistent American was at the front desk, demanding his signature on a receipt. A courier from the Defense Attaché's Office at the American embassy in Tel Aviv had come to deliver a package, Isa said, so Newman had hurried down, signed for the package, and brought it back upstairs.

Back inside his apartment, Newman tore open the Tyvec pouch and found another Iridium phone, ten thousand dollars in cash, and a "back-channel" cable from Incirlik, Turkey, to the assistant Naval attaché, a Marine major, containing General Grisham's instructions to Newman for linking up with Bill Goode in Turkey.

Newman waited for another call from the Russian; but when he hadn't heard from Komulakov by midnight, Newman decided to get some sleep. He kicked off his shoes and lay down on top of the bed, still dressed in slacks and a T-shirt.

He was too tired to sit up and turn off the lamp beside the bed; he fell asleep immediately. The call awakened Newman from a fitful dream at a little after four A.M.

"I am just calling to see if there is anything you need for your assignment," Komulakov said in a voice like a friendly uncle's. "Do you need passports . . . airplane tickets . . . money . . . weapons?"

"I'm fine."

"Really? What does that mean?"

"It means I'll take care of getting my own tools. I'm a little touchy about those things. I have more confidence in my own contacts. Besides, you ought to know by now that I get nervous when you offer help."

Komulakov chuckled. "As you wish. Do you have a plan worked out yet?"

"I'm still working out the details, but it seems to be coming together. I've pulled in an old friend to help me. He's the only one who can get me back into the U.S.

"But I have to tell you . . . we're concerned that your spy is so highly placed we'll set off alarms just by making inquiries. If what you say is true, your guy Morales has looted the classified files of every single American intelligence agency. I'm going to have to be very careful not to spook this guy. I still don't see why you don't just signal him to meet one of your SVR or GRU types in Washington and take care of him yourselves."

"Ah, believe me, Colonel Newman, if I thought he would respond to an invitation to dinner, I would have sent him one a long time ago."

"Well, why don't you signal Morales that you think he's about to be caught—tell him to come to your embassy in Ottawa or Mexico City so you can help him escape—and then grab him and kill him yourselves?"

"You are intelligent, my dear Colonel Newman," said the Russian, "but once again, I've already considered this. Julio Morales would be highly unlikely to respond in that way. Given how meticulous he has been, and how much money we have paid him over the years, we believe it is much more likely, if we sent him a message like that, he would simply flee on his own and *no one* would ever see him again."

Newman grunted.

"I'm going to need to stay in close contact with you, Colonel Newman. How can I reach you while you're working on this . . . task . . . when you are back in your country?"

"Well, I'll be carrying an Iridium satellite phone, since I don't have an office back in the States." Newman gave him the number. "Or you can call here at the hospice and leave a message. I'll be calling back here periodically."

"All right. Just remember, Colonel—no games. You seem to have the right attitude about this. I like the way you're going about this so carefully. Just stay on that plan and don't raise any suspicions. But, Colonel . . . make sure you are successful. Your wife is depending on you."

"I want to talk to her. I need to know she's all right." Despite his attempts to control it, Newman could hear his voice rising.

"I'm sorry . . . perhaps another time. I have to hang up now before those who tap your phone are able to trace the call. Good-bye."

Newman slammed the telephone handset back into its cradle and pounded the headboard of the bed with his fist. He was hoping for a few words with Rachel, to reassure her that he was doing everything he could to get her released.

Ah, well . . . maybe it's for the best. Knowing Rachel, she would have heard something in my voice that would've scared her. . . .

Newman got up, showered, and dressed. Then he threw some things into his flyaway bag. When he checked his watch, it was nearly five o'clock. It wasn't quite light in the east, and he stood for a moment looking out the window, lost in thought about his course of action. General Grisham's instructions, contained in the cable that had arrived with the sat phone, provided very specific arrangements for him to get to Turkey and for establishing contact with Bill Goode, Samir Habib, and a Turkish intelligence officer Grisham said he could trust.

Newman was jotting down a list of instructions for Isa Boyian to follow for running the hospice in his absence when General Grisham called on the encrypted phone.

"Pete," said the general, "I just got a flash call from my friends at NSA. Did you just receive a call at the hospice from Komulakov?"

"Yes."

"I'll get the transcript in a few hours and anything they may be able to figure out regarding Komulakov's location. Did you ask him the questions I suggested?"

After Newman related the conversation, the general said, "Trust us, Pete. I've got the best guys in the world working on this. But now . . . I really need you to get your mind focused on trying to find those loose nukes."

"I understand, sir. I fly out to Turkey later this morning."

"I don't want to sound callous, Pete. I know you want more than anything in the world to be reunited with Rachel and have the Komulakov business behind you. But we'll take care of it. Meanwhile, time could be running out on the other matter. Our guys think the Iraqis may try to use the nuclear weapons just as soon as they're located—probably against Israel or some American military base in Kuwait, Turkey, or Saudi Arabia."

The two men talked for another few minutes, and then Newman hung up and checked to see if his ride had arrived.

Surprisingly, the taxi arrived less than twenty minutes after he called. It was almost dawn when Newman walked through the front door of the hospice and climbed into the cab.

Police Station
Patriarchate Street
Old City of Jerusalem
Sunday, 22 March 1998
0533 Hours, Local

Police Sergeant Ephraim Lev watched the video monitor aimed at the entrance of the Hospice of Saint Patrick. His attention was on the taxi that had just pulled up in front of the building and on the man who got inside, carrying a small travel bag. He zoomed in to get a better look. This was the second unusual event of his shift. A little more than six hours earlier, a car with diplomatic plates had stopped for about five or ten minutes. Lev had made entries in his log and recorded the car. There was no mistaking who got in the cab when he came out of the hospice; it was the husband of the woman who had been kidnapped, the one called John Clancy.

As the taxi pulled away in the still, gray dawn, Sergeant Lev reached for the telephone. He maneuvered the video controller to keep the picture locked on the red taillights of the taxi as it drove away. A tired voice answered on the third ring.

"Major Rotem, this is Ephraim Lev in the Patriarchate Street Police Station Command Center. You asked me to report to you any unusual activity at the hospice. Well, this wasn't exactly unusual, except for the time. Clancy just left his home in a taxi . . . number 8344. It went out the Damascus Gate and is turning left. It just now drove out of camera view, heading west."

Rotem Apartment
Derekh Sur Bāhir
Ramat Rahel, Israel
Sunday, 22 March 1998
0535 Hours, Local

Ze'ev Rotem hung up the phone and looked at the clock on the bedside table. Five A.M. Where was Newman going in a cab at such an hour?

He picked up his mobile phone and punched one of the speed dial numbers.

As the phone rang, Rotem walked over to the bedroom window and looked out into the Ramat Rahel section of modern Jerusalem. He saw scores of multistoried condominiums, newly constructed on a high hill, between the road to Bethlehem and the Palestinian-controlled West Bank. But this upper middle class suburb of Jerusalem came with a price much higher than just a mortgage. Unfortunately for the homeowners, Arab terrorists routinely used the buildings for target practice, shooting directly into the spacious windows, aiming at the occupants. The tenants had learned to cope. Some installed bulletproof glass. Others stacked sandbags on the balconies to obscure and protect the windows. The government had also constructed a high concrete wall on the slope beneath the east side of the buildings. The wall was more than ten feet high, tall enough to prevent a sniper from shooting over the top of it into the yard or blasting out a first-floor window. Nevertheless, the newly constructed buildings were pockmarked by bullets that came from some distance away in the West Bank, a warning that there were those who were violently militant about Jews moving into the neighborhood.

Major Rotem was one of those who had installed expensive panes of Mylar-laminated, bulletproof glass in his windows. Still, he was cautious; he and Dyan usually kept their shades closed and had dark drapes to conceal their shadows when they walked past the windows at night. However, when he was alone in the apartment, he would often take the risk of opening the shades and drapes in order to see the magnificent view of the valley.

"Hello?"

"Captain Moysche, this is Major Rotem. Have you any information from the American with whom I have been working? Yes, of course . . . Clancy . . . the one who lives in the Old City." Rotem listened while the night duty officer checked with someone else before responding that he had nothing to report.

"Did he leave word with any of our men that he was going somewhere today?" asked Rotem.

"No, sir."

"I want you to initiate a search for him. It should be easy. He has a location transponder implant, and our guys in Duvdevan HQ tracked him in Syria on the rescue missions. Tell Duvdevan to put the American back on the tracking roster—they have the frequency of his transponder. I want to know where he goes. Meanwhile . . . I'll be in by eight. If anything unusual happens before I get in, give me a call right away."

Rotem disconnected the call and put the phone back on the dresser while he walked into the kitchen to make some coffee. It irked him that the American hadn't told him about his plans. Rotem hoped he wasn't hatching some kind of rescue operation with the American military or the CIA. After all, his own wife's safety was at issue as well—and that of their unborn child.

✪

Ze'ev Rotem wasn't an observant Jew. In fact, he had been in a synagogue only a handful of times since his Bar Mitzvah. But the day before, knowing that time and options were running out for rescuing his wife, Rotem had gotten up early and driven to the Old City. He maneuvered his Toyota through Zion Gate, turned right, passed En Nabi Dawoud Square and the Armenian quarter, then drove downhill on Batei Kakhase Street. That place held sad memories for him. It was near here that his father had been killed on June 7, 1967, on day three of the Six-Day War. His father had been one of the first fifty paratroopers of the Jerusalem Brigade to enter the city through Zion Gate, and he had been felled by a sniper's bullet as his unit had rushed down this very hill into the Jewish quarter of the Old City.

Rotem had turned left on Hakehuna and pulled his little sedan into an open space at a car park just south of the Sephardic Synagogue. He had gone into the temple for a few moments, stood for awhile in the back praying silently, and then left. But when he exited, instead of going back to his car, he had walked east on Beit El Street to Khayei Olam and then wandered through the winding alleyways of the old Jewish quarter until he stood in the square below the Western Wall.

For several minutes, the IDF major had simply stood and stared at the massive ashlars King Herod had erected as a retaining wall for the Second Temple—now the only remnant of what the ancient Romans had destroyed in A.D. 70. Rotem then placed his yarmulke on his bare head and, removing a three-by-five-inch card from his pocket, he passed through the small crowd of others who had come here to pray on the Sabbath. Arriving at the face of the wall, Rotem rolled up the card and inserted it between the giant stones. On the card he had written, "Oh King of kings, who delivered your people safely out of Egypt, return Dyan safely to me."

✪

The IDF major had spent the rest of Saturday, well into the early morning hours, working with his unit's intelligence officer, trying to determine the whereabouts of the missing women. He then returned home and slept a short time before Lev's call had waked him.

Time is running out. What if their captors lose patience? What if they kill one of the women to force their demands?

Incirlik Air Base
Adana, Turkey
Sunday, 22 March 1998
1155 Hours, Local

Newman nodded his thanks to the Navy crew chief as the C-2A Greyhound pulled up to the big U.S. Air Force hangar at Incirlik, its propellers winding down. "We're five minutes early."

"Glad to be of service, sir," said the Navy petty officer as he moved aft to put down the aircraft ramp.

The mission had begun in typical Grisham fashion, Newman reflected. The taxi had dropped him off at the U.S. embassy in Tel Aviv at 0630. Fifteen minutes later, he was in an embassy vehicle, driven by a tightlipped U.S. Marine security guard, enroute to the U.S. Defense Attaché Office at Ben Gurion Airport.

Then, as the car pulled up next to the DAO hangar, a haze-gray U.S. Navy Seahawk helicopter with the words USS *Mobile Bay* stenciled on its tail started to "turn up." They had taken off at exactly 0715 and headed directly out to sea. By 0840 the Seahawk was being refueled on the flight deck of the USS *Mobile Bay*. Ten minutes later, the SH-60B was airborne again and headed northwest for the big deck of the USS *Theodore Roosevelt*, "The Big Stick."

When the helicopter landed on the flight deck, a crewman in a white vest slid open the starboard door and escorted the Marine to a waiting C-2 COD with both engines turning, its tail ramp down. As soon as Newman was aboard and strapped into one of the aft-facing seats, the ramp came up and the bird was maneuvered to catapult 1. Then, with the engines racing at maximum RPM, there was the explosive sound of the steam catapult firing, and the aircraft was thrown into the air. Once airborne, Newman had promptly fallen asleep and did not awaken until the sound of the deploying flaps and the lowering landing gear, just before the plane touched down at Incirlik. Newman smiled to himself at General Grisham's precision planning.

Now, as he stepped off the aircraft ramp, Newman had an incredible sense of déjà vu, followed by a feeling of overwhelming sadness. He remembered the last time he had been at Incirlik—almost exactly three years ago—with a hand-picked team of courageous U.S. Delta Force and British SAS commandos.

As Newman approached the hangar that had once been his command post, General George Grisham stepped out of the personnel door, shook his hand, and yelled over the roar of the departing C-2, "It's good to see you, Pete. Come on inside. We'll get a bite to eat and then get you on your way."

Over a sandwich and Coke in the hangar office, the general updated Newman on the plans for the next leg of his mission.

"Skillings is over at the motor pool getting a staff car to drive you to Karatas, about twenty-five miles south of here. Bill Goode was docked at Iskenderun yesterday, but he sailed across the bay this morning. It's only about thirty nautical miles, so he's probably there already. He'll meet you in Karatas, at the docks, then he'll bring you back to Iskenderun. There, you'll meet with Samir and Yusef. They'll outline the plan from there. The idea is for you to go with Samir into Syria and drive east across the country into Iraq, directly to Baghdad."

Newman raised his eyebrows. "Right through the front door? Isn't that kind of risky?"

"We hope not. You'll have an Indian passport. And the boys from ISA have worked up a pretty good cover that Bill Goode will flesh out when you see him. You'll be an Indian national, from the former

Portuguese colony of Goa . . . and you'll be in Iraq to sell computer software developed in India."

"India, eh? That's good. I like the idea of being from a part of the world where only the Pakistanis won't like me."

"Well, to be quite frank with you, I'm less concerned about getting you *into* Iraq than I am about getting you *out*. Anyway, you should be all right—they'll check your passport and papers, but if they ask you questions about your work, I doubt any uniformed Iraqi will know enough about computer programming to spot you as a phony. And this time you have something working for you that you didn't have last time—you have three years of Arabic languages under your belt. It makes a difference."

"What's the ingress and egress plan?"

"Getting you in is fairly simple, as I said. For ingress, I've made arrangements for an ISA civilian operating under nonofficial cover to board a flight from India. He's using your cover identity, and he'll fly the regional airline from Bangalore to Mumbai. Then he'll fly India Air from Mumbai to Damascus. That way there'll be a document trail showing you traveled from India to Syria. As you'll see when you get the Indian passport from Bill Goode, it already has the appropriate exit and entry visas and stamps, indicating you arrived in Damascus from India, complete with boarding passes. In case anyone checks your documents against the airline and immigration records, the data trail should verify it was you who made the trip. You'll meet Samir, whose business is located in the Christian quarter of the Old City in Damascus."

General Grisham pulled out a street map of Damascus from his inside pocket. He pointed to the place he had just mentioned, then ran his finger over to the left a few inches. "But you'll meet him here . . . at the Ministry of Tourism . . . on Shukri Al Quatli Street."

"Yeah . . . looks like the building sits back from the highway."

"Yes, and it's two blocks east of the museum . . . right here," the general said, pointing.

"How do I get to Damascus? Fly?"

"No . . . we want you to avoid the airport. According to their records, you flew in to Damascus this morning from India. Besides, you don't want your things to have to pass through security. Your sample case is supposed to be filled with computer gear, but if they X-ray it, I don't think the radiation detection gear will pass."

"Uh-huh, I see. Then what's the best way in to Syria?"

"Yusef Habib has a new truck that he's dying to show you, Samir says. He'll be in Iskenderun when you get there and will take you over-land to Damascus. It's not quite three hundred miles, but the highway is fairly good and, from Aleppo south to Damascus, it's all four-lane. Yusef's son Samir will take the train from Iskenderun to Aleppo, and then change trains there for Damascus. That's where you'll rendezvous tomorrow."

"All right, that gets us through the first part of this drill, but how about the rest of the way in and then back out?"

"Bill Goode has some ideas on the ingress from Syria into Iraq that he's ironing out with Samir and Yusef right now. Samir is a licensed tour guide and can drive you from Damascus to Baghdad. Before you go in, we'll have that worked out as best we can. As for egress, a lot depends on whether you can find the nukes and whether you're discovered. If all is routine, you'll come out according to the plan worked out by Bill Goode, Samir, and Yusef. If there's an emergency, I've got a contingent from 24th MEU conducting joint training with the British Four-Two Commando unit in the Saudi desert, about thirty kilometers south of Rafha. They have the equipment you will need if called upon. Obviously, they can't go all the way to Damascus, but if you can make it back into the Western Desert, we can certainly put fixed wing cover over you from Kuwait and, depending on where you are, arrange for some kind of extract support."

Peter Newman nodded, thinking about all he had been told, realizing it meant that he was going to have to rely more on Samir and Yusef Habib than he had anticipated. "I understand; I just don't want to put more people in jeopardy than we already have—especially the Habibs—they're civilians."

"I appreciate that, Pete. Believe me, if there was any other way to do this, I would. And I also know you're carrying a terrible burden about Rachel. If I had anyone else I could send on this mission, I would."

"Any late word?"

Grisham shook his head. "I have everyone in the region with an antenna and every overhead asset available listening for any transmissions from the kind of handheld radios you told me the kidnappers were carrying. In addition, NSA and GCHQ are trying to capture any relevant telephone communications. They've been at it more than twenty-four hours, but so far . . . nothing. I'm sorry."

"But you aren't giving up?"

"No, of course not. We're trying to guess what part of the country they took the women to. But that seems impossible; so we've started a grid search, moving out from the Hims-Hamah area. We're looking north, east, and south . . . and we'll try to the west if we don't turn up something in the other areas. I want you to know we have our best people working on it, and when we find Rachel, we'll let you know right away. Just have faith, son."

Newman shrugged. "I guess there really isn't anything I can add. I'll stay focused on this mission. But, General—" he looked Grisham in the eye. "I trust you."

The general put his hand on Newman's shoulder. "We'll find her and bring her back. Meanwhile, Pete, you've got a job to do."

Duvdevan Headquarters
Tel-Nof Air Force Base, Israel
Sunday, 22 March 1998
1445 Hours, Local

The Ops Center had activated the tracking device in Peter Newman's foot within minutes of Rotem's call from home. When the IDF major arrived at the Ops Center, he was handed a page of notes showing that Newman had left the Old City, gone to the American embassy, and from there to Ben Gurion Airport. Major Rotem had also been advised of the helicopter sent from the USS *Mobile Bay* to pick up the American.

And now Rotem was tracking Newman himself. His computer screen initially followed the signal all the way to Turkey, where it eventually stopped at the Incirlik Air Base.

The Israeli major guessed that Newman had decided to be with his friend, the American Marine general, who was probably trying to help Newman find his wife. Rotem expected the signal would stay at that site in Turkey for some time, as they worked on the search.

Having the American military involved would likely complicate things.

He stared at the computer screen and then blinked as the icon began to move across the map in front of him. *Newman is leaving Incirlik!* Rotem deduced that he was following the highway from Adana to Yakapinhar. Rotem busied himself with some reports and checked back occasionally to see the progress of the Marine's transponder. The next time he glanced at the screen, the icon had passed Yakapinhar and was nearing Dogankent—heading for the seacoast. A half hour later, the green arrow stopped at the city of Karatas.

Rotem reached for his mobile phone and dialed the number of the phone that the Israelis had issued Newman.

Newman answered it right away.

"Colonel," Rotem said, "I've been wondering what happened to you. I couldn't find you at your apartment. Where are you?"

"I contacted my friend General Grisham, and he arranged for me to fly to Incirlik to see if they could help us find our wives. He's got some of our satellites looking in Syria. And I'm waiting for more instructions from the kidnappers. How are you doing?"

"I'm at an impasse," Rotem said. "I don't know what to do. We are also using our satellites, but without those transponders . . .

"Will you be coming back to Jerusalem?" Rotem added, after a pause.

"Not right away. I'm sorry to leave you alone in this, but I really felt out of place there, not knowing the Israeli SOP and all. . . ."

"I see." Rotem sensed Newman was holding back something.

There was another long pause, and then Newman spoke. "Listen, Ze'ev, General Grisham has promised to give this matter everything he's got. He'll get back to me as soon as they find *anything*. I'll call you the minute I hear. And please . . . do the same if you find something."

"Then you will be staying at Incirlik?" *Does he really think I don't know where he is?*

"Well, in the general area. It's where I feel comfortable . . . and where I can see how things are going."

He's definitely hiding something, Rotem thought. The American had already departed Incirlik, headed toward the coast. Rotem knew he could follow Newman from his laptop, wherever the Marine was going, but he couldn't help feeling betrayed by this man with whom he had already shared so much danger. Rotem decided to keep an eye on the American and make certain that he was not left out of the loop being constructed in Incirlik.

Tall Ajrab Ruin
34 km East of Baghdad, Iraq
Sunday, 22 March 1998
1455 Hours, Local

Leonid Dotensk took a long drink of water from a plastic bottle as he took refuge from the sun in the shade on the north side of the truck. It wasn't that hot in Iraq this time of year, but the sun was unrelenting and lately the arms merchant had been reading much about skin cancer. He looked over at the four "retired" KGB officers he had brought from his homeland to help him. He was sure they had found the hidden weapons.

Dotensk was proud of his memory, for having remembered and found this location after three years, and with no map to consult. He recalled the place clearly in his memory, although he had been here only twice—both times when Hussein Kamil had brought him. Kamil had told Dotensk then that, in addition to his other duties, he was assuming the vacant position of Minister of Antiquities. He'd had his

predecessor executed for allowing "foreign elements" to pillage histor-
ical sites. Kamil had proudly announced that this place, the Tall Ajrab
Ruin, had been declared off limits to all archeological exploration.

But this was the right place—he knew it. When they had arrived
here that morning, Dotensk had one of the Ukrainians take readings
with the expensive electronic equipment that the Chernobyl scientists
had left in his Baghdad offices when they delivered the nuclear weapons
to Iraq in 1995. The sensors were designed to locate even a minute
source of radioactive emissions. He had expected it might take an entire
day or more. But it had taken them only an hour, and Dotensk was
elated. He congratulated himself on his good luck.

Kamil had hidden the weapons well; he had placed the warheads,
in their lead-shielded crates, within the ancient ruin of a pagan temple
that Kamil had said was constructed during the Babylonian Empire
more than two thousand years before. Dotensk recalled something
about the temple site having been razed by the Caliph Mansur in the
eighth century, but it wasn't its history that had given it away. What
Dotensk remembered was that one of the structures had been built
against the side of a hill, and the Ukrainian had guessed correctly that
the back wall might well hide the entrance to a cave, perhaps an ancient
spring.

There had been several minutes of uncertainty, for the radiation
detector gave no indication until they approached the back wall of the
ruined building. But when the sensor began to beep and the needle on
the dial began to move, Dotensk was certain he had found Kamil's hidden weapons.

"They are under this pile of stones," he said confidently to the men
he had brought along. He had them start removing the piles of sand,

stone, and debris piled against the semicollapsed stone wall. As they dug, it became apparent that Saddam's now-deceased son-in-law had chosen the site well—and hidden the evidence of his heinous deed well too.

It only took them a few minutes to find the first body—remarkably well preserved by the dry desert air. The corpse was that of a man in an Amn Al-Khass Special Security Service uniform—one of Kamil's bodyguards, shot in the back of the head. In another hour, enough stones and sand had been removed to reveal three more bodies. All had died the same way.

Dotensk had the bodies dragged over against the far wall. He pointed to where they had been buried and said with certainty, "The next thing you will find are the cases for the weapons. But take care not to break them open with your tools."

As his four accomplices worked with their shovels and pry-bars, Dotensk mused about how Kamil must have done it. He probably had his most trusted bodyguards bring the weapons here and bury them. And then, after that task was finished, Kamil had no doubt killed these four and buried them beside the hidden weapons. What was the line from the famous American pirate story? "Dead men tell no tales."

Out here, in the middle of nowhere, the site would have never been discovered by accident. It was the perfect spot—even Saddam and his sons would never have been drawn to this place to search. But the former SSS commander had overlooked two critical factors: the memory and the intuition of one Leonid Dotensk. The Ukrainian was feeling very satisfied with himself.

For more than five hours, Dotensk's men labored without stopping, except for an occasional drink of water. They used sledgehammers, crowbars, shovels, and chisels to clear away the sand and debris. They finally broke through the masonry wall at the back of the structure and there, just as Dotensk had guessed, was a shallow cave. One of the workers pointed a flashlight into the darkness. There, stored as they had been when Dotensk had last seen them three years before, were three Soviet nuclear artillery rounds.

It took Dotensk and his men another hour to wrap cables around each of the heavy crates and drag them out of the cave into the center of the ruined structure. The arms dealer let the men rest while he turned the truck around and backed it up as close as possible to the weapons crates. Then he climbed into the bed and, with the help of his workers, lowered two long steel ramps for the small forklift that had been chained down beneath the canvas cover over the back of the truck. Dotensk climbed aboard the forklift and carefully drove it down the ramp toward the three wooden crates. The small wheels of the forklift spun in the sand, fighting for traction. Two of the workers pushed it when it got stuck, and Dotensk eased it toward the first crate. He lowered the tongues of the lift and thrust them under the skid holding the crate to lift it. The forklift strained at the load and struggled through the sand. It took twice as long as it should have to get the crate into the truck.

Looking at his watch, he urged the men to help him get the other two crates into the truck before dark. Once that was done, Dotensk wanted to have enough daylight to go over the area and erase their tracks from the sand.

Finally, all three crates were manhandled into the truck, chained down, and covered with a tarp. The men pushed the forklift sideways against the load to conceal it further, and then began working on the ground. By the time Dotensk was satisfied that their tracks were sufficiently erased from the sand and no one would ever suspect what had been taken from the ruins, it was getting dark.

Dotensk decided to ride with the driver in the cab of the truck back across Iraq, in case his talents and bribe money were needed at some border crossing or checkpoint. Dotensk sent the three others in his own Mercedes. They looked grateful.

Leonid Dotensk was inordinately pleased with finding his great treasure and couldn't wait to show off to General Komulakov.

Just before they left in the gathering gloom, one of the men asked what should be done with the bodies of the four Iraqis they had discovered.

"Leave them there. The vultures and the elements will take care of them."

Habirah Prison
Near Salman Pak, Iraq
Sunday, 22 March 1998
1755 Hours, Local

Bruno Macklin felt energy course through his body as he lay on the cement slab "cot" in his prison cell. Adrenaline had begun to flow nearly an hour earlier, when an English-speaking guard came by to tell him he was being transferred to another prison, ordering him to be ready to move when he returned.

The SAS captain heard the opening of the iron door at the end of the hallway and the footsteps of the two guards coming to get him. Macklin felt excitement—and not a little nervousness. He stood up in his cell to wait for the men coming toward him.

They stopped at another cell a short distance away. Macklin could hear the door opening and the rustle of someone shuffling into the hallway, followed by the familiar clink of the ankle chains and wrist irons the guards put on each prisoner.

Just as the prisoner and his detail were moving past his cell, one of the guards used a hand transmitter to unlock the steel door to Macklin's cell. The young Iraqi guard, Macklin noticed, was attempting to grow a mustache—and failing at the task. The guard motioned for the British soldier to come out. Macklin had no belongings to take with him—only the ill-fitting prisoner's uniform and sandals he was wearing, just like the emaciated man standing before him. The guards put arm and leg manacles on Macklin and chained him to the other prisoner; neither man spoke as they walked down the hallway that echoed with the sounds of the heavy-booted guards marching ahead of and behind them.

Another guard waited behind the massive wire-mesh glass door at the end of the hallway. One of the two guards showed him a clipboard with a letter of instructions. The man on the other side of the door nodded, opened it, and escorted the group across this anteroom.

Four other prisoners, also in chains, waited by the opposite door. There were no windows in the room, only the other door—the one that opened to the outside. The outside door opened, and the six prisoners were shoved roughly toward an old Soviet-era military truck and made to climb into its cargo bay, a difficult task to accomplish with the chains shackling them all together.

So far so good, Macklin thought as he sat on one of the two wooden benches that ran the length of each side of the truck bed. The driver threaded the hasp of a large padlock through an end of the heavy chain, then snapped the lock onto a steel bracket in the truck bed.

The other guards went back inside the prison while the prison commandant walked around to the passenger side of the truck cab. The youthful driver had counted on one of the other guards accompanying him to share the driving. It was obvious now that he was going to have to do all the driving, and he also seemed a little flustered to have his boss riding with him.

"Sir, you are not going with the prisoners, are you?"

"Yes. These are important prisoners, and I want to make sure there are no problems." That closed the matter.

Just as the driver started the engine, an officer came running out of the guardhouse and up to the passenger side of the truck. Macklin, who was seated all the way forward on the right side of the vehicle, could hear bits and pieces of Arabic conversation but couldn't make out what was being said over the sound of the engine; then suddenly, the engine stopped, the passenger door slammed, and a moment later the tailgate at the rear of the bed slammed down.

"All right, take the Americans off then," said the clearly agitated prison commandant, who had dismounted and was once again standing behind the truck in the growing dusk.

The driver unlocked the chain. Four guards clambered aboard and started to remove two of the prisoners, who now had a look of absolute terror on their faces. One of them, the prisoner who had been taken out of his cell just before Macklin, tried to resist.

"No! No . . . we're supposed to go too! Don't do this to us! Take us with you—"

The protest was cut short by a guard's truncheon against the side of the man's head. The prisoner collapsed onto the steel bed of the old truck, and his unconscious body was dragged head first off the truck and dumped in the dirt. As the four helpless British prisoners watched in horror, the other American knelt beside his inert comrade. Suddenly a phalanx of guards came rushing out and dragged the two men back inside the building. It was all over in a matter of minutes, leaving Macklin and the other three sitting in the truck stunned.

The prison commandant tried to regain his composure. He ordered two of the guards to reshackle the remaining prisoners, one to each corner of the truck bed. When they had done so, the tailgate was once again slammed into place. The commandant resumed his place in the cab of the vehicle. Then the starter ground for a few seconds until the diesel engine caught, and the truck pulled onto the access road leading to the guarded fortress-like doors in front of the prison. They stopped while the commandant explained their trip to the armed guards at the gate and assured them all was in order. Macklin held his breath while the guards poked their rifles past the canvas flap in the back, and then, after counting the prisoners in the truck to make sure that the number corresponded with the corrected manifest handed to them by the commandant, they waved the truck through.

Everyone began to breathe again when the vehicle pulled onto the highway outside of the prison and started heading southwest toward the sunset.

Macklin heard snatches of conversation from the cab: the driver asking for the destination, and the commandant answering. The highway and engine noise made it impossible to get many details, but it sounded to Macklin as if they were headed toward someplace called Al Najaf.

Macklin had been in and out of many prisons during his captivity, but he'd never heard of Al Najaf. He hoped that was a good sign.

Macklin sat hunched against the canvas, giving him a meager shield from the breeze. The air, growing cold now, rustled the SAS commando's hair, and he shivered.

After a few miles, Macklin had gotten the attention of the prisoner shackled across the truck bed from him and said over the noise of the truck and the flapping canvas, "What about the Americans?"

The RAF pilot leaned as far forward as his bonds would allow and said, just loud enough to be heard, "I don't know. They were supposed to be part of the deal. It's a bloody shame . . ."

Captain Bruno Macklin shivered again. And this time he knew it wasn't from the cold.

TOO MANY
SECRETS

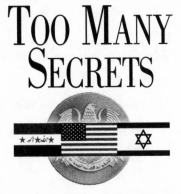

CHAPTER SIXTEEN

Duvdevan Headquarters
Tel-Nof Air Force Base, Israel
Sunday, 22 March 1998
1820 Hours, Local

At first, Ze'ev Rotem had simply felt confused. Now, he felt betrayed and angry.

For the better part of the day, the IDF counter-terror expert had watched as his computer screen repeatedly indicated Peter Newman was no longer anywhere near the big Incirlik NATO Air Base in Turkey. Newman, the liar, had led Rotem to believe that he was going to stay there, working on a way to rescue their wives.

Rotem knew the transponder wasn't lying. When transponders failed, the signal was simply lost. Instead, it was now plain that

Newman had meant to deceive him. The tracking system clearly indicated the American had crossed Iskenderun Bay to Iskenderun, on the coast of Turkey. For the past hour, the computerized tracking program indicated that Newman had not moved from that spot.

Rotem decided to call Newman's special IDF mobile phone for an update to see what the American would tell him. But before he had a chance to place the call, someone knocked at his office door. He looked up as two men came inside and closed the door behind them. He recognized one of the two as Ben Yakib, a Mossad agent, and he guessed the other man was also working for the Israeli intelligence agency.

"Ze'ev, how are you?" Yakib said, extending his hand as Major Rotem stood to greet them. "Meet my associate, David. David, this is Major Ze'ev Rotem of the Duvdevan."

"I heard about your wife . . . I'm sorry. What's the latest?"

Rotem briefly gave them a summary of what had taken place and what they were doing to find his wife. Then he asked, "What brings you here, Ben?"

"Mossad has received information that maybe your wife's kidnapping has something to do with one of our operations. Have you heard about the 'Three Wise Men' operation?"

Rotem shook his head.

"We've gotten some pretty reliable information that Saddam has at least three nuclear weapons that can be made operational very quickly, posing an immediate threat to Israel," David said. "Apparently they were acquired from an old Soviet stockpile several years ago by his murdered son-in-law, Hussein Kamil."

Rotem's jaw hung open. "Three? Three nukes? But Kamil's been dead for almost three years. If this information is correct, why haven't we taken them out, like the Osarik reactor in '81?"

"Good question," Yakib said. "And the answer is simple—we don't know where they are."

"The good news, at least for now, is that no one else seems to know where they are either, not even the Iraqis," David said.

"We got tipped to this because there now seems to be an all-out effort on the part of the Iraqis to find the missing weapons—which we believe to be tactical nuclear artillery rounds. We've had a team on this project for several weeks, apparently even before Saddam knew the weapons were in his country. I can't give you any more details about how we found out, but it's only a matter of time before these weapons are found," Yakib said.

"I don't understand. How does this—"

"Ze'ev, we think that your wife's kidnapping has some sort of connection to the 'Three Wise Men' operation, but we haven't been able to figure out what it is," Yakib said. "We were able to learn about the matter because, even before the kidnapping, we had our men in Syria watching the growing cooperation between the PFLP and the Hezbollah. Then suddenly a few days ago, some European guy shows up in Damascus, and the PFLP guys drop everything to help him. As it turns out, he's likely the guy you shot when you raided the safe house in Hamah."

"Well, if that's the case, I can tell you he's a Russian. But what makes you think there's a link?" said Rotem. "We haven't been able to connect any of the terrorists to Iraq. It looked to us as if they were just gangsters . . . kidnapping and break-ins were their specialty. The kidnapping of my wife and the other woman seemed to be some kind of contract job for the Russian. In fact, I think my wife was just in the wrong place at the wrong time. It was the American woman he wanted . . . in order to get to her husband."

"Yes, we know that," David said. "But our intelligence indicates that even *that* was a case of 'wrong place and time.' The Russian didn't want the American woman or her husband because of any ties to Iraq. I don't think that the Russian or those PFLP terrorists even knew about the Iraqi nuclear weapons. No, we think something else was going on.

"We read your report about how this man Newman has been living here three years under Irish cover identity as John Clancy, because he was accused of being a wanted IRA terrorist named Gilbert Duncan," David said. "Frankly, we were skeptical and, after checking, we found that there really is no Irish terrorist named Gilbert Duncan. In fact, the name and photograph appeared out of nowhere in a UN report and then the Interpol BOLO notice in March of '95."

"So that made us wonder, who is this fellow, Clancy/Newman—and what is he doing here?" Yakib said. The two Mossad men looked at Rotem, and the silence widened uncomfortably.

"He's an American Marine," Rotem said, finally.

"How do you know?" Yakib said.

"Ben, come on! How many years have we known each other? He told me. That's how I know. And then the Deputy Minister of Defense told me to let him help us get back our wives. Apparently he's some pro-tégé of the general in charge of the American Central Command."

"What else do you know about Newman?" David asked.

"Well, according to him, he was the commander of that UN assassination fiasco in Iraq back in March of '95. And, again according to him, the guy who set him up and compromised that mission is the same guy I shot a few days ago—a former KGB officer."

Yakib nodded and looked at David. "That fits," David said. "The Russian is probably Dimitri Komulakov, a former KGB general who served until June of '95 as a Deputy Secretary General of the United Nations. Mossad has a rather extensive file on him. Your U.S. Marine has good reason to dislike the man. But even your American friend probably doesn't know that the Russian may also have been the one who was behind the sale of the three weapons to Iraq in the first place, through one of his associates from Ukraine."

Rotem's eyes widened. "You mean that the Russian kidnapped the women in order to get Newman to find those nukes for him?"

David shook his head. "We don't think so. In fact, the subject never even came up when they were in Hamah. They talked about a different assignment . . ."

Rotem looked at the younger Mossad agent. "You had an eaves-dropping device planted at the PFLP safe house when Newman was there?"

Neither man answered, but Yakib returned to the original subject. "The Russian wanted Newman for a different job—and we're on top of it—but we can't talk about it. We also know Newman is working with the American military. They were the ones who contacted him a few weeks ago to go look for those nuclear weapons."

Major Rotem was astonished at how much the Mossad knew. "Incredible . . ."

"We think that's why he left Incirlik this afternoon, headed for Syria. We believe he's going into Iraq to meet with either the CIA or the

Kurdish resistance to get information on possible hiding places for the weapons."

"And you've been tracking him, too?" the dumbfounded Israeli major asked.

"Yes."

"Why have you told me all this?"

"Because we need to get closer to this American. At first we thought of removing him from the scene because he could complicate our own efforts to find the weapons. But then we figured, if we could assure a cooperative association, it might be useful to have him involved. Do you think you can gain his trust and have him keep you informed on his progress?"

"I don't know . . . I can try. How much can I tell him? If I'm going to get him to trust me, he'll have to be included in some of this or he won't let me in."

"Well, don't let him know we're getting intelligence from a source with access to American information," David said.

"I don't want to have anything to do with spying on the Americans. We've had enough problems with them over the Pollard matter. We don't need another mess like that."

"Don't worry, Major," David said, "our source isn't an American."

Rotem shook his head, still doubtful. "Assuming I can gain the trust of this Marine, what can I tell him?"

"You can tell Newman about our eavesdropping when the Russian had him in the PFLP house in Hamah. And you can tell him about our own searches for the weapons. You can even let him know that the Russian may have been implicated in the original deal with Hussein

Kamil. I think the American can be trusted with those secrets. He wouldn't want that information to be leaked either," Yakib said.

"I can't believe this. The whole situation is bizarre. Do you think Mossad or the American can find those weapons before Saddam discovers them?"

"We'd better," David said. "Because if we don't, and Saddam or one of his sons finds them first, we may have to take the most severe preemptive measures."

Rotem's mouth dropped again. "The Jericho Sanction . . . ," he muttered, almost to himself.

"What do you know about that?" David asked sharply.

"Before I joined the Duvdevan, I was a strategic planner for the National Defense Committee."

"I thought strategic planners were barred from serving in units where they stood the risk of capture," David said.

"Most are, but an exception was made for me in deference to the way my father was killed."

The two men from Mossad knew the story; they decided not to press the matter.

Ze'ev was uncertain how much the two men from Mossad knew about the Jericho Sanction, so he did not elaborate. If they understood, it would not have to be explained. And the way that David had asked the question led Ze'ev to believe the two of them knew precisely what he was talking about. Rotem was beginning to feel a sense of real dread, not for himself, not even for his wife—but for his country.

The Jericho Sanction was the code name for an Israeli preemptive action against any hostile nation threatening to attack the Jewish state with a weapon of mass destruction. The code name referred to the

Jericho 2 nuclear missiles deployed at Zachariah, west of the Dead Sea, south of Hebron.

Israel had often told the world publicly that it would not *introduce* nuclear weapons into the Middle East. However, that statement contained enough ambiguity to confound anyone who questioned its real meaning. Besides, nearly every intelligence service in the world knew that Israel already had "the bomb." The only question was how many.

The Jericho Sanction called for a limited, preemptive nuclear first strike. But there was another plan that kept potential enemies guessing. In addition to the Jericho Sanction, Israel also had plans for an all-out nuclear war, its strategy of last resort. Dubbed "the Samson Strategy," after the biblical character who was killed while destroying his enemies, the plan called for an *in extremis* strike, using Israel's entire nuclear arsenal, even if it brought Armageddon to the land.

Though it was illegal to write or talk about the subject in public, the Israeli nuclear weapons had been around since right after the birth of the Jewish state in 1948. The rationale was simple: Israel was home to fewer Jews than Hitler had killed in the Holocaust, and these survivors, living in the Jewish state, regardless of their political ideology, were committed to the survival of both the nation and the Jewish people. "Never again!" were their watchwords. They built their first nuclear weapon in 1964, and then acquired the technology to keep improving it and others. Most foreign intelligence agencies currently estimated that the Israelis had some two hundred nuclear weapons. In reality, they had many more.

The Jericho 2 nuclear missiles had a range of from 1,500 to 4,000 kilometers with the Shavit space launchers. This was a strategic improvement over their Jericho 1 missiles and their limited range of only five hundred kilometers. Unlike the Russian and American nuclear missiles launched from submarines or fixed land-based silos, the Israeli missiles were each mounted on a forty-two-foot TEL, a mobile transporter/erector/launcher. Most of these were housed in limestone caves in western Israel, not far from the Tel-Nof Air Base. Other nuclear missile sites were scattered across the nation to give the nation a strategic advantage against enemy attacks from any direction. These well-dispersed sites also insured that some would survive an enemy preemptive strike and ultimately prevail in a nuclear conflagration, since Israel possessed more weapons of mass destruction than its adversaries did. Even if all of their potential enemies launched all of their combined weapons of mass destruction at the same time, Israel would still be able to respond with enough nuclear firepower to destroy any number of enemy cities, enough firepower to unleash a horrific Armageddon.

While the Israelis were cognizant of the potential apocalyptic consequences of using nuclear weapons, they also knew they could not permit themselves to be intimidated by a madman like Saddam, or some militant mullah bent on launching a doomsday *jihad.*

None of these thoughts brought any comfort to the already troubled mind of Major Rotem as he sat in his office. His two visitors left after relaying their information about Newman's true mission. This was pretty heady stuff for the Duvdevan major to consider. But he knew two things: he needed to get to Newman right away and make him aware of what was now known; and right now, from what he could see, nobody was working on rescuing their wives.

25 Piers Harbor

Iskenderun, Turkey
Sunday, 22 March 1998
1835 Hours, Local

Peter Newman excused himself and went topside of the *Pescador II,* now anchored at the docks in Iskenderun Bay. The short trip across the bay had been relaxing and comfortable. There were small swells and only a few whitecaps as they sailed from Karatas to Iskenderun that afternoon. The rest of the day was spent going over his cover story, the phony documents, the maps, and the pocket litter Bill Goode had provided while they waited for Samir Habib and his father, Yusef.

When the two Christian Arabs arrived, they had a warm and emotional reunion. Both of these men had risked their lives several times to save Newman three years earlier, and the transparent goodness of their unselfish acts had remained with Newman since those difficult days. And while he had seen Yusef once since then, at Christmas '95 in Bethlehem, he had not been with the father and son together since those desperate days when he was trying to escape Iraq as the sole survivor of a betrayed mission.

Now, with Bill Goode below in the galley preparing the evening meal with the help of his two rescuers, Peter Newman had climbed back on deck for a few minutes of solitude. He looked past the calm seas into the western skies, to the slowly setting sun and the radiant edging it gave to the cumulus clouds forming in the distance. The evening breeze was picking up, and Newman felt its soft presence, tinged with cool saltiness, blowing through his hair and across his face.

He took time to think about Rachel . . . and little James. How he missed them both. He felt a tug of emotion at his helplessness and loneliness and wished for the thousandth time he had not left them alone on the day Rachel had been kidnapped. He also wished he could talk to his wife on the phone, reassure her, and tell her that he loved her. But he had already tried that tack with Komulakov and had gotten nowhere.

Newman looked at his watch—it was midmorning in the eastern U.S. Maybe he could at least check in with his sister and see how his son was bearing up. Newman went below to his spacious cabin, retrieved the satellite phone from his duffel bag, returned to the deck, punched in a number, and waited for the overseas connection to engage.

His sister Nancy answered and recognized his voice right away. "Oh, Pete . . . I'm glad you called. We've been so worried about you and Rachel. Are you all right? Have you heard anything from Rachel? Is she all right? What's happening?"

He told Nancy he had met briefly with Rachel and the kidnappers, and that Rachel was alive and well. "We're working on trying to deal with their demands . . . and looking for ways to get her back safely."

Nancy had many more questions about what was being done, who was doing it, and many others he couldn't answer; and he deflected her queries with other information, hoping Nancy would understand.

"Is James OK? How is he adjusting?"

"Well, he keeps asking about his mommy and daddy . . . and cries at night when I put him to bed. He says that his mommy tucks him in bed, and that his daddy helps him say his prayers. It isn't quite the same when we try to do it."

Newman choked a little on her words, and felt tears welling up in his eyes. He had been too busy, first in trying to rescue Rachel and now with the nuclear weapons recovery, to permit himself many thoughts about his son. Now hordes of feelings and memories flooded over him, and his shoulders sagged with the heaviness of his loss.

"What's he doing now?"

"He's playing with some toys that we bought him, and his teddy bear," Nancy said softly. "He's doing fine, Pete . . . don't worry. You'll see him, and Rachel, soon."

"Put the phone by his ear . . . let me talk to him . . . see if he recognizes my voice."

He heard her talking to James. "James . . . do you want to talk on the telephone? Your daddy is calling on the phone. Here, why don't you talk to him?"

Newman heard the rustle of the phone as it was placed in his toddler's hand.

"Hey, buddy . . . how's my boy? Are you having a good time visiting Aunt Nancy?" He tried to keep his voice upbeat, despite the tears running down his face.

"Daddy . . . ," James said, so softly that Newman barely heard his voice.

"Yeah . . . this is Daddy, son. Can you talk to me?" There was silence at the other end. The little boy did not know how to use a telephone but was likely transfixed by hearing his father's voice. Newman tried to coax some kind of response, asking leading questions about what he was doing. But the boy said nothing.

Eventually Nancy came back on the line. "He knows that it's you, but when you ask him questions, he just nods or shakes his head. He doesn't know he's supposed to talk. But his eyes lit up when he heard your voice. I'm sure you made him happy by calling."

"Yeah . . . uh . . . listen, Nancy, I've got to get going. I really appreciate what you're doing for us. I hope we can get things sorted out and find Rachel soon. Keep us in your prayers, OK?"

"Of course, Peter. And don't worry about James. He'll be fine. Just concentrate on finding Rachel. And be careful."

"Thanks, Sis . . . I will. Good-bye."

As he hung up, the breeze that had been so exhilarating just moments ago now made him shiver. As he looked to the western sky, the sun had fallen behind the clouds and their once-golden edges were now dark gray and foreboding. Newman clenched his jaw and turned to go back to work. He headed toward the salon of the *Pescador II,* where Bill Goode, Samir, and Yusef were waiting.

MI6 Ops Harbor Site
Judayyidat Ar'ar, Saudi Arabia
Sunday, 22 March 1998
1845 Hours, Local

British MI6 Agents Thomas and Blackman and their contingent of shooters had flown from Rafha aboard two U.S. Marine CH-53s earlier in the day. The big U.S. helicopters, ostensibly part of a joint U.S.-UK desert training exercise, had landed in a wide *wadi* just west of the hilltop now being used as an observation post by the MI6 operatives. The twenty-one Four-Two Commando Royal Marines were now deployed in a perimeter around a grimy little one-story cinder block building that had once been a monitoring station for the now defunct pipeline between Karbala, Iraq, and Badanah, Saudi Arabia.

Inside the structure, Thomas and Blackman had set up their communications gear and night-vision equipment so they could keep an eye on the dusty border station on the boundary between Iraq and Saudi

Arabia. With binoculars, Thomas could see the Iraqi outpost at Judaiat al Hamir about a kilometer away, where the truck carrying the four prisoners was supposed to cross.

Beyond the isolated border post, he could see the ribbon of highway running to the northeast that the truck was due to come down. Aside from the border post itself and a few stone buildings beyond, there was nothing but desert as far as the eye could see. While that was good from the standpoint of not drawing unwanted attention, it also left them vulnerable to any breakdowns the truck might suffer, as well as make the truck an easy target for Iraqi aircraft if the plot was uncovered and reported before the truck could get across the border.

Blackman, meanwhile, had set up a flat plane antenna plugged into a sat comm transmitter/receiver, which was in turn plugged into a port on his laptop computer. The whole setup was being run by a tiny, gasoline-powered generator that was humming away in a small sand pit on the bank of the Wadi Ar'ar.

"Joe . . . take a look at this," Blackman said to Thomas.

"What do you have?" Thomas said as he stepped away from the window.

"Some very interesting stuff," Blackman said, peering at the screen. "This is the new 'Battlefield Threat Warning System' our chaps built with the American satellite wonks. It's designed to give units in combat some real-time intelligence information from every overhead platform that NSA, NRO, and GCHQ can access."

"Quite some toy. How does it work?"

"The computer automatically displays a terrain map of the area where we're located, based on our GPS plot. Then, each successive overlay shows what the thermal, RF, visual, radar, and laser sensors are picking up on each satellite pass. Here," Thomas said, pointing to the lower right side of the screen, "it tells me how old the information is and how much longer before this particular sensor will pass over us again. According to this, the last satellite visual pass, twelve minutes ago, shows that the truck with the four prisoners and two Iraqis is proceeding as planned. It crossed the Euphrates at Al Musayyib. At Karbala, instead of turning south down toward An Najaf, it took the right fork toward An Nukhayb. They should be about halfway there by now."

Blackman nodded and consulted a map on his own computer screen. "At that rate, I put them about ninety-two kilometers north of the border." He zoomed out to reveal a larger portion of Iraq, and said, "I sure hope Saddam doesn't have any of his aircraft up tonight, 'cause according to the terrain map, it sure is open out there."

"Can you make that thing give you the latest NRO radar imagery?" Thomas asked.

"Yeah," said Blackman, "I can get all kinds of different overhead readouts from the birds. Watch this." The MI6 agent typed in a series of numbers and letters and hit the Enter key.

"This view shows radio frequency spectrum in the area of interest. If Saddam has any aircraft up and they so much as key a mike, this'll show it . . . Hey, what's this?"

In the upper left corner of his screen, a blinking icon showed tactical UHF radio transmissions emanating from just across the Iraqi border in Syria, at a place called At Tanf. He was puzzled. The frequency in the blinking icon showed a spectrum reserved for NATO military use.

"Hey, Eddie," Blackman called out across the room to his RTO. "C'mere, will you? Can we check on this signal?" The young radio operator looked at the computer screen. "Any idea what this is?"

Eddie looked at the flashing icon on the screen, broke open a small spiral-bound notebook, checked the frequency against the list on one of the pages, and said, "Well, it's not a taxicab."

"Yes, well, thank you, Sergeant Willis. Now that we know what it isn't, can you tell me what it *is?*"

"Well, according to this GCHQ manual, and assuming the satellite is correct, there are at least two Marconi DM-3 high-power, hand-held, UHF radios broadcasting in Syria on a frequency assigned to NATO."

To no one in particular, Blackman said. "That's very strange."

"Yes, sir, quite. Shall I notify Riyadh?" asked Willis.

"Good idea. Do that, Eddie," said Blackman. "They may not have seen this. That's one of the problems with this system. It pulls in so much information that something important can get lost in the noise. A little bit like drinking from a fire hose."

"Shall I also alert the Americans down by Rafha?"

"Yes . . . alert the Marine helicopter detachment, but don't bother with their CIA or NSA people. They always tell you they know everything. The last time I tried calling them about a matter like this, I was told, in so many words, to mind my own business."

Qadi Sh'Iyah Cafe
Ar Ramadi, Iraq
Sunday, 22 March 1998
1855 Hours, Local

The restaurant Leonid Dotensk had finally chosen was well below his usual standard. But this little town on the west bank of the

Euphrates wasn't Paris, Amman, or even Cairo. And to his hungry crew, it hardly mattered. Their appetites honed by a full day of manual labor, they had grumbled constantly as he pressed on right through Baghdad and past the pleasant ambiance of the Al Rashid Hotel.

"I should think we deserve a reward after finding these, Mr. Dotensk," the man driving the truck said when they headed out of the capital, past the grotesque statue of Saddam's two huge forearms rising up out of the ground and grasping two enormous crossed swords.

"Quiet, Yuri. You are being well paid. And I am not going to stop until we get beyond the military checkpoints near the Markab and Habbaniyah air bases." But even after breezing past the air bases, he had the drivers continue on for another twenty-five kilometers in the gathering darkness.

Dotensk finally stopped at this nondescript place, not because he knew the restaurant had good food, but because it was next to the highway and it was open—increasingly rare these days, outside of Baghdad. He told the men to eat in shifts and, now that he had finished, Dotensk came back outside to the two men guarding the truck.

"You may go eat," he told them. "I will stay here and watch the truck. Tell the other two to come out when they're finished." The two former KGB thugs who had been waiting in Dotensk's Mercedes eagerly complied—they were starved.

Dotensk lit up a cigar and a huge blue cloud of smoke rose around his face. The evening wasn't as cold as expected for this time of year, and he sat on a nearby bench to keep an eye on the truck. Only a few people were out on the streets. Most were at home having their own meals. Those who were still walking by were mainly laborers whose hours were longer than office workers'.

As he sat there enjoying his after-dinner cigar, a dark green Nissan Pathfinder with the insignia on its door of the Amn Al-Khass, the much-feared Special Security Service, pulled up behind the truck. As Dotensk watched, two men in uniform got out of the vehicle and walked up to the truck that was carrying the three nuclear weapons. The Ukrainian arms merchant quickly rose to meet them.

"Good evening," he said in Arabic. "Can I help you? I am the owner of this truck."

"Let me see your identification," one of the policemen said. The other man moved behind the Ukrainian, causing the hair to stand up on the back of his neck.

"Of course." He offered them the documents showing that his truck was carrying computer mainframes and other industrial equipment. "You will see that everything is in order."

The two uniformed policemen ignored him and climbed into the back of the truck, shining their flashlights onto the cargo. One of them took his truncheon and struck the wooden cases. He pulled on the metal strapping to see if it was intact. Dotensk winced, hoping they wouldn't ask him to open the crates. If they discovered the lead lining in the boxes, they would certainly be suspicious.

"Uh . . . are you looking for something in particular?" He kept his right hand inside his jacket pocket, closed around his 9mm automatic pistol.

One of the policemen held a sheaf of faxes in his hand. Dotensk could see mug shots of several men. The Iraqi took them one by one and reviewed them, looking at each one and comparing them to Dotensk's face. Satisfied, he handed Dotensk his identity papers. "Are there others with you?"

Dotensk nodded. "Inside the restaurant having their evening meal."

"Come with me and point them out."

They went inside and Dotensk took them to the table where the four were eating. The policeman with the faxes shuffled through them again, comparing each one to the faces before him, while his partner stood next to him with his hand on the butt of a 9mm Makarov pistol, holstered on his hip. When he finished looking through the faxes, the Iraqi then asked to see the ID papers of the four men. They complied, all the while continuing to eat casually.

Finally, the two policemen conferred and determined there were no reasons to hold these men.

"Tell me for whom you are looking, and we will keep an eye out for him," Dotensk said. "We have quite a distance to travel and . . . you never know. . . ."

The policeman hesitated. "There was an escape from a prison today. It took place less than eighty kilometers from here. Four criminals escaped in a truck similar to yours, with canvas over the top. There may be an Iraqi officer and another man with them—probably accomplices but maybe hostages. That is why we had to check."

"May I see the photos, in case we run into them?" Dotensk asked. Dotensk couldn't care less about four criminals who escaped an Iraqi prison, but he thought it wise to feign some interest at least.

The two policemen looked at each other, and the senior officer shrugged and gestured to his subordinate, who held the faxes out to the Ukrainian.

Dotensk pretended to examine the first picture carefully—the caption described him as Major D'awd al Khidir. The second photograph was that of another Iraqi, apparently an enlisted man in the Special

Republican Guard. The third, fourth, and fifth pictures surprised the arms merchant; they were all clearly either European or American. Unlike the first two photos, there were no names or descriptions beneath their faces. But when he got to the final photograph, he was stunned, though he studiously tried to avoid any evidence of recognition.

The picture was of the only survivor of the Anglo-American raid on Tikrit that he had witnessed with Hussein Kamil in March of 1995. The man in the photo was undoubtedly the wounded British SAS officer who had been captured when the rest of his team was annihilated. Dotensk remembered the occasion vividly, though much had happened in the three years since.

He handed the faxes back. "We will keep our eyes open for anyone suspicious and notify the authorities if we see anyone who resembles these men."

The policemen nodded, left the restaurant, climbed back into their vehicle, and were gone.

Dotensk walked back outside. *Four criminals . . . escaped prisoners . . . they must all be British or American captives. And the only prison that close is that newly constructed one near Salman Pak where Kamil was eventually going to store the nuclear weapons. An escape like this from one of Saddam's best prisons requires outside help. No doubt the British or American intelligence agencies are behind it.*

But the most troubling thought that concerned Dotensk was based on the man whom he recognized. *If this British survivor gets away and talks to his superiors about the Tikrit mission, General Komulakov might have even bigger problems than that spy inside the American intelligence apparatus.*

Dotensk had absolutely no idea how much the British SAS prisoner knew, but he was more convinced than ever that he needed to consummate some kind of deal with Qusay Hussein as quickly as possible, before things began to blow up in his face.

Iraqi Security Checkpoint
Near An Nukhayb, Iraq
Sunday, 22 March 1998
1910 Hours, Local

The truck carrying the four prisoners had been traveling with its headlights off for the past hour, encountering little traffic. "Pull over," Major D'awd al Khidir told the driver. He saw the lights of a checkpoint more than a kilometer down the deserted highway—well before the soldiers or policemen manning the roadblock could see them. The checkpoint made him very nervous. This wasn't supposed to happen this far from the border.

"Shut off the engine and do not use any lights," al Khidir said. The commandant got out of the cab and peered at the checkpoint.

The prison chief climbed back in the cab. Taking a pair of binoculars out of the duffel bag beside him on the seat, he again studied the lights down the road. "It is a roadblock . . . they have set up a military checkpoint."

The driver shifted in his seat. Al Khidir guessed he was getting nervous; driving at night with lights off was not standard procedure. "We do not want to go through the checkpoint," he told the driver. "I want you to turn off the highway and go to that *wadi* over there to the left. Its bed is dry, and we can follow it to beyond An Nukhayb to where it meets the Wadi al Ubayyid. Then we can follow it west until we get back onto the highway."

"Sir . . . why are you trying to avoid the checkpoint? Are we not tak-ing the prisoners to another prison?"

"No, Omar . . . we are not. We are going to cross the border with these men. You can go with me, or you can return with the truck to the prison. I will let you decide."

"But sir . . . I—that is—my family is here. I cannot abandon them. I must stay here."

"I can pay you a full year's salary to come with me, and you can try to get your family out of Iraq later."

"I would not know how . . . sir. I must stay here, with my family."

"I understand. I will release you and the truck when we have made the arrangements for the prisoners to be set free. I need you now . . . and later you will be permitted to leave us and return to Habirah Prison. Now, drive over to that *wadi.*"

The truck pulled out onto the highway and crossed the road into the flat desert. It lumbered and bumped over and through the gravel and soft sand toward the dry creek bed that Major Khidir had pointed out on the map. Once the vehicle made it to the harder ground, the commandant ordered the driver to stop.

"Come with me to the back of the truck. We are going to unlock their chains and give them a change of clothing to replace the prison uniforms."

Shackled in the back of the truck, SAS Captain Bruno Macklin was more than a little nervous when the vehicle pulled off the highway and stopped in this desolate location. He and the other three men chained in the bed of the vehicle all remembered what had happened earlier in the day when the two Americans had been dragged out of the truck. He was still not convinced that this was indeed an escape—this would be a perfect spot to dump four bodies.

But Macklin felt reassured when the younger guard unlocked the padlock of the chain that bound them all together and then released their handcuffs and leg manacles. And when the Iraqi in charge explained to RAF captain Robbie Blake that he had brought some clothing to replace their prison uniforms, then opened a large canvas bag to distribute them, the SAS officer finally began to have hope that he really was on his way to freedom.

As the men quickly changed clothes, the commandant told the driver to dispose of the chains and prison uniforms.

"There is a slight change of plans," the prison chief told Captain Blake. "There is a police or military checkpoint on the highway this side of An Nukhayb. We cannot take the chance of going that way. I have chosen a detour, following these *wadis* until we can get back onto the highway southwest of An Nukhayb. But this detour will slow us down at least thirty or forty minutes."

"Do you have some weapons we can use, in case they come after us?" Blake asked.

"I do have some extra weapons," the commandant replied, "but I am afraid I cannot give them to you. I am sorry . . . but the guns will stay with me for the time being."

"Yeah, well . . . let's get going. If we can see the lights of that road-block from here, maybe they can see us. And I wouldn't want to have made it all this way only to be stopped by those guys at the check-point."

"Yes, but remember, there is another checkpoint at the border crossing. The authorities are apparently already aware you have escaped, so we should expect an alert throughout all Iraq. You are special prisoners and every attempt will be made to prevent you from escaping."

Blake nodded. "No doubt we're very special, eh mates? Don't you all feel special? So . . . what's 'Plan B'?"

"Plan B?"

"Did your contact give you an alternate plan if the border crossing was closed?"

"Yes . . . they gave me a device with a magnet on it and told me to fasten it to the truck. I assume it is some kind of tracking apparatus. I put it inside the back wheel well. Your British friends instructed me that if we leave the truck, I should take the device with me so that they will 'see' that we are taking an alternate route. There is another *wadi* about twelve kilometers before we get to the border. It crosses the highway where the road curves south. We must assume the border posts have now all been alerted, and so we will follow the Wadi Hamir two kilometers north of the highway. There we will be met by your people."

Blake nodded appreciatively. "I was hoping you had something up your sleeve." He picked up a large rock and went over to the back of the truck. With two great swings, he struck the taillights and smashed the bulbs inside. "Your brake lights might give us away. We'd better get going now."

MI6 Harbor Site

Judayyidat Ar'ar, Saudi Arabia
Sunday, 22 March 1998
1955 Hours, Local

"Well, look who has finally gotten himself out in the field!"

Joe Thomas was peering through the long-range night-vision binoculars, out the doorway of the dingy concrete-block structure.

Downhill to the west, a U.S. Marine CH-46 helicopter had just shut down next to the two CH-53s, showering the whole area in a furious cloud of dust that obscured the horizon.

"Who's that?" Lloyd Blackman asked as they looked down the hill.

"Well, it appears to be good old Dwayne Wardell, our MI6 base chief in Riyadh."

"What's *he* want? Doesn't think we can handle the assignment without direct supervision, or what?"

"Maybe he got tired of sipping tea and eating scones with all the Riyadh royalty."

A Royal Marine sergeant in full battle gear escorted the man up to the door of the building. "'S'cuze me gents, this chap says he belongs here. He's got a badge says he's in Her Majesty's service."

"Thank you, Sergeant. Please let Mr. Wardell into our humble abode."

The Royal Marine stepped aside and a man entered who was at least ten years older than Thomas. Though the room was illuminated only by the laptop computer screens and a single chem-light resting on a map spread over two equipment cases, Thomas could see he was resplendent in a tailored bush jacket, matching khaki trousers, and desert boots that had been highly polished before walking the five hundred yards in the sand from the LZ.

"Good evening, Thomas, Blackman," the new arrival said, looking around. "I got to thinking you might be a little lonely up here, so I asked our American friends for a few more of their toys."

"Sir?"

"Yes, well, it seemed to me if things get a little dicey, a bit of fire-power might be in order, so I asked the American Marines if they wouldn't mind posting their two Cobra gunbirds up here to keep their other helicopters company—just until tomorrow."

Thomas smiled. He'd wanted the extra firepower, but London had counseled against asking the Americans for too much. "Great! When will they arrive?"

Wardell looked at his watch. "They were to have left Ar'ar at 1930 hours. That means they should be here any moment. The helicopter I came on also had something the yanks call a 'fuel bladder' in it to refuel them when they get here. Where're our escapees?"

Blackman, pointing to the map display on his computer screen, said, "Based on what the tracking information tells us, the truck is headed for Point Bravo, and that will be the pickup point."

"Do you have an ETA for them yet?"

"The satellite is tracking them at about twenty kilometers south-west of An Nukhayb," Thomas said. "I'm guessing they're about fifteen to twenty minutes from the point where they'll leave the highway, then it's a few minutes more to the rendezvous point."

"Any sign of hostiles?"

"No . . . there was a roadblock northeast of An Nukhayb, but the truck bypassed it safely. They've been moving steadily since then and are only thirty-three minutes behind schedule. Not bad . . . except for the curfew."

"What curfew?"

"Right about 1930, a half hour ago, we intercepted a broadcast by the regional commanders at An Nukhayb and further south at Ash Shabakah," Blackman said, "that they were imposing a curfew for all vehicle traffic until dawn. That means the only vehicles moving in the

Eastern Desert will be Iraqi security and our truckload of escaping POWs."

"Well, let's keep our fingers crossed. The Iraqis will have a force at all their border crossings, given the nationwide alert. If some local commander gets ambitious and sends out a recon patrol to look for the truck, our boys may get caught before they ever get to the border. As soon as the Cobras get here, establish an encrypted radio link with them so they know everything that's going on."

"Yes, sir." Blackman turned. "Sergeant Willis, come here, please."

The RTO came up from his seat in the corner, removing one side of his headphones. "Yes, sir?"

"Eddie, go down to the LZ. When the Cobras land, ask the section leader to come up here and bring with him the settings for his KY equipment."

As the young man headed out the door, Thomas said, "And you might tell him we suggest he take on as much fuel as possible as soon as he can."

The RTO had hardly exited the building when two red icons began to blink on the computer screen in front of Blackman.

"Uh-oh."

"What is it?" Wardell asked as Thomas pressed toward the screen.

"I'm showing a launch of Iraqi MIGs out of Markab, just west of Baghdad," Blackman said. The three of them watched as the computer updated itself from a satellite traveling more than twenty thousand miles per hour, one hundred thirty miles above Iraq. "It looks like the MIGs are headed toward An Nukhayb . . . two of them. That's the town just a few kilometers east of where the truck had to leave the highway to avoid a checkpoint."

"But if the officer at the checkpoint called for the MIGs, wouldn't we have detected his radio transmission back to Markab or Baghdad?" asked Thomas.

"Not if he made the call by telephone," said Blackman. "Remember, thanks to their friends in Beijing, these guys now have buried fiber optic cable connecting all their command centers."

"Where are the MIGs now?" asked Wardell.

"They're getting close to the truck," replied Blackman, pointing to the screen. "I'd say they're only ten minutes out. And it looks like they're flying a search pattern, parallel to the highway. If they spot the truck before it makes the rendezvous point, they'll be able to lock on and destroy the truck and everyone in it."

"Dwayne, what happened to our request for fixed wing air support for this mission?" Blackman asked.

"Sorry. No direct support . . . London has set up a diversion with our aircraft in the no-fly zone, but we've got nothing this far south," the senior MI6 man said. "We only have the CH-53s and the Cobras." As Wardell said the word, they heard the sound of the two gunships settling on the LZ to the west.

One of the technicians who had been monitoring the radios across the room said, "Sir, I've got Sergeant Ellis on the LZ, asking for Mr. Blackman."

The MI6 officer jumped to his feet, grabbed the handset, and depressed the button on its side. He waited a second for the electronic *ping* of the encryption, and said into the mouthpiece, "Ellis . . . this is Blackman, go ahead."

"I've just talked to Captain Drummond, the Cobra section leader. He's coming up on our VHF frequency, and he's loaded for bear with air-to-ground and air-to-air. His call sign is 'Snake Two-One.' He wants you to try to raise him, over."

Blackman keyed the headset. "Snake Two-One, this is Control, over."

There was a momentary delay for the electronic handshake and then a voice with a heavy Southern drawl came through the earpiece. "Go ahead, Control, what can the U.S. Marines do for you boys?"

Blackman's heart was pounding. The request he was about to make exceeded his authority, but time was running out.

"Our POWs aren't going to make it to the border. The Iraqis are hunting them on the ground and in the air with two MIG-25s about twenty kilometers east of here. Can you escort one CH-53 with some of our Royal Marines and go pick them up?"

"Let me check. Stand by."

Blackman looked up at his two superiors who said nothing. A minute went by, then another. Then he heard the *ping* as the helicopter pilot came back on the air.

"We're good to go," Drummond said. "But one change, we're going in with both CH-53s just in case we lose one—that way we can still pick people up. We're loading up fifteen of your Royal Marines to take with us just in case things get dicey on the ground, if you know what I mean. We'll be out of here in about five."

No one in the room said a word. Below them to the west, they could hear shouted orders as the Royal Marine NCOs and officers saddled up the men of Four-Two Commando. Then there was the whine of the big CH-53s starting up. Captain Drummond's voice came over the radio. "Give me the best you've got on where everybody is so we can plug it all into our GPS and weapons systems."

Blackman gave him the most recent coordinates for the truck and the track of the Iraqi MIGs.

"Roger that," Drummond said. "We're locked and loaded."

The roof of the building shook as the four helicopters took off directly over them, headed east with their lights off.

The three men in the control shack were surrounded by a sudden eerie silence, except for the quiet hum of computers and the intermittent static of the radios. They stared at their screens . . . and prayed.

✪

As they crossed the border into Iraq, the helicopters were at fifty feet and 120 knots with Captain Drummond's Cobra in the lead, followed by a CH-53 carrying eight Royal Marine commandos. Further behind and to the left was the second Cobra, followed by the other 53, also carrying eight Royal Marines. Their track took them north of the Iraqi border post at Judaiat al Hamir, but the sound of their rotors carried across the desert, sending the guards rushing out of their barracks and into a nearby bunker, fearing that they were under attack.

Four minutes later, heading due east to the last reported position for the truck, Captain Drummond's weapons systems operator, sitting in front of him in the cramped cockpit, came up on the intercom, "Bogey . . . ten o'clock. Eight miles. Fast mover. Headed our way. Sidewinders going hot."

Drummond was scanning the sand in front of him through his night-vision goggles, concentrating on avoiding flying his aircraft into the ground as he traversed the terrain at just above rooftop height.

"Roger that," he said. "I'm looking for the truck. Let the bogey alone as long as he leaves us alone. But if he messes with us, fry him."

✪

Back in the MI6 harbor site, Wardell, Thomas, and Blackman watched the icons converging on the laptop screen. It was like a surreal video game. In the center, the blinking blue square that was the truckload of POWs was slowly making its way west up the Wadi Hamir—so near, yet so far from the Saudi border. To the east, moving fast, two red blips—the Iraqi MIG-25s—were searching for any vehicles violating the curfew. And finally, on the left side of the computer screen, were four green icons—the two CH-53s and their Cobra escorts, trying to get to the truck before the Iraqis.

4,000 Ft. Altitude
12 km SW of An Nukhayb, Iraq
Sunday, 22 March 1998
2035 Hours, Local

Major Abib Al Hillal was flying the lead MIG-25 Foxbat in a low-level search pattern parallel to the highway. While looking for the truck, the Iraqi fighter pilots were taking a gamble by flying along the edge of the no-fly zone. The pilots had been briefed that the vehicle was to be found at all costs, and if a ground unit could not get to it, the vehicle and the criminals who had stolen it were to be destroyed.

Major Al Hillal thought this mission was a terrible waste of scarce flight hours, but it was better than no flying at all—something altogether too common in the Iraqi Air Force these days. From fifteen hundred feet, at 250 knots, he was having a hard time seeing the ground below, especially since the night-vision equipment he was using was of an old Soviet design and poorly maintained. He noticed a few parked trucks here and there alongside the highway, and he called in with their positions for ground units to check them out.

This was turning into a rather boring mission, although he didn't dare say that over the radio to his wingman. One never knew who else was listening these days.

His wingman, in a second MIG-25 was three kilometers off his port wing as the planes flew south by southwest along the Tubal riverbed.

Ironically, Major Al Hillal felt at a disadvantage chasing a truck with a supersonic jet. It was all but impossible to determine if it was the truck carrying the escapees from Habirah Prison. Nevertheless, his instructions were to stop *any* truck that fit that description, by any means at his disposal, if it could not be stopped by the ground units.

In just a matter of minutes, the MIGs were approaching the Iraq-Saudi Arabia border. Al Hillal had no wish to be pounced on by some U.S. or British jet vectored down on them by an invisible AWACS plane somewhere over central Saudi Arabia. They each banked and turned to retrace their paths, only this time at a slightly lower altitude. As his fighter jet leveled off and returned, flying in a northeasterly direction, Major Al Hillal's attention was captured by a movement almost directly below him. He put his MIG into a sharp angle, nose up, to brake the jet. He banked into a right turn to get another look. Then the moon broke through the clouds, and he saw what had caught his attention. He almost choked in his oxygen mask. There, almost directly below him, were four sets of rotor blades—headed into his country.

He waggled his wings to catch his wingman's attention. It did no good. He thought of engaging alone, but remembered he had been told to get permission before firing. Uncertain about what to do, he decided to play it safe and call for permission to engage. It was a fatal mistake.

✪

When Major Al Hillal toggled the radio switch on his stick, the transmission was immediately monitored by the RF sensors aboard the invisible satellite in geosynchronous orbit miles above him. In less than a second, the transmission was displayed on the screen in front of Blackman. The MI6 officer immediately reached for his radio handset.

"Snake-two-one. Be advised, an Iraqi MIG-25, closing on your six, has just transmitted on a command frequency. He may have spotted you. He's probably above you."

✪

Captain Drummond keyed his mike.

"Roger."

He cranked on full military power, pulled the collective in his left hand all the way to its stop and, with his right hand, he pulled the stick between his feet as far back as it would go.

"Engaging Bogey. My Six. High! Scatter!"

As the nose of Drummond's Cobra came screaming up, the other three helicopters darted right, left, and down even lower. Now, almost inverted, Snake Two-One was searching the sky above him for the MIG. An instant later, the heat sensors mounted on the sides of the Cobra in the Sidewinders began to screech and Drummond's weapons systems operator, Lieutenant Dave Allen, said, "Missile away."

Drummond ducked his head so that the flash of the missile's rocket motor wouldn't flare in his night-vision goggles. Immediately after the missile fired, he rolled the helicopter to the right and down, picking up airspeed and heading for a hill just to the southeast.

Behind him, the Sidewinder, streaking at two-and-a-half times the speed of sound, found its mark in the fuselage of Major Al Hillal's wingman. An instant after the missile warhead's detonation, shards of steel ripped into the big jet's turbine—breaking blades that instantly cut fuel lines. There was a sudden orange fireball, four thousand feet above the Iraqi desert.

★

As his wingman's MIG burst into a fireball, Major Al Hillal broke off his attack and dove for the ground, heading away to the northeast while he called over and over again into his radio that he and his flight had been ambushed by enemy jet fighters.

Meanwhile on the ground, an Iraqi Republican Guard contingent raced for their trucks and pulled onto the highway. They had been delayed for the night, just west of An Nukhayb. Unaware of the helicopters, the Iraqis were convinced that one of their own surface-to-air missiles had brought down a U.S. or British aircraft.

Within minutes, the Republican Guard unit arrived at a point several kilometers from the burning aircraft. The officer in charge ordered one of the trucks to remain on the highway while the other three left the road and raced across the desert floor toward the flaming wreckage.

It took another eight minutes for the three trucks to get to the site. The ruined hulk of the MIG was still too hot to approach, but within a few seconds one of the NCOs came running up to his commander, carrying a logbook that had spilled from the wrecked aircraft. On it were the markings of the Iraqi Air Force. The stunned officer immediately got on the radio to report what Baghdad already suspected—the downed aircraft was one of theirs. Three minutes later, Air Force Command in Baghdad ordered a general alert and launched four more MIGs: two from Markab and two more from Tikrit South.

Wadi Hamir

N of Judaiat al Hamir, Iraq
Sunday, 22 March 1998
2100 Hours, Local

The four British prisoners, their former jailer, and their reluctant driver had watched the whole fireworks display from the lip of the *wadi*, just two kilometers from where the Iraqi MIG crashed into the sand. When the MIGs flew over them on their initial pass, headed from east to west, the warden and the four POWs had jumped from the truck and run for cover, expecting to be strafed. The Iraqi driver, afraid for his life, stayed inside the truck. His commandant had taken the guard's weapon as a precaution.

Now, with the burning wreckage off to their north and Republican Guard trucks on the highway not far from them, the escapees didn't know what to do. The commandant estimated that they were still a good ten kilometers from the border. They were debating whether to try to take the truck further up the *wadi* toward the Saudi border or, in their weakened state, to try walking—when they heard the sound of helicopters.

A look of terror came across the commandant's face, and he turned to Macklin, the former prisoner who was nearest to him, as they hunkered down on the lip of the dry riverbed. Below them was the truck, the petrified driver still in the cab. With a trembling hand, the warden handed Macklin his pistol and said in broken English, "Shoot me. If they strafe us with the HINDs, we will all die anyway; but if they take me prisoner, I will be tortured until I die. Please shoot me now."

Macklin was still looking at the terrified man when the first helicopter came flashing overhead, flared, and landed about twenty feet away in a roaring cloud of dust. He peered up over the lip to see, not an Iraqi HIND but a CH-53E, its lights off and armed men rushing out of its tail ramp.

The first rifleman, wearing night-vision goggles, ran directly to Macklin and kicked the gun out of his hand, grabbed him by the shirt, and started dragging him toward the helicopter. As Macklin stumbled in the man's grasp, he could see two smaller helicopters firing their miniguns and rockets toward the road where the Republican Guard unit was positioned.

Before one of the British commandos could grab him and drag him off to the helicopter, the commandant scrambled back down into the *wadi* and ran up to the driver's side of the truck. He looked up at the guard still sitting behind the wheel. "Are you sure you do not want to come with us?"

"I—I cannot. I need to go back, sir."

"All right. You can go now. Just keep your lights off or you will attract the attention of those MIGs."

The guard wasted no time. The MIGs might be getting ready to bomb this area even now, and he wanted to be as far away from this place as possible. He spun the truck around and accelerated across the sandy desert floor back toward the highway.

The commandant watched him go, then hurried to join the others as they struggled up the loose rocky soil of the embankment to the waiting helicopter, the commandos helping them as best they could.

A few moments after all four of the ex-prisoners and their former warden were aboard, the Royal Marine sergeant in charge of the commandos came running up the tail ramp and shouted at Macklin, "There are supposed to be two more; where are they?"

Captain Macklin, trying to make himself heard over the din of the engines and the whirling rotors yelled, "They didn't make it."

"What do you mean?" shouted the Sergeant.

"They aren't here," Macklin bellowed. "The Americans weren't released."

The Royal Marine flipped up his night-vision goggles and yelled, "Which one of you is the warden?"

The defector raised his hand, and the sergeant yelled in his ear, "Where are the two Americans we're supposed to bring out with us?"

"It could not be helped. They were taken off the truck before we left Salman Pak."

"Why?" The commando was obviously angry but gave the signal to lift off anyway.

A cloud of dust enveloped the big helicopter as it clawed its way into the night sky. Once it was fifty feet in the air, the pilot tipped the nose forward, and a cold wind rushed through the cargo bay as the chopper gained speed, heading southwest toward the Saudi border.

Once he was satisfied all his men were all OK, the sergeant came back to the Iraqi defector and repeated the question again, shouting in his ear. "Why?"

The man looked perfectly miserable. Tears came to his eyes as he said, "I do not know. I tried to bring them with us but was prevented." He shook his head and stared at the floor. *"In sha' Allah."*

PLANNING FOR WAR

CHAPTER SEVENTEEN

International Scientific Trading, Ltd.
At Tanf, Syria
Monday, 23 March 1998
0235 Hours, Local

The small sign on the front of the big warehouse read "IST, Ltd. Logistics Center" and listed a Damascus phone number. In 1983, when Leonid Dotensk urged the KGB to purchase the facility from a French petrochemical company, Komulakov had objected.

"We have nice offices and *Rezidenturas* at embassies in all the capitals. Why would we need a bunch of buildings stuck on a lava bed in the middle of a desert, so far from our clients?"

But Dotensk persisted, claiming the KGB needed a place that was easily accessible, yet away from inquisitive eyes and nattering tongues. This warehouse complex beside the Baghdad-Damascus highway—

225 kilometers east of Damascus, and about twice that distance west of Baghdad—filled the bill. And the Ukrainian's foresight had been confirmed; even the 7,000-foot runway adjoining the facility had proven invaluable.

Over the years, the three buildings in the walled and gated compound had been used as a refuge for a veritable "Who's Who" of international terror. George Habash, founder of the PFLP/GC, found sanctuary here. Abu Nidal was a guest while arrangements were being made for his move to Baghdad after he fell out of favor with Hafez al Assad. And Abul Abbas, the mastermind of the *Achille Lauro* hijacking, had hidden here after the Italians helped him slip away from the Americans in 1985. Dotensk had personally arranged for a chartered Lear jet to fly the PLO terrorist here from Yugoslavia, before sending him on to Baghdad.

Prior to the collapse of the Soviet Union, the site was routinely used for schooling new KGB and GRU intelligence operatives; training PFLP/GC terrorist recruits; storing weapons, ammunition, explosives, and equipment; and for harboring KGB officers in transit throughout the Middle East. Even today, it is still part of an underground railroad for moving Hezbollah and Islamic Jihad actives between Tehran and Lebanon's Bekaa Valley.

But all of this paled in comparison to the use Dotensk now had for the warehouse complex. When the Ukrainian arms merchant and his four associates arrived in their two-vehicle convoy at the gate, it was already the middle of the night. It had taken them nearly two hours to get through the double checkpoints at the Iraq/Syria border crossings, and it had cost the Ukrainian almost twenty-five thousand dollars in bribes, but Dotensk knew it was worth every penny.

General Komulakov had not yet arrived, for which Dotensk was also pleased. He wanted to see the expression on the face of his business partner when he showed him the three recovered nuclear weapons, still housed in artillery shell casings and stored in their original crates.

On the long drive from Baghdad, Dotensk had mused about keeping his newfound treasures all to himself. But that was only until he considered the logistics involved. In order to do that, he would have to get rid of the four men who helped him bring the weapons back. And he'd also have to eliminate the two people who helped him prepare the phony shipping documents for his trip from Iraq into Syria. Such a loss in personnel would be too difficult to explain, even though it meant hundreds of millions more Swiss francs. And then Dotensk considered the matter of what Komulakov would do to him if he ever learned about a double cross.

That's when Dotensk decided he could be content with his share of the gains. After all, Komulakov still had six more nuclear weapons and could probably get his hands on more, so there was still plenty of opportunity to get obscenely rich. But one thing was certain: this time Dotensk would lay claim to a fatter commission than when the weapons were originally sold to Saddam. He wanted 50 percent, but he wasn't sure he could push the general that hard. Still, he was certain Komulakov would agree to a 40 percent share for his efforts.

The Ukrainian was tired and, as the other men went off to their wing of the compound, Dotensk went toward his own living quarters. As he passed one of his men sitting in a chair outside one of the bedrooms, he stopped briefly to chat.

"How are the prisoners?"

The man shrugged. "No problems. They were troublesome at first, but when it became apparent they were not going to be rescued, they seem to have grown despondent and quiet. They are no trouble."

"Good. Perhaps the general will have new information when he comes later today. Has he called to say what time he is arriving?"

"I think he is expected about noon."

"When do you go off duty?"

"At seven in the morning."

"Then knock on my door and wake me when you go off duty. I have some things to do before the general comes."

Visiting VIP Quarters
Incirlik Air Base, Adana, Turkey
Monday, 23 March 1998
0010 Hours, Local

General Grisham had just finished reading the afternoon dispatches from his headquarters at MacDill. His eyes were red-rimmed with fatigue, but when the STU-III secure telephone on his desk began its insistent, electronic chirp, he reached for it instantly.

"Sir, we have an incoming encrypted Iridium sat phone call from someone named Mr. Ram Fales," the base signal operator said. "He says it's important, sir. Shall I put it through?"

"Yes, I'll take it."

He waited a moment for the encryption system to synchronize. Once it did, anyone intercepting their telephone conversation would only hear the garbled electronic data streaming like the sound of a fax line. When Grisham heard the distinctive *ping*, he said, "Pete? Where are you?"

"I'm in Baghdad, Room 332 of the Al Rashid Ho—"

"Stop! Answer yes or no. Are you alone?"

"Yes."

"Are you on the balcony?"

"Yes."

"Close the door to your room."

"OK."

"Good," said Grisham. "That won't guarantee they can't pick up your end of this conversation and try to piece things together, but it'll make it harder."

"Yes, sir . . . you taught me well. I assume every room in Baghdad is bugged by the Amn Al-Khass or the Mukhabarat, or both," Newman said.

"Yes . . . well, I just want to make sure we don't get compromised on the little details. Don't ever say my name or rank when you call. Don't use anyone else's real name. Did you ask for me by name when you called the signal operator?"

"No. I asked for the boss like you told me before I left."

"All right. I'm sorry to have jumped on you. It's just that you're in one of the most dangerous places on earth for an American military man, and there's an awful lot riding on your mission. How was your trip in—any problems?"

"No problems. Just a long drive from Damascus with 'The Salesman,'" said Newman, using the agreed-upon cover name for Eli Yusef Habib. "He's gone to his daughter's house, but I have his phone number if I need him in a hurry. His son has gone to do some checking on where we might find our three customers."

"I understand. There's another piece of news that could affect your . . . uh . . . sales trip. I just got a cable from MacDill that a joint operation we've been planning with the Brits went down earlier tonight. The good news is that it succeeded . . . but the bad news is that it may result in even greater than normal scrutiny of foreigners in Iraq."

"What was it?"

"It was a prison break." Grisham was still reading the message with the bold heading: FLASH/TOP SECRET. "With a little help from one of our CENTCOM units on a 'training mission' in Saudi Arabia, the Brits rescued four of their POWs from an Iraqi prison at Salman Pak. We thought they were all airmen and that we were also going to get two Americans out with them. Unfortunately, we didn't get the Americans . . . but the good news is that the Brits say one of the POWs is an SAS captain named Macklin and that he was captured three years ago following your UN operation. Does the name ring a bell?"

There was a long silence on the line.

"Yes! He was one of my . . . my best, uh, programmers . . . and I'm glad to know he's still . . . uh . . . in the business. Please give him my congratulations on his promotion . . . and be sure to ask him if he can give me any . . . ah, advice about my sales territory."

"I understand, Pete, will do. I'll make sure each of the rescued POWs are asked. They're all resting right now, after a shower and hot meal. We'll start debriefing them in the morning in Riyadh. I've asked the Brits to hold off on any announcement about their rescue for at least forty-eight hours, to buy you some time. Once the news of POWs in Iraq becomes public, the regime will deny that they were ever there and claim it's some kind of British trick or publicity stunt, but they're also likely to clamp down even tighter on travel to keep the UN inspectors and the international press from poking around."

"Well, thank you for the update. I don't guess there's anything new . . . on the home front?"

"I'm sorry, Pete. Nothing new on Rachel, but be assured we're still doing all we can."

"I have to believe that you are—otherwise I wouldn't be able to . . . I have some interesting news for the home office."

"Yeah, go ahead," said Grisham.

"You know the gentleman I was working with whose wife has the same problem as mine?"

"Yes."

"Well, he called me on the other sat phone a few minutes ago, the one his marketing organization gave me. He asked me if I was enjoying my stay at the Al Rashid Hotel . . . and told me he knew the three customers I'm here to see."

Grisham was silent for a moment. "I'm not surprised that they know where you are. We should have removed their tracking device from your foot before sending you in. What bothers me, though, is that the Israelis have knowledge of your mission. Did he refer specifically to the nukes?"

"Yes. In an oblique way, of course."

"Had you ever mentioned anything about the nukes to Rotem or anyone else in his unit while the two of you were looking for your wives?"

"No. But now he's telling me to forget about my business here and to come home early. It sounded like a warning."

"Then we have a leak. It may be at MacDill—but I doubt it—it's more likely here in Turkey. And what's worse, if Rotem knows, that means the Israelis are also looking for the nukes."

"Why is that a problem?"

"Because loose nukes would make the Israelis nervous. And unless the weapons are found and disabled very soon, they're more likely to act preemptively on their own. They can't afford to take the chance that Saddam, Hezbollah, Al-Qaida or someone else gets their hands on these things first. Israel has made it known—at least to the United States— that they have a 'first strike' plan they'll use if they believe their country is threatened with imminent attack by a weapon of mass destruction—particularly if it's nuclear. Rotem's comments to you suggest the Israelis may be planning a nuclear strike on Iraq."

"Oh, man—" There was a long pause. "Any idea how much time we have?"

"No. Has Eli Yusef or Samir been able to make contact with the people there that they believe could be helpful to you?"

"Not yet. We're supposed to meet tomorrow. Let's hope the meeting is successful and that I can be introduced to our three customers."

"I'm going to pray that Eli Yusef and Samir come up with something quickly because now I'm going to have to inform Washington."

"Why? You told me we couldn't trust the people there."

"We can't. And I don't want to. But I have no choice. My duty requires me to warn the Pentagon that the Israelis may be preparing for a nuclear attack on Iraq."

The Knesset
Jerusalem, Israel
Monday, 23 March 1998
0045 Hours, Local

It had been a particularly contentious meeting of the War Cabinet, and the Prime Minister was still in his office when the red phone on the credenza behind his desk began to ring. He looked at the clock on the wall labeled "Washington," noted that it read 1745, and picked up the handset of the telephone that connected the Israeli Head of State to the

top echelons of the U.S. government. The secure phone system had
been installed after the 1967 Six-Day War at the request of Lyndon
Johnson and had been upgraded every few years since then. Unlike the
hot line between Moscow and Washington, this phone system had several extensions and was used routinely by senior officials in both governments as a shortcut for issues deemed too sensitive for their respective embassies. As he put the receiver to his ear, the operator said, "Sir,
it is the American Secretary of State for you."

*I wonder what brings the Secretary of State to work on a Sunday in
Washington,* he thought.

"Madam Secretary . . . to what do I owe the honor of your call?"

"I hope I didn't wake you, Mr. Prime Minister, but I'm calling
because of a grave matter that has just come to my attention."

"Oh?"

"Mr. Prime Minister, I am deeply concerned that Israel may be
planning a preemptive nuclear strike against Iraq because of some mis-
guided belief that Iraq has somehow obtained nuclear weapons. The
President has asked me to call you and to tell you that this is totally
unacceptable to the United States and such an action risks all-out war
in the Middle East. You must make certain that such an act does not
take place."

If the Prime Minister was shocked to hear the topic of his late-night
meeting with his closest advisors as the subject of a call from the
American Secretary of State, his voice didn't betray his concern.

"Madam Secretary . . . the United States is welcome to communicate
its concerns to Israel, and you know we always listen. But you also know
that ultimately *we* are the ones who must live with any serious decisions
affecting our national security. Please convey my appreciation to the

President, but tell him that Israel stands by its policies of self-defense, and that we will do everything necessary to prevent an attack upon Israel's sovereignty and its people, *especially* regarding weapons of mass destruction by a nation that has publicly called for our annihilation."

"But Mr. Prime Minister, we are only asking for restraint. We have no evidence that Iraq has such weapons. And even if they do, I am certain that the United Nations can address this matter before it gets completely out of hand."

"Madam Secretary, forgive my candor, but the UN is part of the problem, not the solution. They are letting this madman thumb his nose both at them and at the United States. Saddam has been given ultimatum after ultimatum, and he ignores them all. If the United Nations and the United States want to prevent, as you say, 'all-out war in the Middle East,' then I suggest you ask the President to do something *immediately* about Iraq's recklessness and its drive to acquire and use weapons of mass destruction. So far, I don't think the President has shown much thoughtful or forceful leadership in that direction."

The former IDF paratrooper-turned-politician took a breath and softened his voice a little.

"Look . . . the White House did nothing when the Iraqis invaded the northern provinces in '95. It just stood by and let Saddam destroy the Kurds and the INC opposition. This past year alone, Saddam has executed more than fifteen thousand political prisoners, and we didn't hear any UN human rights protests over *that*. Think of it! He killed *fifteen thousand people*, thousands tortured before they were killed. And when their relatives were called in to claim the bodies, Saddam made *them pay* for the bullets used to kill their loved ones before the bodies would be released.

"In the three years since the invasion of the north, the White House has done virtually nothing to stop Saddam from building weapons of mass destruction. Saddam has made a joke of the UN weapons inspectors. Contrary to the UN resolutions and the terms of the Gulf War cease-fire agreement, Saddam has gotten away with whatever he wants.

"I suggest that, if the White House really wanted to prevent all-out war in the Middle East, then you should talk to whomever it was that told you about *our* supposed plans. Ask them *who* is going to stop Saddam from launching nuclear and biological or chemical weapons on Israel if we don't. Ask them what *they* are doing to stop Saddam. I predict you will come up with the same answers that I have—that no one else is willing to take the measures that we're willing to take.

"Madam Secretary, Israel was asked to show restraint during the Gulf War. When Scud missiles fell in our cities and villages, we did not respond in kind—because the United States asked us to show restraint. Lives were lost. Israelis died in those attacks . . . still we did not retaliate. We have waited seven years, Madam Secretary, for the United States to come up with a satisfactory plan to bring stability and peace to the Middle East by doing away with all of Iraq's WMD programs, and getting rid of Saddam. Yet now, when we're in imminent danger of a nuclear attack, you call on us once again to show restraint?"

The United States Secretary of State stammered something about having to consider what effect Israel's actions would have on the entire region, but she offered no alternatives to the Prime Minister's points. "B-but such things take time," was all she managed to say.

"Madam Secretary, we are patient people. We understand that things take time. But we are running out of time because of the inaction of those we call our allies.

"I understand that the United States CENTCOM is trying to locate the nuclear weapons that Saddam acquired several years ago. Such an effort is commendable, but it should have been done long ago. If your military succeeds in finding the nuclear weapons and removes the threat in the next seventy-two hours, Israel will have no need to act in self-defense. Quite frankly, Madam Secretary, our people don't believe the CENTCOM efforts have much hope of success at such a late hour—and we cannot give the White House the luxury of doing nothing. We must, and will, take action."

There was a pause on the line. Did the Secretary not know of CENTCOM's mission?

"Aren't you thinking of the CIA when you mention efforts to locate nuclear weapons in Iraq?" she asked.

"I am told your CIA's efforts have been totally unsuccessful, and that is why your military is now involved."

"CENTCOM? You heard it was CENTCOM?"

"Yes. We have our ears to the ground in many places because for us it is a matter of survival. We are few, and our enemies are many, and all around."

Another long silence. "Well, I'll pass this on to the President. He may want to call you himself. Thank you for your time."

The Prime Minister hung up the phone and buzzed his aide.

"Please ask Security to bring my car. I want to go home."

He stood and walked over to the large window overlooking Eli'Ezer Kaplan Street and stared off in the distance toward the western suburbs of Jerusalem. The city was quiet, most of its population already asleep. He was grateful the City of David was peaceful tonight. He had made a promise to God that he would do everything in his power to protect

Israel. And he knew the sleeping citizens of Jerusalem were expecting him to do exactly that.

The State Department
Washington, D.C.
Sunday, 22 March 1998
1805 Hours, Local

The Secretary of State sat and thought for a few minutes about what she had just heard. Then she turned to her secure notebook computer and drafted a terse message.

TOP SECRET/FLASH
EYES ONLY FOR: THE PRESIDENT
                       THE SECRETARY OF DEFENSE
                       DIR OF CENTRAL INTELLIGENCE
SUBJECT: ISRAELI MILITARY PLANS

    THE PRIME MINISTER OF ISRAEL INFORMED ME AT 6 P.M.
EST THAT U.S. CENTRAL COMMAND HAS AN EFFORT UNDER-
WAY TO LOCATE AND RECOVER NUCLEAR WEAPONS IN IRAQ.
HE INTIMATED THAT IF THE EFFORT DOES NOT SUCCEED IN 72
HOURS, ISRAEL IS PREPARED TO LAUNCH A PREEMPTIVE
NUCLEAR ATTACK ON IRAQ.

She didn't bother to suggest what U.S. government actions needed to be taken, nor did she include copies to the Vice President or the Chairman of the Joint Chiefs of Staff. After reviewing the text, she simply sent it via a secure e-mail link to the State Department's message center, just down the hall from her office, where it would be distributed.

She was still fuming over the embarrassment of learning about an incredibly sensitive U.S. operation being carried out in the Middle East—from the Prime Minister of Israel, no less! *Most powerful nation on earth, and I have to sit still for a dressing-down by the Israeli PM.* She clicked the Logoff button on her screen and closed the notebook computer, then shoved it hastily into her briefcase.

It was shaping up to be a hectic week. She walked out of her office complex toward the elevator that would take her downstairs to the security desk, where her driver and security detail were waiting.

But as she got to the elevator, she began to have misgivings about the message she had drafted.

Before that message is distributed, I'd better check to make sure that business about CENTCOM is true.

She returned down the hall to her office suite. Depositing her briefcase on the desk in the reception area, she went into her inner office. When she got to her desk, she picked up the phone and called the Communications Center. The duty officer answered on the fifth ring.

"What took so long?"

"Sorry, ma'am. We're trying to locate the Sec Def and the DCI so we can send out that Flash/Eyes Only cable you sent us."

"Have you sent it out yet?"

"No, ma'am."

"Good, hold it. Don't send it until I tell you to." She hung up and picked up the red phone that connected her directly to the White House signal operator.

"Connect me to the Commander in Chief of CENTCOM."

"Yes, ma'am. Wait one."

Several minutes passed.

"Ma'am, the Command Center at MacDill informs me General Grisham is out of the country and is not expected back for three or four days."

"Then track him down and get him on the line for me."

"Ma'am, he's in Incirlik, Turkey . . . there's a seven-hour time difference . . . it's after midnight there. Do you still want to call?"

"Yes. And hurry up."

Finally, the call went through.

"Hello . . . General George Grisham speaking. What can I do for you, Madam Secretary?"

"General, I just concluded a telephone call with the Prime Minister of Israel. He informed me that the United States Central Command has some kind of covert operation underway in Iraq, looking for nuclear bombs."

She waited.

"Did the Prime Minister say where he got that information, ma'am?"

"No. I expect he got it from Mossad. Is it true?"

"What's true, ma'am, is that I have CENTCOM military personnel operating over, around, and inside Iraq every day. And nearly every day some of my pilots get shot at in the skies over Iraq."

"So, General," she said angrily, "exactly how many military personnel do you have on the ground in Iraq at this minute?"

There was a long pause, and then Grisham replied, "One. His name is Newman. He's a Marine officer."

"A Marine officer named Newman? Did this plan originate in the White House or the Pentagon?"

"Neither. It originated with me, as part of the authority given me as Commander in Chief of CENTCOM operations in the Middle East.

It's a military operation within my purview of operations. It is highly classified, and lives are at risk."

"Who else knows about it?"

"Respectfully—why do you ask, ma'am?"

"If you're running a secret operation in Iraq, you've crossed the line, General. You are now into areas of international diplomacy. You had no right to take this on without White House or Pentagon approval. From what I gather, you haven't informed either office—is that true?"

"Madam Secretary, the reason why this operation is so closely held is that—"

"I don't *care* about the reasons. Listen to me, General . . . the decision to put Americans on the ground in a hostile country should only be made with the knowledge of the President, with input from the State Department, and with notice given to the United Nations. I want you to stop your meddling—right now! Get your men out of Iraq and stay out of the way. Israel is making my life miserable as it is. I don't need our own military to add to my troubles. Do you understand?"

There was a long pause.

"Madam Secretary, I want you to understand something. I am neither usurping your responsibilities nor encroaching in areas of diplomacy."

The general's voice was calm and quiet. It put the Secretary even more on guard.

"God knows I have plenty to do with my own job description. However, if I may speak freely, you're overstepping *your* authority. I am conducting *military* operations here . . . not diplomatic missions. I am charged with making sure that conflicts between the nations of the Middle East don't escalate and get worse on my watch. To that end, I sent out a *flash* message less than an hour ago, notifying my government that Israel may be planning a preemptive nuclear strike on Iraq. It is my belief that if I can find the weapons that Israel is justifiably concerned about, we may just be able to prevent such an attack. I believe this to be within the scope of my duties and responsibilities. Now, if you disagree, Madam Secretary, I suggest that you take the matter up with the Commander in Chief and the Secretary of Defense. That's my chain of command. If either of them wishes to modify my assigned duties, I will, of course, obey those orders. In the meantime, Madame Secretary, the Iraqi mission stays on track."

The Secretary slammed the phone down. She got up from her desk, grabbed her coat and purse, and strode out of her office.

As she exited the inner office, she almost collided with a man she didn't recognize—and he was holding *her* briefcase.

"Who are you? What are you doing on this floor? And what are you doing with my briefcase?"

The man smiled warmly and extended his hand. "Good afternoon, Madam Secretary. My name is Bob Hallstrom, FBI, and I work here in the building too. My office is on the second floor. On weekends, whenever I'm in, I make a security check of the various floors. I get off the elevator and look around on each floor, you know? Well, I got off on this floor and saw the door of your suite open, and this briefcase on the front desk, in full view of the hallway. Since I noticed your initials by the handle and I thought it might have some important documents in it, I was on my way to call the security desk in the lobby and have them lock it up. I thought you might have accidentally left it here when you departed for the weekend on Friday. Sorry for startling you."

The Secretary of State looked at the man's identity badge. His name and *"FBI"* were prominently displayed on it, along with his photograph.

"I wouldn't want just anyone finding your briefcase and pawing through your private papers," Hallstrom said, handing her the briefcase.

The Secretary gave an inward grimace. She had carelessly left valuable classified documents and a notebook computer containing top secret data in view of the hallway, where it could easily have fallen into the wrong hands.

"Thank you . . . Mr. Hallstrom." She put the case under her arm and headed for the elevator.

"No problem, ma'am. Enjoy the rest of your Sunday."

✪

When the elevator doors closed behind her, Hallstrom reached into the drawer on the table where the briefcase had been left. He removed the ten pages of material he had photocopied from documents in her briefcase, pages that he had run off on the nearby copier while she was in her office on the telephone. Then, after looking both ways down the hallway, he reached into the drawer again and retrieved the two 3.5-inch computer disks onto which he had downloaded files from her notebook computer.

The Secretary of State had been in a hurry, Hallstrom guessed—too big of a hurry to finish shutting down her computer. When the Shutdown box had come up on the screen in the closed computer and gotten no password-protected command to completely power off the device, the screen had simply reverted to the most recently opened window—the e-mail message to the President, sent via the State Department's message center.

It wasn't the first time he'd gleaned sensitive data from an unguarded computer. He'd even begun carrying blank disks with him on his weekend "security" tours of the building, against just such a possibility. He put the disks into his trousers pockets, folded the papers, and slipped them into his inside coat pocket. Then the spy walked over to the elevator.

In his office for the next hour, FBI Special Agent Robert Hallstrom busied himself with reading the purloined material. When he had finished, he carefully wrapped the documents around the two disks containing the downloaded files from the Secretary's computer and placed them inside a plastic bag. Then, he turned to his computer and began typing.

"Dear General Komulakov . . ."

Armenian Church Grounds
Port Said Street
Baghdad, Iraq
Monday, 23 March 1998
0730 Hours, Local

A note was shoved under Peter Newman's door at the Al Rashid at about 0300. Newman knew the time because he heard several hard raps on the door and he had looked at his watch when he sprang out of bed. But when he got to the door, there was no one there—only the scrap of paper on the floor by his feet, with the words, written in block letters in English, "Meet me at the Armenian Church on Port Said Street in the morning, as soon as possible after the curfew is lifted."

Newman might have dismissed the note as a trap or a setup, except that at the end of the note, instead of a signature, he recognized the twin overlapping curves of the symbolic emblem carried by Bill Goode, George Grisham, Eli Yusef, and Samir Habib—the same one that was on the door of the hospice in Jerusalem—the simple outline of a fish.

He left his hotel as soon as it was light and legal, and walked up Sa'adon Street, then north a few blocks past Tahrir Square. As he walked, he noticed that despite the stories he had read about the hardship and starvation caused by the UN embargo, the people he saw on the street seemed reasonably well off and appeared to be making their way to their places of work, albeit with relatively few cars.

He occasionally stopped at a stall or a storefront to check for anyone following him, but he concluded that either there were dozens on the surveillance detail or none; he could find no trace of a tail.

He crossed Port Said Street and walked east to Al Khifah Street, where he turned and continued walking toward the Al Gailiani Mosque. When he came to the mosque, he turned and walked parallel on the walkway alongside the huge building for a block, until he got to Nidhal Street; then he doubled back in the direction he had come. Quite certain by now that no one was following, he continued down Nidhal Street, back across Port Said Street, until he came to the Armenian Church.

In the churchyard, Newman waited for several minutes under a huge shade tree on the corner, keeping well inside the shadows. Then, checking his watch, he strode along the old stone path toward the back of the church grounds, where there was a small courtyard. He waited for another moment, then walked over to a bench near the ancient cemetery. He sat down to wait.

Less than five minutes later, Newman saw another figure approach from the direction he had just come. The slightly built man, dressed in dark slacks, a black cotton shirt with an open collar, and a dark brown suit coat that didn't match his trousers, looked around almost furtively. He saw Newman, walked over to the bench, and sat down. Newman guessed from his face that the man was in his late thirties, but his gait was that of a man much older.

"How do you do?" the man said in perfect, Arabic-accented English. "My name is Dizha. My friend Samir said you are looking for a guide." At this the young man held up something in the palm of his hand—a tiny metal fish, little more than an inch long.

Newman relaxed, smiled, pointed at the tiny emblem, and said, "He is my guide too." He then held out his hand. "My name is Ram Fales."

Dizha continued to look about the churchyard as he spoke. "Samir told me what you are looking for. I have made some inquiries among my friends who carry the sign of the fish, and I am afraid that what you are seeking is no longer here."

"No longer here? How do you know?"

"Mr. Fales," Dizha began, "you must understand, my information is credible. I am not entirely what I appear. I may be a poor, humbled man today, but until 1994 I held an important position . . . a Ph.D. and assistant to Dr. Khidir Hamza . . . the man in charge of our atomic energy program. I worked at the Tarmiya magnetic enrichment plant, and I was one of his engineers at the Al-Atheer facility when he defected. Because I was close to Dr. Hamza, I was imprisoned on suspicion of having helped him escape; but by the grace of God, I was not killed with the others. Still, since I got out of prison, I am only allowed to work as a laborer on highway projects."

"Not many are lucky enough to get out of prison alive. Were you tortured in prison?"

"Yes . . . many times . . . nearly every week. Some days I used to pray that God would let me die." And then he added with a wry smile, looking directly at Newman, "Isn't it good that we have a merciful God who knows better than we how to answer our prayers?"

Newman nodded. Dizha continued in a voice just above a whisper.

"It is my understanding from the inquiries I made at Samir's request that, much to my surprise, there really must have been three nuclear devices hidden here. I had heard rumors about it ever since Hussein Kamil had defected, but I thought that if Iraq had acquired them, the government would have probably used them by now. Strangely, just a week ago—after I had dismissed the rumors as false—one of my former colleagues at Atomic Energy told me about Saddam's son, Qusay, searching all over the country for three nuclear artillery rounds that Kamil had purchased from the Russians."

"The Russians? Are you sure?"

"Well, I cannot be positive, because I did not see them. But from what I know of Soviet nuclear weapon design, it sounds right. That also fits with another story I learned from a fellow believer who works with me at the Department of Highways. My friend is in Division Three, the place where they keep the records of who uses the highways, what vehicles go where, what trucks are carrying, and where they are going. It's supposed to help stop the black market. My friend says that a few days ago, a Ukrainian—well known here for acquiring materials and equipment banned by sanctions—arrived in Baghdad. Coincidently, he has offices in the same hotel where you are staying. According to my friend, the Ukrainian arrived with an empty truck, significant amounts of money, and four of his countrymen."

"Where are they now?"

"They are gone, and if my friends are correct, they took with them what you seek."

"Where did they go?"

"I am not sure, but my friend in Division Three told me he saw a routine report from two nights ago, from a police unit in Al Habbaniyah. The police inspected a truck transporting three large crates. Two men, carrying Ukrainian passports, were driving the vehicle. Three other Ukrainians were in a Mercedes sedan, accompanying the truck."

"And you guys get all that information just from your daily traffic reports? Amazing—but where could they have gone?"

"I do not know yet," said Dizha, getting up to leave. "But my supposition is the truck and its cargo are now back where they came from. If I am correct, I should know for certain this afternoon. But Mr. Fales, it is too dangerous for us to meet again. I will tell Samir when I find out for sure."

Newman rose as well; as the other started to depart, he put his hand out and said, "Thank you for all you have done, Dizha. You may have helped to prevent a terrible tragedy. I'll pray for you and your family— it's got to be tough to be a Christian here."

"Thank you. And I shall pray for you . . . and your wife. Samir told me about her."

"One last question: Dizha, if you were to make an educated guess, where do you think the weapons have been taken?"

The Iraqi looked Newman in the eye.

"Syria."

FREEFALL
TOWARD DISASTER

C H A P T E R   E I G H T E E N

International Scientific Trading, Ltd.
At Tanf, Syria
Monday, 23 March 1998
1115 Hours, Local

eneral Dimitri Komulakov's Lear 35 touched down on the east end of the runway precisely on time. He loved this fast little jet and the exquisite irony of having two Swiss pilots flying a "retired" Russian KGB officer in an American-made aircraft to this tiny spot in the Syrian desert. The plane taxied into the hangar with *IST Ltd.* printed above the door and began the shutdown routine. When the copilot finally opened the hatch in front of the left wing, Leonid Dotensk was standing there, wearing the biggest smile Komulakov had ever seen on the Ukrainian's face.

The two men shook hands, and Dotensk gave the former KGB officer a great bear hug that made the general wonder whether his friend had been drinking. The Ukrainian asked, "Did you have a good flight, General? I thought maybe you would bring your friend, Miss Sjogren. Are you rested, General?"

"Leonid, take a breath. What are you prattling on about? Why are you so excited?"

"Come with me. I have something to show you."

Komulakov resisted at first, then followed Dotensk to the large, adjoining building that housed the vehicles. Dotensk bounded up on the back of the truck and threw off the tarpaulin that covered the cargo that was still inside. He made a grand gesture and bowed.

"Do you recognize these?"

"No . . . should I?"

"My dear General . . . This truck contains our newest and sweetest fortune."

"Are you drunk, Leonid?"

"Yes! Yes! *Yes!*" Dotensk laughed. "I am drunk with success! These are the three nuclear weapons we sold to Hussein Kamil in '95. He had hidden them—buried them in a remote part of the Iraqi desert. And *I* have recovered them!"

"You're joking."

"No, General. I recalled a place Kamil took me—without his bodyguards, a place he assumed no one else knew. Anyway, I went there yesterday . . . found them . . . dug them up . . . and, here they are! Now I can sell them *back* to Saddam."

Komulakov smiled. "You never fail to surprise me, Leonid. I always seem to underestimate you. I'm sorry. You are to be congratulated."

"Oh, my dear General. I want more than your congratulations this time. I want a bigger commission for my sale. After all, without me, we could not be selling this shipment back to the Iraqis at a fat profit. You owe me that, General."

Komulakov smiled. "What do you think is fair?"

"Fifty percent."

"Thirty-three percent," Komulakov said, evenly. "It's a far better deal than I gave you the first time. Besides . . . greed only leads to other sins."

Dotensk blinked, and for a moment was silent.

"All right. Thirty-three it is."

Komulakov studied the Ukrainian's face carefully for a moment, then turned toward the offices and living quarters.

"Leonid, get on the phone with Saddam's second son and tell him we can deliver these right away. But be careful. Remember whom you're dealing with. They must not know you're selling them something they've already paid for."

"Don't worry, General. I'll take care of everything." Dotensk jumped down from the truck and followed Komulakov toward the offices.

Komulakov pointed toward the two-story barracks building next to their living quarters. "How are our two female guests?"

"Fine."

"I'm going to pay them a visit," said the general and ordered one of the pilots, "Have my bags put in my room."

As Komulakov entered the front door of the building, a large man in an unpressed khaki uniform rose from behind a desk.

"Show me where the women are kept," said Komulakov.

They walked up the stairs and down the hallway to a solid steel door, where another armed man was posted.

"Open the door for me, Vasili," Komulakov said.

The guard produced a key and unlocked the door. The general walked inside the room.

The two women, seated at a small, plain, wooden table, looked up, startled, from the books they were reading. Both of them stood and backed away from him, toward the rear wall.

Komulakov looked at the austere furnishings: two steel beds with thin mattresses and coarse woolen blankets, the small desk, two chairs, a single overhead light bulb, and one small, high window with bars on the outside. He nodded approvingly.

"Good morning, ladies. I trust your accommodations are suitable. Have they fed you yet today?"

Dyan shook her head, while Rachel gave no response.

"I'm sorry to hear that. I will see that you receive a hot meal within the hour."

"When are you going to let us go?" asked Rachel.

The Russian looked at the American woman. She was wearing the same black robes she had been given shortly after her capture, and she looked as if she hadn't bathed or brushed her hair in some time. Still . . .

"Mrs. Newman . . . come over here."

Rachel did not move.

"Please. I want to talk to you about your release. Please come over here."

Rachel inched toward him.

"While you are waiting for your meal, I will permit you both to use the bath. There are hot water, soap, shampoo, and towels. You may want to clean up before you eat. And I'll get you some clean clothes."

"Thank you," said Dyan quietly.

"When are you going to let us go?" Rachel said again. Her voice had even more edge this time.

"It shouldn't be long. Meanwhile, I'll try to make your stay as comfortable as possible," Komulakov said. "I'm sorry I can't permit you to telephone your husbands because they surely would try to trace the calls . . ." He stepped closer to Rachel. " . . . and that just wouldn't work, I'm afraid." The Russian reached out and stroked Rachel's face with the back of his hand.

She pulled back and glared at him. "What kind of man is such a coward that he has to kidnap a woman and take her from her baby just to blackmail her husband? You're really some piece of work, you snake!"

Komulakov laughed. "Now, now . . . I don't want to have to take away your bath privileges for such impertinence. But I will if you persist in such ill manners."

Rachel turned away angrily, shook her head, and looked back at Komulakov with a fierce, unflinching stare.

He laughed again and left the room, locking it behind him. He almost collided with Dotensk in the hallway.

"Excuse me, General . . . I wanted to make sure that you found the prisoners' situation satisfactory."

"Yes, well, Leonid, you've never had much sensitivity when it comes to women. I told them they could have a hot meal . . . and bath . . . and have a change of clothing on a regular basis. See to it."

"Yes, General. I will see to it right now."

Komulakov grabbed his arm. "Just a minute, Leonid. I thought of something else."

"Yes?"

"I was thinking, after you sell the weapons back to Saddam, you should contact some of our friends and spread the word that Saddam has the weapons. But make sure to tell them the weapons came from Chechnya. I want to stir things up in Moscow and keep Yeltsin busy. I want him putting out so many fires and answering so many questions from the international press and foreign diplomats that he doesn't have time to think about the presidential elections in 2000. In fact, we need an entire strategy to keep him occupied. We must find more ways to discredit Putin, since he's apparently Yeltsin's intended heir. See what you can come up with for our friends in Chechnya."

"Yes, General. So . . . your political plans are still on track?"

"Of course. Why wouldn't they be? I am the best candidate, after all."

Euphrates Café
Ar Ramadi, Iraq
Monday, 23 March 1998
1330 Hours, Local

Peter Newman and Samir Habib sat at a table in an outdoor café on the outskirts of Ar Ramadi, an hour's drive west of Baghdad. Newman had skipped breakfast; he was glad for the light lunch the waiter brought to their table.

That morning, Newman had felt as though his life was on fast-forward. After his early-morning meeting with Dizha, Newman had first called General Grisham. He conveyed to the general what the former scientist had said. He had then taken the phony briefcase, along with his bogus business cards, and called on two nearby Baghdad businesses, posing as Ram Fales, a Portuguese-Indian salesman for a complicated computer program. Both of the managers were completely baffled by his presentation and turned down his sales pitch, as did the supervisor at the small pipeline services firm across from the petrol station where Samir had refueled his diesel-powered pickup.

"Good thing I'm not a real salesman, Samir—I'd starve to death," he told his friend. "Oh, well . . . the sales calls corroborate my cover identity. I can give those guys' names if I get picked up for questioning."

He had been back in his room at the Al Rashid less than two hours when Samir called on the hotel phone. "Mr. Fales . . . this is your guide, Samir. I have just talked to the man you were with early this morning. He is certain he knows where your three customers are, but we must leave soon."

"Is it far?"

"Well, we should depart right away so we can get back before curfew tonight. I will pick you up at noon. I must first obtain a travel authorization."

Samir arrived at the front of the Al Rashid at 1200 hours in the pickup, and Newman got in, carrying only his briefcase and a dark blue windbreaker. As they pulled away from the front of the hotel, Samir said, "Good. You left your travel bag. That will lead anyone who is suspicious to believe you will be coming back. You have your passport?"

Newman nodded and smiled. "You're good, Samir. Anybody eavesdropping on your phone call would never suspect a thing."

Samir shrugged. "To stay alive, we have to be careful."

"Dizha contacted his friend in the Highway Department records office and another one in customs," Samir said as they drove. "They confirmed that a heavy truck, accompanied by a Mercedes and at least four Europeans, was on this road last night. The truck is one used routinely by a contraband smuggler named Leonid Dotensk.

"This man Dotensk often delivers equipment, chemicals, weapons, electronics, and the like to various government agencies in Baghdad. Dotensk very rarely takes anything *out* of Iraq. But this time he did. Three large cases—big enough and heavy enough that they also had a forklift in the truck to load and unload them."

"How do you know this, Samir?"

"My dear Peter—oh, excuse me—Ram." Samir grinned at his slip-up. "Our family is in the import/export business. We carry commercial goods across all these borders year-round. We get to know the border police, the customs agents, and the interior ministry officials. Sometimes we expedite a shipment with a little consideration for a poor man's family. Do you understand?"

Newman smiled and nodded. *"Bakshish."*

The young man looked offended. "Oh no, Ram—that would be bribery. What I mean is that when we get to know these men, sometimes we learn of a need they have—sometimes for a particular kind of medicine, or a tool, or a part for a water pump. They know we travel to where these things are available. It's a small thing for us to help them. When we provide what they need, they sometimes repay the favor by providing what we need. But they know we are Christians and that to us, bribery is wrong. Do you understand?"

"I think so," said Newman. "I'm sorry if I offended you."

"It's all right," said Samir.

Al Ramadi was coming into view. "We will be here only long enough for you to meet with the business across the street," Samir said, "while I fill up the extra drums in the back with diesel fuel and water. Then we must find a bit of food and get underway. We have a long drive ahead of us."

They were nearly finished with their light lunch. Newman looked at Samir.

"Tell me about your family. Do you have any more children?"

The Christian Arab smiled. "No more. But all three are in school now, and my wife thinks perhaps we should have another. What about you? Do you have any more babies?"

"No . . . just our little boy." Newman smiled, but his face clouded a little as he thought of James, now thousands of miles away in the U.S.

"Well, we'd better be on our way, Samir. How long do you think it'll take us to drive to Ar Rutbah?"

"It is about three hundred kilometers. My father and I have driven this road many times, and it takes about five hours. We have plenty of fuel and water, but the road is not good enough to travel very fast.

They went outside and, as they climbed into the truck, Samir said, "We will meet my father and another man in Ar Rutbah."

They had traveled only a few miles on the highway when Newman heard the *chirp* of the sat phone from inside his briefcase. He opened the case where the two Iridium phones—one given to him by the Israelis, the other by General Grisham—had been placed beside the radiation test gear, disguised as sales samples of computer equipment.

The small screen on the face of the Israeli sat phone blinked the message, Incoming Call. He listened for the electronic *ping* of the encryption synchronization.

"Newman."

"This is Major Rotem. Tell me where you are."

"Uh . . . I just finished lunch. Why? Do you have some news?"

"Yes, I do have some news. Can you talk freely?"

Newman glanced at Samir. "I can talk. What do you have?"

"Our locator system tells us you are still in Iraq. If you are, you must leave immediately."

He's trying to tell me something without saying too much.

"Go on."

"We have intel that the Iraqi nuclear weapons have been discovered," Rotem said. "We're mounting an operation to find and recover them. If we can't do that in forty-eight hours . . ."

"How did you find out about the nukes?"

"Our intelligence came through with the information this morning. They're trying to locate them, even now. Can you come back to Jerusalem? I'd feel more comfortable if we were working together to find our wives."

"Well . . . first I need to find a way to clear the deck. Let me get back to you."

He pushed the red button on the Israeli sat phone, terminating the call. He then replaced it in the briefcase and removed the unit General Grisham had given him and punched in the memorized emergency number.

"Grisham here."

"General, Newman. Have you received any new intelligence about the nukes since my call this morning? I just got another call from Major Rotem, and he says the Israelis are close to locating them and are prepping for an op to get them or take 'em out."

"I have nothing new. We've asked NRO to review the imagery tracks for western Iraq, but the Brits had things pretty tied up with their little POW prison break in that time frame, so we're probably not going to get much help there. I thought you were on your way with Samir to see if you could get more information from their people where they think the truck crossed the border into Syria."

"I am . . . but I'm still several hours away." Newman looked at the map spread out on the seat. "General . . . Major Rotem hinted the Israelis were planning a preemptive strike on Iraq if they didn't recover those weapons in forty-eight hours."

There was silence on the other end of the phone, and Newman thought for a moment the call was lost. "General . . . did you hear me?"

"Yes, Pete. I've heard the same thing through my channels. I . . . I'm praying the good Lord put you where you are in order to use you to do something . . . and I'm praying the people Samir and Eli Yusef know in Iraq can help us. It's got to be an answer to prayer that those nukes have surfaced before Saddam could get his hands on them. But we've got a long way to go before we can get them into *ours*. Call me after you debrief Samir and Eli Yusef's contact."

"Yes, sir." Newman disconnected the call.

He looked at Samir. "We don't want to attract undue attention, my friend, but we need to be at Ar Rutbah as quickly as possible."

GCHQ Echelon Station
Morwenstow, Near Bude
Northern Cornwall, UK
Monday, 23 March 1998
1050 Hours, Local

The remote satellite Signal Intelligence station did not blend in well with the scenic rolling meadows and sheer cliffs above the seas. The facility was part of an enormous joint venture between the UK's GCHQ and the United States' National Security Agency. The Echelon network included clandestine listening stations in Canada, New Zealand, Australia, Japan, Taiwan, Cyprus, Hungary, Pakistan, India, Oman, Kenya, and, of course, Israel.

All these listening posts fed intercepted signals and communications to Fort Meade, Maryland, or to the GCHQ station in Morwenstow, where, in a dozen buildings scattered over the site, more than a thousand people were glued to computer terminals and audio monitoring equipment or analyzing reams of printed documents. Engineers tweaked the twenty-two giant and midsize satellite dish receivers, trolling for secrets.

The governments that sponsored Echelon placed a high value on their ability to eavesdrop on almost any kind of communications: data, voice, fax, video—it hardly mattered. Much of the top-secret work at Morwenstow was aimed at intercepting written messages—telexes, facsimile documents, and e-mail. But the site also intercepted voice and other messages via landline telephones, cell phones, instant messaging devices, computers, satellite phones, and various kinds of radio traffic—everything but smoke signals.

Loretta Morris, a forty-eight-year-old single woman who lived with her mother in nearby Bude, had been working in the Echelon computer network for more than two decades, through half a dozen project name changes. For years she had come in every morning at nine, booted up her computer, and sifted through the accumulated overnight intercepts. Her duty now was to sort through all the written messages, looking for any references to weapons of mass destruction. To aid Loretta in her search, the computers flagged any overnight ingoing and outgoing communications that carried key words relating to her subject category. Then the computer retrieved those communications and routed them into separate files, ready for Loretta when she got to work in the morning.

Most of the references were spurious, of course; the software filters, despite the tens of billions of dollars spent on them, were still unable to put words into context. For example, today one transcript told about a "big bomb," which seemed like a "hit." However, after reading the entire text, Loretta saw it was simply an innocuous theater review of a new *avant garde* play. But there was no way of knowing that without reading the entire text. She had learned after so many years on the job to skim over the material and visually grab phrases that made sense in the context that was expected.

Loretta's work had been so exceptional that on the first of March she had been selected to participate in a new experiment. The officials running NSA and GCHQ had decided that "overnight" was no longer fast enough in an era of proliferating weapons of mass destruction, so they had designated about a hundred intercept specialists to provide "near-real-time review" of communications as—or shortly after—they were made, and then to flag these intercepts for prompt review by a senior intelligence officer.

It took extraordinary attention and concentration to perform this task but now, in her third week of this experiment, Loretta was still excited about her new assignment—although it sometimes seemed a bit voyeuristic. As she told one of her coworkers, she felt like she was "looking over someone's shoulder as they wrote a love letter."

She had been scrolling over live copy for about half an hour this morning when she hit the pause key. On the screen was a transcription of a satellite telephone conversation that had taken place in the Middle East only minutes ago. It was being converted into text by proprietary NSA software that transposed the intercepted digital voice stream into written copy. At the top of the screen was the keyword: NUCLEAR, and the phone numbers of both parties, the identifier codes that relayed the messages to and from their locations, and the time and date stamp. It showed that the parties were conversing over the Iridium Satellite Phone System, using a commercial encryption algorithm for which NSA and GCHQ had the key. Having first skimmed the content, Loretta now read the message carefully. She was more than halfway through before she saw the keywords that had caused the computer to target this message for review.

TEXT OF CONVERSATION:

Male Voice 1: . . . Newman . . .
Male Voice 2: This is Major Rotem. Tell me where you are.
MV1: I just finished lunch. Why? Do you have some news?
MV2: Yes, I do have some news. Can you talk freely?
MV1: I can talk. What do you have?
MV2: Our locator system tells us you are still in Iraq. If you are,
          you must leave [unintelligible].
PAUSE
MV1: Go on . . .
MV2: We have intel that the Iraqi NUCLEAR WEAPONS have
          been discovered. We're mounting an [unintelligible] . . .
          to recover them. If we can't do that in forty-eight hours . . .
MV1: How did you find out about the NUKES?

MV2: Our intelligence came through with the information this
morning. They are trying to locate them [unintelligible] . . .
Can you come back to Jerusalem? I'd feel more
[unintelligible] . . . working together to find our wives.

MV1: Well, first I need to find a way to clear the [unintel-
ligible] . . . Let me get back to you.

END OF CONVERSATION.

Loretta printed the text and placed it in the box on her desk marked
Urgent. A few minutes later, a runner took the papers from that *Urgent*
box and carried them to the second floor for the supervisory intelligence personnel to read and evaluate.

Petrol Oasis
Near Ar Rutbah, Iraq
Monday, 23 March 1998
1830 Hours, Local

Samir saw his father's truck and pulled up beside it in the crowded
truck stop. This was the last place to get petrol and water before crossing into Syria, where the prices for both were much higher. Eli and
Samir Habib knew this place well; they could no longer count the
number of times they had stopped here, carrying everything from toast-
ers to baby incubators. Eli was well known to all the men who worked
the pumps and even had the grudging respect of the black-market truck
drivers who plied their tandem tankers and box trailers back and forth
between Iraq and Syria.

Eli had parked his pickup in the shade of a large date palm, and
when Samir pulled up beside him, the old man seemed to awaken from
a nap.

"Ah, my son!" he said through the open window of his truck, "I was just praying that you and our friend would arrive safely and soon, for Nazir must soon go to work. He is on the night shift at the border station."

As the three men embraced in the sandy parking area, Newman noticed the person Eli had referred to as Nazir. He remained in the passenger seat of Eli Yusef's truck, hunched down in the seat, peering furtively over the dashboard.

"Please," the old man said, "let me introduce you." Eli Yusef walked Newman by the arm over to the passenger door of the truck, saying, "Nazir, this is my friend Ram Fales, he is a dear friend of mine. Mr. Fales wants to ask you some questions about the truck belonging to International Scientific Trading, the truck we talked about this morning. You can trust Ram as you do me."

Then turning to Newman, he said, "Nazir is an old friend. He is Chaldean and knows the Lord. But he is quite worried about getting in trouble with the authorities. You may speak in English, for he studied the language at the Christian school before it was closed."

The American nodded and smiled at Nazir.

Eli said, "Very well. My son and I will go and get some water. You may talk but should not tarry. Nazir must be at the border post in time for his shift, and I have promised to drive him there." The old man and his son went into the petrol station as Newman walked around and got into the driver's side of the truck.

"Nazir, please trust me," Newman said. "I will not betray your confidence. Can you tell me what you saw last night?"

The slight man in the uniform of the Iraqi Customs Service looked at Newman, took a deep breath, and began in a voice barely above a whisper.

"I have been on night duty at this post for more than a dozen years. Eli Yusef is a friend. He says I can trust you."

"You can; I promise you that. What happened last night?'

"Ever since I have been at this post, trucks and lorries from International Scientific Trading come and go through this checkpoint to and from Syria, carrying all kinds of things. Always we are told in advance by the Interior Ministry officer on duty that a lorry or a convoy of trucks will be coming and that we should simply stamp the import forms as paid. We are not to inspect the vehicles.

"On Saturday evening, a Scientific Trading lorry with a canvas cover came through from Syria, but it was totally empty except for a forklift in the bed.

"The same lorry came back last night carrying three large crates . . . the one that set off all the detectors."

"Detectors—what detectors?"

"I do not know what they are supposed to measure, some kind of radiation, I think. They were just delivered to us a few weeks ago. But no one ever explained to us what they were supposed to do, or how to use them. You see, Mr. Fales, the Scientific Trading trucks have always come from Syria loaded and gone back empty. But this time, it was just the opposite."

"Did they declare what the cargo was, Nazir?"

"Oh yes, when it set off the detector, the man in charge, Mr. Dotensk—he is a very important man and even has an Iraqi diplomatic passport—he showed me the bill of lading indicating that the cargo was three X-ray machines he was taking to Syria for repairs."

X-ray machines don't emit radiation unless they're operating. "Do you remember where in Syria the machines were being taken for repair?"

"Of course. They were taking them to the big International Scientific Trading logistics center outside of At Tanf. Mr. Dotensk owns it. Eli Yusef and Samir have driven by it many times on their trips to and from Damascus. I am sure that they know the place well."

Newman's heart began to race. He looked down at the map he had brought with him from Samir's truck. With his finger, he traced the road from Al Rutbah, where they were now, to At Tanf. It was just across the border in Syria, less than 175 kilometers from here—fewer than three hours' drive unless there was a holdup at the border crossing.

"This is very helpful, Nazir. Was there anything else?"

The border guard thought for a moment and said, "No I don't think so, but if you want, I can tell Eli Yusef or Samir when Mr. Dotensk brings the X-ray machines back to Baghdad."

"Say that again, Nazir."

"I can call Eli Yusef or—"

"No, the part about bringing them back into Iraq."

"Oh yes, Mr. Dotensk was very explicit about that. He said he would have them fixed in a few days and would be bringing them back. He wanted to make sure the same personnel were on duty, so he would not have to pay an import duty on them. He and the captain joked about it . . . and he filled out a special form we have for that purpose."

"He's bringing them *back?*" Newman said aloud to himself as he stared out the window at Samir and his father approaching. "What do you suppose this fellow has in mind?"

Nazir looked at the American quizzically, shrugged his shoulders, but said nothing. He thought he'd already answered that question.

Incirlik Air Base
Adana, Turkey
Monday, 23 March 1998
1835 Hours, Local

General George Grisham was on his way to the Officer's Mess for dinner when Gunnery Sergeant Amos Skillings caught up with him.

"Excuse me, sir . . . we just got word, there's a secure teleconference call from the Joint Chiefs. They're on the satellite line now."

"All right, Gunny. Is this about that red rocket I sent out last night, warning about the possibility of an Israeli preemptive strike?"

"No sir . . . just some video of a bunch of brass hats sitting in the tank over at the Pentagon, waiting for you."

The general hurried into his conference room, threw his briefcase on the table, and sat down while Skillings adjusted the secure video conferencing equipment. The sergeant aimed a digital video camera at Grisham and used the remote control to turn on a large-screen video monitor. Skillings handed the remote to the general and left the room. Grisham switched the tabletop control to *VID/VOX,* and a picture flickered on the screen showing a conference table surrounded by the highest-ranking officers in the U.S. military.

"General Grisham here. Good day, gentlemen."

General Dwight McKee, the chairman of the Joint Chiefs of Staff, was seated at the end of the table. Grisham could see from Dwight's body language that he was not having a good day.

"Hello, George, good to see you. As you can see, I've got General Michaelson, Admiral Stratton, and General Hoisington here with me. We need to talk, George."

"Yes, sir. What can I do for you gentlemen?" *Where's the commandant of the Marine Corps?*

"Well, George, we've been sitting here for the past hour and a half trying to come up with a polite way to deal with this problem we've had dropped in our laps . . . but there's no easy way."

Something was not right. Grisham had known these men for years. Michaelson, the Army Chief of Staff, had served with him in Vietnam. He and Admiral Vince Stratton were Naval Academy classmates. And Hoisington, the Air Force Chief of Staff, had been his neighbor when they were students at National War College. But none of the faces looked particularly friendly now.

"What's the problem, sir? Is it about the nuke warning I sent out about Israel?"

McKee looked as if he'd swallowed a pin cushion. "Actually, *you're* the problem, George. Do you recall having a conversation with the Secretary of State yesterday?"

"I do . . . only it wasn't yesterday, it was just after midnight today, my time."

"Yes . . . well, it seems you've crossed swords with Madam Secretary of State, and she didn't like it. She went to the President, and the President called the Secretary of Defense, and the SECDEF called me. Now George, I know you well enough to know you don't go out of your way to tick somebody off, especially somebody with as much clout as she has. What in the world did you say to her?"

General Grisham shook his head and rolled his eyes. Then he sighed quite audibly before speaking. "General McKee . . . what I said was inconsequential. It's what *she* said that's got the water boiling there at the Pentagon.

"The reason she called me to task is that she claimed I was intruding on her turf . . . meddling in international diplomacy. Well, I told her that was nonsense . . . and what I was doing was fully within the scope of my duties as CinC CENTCOM . . . and I left it at that. End of story."

"Uh . . . George, listen . . . the SECDEF took a real beating from the President on this," Admiral Stratton said. "They're both pretty rankled. SECDEF says the Secretary of State got information about an operation you have going in Iraq, and she was embarrassed she didn't know anything about it. And the fact is, neither did the Secretary of Defense, George . . . neither did *any* of us. What's going on?"

"I wouldn't call it an operation, Admiral. The matter is so small I didn't think it was worth reporting until I had something to put in the report. I've got just one man doing some on-site intel gathering and recon . . . that's it." He watched the faces of the men in the other conference room, but he couldn't tell what they were thinking.

"What's this Marine looking for that the UN inspectors can't find or you can't get through satellites, the CIA, DIA, or allied channels?" General McKee asked.

"Uh . . . well . . . I'd prefer not to go into that right now, sir. I'd like you to take my word that it can wait until I get more information to—"

"George, cut the bull. She told us you've got a man inside Iraq looking for nukes. And she says she heard it first from the Prime Minister of Israel. If the Prime Minister of Israel knows it, so does the entire Middle East. Now tell us . . . is it true that your one-man operation in Iraq is there to find Saddam's missing nuclear weapons?"

"You can't seriously think that's even remotely possible," General Michaelson said.

"What are you asking of me, gentlemen?" Grisham said. "What does the SECDEF want?"

"He wants you to call off your operation immediately," McKee said. "That means right now! And then—and I quote the Secretary of Defense, who left this room just minutes before we called you—'Tell that knucklehead to get his rear end on the next flight out and report back here to the Pentagon. I want him in my office by this time tomorrow.' Unquote."

"But gentlemen, I can't call it off right now. I'm not even sure we can get in touch with my man, let alone pull him out, in such a short time."

"Nothing's impossible, George," said Admiral Stratton. "Listen . . . the SECDEF . . . well, I've never seen the Old Man so ticked with you—or with us, for that matter. He thinks we should've had a tighter rein on you."

"You should have brought us into the loop, George," General McKee said. "We might have been able to explain your plan a little better. But not knowing anything about it caught us all off guard, You'll have to make things right when you get here tomorrow."

"But how can I get there tomorrow? I've got a serious mess here, gentlemen. A mess we're *this* close to solving. General McKee . . . Admiral . . . gentlemen, I need your help. This problem you've given me is just about politics. I can apologize and explain my plan, but not now—or even tomorrow. Can't you buy me a little more time?"

"Sorry, George. It's a direct order from SECDEF," McKee said. "It's out of our hands. See you tomorrow. Call off the operation and get back here ASAP. That's an order."

"I'll do my best, sir. Grisham out."

He turned off the video and voice feed to the conferencing equipment and sat for a moment with his chin resting in his cupped hand.

Dear Lord, what do I do? How can I follow the order I've just been given without jeopardizing the lives of Pete and Rachel? God, . . . I need answers—quick.

The STU-III secure phone on the pedestal table in the corner buzzed. Grisham reached for it.

"General Grisham, this is the Comm Center signal operator. I have an incoming encrypted Iridium call from a Lieutenant Colonel Newman."

"Put him on."

There was the usual sound of the two encryption systems synchronizing, and then he heard Newman's excited voice.

"General, I think I've found the nukes!"

Grisham sighed and rubbed his forehead. "What have you got?"

"I just spoke with an Iraqi customs official . . . ." Newman said something about radioactive cargo, some place in Syria, and some outfit called "International Scientific Trading." He was speaking quickly. Then he started talking about the location in Syria where he thought the nukes were being held.

"Samir and Eli have been by this place hundreds of times. They can tell us everything we need to know."

"Hold on . . . let me get a pen. I need to write this down," General Grisham said. "You said that the name of this place is At Tanf? And it's in Syria, just across the border from Iraq."

"Yes, sir, that's right. And I have the approximate coordinates where that building should be located—where we think the weapons are being stored. Do you think you can twist the tail of one of the spy birds and have it look down in that direction and see what it can make out?"

"Give me those coordinates." The general wrote down the numbers that Newman read to him, and he read them back for accuracy. Then he said, "Let me look into this, and I'll get right back to you. Stand by where you are for about thirty minutes or so."

When the call ended, General Grisham called out loudly, "Gunny! Are you still here?"

"Aye sir!"

"Walk with me to the command center. I'll tell you on the way what I need. And we've got to work fast!"

"Aye aye, sir!"

"I think our friend Colonel Newman may have found the pot of gold at the end of the rainbow."

Petrol Oasis
Near Ar Rutbah, Iraq
Monday, 23 March 1998
1900 Hours, Local

Peter Newman and Samir were growing restless. Eli Yusef had already departed with Nazir in order to get him to the border outpost in time for his duty shift. Newman and Samir had intended to follow shortly thereafter, but Grisham had ordered him to stay put. Now the two men had overstayed their refueling stop at the desert gas station and, as they feared, they were beginning to draw a certain amount of attention from the laborers and mechanics who worked there. They tried to remain as inconspicuous as possible, but the traffic in the petrol station was beginning to dwindle as the sun set. If they didn't get moving soon, they would be on the highway headed for the border after the curfew, an invitation for far more attention than either man wanted.

As Newman checked his watch for the fifteenth time in as many minutes, his phone began to chirp. He immediately answered and waited for the encryption to sync.

"Sorry it took so long, Pete, but I think you may have found more than we hoped."

"What do you mean, General?"

"Well, first, we got a real-time scan from a passing bird with a long lens, looking for buildings and an adjoining runway that fit the description your contact gave. While we were confirming we have the correct site, one of the techs remembered something GCHQ picked up while the Brits were doing their POW extract on Sunday the twenty-second. He recalled that they had observed transmissions from that same general area. This tech said they thought it was strange because the transmissions were coming from Marconi DM-3 UHF hand-held radios in the NATO broadcast spectrum—and they were coming from At Tanf. Didn't you tell me those were the radios the terrorists holding Rachel were carrying?"

"Yes, sir!"

"Well, he just checked with GCHQ. Those transmissions have been emanating from that site almost nonstop since Sunday. And this afternoon, one of them broadcast the following message . . . now where did I put it?" Newman could hear the sound of papers rustling on the general's end of the circuit. "Here it is . . . 'Mr. Dotensk says the general wants the women to have a shower every day and fresh clothing every two days.' Pete, it looks and sounds to me like we've found both the nukes and Rachel."

Newman leaned forward in the seat, his head almost touching the dashboard. "Are you sure, sir?"

"Well, Pete, I can't prove it, but my gut tells me this is right. It's the same name as the fellow your border guard mentioned. So it's the right place for the nukes. And then, the reference to 'the general' and 'the women'—somehow I just have this feeling this transmission is also about Rachel and her friend."

"Thank God!"

"We're checking now, but it appears everything we're looking for is right there in one place—and it doesn't seem to be going anywhere."

"Sir . . . I can't believe it! That's the best news I've had all week. Now all we need to figure out is how to get the nukes and the women out of there."

"Pete . . . listen to me. We need to think this through very carefully. If we're right, this may be a whole lot bigger than anyone ever imagined. If we're correct, and Rachel and her friend are being held in the same place as the nuclear weapons, then this man Dotensk is somehow affiliated with your old nemesis Komulakov. That could mean there's some kind of official Russian connection to the whole thing—including the sale of Russian nukes elsewhere."

"General, I don't want you to think I'm going off half-cocked, but I don't think this is going to keep very long. What are the possibilities you can get me some help, sir? Do we have any idea how many bad guys there are at this facility outside of At Tanf? We can't let this wait too long. The Iraqi customs fellow I talked to says those three crates—which are undoubtedly the nukes—are going to be brought back *into* Iraq in a matter of days."

There was a pause at the other end.

"Colonel, I don't know how to tell you this. I've been given a direct order to end your mission. It was supposed to end an hour ago. And I'm supposed to be catching the next flight back to Washington."

"What . . . How can they—?"

"Pete . . . there's nothing I can do to help you in the next twenty-four hours. I'll have to go upstairs to get the kind of help we need, considering the international consequences of what you've found. Let's pray these characters don't move the nukes or the women in the next twenty-four hours. As soon as I get to Washington for some face time with the SECDEF and/or the President, we'll figure out a way to do this job. Until then, I'm asking you just to hang loose. I know that that's not going to be easy . . . but for reasons I can't go into now, it looks as if I'm going to have to do this one strictly by the book."

TOUGH CHOICES

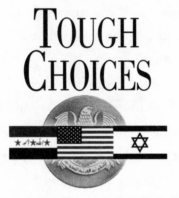

CHAPTER NINETEEN

Duvdevan HQ
Tel-Nof, Israel
Monday, 23 March 1998
1915 Hours, Local

Major Ze'ev Rotem sat deep in thought at a desk in the Special Operations Command Center with his hands clasped below his chin. Displayed on the desk in front of him were printouts of the satellite images of the Jericho 2 training exercise held earlier that day. The satellite photos showed very clearly that six of the transporter-erector-launcher vehicles were in place, ready for the launch procedures. The Jericho 2 base at Zachariah housed some fifty nuclear missiles; the six in place for a launch were enough to do horrific damage anywhere within a range of fifteen hundred to four thousand kilometers.

The warheads on these ballistic missiles put every square inch of Iraq within reach of Israel's nuclear arsenal. And Rotem knew the Jericho 2 rockets in the photos on his desk could also reach targets in Pakistan, Egypt, Iran, Saudi Arabia, Syria, Afghanistan, Turkmenistan, Chechnya, Uzbekistan, Yemen, and Kuwait.

Although the satellite pictures were clear, Major Rotem wished he had copies of some IRS-C high-resolution off-nadir prints from one of India's new satellites. The Indian Defense attaché had shown him a sample a year ago, and it offered not only higher image clarity but also a 3-D "slant-view" of the geography around the TELs deployed at Zachariah. Rotem liked this perspective better for evaluating an area's vulnerability to attack.

Unlike the U.S. and Russians, Israel had no weapons on submarines or in hardened nuclear missile silos with blast doors that could withstand a nearby nuclear hit. Confronted by the stark realities of size, geology, and enemies on every side, Israel had opted instead to mount its strategic deterrent missiles on mobile launchers—the TELs—stored for protection in reinforced limestone caves. But what Rotem and few others knew was that the protection afforded by these reinforced caves was wholly inadequate if a nuclear weapon detonated nearby.

The IDF major was also worried that if India could watch Israel's Jericho 2 launch exercises, it was entirely possible that a half dozen other countries, including the French, could also.

If the French have a satellite shot of this, would they share it with the Iraqis? Knowing what he did about certain French financial and business interests in Iraq, he felt he knew a potential answer to that question.

Rotem had checked the intel just an hour ago. The most recent pass by an Israeli satellite showed no new activity in Iraq. There were no communications intercepts or agent reports indicating the deployment of Iraqi Scuds or any heightened level of alert in their Rocket Forces.

But Rotem also knew, as did every other officer in the Israeli Armed Forces, that during the 1990-91 Gulf War, the Iraqis had succeeded in launching thirty-nine high-explosive-tipped Scuds against Israel. And he also knew that despite claims to the contrary, every one of them had penetrated the Patriot missile defenses that the Americans had hastily installed.

Since then, the improved Patriot PAC III missile defenses and Israel's own Arrow antimissile system had been deployed, but none of these offered absolute assurance that an Iraqi warhead wouldn't get through. That's why Israel was making it known that its Jericho 2 missiles were being readied—as a signal to Iraq or anyone else that even the threat of a nuclear assault on the Jewish state would result in a massive counterstrike or, if necessary, even a preemptive attack.

Now, Major Rotem confronted the personal realities of the situation. His wife was still missing, presumably still held with the wife of the U.S. Marine officer, probably in Lebanon, Syria, or Iraq. Newman was wandering around in Iraq looking for MIA nukes. And now the whole world knew Israel was prepared to launch a deterrent attack on Iraq.

Rotem had accompanied the IDF's Chief of Staff to an emergency meeting of the War Cabinet where the Prime Minister had issued a grave warning that Israel could be at war in less than forty-eight hours.

And now, with all this weighing on his shoulders, Major Rotem had been told to prepare his Sayeret Duvdevan unit for two entirely different missions: either to protect the Jericho 2 launchers from some kind of terrorist attack or to get underway on a moment's notice on a mission to capture and destroy the Iraqi nuclear weapons if they could be found.

Rotem devoutly hoped the word would come down shortly for the second mission, for it would mean there was at least a chance of averting a nuclear holocaust. No one really wanted to think about the possibility of starting a chain reaction leading to a Middle East apocalypse. Yet, he knew that if a weapon of mass destruction threatened Israel, his government would make that choice—they would choose to respond in kind. That was the sole rationale behind the billions spent developing the Jericho Sanction.

But he also knew that a launch of the Jericho 2 nuclear missiles would change everything in the world—forever. He didn't fear retaliation in kind by the Iraqis, but he wasn't so sure about Pakistan, which also had nuclear weapons. Would the Pakistanis intervene for another Muslim nation, as the Indian Defense attaché had warned they might?

If we launch those Jericho missiles at Iraq, will I ever see my wife again? Will I ever know the child she carries? Or will Dyan be incinerated in the conflagration. . . .

The IDF officer sighed and swore softly. Now was a terrible time for him to be distracted by personal concerns. Still, it was impossible not to think of Dyan. He paced back and forth across his office.

Why doesn't the American call?

Petrol Oasis

Near Ar Rutbah, Iraq
Monday, 23 March 1998
1920 Hours, Local

"My friend," said Samir, "if we are going to move from here, we must go now. The curfew will soon be on us, and then we will be at great risk for being on the highway."

The Marine looked at the young man as if coming out of a trance. Newman was stunned by his last conversation with General Grisham, and he had been turning over in his mind how he could comply with the order to "hang loose" for the next twenty-four hours while the nuclear weapons he had been sent to find *and* his kidnapped wife were less than ninety miles away.

"You're right, Samir, let's go."

"Go where, my friend?"

"Where is your father going to spend the night after he drops off Nazir?"

"We have a family friend on the east side of At Tanf. He is a Syrian Christian whose family were all killed in the Homs uprising about thirty years ago. He owns a restaurant and keeps some rooms above it where the oil exploration people sometimes stay. My father will probably stay there."

"Can we get across the border and meet him there?"

"Yes, I think so. Nazir will be on duty and he will let us pass, though we may have to pay an 'entrance fee' on the Syrian side of the border."

"Can we get to the border before the curfew?"

Samir checked his watch and nodded. "I think so, if we leave right away. As long as we are in line at the border post when the curfew comes, they will leave us alone. Is that what you wish to do?"

"I don't want to put you in greater jeopardy than you are already," said Newman, "but at this point, you may be the only hope I have of getting my wife back safely. And if the Lord is willing, we may also be able to do something about the three nuclear weapons at the same time."

Samir looked at the American, but Newman was staring straight ahead. Samir started the truck and pulled through the parking area—past dozens of tandem tractor trailers and panel trucks, their diesel engines idling—and out onto the highway, headed west.

"What's in all those trucks?" asked Newman as they picked up speed on the macadam roadway.

"Mostly smuggled goods. They are carrying banned equipment and merchandise into Iraq. They cannot go any further tonight because of the curfew. Tomorrow morning they will continue on to Baghdad or wherever else they are going inside this poor, tortured country."

Within minutes, the glow of the truck stop and the Al Rutbah Oasis faded into the darkness behind them. Newman rode in silence for a few minutes. And then, as though he had just made up his mind about a course of action, he opened the briefcase beside him on the seat, removed the Israeli phone, and plugged its battery charger into the cigarette lighter beneath the dashboard. He flipped the antenna up, extended it out the window, and dialed the number for Ze'ev Rotem. The major answered on the second ring.

"Rotem."

"Major, this is Peter Newman."

"Yes, go ahead."

"I have found our wives—and the nuclear weapons. I'm headed toward them right now. Are you still tracking my location?"

"Hold on."

Newman could hear computer keys clicking.

"Yes, I have you." Rotem said.

"Good, because where I'm headed, I'm going to need some help."

"Help? What kind of help?"

"Enough help to rescue two wives and recover three nuclear weapons."

There was silence from Rotem. Then he spoke, his voice low.

"Colonel, I don't have that kind of authority. My country is, right at this minute, preparing to launch a preemptive nuclear strike on Iraq. In the midst of this crisis, nobody is going to authorize me to launch a rescue mission for two women. I can't help you, even if . . . even if it means placing my own wife at risk."

"Major . . . if we can get those rogue nukes back, Israel would have no point in striking Iraq. The weapons aren't even in Iraq. They're in Syria. And so are our wives. I know precisely where they are—at least within a few hundred meters. If I had some help, I believe we could recover the weapons and bring our wives home safely."

Suddenly, a new voice was on the line. "Lieutenant Colonel Newman, this is Brigadier General Meir Hofi. I am the commander of the Duvdevan units to which Major Rotem is assigned. Forgive me for intervening in this conversation, but as I'm sure you understand, all calls into this headquarters are monitored for obvious reasons. Unfortunately, Major Rotem is distraught and has given you information that should not have been spoken. I'm sure you understand."

Newman was so astonished by the new voice on the circuit that at first he said nothing.

"Ze'ev?"

Rotem's voice came back on. "Colonel Newman, that's correct. General Hofi is my commander."

"Thank you, Major," said the voice of the IDF general. "Colonel Newman, are you still there?

"Yes."

"Good. Now you say you are certain where these weapons are— that they are not in Iraq but in Syria?"

"That's correct, General."

"Well done! Now if you will please provide me with the location and any other information that you know, we will ensure that all of this is taken care of and you and your government will have no further need for concern."

Newman's mind was racing. "Before I give you that information, General, do you mind telling me how you intend to 'ensure that all this is taken care of,' as you put it?"

"Colonel Newman, my government will respond in a way we believe appropriate to protect the state and people of Israel."

"Yes, General, as you should," said Newman, regaining his composure. "But I was just wondering if that means a heavy air strike on the location where the nuclear weapons are hidden, or does it involve a raid to rescue our wives and recover the weapons? Because if it's the former and not the latter, with all due respect, sir, I may have a hard time remembering where this place is."

There was moment of silence that went on so long Newman wondered if the signal had been lost. Then the voice of General Hofi came through the earpiece, dripping with sarcasm. "Excuse me, Lieutenant Colonel Newman, but Major Rotem wants to give me the benefit of his wisdom as well. Please hold . . ."

After what seemed like another eternity, the general's voice came on again, this time softened considerably, "Colonel Newman, Major Rotem has convinced me I should hear what you have to suggest. Will you tell me what you are proposing?"

Newman sighed deeply and spoke carefully into the phone. "I'll arrive in the vicinity of the site tonight and conduct a reconnaissance. I'll brief you on what I find, and you can tailor a force to be inserted by HALO tomorrow night. We will rendezvous at a predetermined location, conduct a movement to the objective, raid the facility, recover the hostages and the weapons, and then you pick us up in CH-53s to bring us all back out."

"Ah, you make it sound so easy, Colonel," said the IDF general. "Let me confer a moment with your young friend."

After another lengthy silence, the general said, "I hope that after the two of you are court-martialed, you don't decide to become shoe salesmen. After listening to the two of you sell me, I judge you could outfit my wife with a footwear collection to rival Imelda Marcos! But Colonel . . . I like your idea. I will brief the Minister of Defense, and Major Rotem will get back to you. However, I assure you that tomorrow night has to be the deadline. We are not going to stand-down our nuclear forces just on the hope that this high-risk venture succeeds. I am also going to suggest to the minister that the force Major Rotem brings with him should be very small—because if those weapons really are there—and you do not succeed—we will put every bomb I can authorize on top of that site to make sure those nuclear weapons can never be used. Do you understand me?"

"Yes, sir . . . perfectly."

As Newman pushed the red button on the left side of the phone to terminate the call, a small sliver of moon appeared from behind some clouds in the otherwise black sky. As he stared at the moon, Newman pondered the consequences of the insubordination he had just set in motion.

International Scientific Trading, Ltd.
At Tanf, Syria
Monday, 23 March 1998
2000 Hours, Local

General Dimitri Komulakov had just sat down to dinner when one of Dotensk's men knocked on the door of the dining room. The KGB general, chewing a generous portion of lamb chop, motioned for the man to enter.

"General," he said, glancing enviously at the sumptuous fare, "I am sorry to bother you, but there is a secure call coming in for you from the *Rezident* in Washington. Shall I tell him you will call back?"

Komulakov looked at his watch and took a gulp of wine to help wash down the mouthful.

"Well, it must be very important if it keeps our friend Viktor Martynov from lunch with some American capitalist. Perhaps Yeltsin has drunk himself to death, and they want me to return to Moscow to restore order, eh?"

The general rose and followed the messenger. Outside the "guest house," they headed to the south end of the compound, toward a windowless, concrete building with a metal door that resembled a blockhouse. There was no knob or handle on the door. When they arrived at the portal, the general pushed a button on a metal box with Russian Cyrillic letters that said, *General Komulakov.*

A voice from the speaker beside the box asked him to look up to a mirror-like portal recessed into the wall beside the door. When the guard inside verified that the man standing outside was indeed his superior, there was the sound of a lock being turned, then a deadbolt being thrown, and the heavy door slowly swung out.

This was the "Sanctum" space for the facility. Constructed of steel-reinforced concrete, with walls and ceiling both more than a meter thick, only Russians—never their proxies—were allowed inside. The building, erected in the early '80s, right after the Soviets had purchased the property, had been designed to hold all the classified materials used by the KGB and GRU at this remote site. It had once been the repository for a KAPELLE device, the encoding/decoding machine that the Soviet intelligence services had used for transmitting all their sensitive traffic. Such a device would ordinarily still be here, but in 1987, a daring CIA team had managed to steal one of the devices, forcing the Soviets to change all their equipment and procedures for sending and receiving classified material. The Sanctum at At Tanf was still a repository for classified material, but its encryption equipment was for a much lower level of security and relied on the same kind of electronically generated digital algorithms used by the Americans. The Soviets had learned how to do all this from one the most effective spies they had ever recruited—John Walker—a U.S. Navy cryptologist turned spy.

Komulakov was admitted to the interior room where the communication officer held a telephone handset. The heavily shielded cord from the handset was connected to a large box that sat on a pedestal in the corner. Nicknamed "Piano," the machine scrambled the sound being sent through it to make it generally indecipherable to someone who intercepted the conversation. Though it worked well enough, the Russians were never completely sure the garbled transmissions weren't being deciphered by the massive Cray computers employed by NSA and GCHQ. Moscow limited what could be said over the phone to relatively low-level communications. The most sensitive information still had to be transmitted by encrypted message.

The operator said, "Washington," handed the phone to Komulakov, and left the room, closing the door behind him.

"Good afternoon, Viktor," said the general.

"Dimitri, how long will it take you to get to the *Rezidentura* in Damascus?" asked the voice in his ear.

Komulakov computed the time-distance factors in his head. Damascus was 240 kilometers by road, a three-hour trip. The Lear would take twenty minutes—if the pilots were sober.

"If it is very important, I can be there in an hour."

"It is very important, Dimitri."

"Can you tell me what it is about?"

"On this line, I can only tell you that we have received an emergency message from your friend Morales."

Komulakov was stunned. Messages from Julio Morales were supposed to be only opened at Moscow Centre. "You've read it?"

"Yes. His message told us to get the information to you by the most expeditious means possible, that it was a serious emergency. And I must say, having now read it, I would have to agree. This really is an emergency. It involves a bright flare."

"Stop!" Komulakov shouted into the handpiece, hearing the code words for a nuclear weapon. "Say nothing more on this circuit. I am on the way. I will be in Damascus in an hour. Reduce the information that you have to a secure encrypted cable, and I will read it when I get to Damascus. Notify the embassy that I am coming and inform the 'pianist' to be ready," he said, referring to the SVR cryptologist.

"Yes, sir."

Komulakov hurried out of the Sanctum and back to the guest house. When he bustled into the dining room, Dotensk was just finishing his meal.

"Leonid, get the pilots, and have the jet pushed out of the hangar. I must go to Damascus right away. Tell them to file a diplomatic flight plan so we get clearance into Assad airport. I will return here in about three hours."

"Yes, sir, but . . . is it Yeltsin? Are you being recalled to Moscow?"

"No, you idiot. It's some kind of urgent message from an American spy. I must go to Damascus to retrieve it since the imbeciles who run Moscow Centre can't figure out a way to put a truly secure communications site out here in this merciless hole."

Incirlik Air Base
Adana, Turkey
Monday, 23 March 1998
2015 Hours, Local

"General, your aircraft is ready to depart when you are," Gunnery Sergeant Skillings said as he walked into General George Grisham's office.

The Commander in Chief of CENTCOM was putting some files into a briefcase when Skillings came in. "I'm just about set, Gunny. What's the weather like over the Atlantic, and in Washington?"

"Looks clear all the way, sir."

"OK . . . let's get going then."

The two men fell in step and walked briskly down the corridor, headed for the front of the building where the general's staff car was waiting. As they entered the lobby of the NATO headquarters, the outer door opened and Colonel Len Buckel, the CENTCOM G-2, entered, followed by two British officers and a small, thin man wearing a Royal Marines sweat suit. Buckel stepped forward while the others waited by the door and said, in a quiet voice that only Grisham and Skillings could hear, "Sir, I need to talk to you."

"Can it wait, Len? I've got a plane to catch, and we're already ten minutes behind schedule."

"Just a moment or two of your time, General. I believe this is very important."

Grisham hesitated. Throughout his career, he had made it his practice to rely on his subordinates and to listen when they had something important to say. In combat, this principle had saved his life on more than one occasion. He turned to Skillings.

"Let's use the conference room right inside the door."

The group turned and re-entered the wing of the building that Grisham and Skillings had just exited, and the six men went into an empty room, just a little way down the corridor.

As the two British officers and the man in the sweat suit entered, Buckel introduced them, each shaking hands with Grisham as he was presented. "Sir, this is Colonel Brighton, the executive officer for the

British base commandant. Major Clift is the Royal Marines liaison officer. And this, sir," said Buckel, introducing the thin man in the sweat
suit, "is Captain Bruno Macklin, SAS . . . he was part of that Iraqi
prison break the Brits pulled off. Captain Macklin wanted to meet you.
He knows you were Colonel Newman's CO and wants to ask about
him."

"How do you know Pete?" asked Grisham.

"Sir, I was part of the UN unit that was caught in the ambush in
Iraq in '95."

Grisham was stunned. "We thought you were all dead, Captain. In
fact, Pete . . . I mean, Lieutenant Colonel Newman thought you were
all killed. I'm glad to see you, soldier."

The general gripped Macklin's hand in both of his.

"Captain, it's a privilege to meet you. Colonel Newman has nothing but good things to say about you."

"Thank you, General." Macklin gave a faint smile. "You'll have to
excuse the informality of my dress, but these were the only clothes the
Royal Marines had to offer when I dumped my prison uniform last
night. They brought me here to fly me back to London. The Colonel
says they want to debrief me on our mission in '95, and whatever I
might know about Saddam's prison system and the like. But before I
left, I heard that Colonel Newman is alive and . . . in the area, so I had
to try and see him. Is there any way for me to get in touch with him?"

"Uh . . . it's great you're alive and safe, Captain Macklin. However,
I'm afraid you're going to have to wait to speak to Colonel Newman.
He isn't here; he's . . . on a special assignment."

"Yes, sir, I know. Our intel folks tell me there's a bit of dust-up brewing between the Israelis and the Iraqis, and Lieutenant Colonel Newman is somehow right in the middle of it."

General Grisham clenched his jaw, irritated that a highly sensitive mission was being discussed around the British headquarters. He looked at Brighton and Clift.

"Sir, as you know, GCHQ is monitoring the situation between Israel and Iraq," Brighton said. "While Captain Macklin was in the NSA/GCHQ SCIF being debriefed on his experience, one of the technicians mentioned Colonel Newman was in some jeopardy inside Iraq."

"General, is Lieutenant Colonel Newman in trouble?" Macklin said.

"Why do you ask?"

"Well sir, if what I've heard since I was released is true, Colonel Newman is in Iraq, and the Israelis seem ready to go to war because they believe Saddam has nukes."

Grisham sighed and pushed his hat back on his head. "Yeah . . . that seems to be a pretty good summation of our headache."

"And Colonel Newman?"

"Yes . . . Pete is in the thick of things. But I hope to be able to get him some help. I'm on my way to Washington right now to see about getting permission to send a special ops team in there to—"

Grisham suddenly paused midsentence, obviously deep in thought.

"What is it, General?" Macklin asked.

Grisham looked at Brighton and Clift. "Where is the Royal Marine unit that went into Iraq to rescue the captain?"

"We have one company from Four-Two Commando, near Badanah, Saudi Arabia, sir," Clift said. "That's the unit that sent a platoon in to pick up Captain Macklin and the other three prisoners."

"What are they doing now?"

"They were doing some joint desert warfare training with your U.S. Marines until this morning when your lads went back to Jordan. Our boys have two more days of independent training scheduled, and then they're supposed to motor back to Kuwait, where they'll rejoin their mates on the amphibious assault ships that are parked at Al Fuhayhil."

Skillings opened his briefcase, withdrew a map of the region, and spread it out on the conference room table. Grisham bent over the map.

"Who has OpCon over that company of Royal Marines?" the general asked.

"Sir, they arrived in theater as part of your Regional Reserve. But at the moment, they are technically under the operational control of MI6," said Clift. "But if you wish, I'm sure London would agree to have them redesignated to CENTCOM right away. Shall I ask?"

Grisham hesitated for a moment. "No. I'd rather MI6 kept them under their OpCon just a bit longer—because it's not likely in the current, ah . . . political environment . . . that I'm going to get a quick decision out of Washington to send any U.S. forces into Iraq to deal with this problem. MI6, on the other hand, doesn't have to answer to the Pentagon.

"Look, what you guys just accomplished with this prison break," he said, pointing to Macklin, "would have taken the Pentagon forever to decide what to do and when to do it—and then the details would have been leaked from Congress before we could put one boot on the ground."

"Shall I query our Joint Staff on this, sir?" Brighton said.

"Let's run this through MI6 and see what they say first, if that's OK with you, Colonel," said Grisham.

"Well, sir," said Brighton, "it just so happens that the two MI6 chaps who ran this little show, Thomas and Blackman, are over at the BOQ right now. They planned to accompany Macklin back home—but they seem to be the adventurous sort. Shall I hustle them over here so you can talk to them?"

"Yes, Colonel, that would be a very good idea," Grisham said. He turned to Skillings. "Gunny, it seems to me our aircraft just developed a malfunction of some kind or other. I think you'd better let Andrews Air Force Base know we're going to be delayed on take-off for awhile."

RACING
TOWARD DOOMSDAY

CHAPTER TWENTY

Babylon Technology Company
Al Mahmudiyah, Iraq
Monday, 23 March 1998
2030 Hours, Local

"Y ou sent for me, sir?" The small, slight man with thick, over-
sized spectacles and a lab coat two sizes too large stood in the
doorway marked Director in Arabic, French, and English.

"Yes, Dr. Aranul. Come in," said Qusay Hussein. "Sit down."

Iraq's leading nuclear scientist fidgeted in the large leather chair.
Educated in Bern, Switzerland, at the two-hundred-year-old French
university for scientific study, École Polytechnique, Dr. Hiran Aranul
was a brilliant man who always seemed on the verge of discovery.
Saddam had placed him in charge of ensuring Iraq's nuclear weapons
capability by the end of the decade, and Qusay, the dictator's son, had

called a late-night meeting at this clandestine laboratory disguised as a computer company.

Dr. Aranul was more than a little fearful. He knew Saddam had a low tolerance for failure—and he knew he was well behind schedule for developing a means to enrich the uranium Iraq was covertly acquiring from France and South Africa.

"Please extend my warm regards to your father. Please tell him we are toiling around the clock to replicate the work being done by Dr. Hamza before he defect—uh . . . before he was kidnapped."

"I am not here to listen to your excuses, and I do not wish to hear anymore about the traitor Hamza. I have something else in mind."

"How may I be of service?"

"What I am about to tell you must not be divulged to anyone. To do so will be a capital offense. Do you understand?"

"Yes, sir."

"I need to know how many Scuds and how many of our new Al Fatah or Al Samoud missiles are ready for configuration to accept nuclear warheads."

The scientist pushed his glasses higher on the bridge of his nose. Qusay could see the sheen of sweat on his forehead.

"None. At least, as far as I know. I . . . I have taken the initiative to study the missiles and their potential to accept nuclear warheads. I have also done some preliminary work on the required modifications, and I believe we could probably modify three Scuds and three Al Samouds fairly quickly. But . . ."

"Well? What is it?"

"It's just that . . . Sir, I regret to inform you that we do not as yet have a nuclear weapon to put in any of them."

"That does not matter. For the time being, I have obtained three nuclear weapons—Russian-made nuclear 152mm artillery rounds—but I am told they are too heavy and too large to be used as warheads on our missiles."

"Yes, that is true. Most perceptive, sir."

"I called you in because I want to see if you can provide us with an alternative."

"Yes, I will do my best, of course."

"I already know it is impossible to modify the Russian nuclear artillery weapons for use in our Scuds. But can you remove the nuclear material from one of the devices I have acquired, divide up the materials, and then place it, along with conventional explosives, inside six of our missile warheads?"

Dr. Aranul thought for a moment. "It would depend on whether we have the PAL codes for the nuclear weapons you have acquired. Attempting to disassemble a nuclear weapon without the Permissive Action Links can be very dangerous, but theoretically, the answer is yes. Of course, if one of these bombs detonated, it wouldn't cause a typical nuclear blast. Instead, the conventional explosive would simply spread radioactive material over a target area. The results of the explosion would be determined by the height of burst, the ground temperature, and the winds at the time of detonation."

"What do you mean 'height of burst?'"

"The altitude above the ground where the warhead detonates. There is an optimum altitude for this kind of weapon—the Americans call it a 'dirty bomb.' If it is too high, the radioactive particles are dissipated into the upper atmosphere by the winds—and if the detonation is too low, it only spreads a short distance. In fact, if the detonation occurs at ground level, it might only spread a few hundred meters."

"Hmm . . . I see. What is the best altitude then?"

"Again, it depends on the temperature and winds—cooler weather is better—a moderate breeze, five to ten knots, would maximize coverage from an air burst at two hundred to five hundred meters above the ground."

"Can the warheads on those missiles be programmed to detonate at that height?"

"Oh, yes. All it takes is a fuse with a barometric—or even better—a radar altimeter."

"Do we have those available?"

"We have them for our chemical artillery warheads," said Aranul. "We could simply reconfigure the fuse to fit the missile warhead."

"How long would all this take—removing the nuclear material from one of the artillery rounds, mixing it with conventional explosives, loading it in six missile warheads, and reconfiguring six of those fuses?"

Aranul thought for a moment. "If we stop all work on the centrifuge for enriching our uranium and keep the UN inspectors away, I think it could all be done in a few days."

"We do not have a few days," Qusay said sharply. "I need it done in less than forty-eight hours. They must be fully operational by Wednesday night."

"But, sir . . . I—I don't believe that such a thing is possible in such a short amount of time."

Qusay leaned across the desk and squinted his eyes as he looked into the eyes of the frightened little man across from him.

"Dr. Aranul . . . you have a way of telling me what I do not want to hear. Start modifying the warheads and preparing the fuses immediately. I will have the Russian artillery shells delivered to you tomorrow. I expect you to have them ready before the deadline."

"I understand, Excellency . . . but a question, if I may . . ."

"What is it?"

"If I am to take the fissile material from only one of your newly-acquired nuclear weapons, what am I to do with the other two?"

Qusay's mouth twisted into a malicious smile. "I wondered if you would ask. You are to disarm the Permissive Action Links on the other two nuclear artillery rounds—I will try to get you the codes—and then, rig them up so that each can be command detonated."

"Command detonated? By whom?"

"By the martyrs who have volunteered for this glorious mission." *This is why my father forged such a close relationship and spent all this money on Osama bin Laden, Hezbollah, and Arafat's Al Aksar Martyrs' Brigade.*

Hiran Aranul sat back in the chair. He was very quiet for a long time.

"Sir," he said finally, "can we be certain that the martyrs will indeed go to their proper targets—in Israel?"

Qusay glared at the little man. "This is not your concern. But who said the two nuclear weapons are to be detonated in Israel? The Scuds and Al Samouds are enough for the Jews. The other two are for the Americans and British."

Aranul pushed his glasses up again. "What you are asking, sir, will take more people and more man-hours than I have at my disposal."

"Tell me what you need, and I will see that you have it. Meanwhile, get the six missiles delivered here from the factory in Al Haytham. I have already ordered two scientists from the research facility in Al Kindi to come here and help you. Make whatever arrangements you need for tool workers, lathe operators, and whatever else you require. I will give you all you need to get this task done. While you are waiting for the three weapons and the missiles to arrive, work on the electrical and mechanical plans you will need for these conversions."

Qusay stared into the face of the scientist. "Be sure you make no mistakes, Doctor. Your life depends on the success of this assignment."

Perhaps he had pushed too hard. Qusay could see the man shaking.

"Don't worry, Doctor; that is just my way of emphasizing the importance of what you do. Don't be afraid. I want you to think only about success. When you accomplish this great task and everything is ready, I will see that you receive a great bonus. I will give you a brand new Mercedes and a new villa near my father's palace in Tikrit—all that for just two day's work."

The scientist tried to smile. "I will do my best, Excellency. I will go directly to the laboratory now."

"Good. I have every confidence in your ability."

As Dr. Aranul stood to leave, Qusay stopped him and handed him a paper. "Here . . . you will need this."

"What is this?" Dr. Aranul asked.

"Those are the coordinates for targeting the six missiles. Make certain each of the warheads is equipped with one of these six sets of coordinates. I want to make sure that when the missiles are launched, each weapon will find its mark. Now leave. I must make some phone calls."

As he watched the scientist walk away, Qusay wondered how long it would take before Aranul realized that all six target coordinates were in Israel.

International Scientific Trading, Ltd.
At Tanf, Syria
Monday, 23 March 1998
2115 Hours, Local

Leonid Dotensk hung up the phone and smiled. The call from Qusay made it abundantly clear that the Iraqi dictator's son wanted the three nuclear weapons very badly—badly enough to pay the agreed upon price without haggling. The Ukrainian arms merchant savored the knowledge for a few minutes and then picked up the phone and dialed a number at the Russian embassy in Damascus. When the operator answered, he said, "Has the general arrived yet?"

After a pause, he heard Komulakov's voice. "Leonid, I just arrived here. Will you give me no peace? What do you want? And why are you calling on an open line?"

"My apologies, my dear Dimitri, but it is a matter of great urgency. Our customer just called, and I must get right back to him on the terms for the three machines he has on order."

"Ah yes, Leonid, all right. I'm all ears."

"Well, first of all, he wants them right away, but I told him he would have to transfer payment in full before we could release them. He became quite agitated. He told me it was imperative that he have them by tomorrow night at the latest."

"Why?"

"I don't know. But he is adamant about immediate delivery."

"Where does he want them delivered?"

"He wants them brought to a research site called Babylon Technologies in Al Mahmudiyah."

"Where is that?"

"Less than twenty kilometers south of Baghdad. I also told him that because of all the American and British aircraft over Iraq, we would have to deliver his cargo overland, by truck from Syria via the Damascus-to-Baghdad highway."

"You didn't tell him where they are now, did you?"

"Of course not."

"I wouldn't put it past him to try to steal them, if he knew where they were," said the general. "Anyway, I don't understand the urgency. It troubles me."

"Look," Dotensk said, "our customer has agreed to deliver one hundred million dollars in gold bars, and wire transfer the balance in Swiss francs to our bank account later in the day when the banks open. I think we should agree to those terms, even though it means he will take delivery before full payment has been received."

Komulakov said nothing for a long while. "I'm a little concerned about the arrangement, Leonid. A hundred million in gold will weigh more than twenty thousand pounds. It would take two trucks to move it. However, we can handle the gold. So . . . I don't think we should jeopardize the deal. The worst-case scenario is that he reneges on the final payment, and we get only a hundred million in gold bars. I guess I can live with that, can't you, Leonid? After all, this is the second payment we're getting for the same merchandise." The general chuckled.

"When will he send us the gold?" asked Komulakov.

"If I call him back and tell him we accept his terms, I will tell him he has to have the gold delivered here tomorrow so we can verify the weight," said the Ukrainian. "As soon as we have confirmed that the weight is correct, I will leave with the three. If our customer gives us an escort so we can travel during the curfew, I could be back here the following morning."

"Very well, I agree," Komulakov said. "If anything new arises from your next conversation with him, let me know. I'll be back later tonight. Make sure you have someone standing by to turn on the lights on the runway."

"Certainly, General. Have a safe flight."

Dotensk thought for a moment, then reached for the Marconi radio to call the barracks where his four Ukrainian operatives were billeted.

"We need to unload one of the crates off the back of that truck," he said. "Meet me in the vehicle shed in five minutes."

MI6 Headquarters
Century House, Lambeth
London, England
Monday, 23 March 1998
1830 Hours, Local

Sir David Spelling pressed the switch on the antique intercom box on the left side of his desk.

"Downs, come in here!"

"C" ran a hand over the smooth finish of the mahogany box. The lads from Signals had tried to replace it several times, but "C" would have none of it. He liked the old squawk box's history: it had been used by his earliest predecessors to summon the staff to the air raid shelter in the basement of Century House during the blitz. He was adamant it wouldn't be replaced until he was.

Ian Downs, Director of Operations for MI6, knocked twice on the door and entered the inner sanctum.

"I trust you've seen this latest missive from Thomas? What've he and Blackman been doing out there . . . chewing *khat?*"

"I rather doubt that, sir," replied Downs. "I've heard they've been chatting with the Americans and believe they've discovered the location of what we've been reading about in all these intercepts GCHQ has been vacuuming up the last few days."

"You mean those rumored Iraqi nuclear weapons?"

"Precisely, sir."

"Well, read this cable and tell me if this makes sense to you."

MOST SECRET
NIACT IMMEDIATE
EYES ONLY FOR THE DIRECTOR
FROM: SAND DOLLAR
TO: OSO, MI6
SUBJ: INTERVENTION OPPORTUNITY

    1. CG CENTCOM SOURCE IN IRAQ ASSERTS THREE STOLEN SOVIET NUCLEAR WEAPS ARE LOCATED VIC OF AT TANF SYRIA.
    2. CG CENTCOM REQUESTS MI6 ASSISTANCE IN RECOVERING THESE WEAPS BEFORE THEY CAN BE DELIVERED TO IRAQI GOVT.
    3. CG CENTCOM SUGGESTS SAME 4-2 COMMANDO ROYAL MARINES ELEMENT USED IN RESCUE OF FOUR UK POWS FROM IRAQ BE USED FOR OP.
    4. SAND DOLLAR PERSONNEL AND EQUIPMENT ARE AVAIL AT INCIRLIK. RIFLE COMPANY OF 4-2 COMMANDO NOW AT BADANAH, SAUDI ARABIA. SAND DOLLAR PRIMARY CAN COORDINATE.
    5. REQUEST YOU ADVISE SOONEST. SAND DOLLAR PRIMARY AND NUMBER TWO STANDING BY.

    BT

When he finished reading the brief text, Downs looked up and said, "Are you asking my opinion?"

"No! Why should we even contemplate this? If the Americans know where the blasted things are, why don't *they* go fetch them?"

"I would guess, Sir David, it's because right now the people in Washington are having rather enough difficulty keeping up with all their president's sexual dalliances. They don't really have time to chase after something as mundane as a few loose nukes."

Spelling glared at his subordinate for a moment. Then he pivoted his chair and looked out his window. "It *would* make a rather nice trophy for the next time I go back to Parliament to beg for a few more pounds, wouldn't it?"

"Yes, sir. And just on the off chance you might think it was a good idea, I inquired at the Admiralty regarding keeping their Royal Marines for a bit longer. They agreed—subject to approval by the PM, of course."

Sir David pondered the matter for a few more seconds, then said, "Very well, Downs. Send off a cable to Thomas and Blackman and tell them to start the planning—but no green light until I get the go-ahead from the PM."

"Yes, sir." Downs gave a faint smile. "Shall I also call the Cabinet Secretary and tell him you require an audience at 10 Downing?"

"Yes . . . and have somebody call up my car."

Downs turned to go.

"And one more thing, Downs. Tell Thomas and Blackman to be careful. I don't want to read about this in *anybody's* newspapers."

Incirlik Air Base
Adana, Turkey
Monday, 23 March 1998
2145 Hours, Local

General Grisham climbed up into the U.S. Air Force Gulfstream IV, resigned to the fact that he was going to get a royal chewing when he arrived in Washington. He calculated he would be about four hours late for his command performance on the carpet in front of the chairman of the Joint Chiefs.

As he handed his briefcase to the waiting Air Force cabin attendant, Grisham saw Gunnery Sergeant Skillings trotting toward the aircraft. The general could tell by the sergeant's expression that the matter was important, so he signaled the pilot to wait. He climbed back down from the aircraft to meet Skillings.

"What is it, Gunny?"

"Sir, it's that call you placed to Colonel Newman. He's calling back and says he needs to talk to you right away."

The general reached for the sat phone. "Pete . . . I tried calling you, but I couldn't get through. Did you get my voice mail?"

"Yes, sir, I did."

"Well, I'm glad you called me right back. Listen, Pete . . . I have to leave for Washington now. The plane is waiting. I just wanted to give you some good news. I've been in touch with MI6 and asked them to loan us the special ops guys who just completed a rescue of four British POWs. They've given the green light for us to use them. So, the good news is that the British are coming! They're ready to help you go after the nukes and rescue the women too."

"Well, General, it looks like feast or famine. Major Rotem put on his boss, General Meir Hofi, and he's dispatching a team of their Sayeret Duvdevan commandos to help too."

"This is getting crazier by the minute. Everybody's willing to step up to the plate except Uncle Sam."

"General, if you leave for Washington, who's going to coordinate all this?"

Grisham sighed. "Lieutenant Colonel Newman, if this were being done right, I wouldn't budge from this HQ until I had you, Rachel, Mrs. Rotem, and those nukes right here with me. Unfortunately, I've got a major fire to put out back in Washington. I've been given direct orders to fly back and be at the Pentagon in the morning. I *have* to go. Now, Colonel . . . I'm sorry. And with the way things are between here and the Pentagon, I can't even give you any CENTCOM assets. You'll have to coordinate on the ground with the British and Israelis. I can't commit so much as a sidearm or a private. It reminds me of the situation in Khafji in 1990 . . . when the Saudis bugged out, there was a young Marine officer and a Force Recon team there on the ground. And somehow, all by himself, that Marine managed to coordinate all manner of naval gunfire, air strikes, and eventually even artillery and armor, to destroy the better part of an Iraqi Republican Guard's armor regiment. He did this and brought all his people out safely. Do you remember?"

Now there was silence from Newman's satellite phone.

"Yes, sir. I remember Khafji."

"I'll say. They gave you the Navy Cross for that one, didn't they, Pete?"

There was another long pause.

"General, there's someone there with you now that I had with me back then. If you can leave him behind to work with me on this, we might just be able to pull this off."

Grisham looked over at Gunnery Sergeant Skillings. "You mean the Gunny?"

"Yes, sir."

General Grisham nodded his head, still looking at Skillings and said, "Very well, Colonel Newman, I'm leaving Gunnery Sergeant Skillings here to be your contact at CENTCOM. I'll give him a TDA with the Brits, and he can officially work for them . . . relay comms from you to the Israeli and British commando units and keep you apprised of real-time intel from here. I'll tell the NATO and CENT-COM staff here I've asked him to monitor the situation and keep me apprised of the matter."

There was no response from Newman.

"Pete . . . did you copy that?"

"Yes, sir . . . I heard. Thank you."

"I've got to go. Pete . . . I know this is very high stakes stuff, but I believe it can all work. You know how to do this kind of thing. You'll have the best British and Israeli commandos helping . . . and Gunnery Sergeant Skillings will coordinate from here. It'll work—and *you're* just the one who can make it happen."

"Aye, aye, sir."

"Where are you now, Pete?"

"We're in the line of vehicles waiting to cross the border. My escort assures me we can still cross, even though the curfew has already gone into effect."

"Be careful. The Iraqi border guards are undoubtedly still alerted and on the lookout for those escaped POWs . . . so they'll probably have soldiers to augment the border officers."

"Yes, I know. We have a friendly who'll be on duty at the border crossing. He'll help us get across. Pray for us, General."

"I've been doing that, almost nonstop, and I'll keep doing it until you're all home safely. God bless, Colonel."

"Thank you, sir."

The general handed the satellite phone back to Skillings. He looked into the eyes of his gunnery sergeant and said, "As soon as we launch, I'll send a message back here letting both the NATO and CENTCOM staffs know you're going to help Newman. I'll make sure they stay out of your way, and that they keep this thing under wraps until it's over. Gunny . . . I hope we don't both end up getting court-martialed for what's about to happen."

Skillings returned the general's gaze evenly. "Sir, we're doing the right thing. Everything else will sort itself out."

The general gripped the sergeant's shoulder, then climbed back into the aircraft to start the long trip back to Washington.

International Scientific Trading, Ltd.
At Tanf, Syria
Monday, 23 March 1998
2150 Hours, Local

It took Leonid Dotensk and two of the other Ukrainians a little more than half an hour to unload one of the nuclear weapons from the truck. Once they wrestled the crate to the floor, they cracked open the lead-shielded container and removed the gray-green artillery round from its cradle inside the box.

"Is this safe?"

Dotensk really wasn't sure, but he said, "Of course. Now help me get this over to the workbench so we can disguise it as something other than what it is."

Once the round was on the workbench, Dotensk and one of his hirelings fashioned a different housing for the deadly weapon from a four-foot section of PVC pipe. After wrapping the artillery round with flexible sheets of lead, ordinarily used to protect film from X-rays, they slid the pipe down over the bullet-shaped projectile. Then Dotensk stuffed heavy plastic foam into both ends and capped the pipe at both ends.

"Will that lead foil protect us from leaking radiation?" the other man asked.

"Certainly," said Dotensk, with more confidence than he felt. "Besides, I don't intend to keep it here for very long. For now, put it on that other truck over there. Then, go get some sand. I want to fill up this empty case so it weighs the same as it did before we removed the warhead.

"By the way, when you go outside for the sand, stop at the hangar and turn on the runway lights. The general should be returning soon."

Dotensk decided Komulakov didn't need to know about this little shell game he'd decided to play. Qusay Hussein would, of course, kill him if he discovered the switch, but Dotensk's instincts told him Qusay had no intention of actually wiring the final fifty million to his numbered account in Aruba. Dotensk reasoned that if Iraq actually started some kind of nuclear exchange, there wouldn't be anyone left in the Hussein family to carry out a vendetta against Leonid Dotensk, the world's smartest arms dealer. Somebody would always be in the market for a good nuke. No sense wasting inventory.

Besides, if nothing happens and Qusay is still around in a week or two, I will just tell him he can have his third nuke as soon as the money appears in my account.

There was also the matter about the gold. Before Komulakov returned, Dotensk had to figure out a way to move nearly ten tons of gold to a bank, where he could get his cut. And he had to do all this without the rest of the men in this compound becoming greedy and taking part of—or the whole—treasure trove for themselves.

Still, Dotensk thought, before worrying about how to divide the gold, they first had to receive it.

"Mr. Dotensk," shouted the largest of the Ukrainians. "We are ready to put this crate back on the truck."

"Did you weigh it?"

"Yes, sir, this crate is now equal in weight to the others."

"Then put it back on the truck," said Dotensk. "But put it all the way to the front of the truck so that, when the cargo is unloaded, they won't have the one full of sand until last."

The two workers complied, using the forklift to shuffle the load. When they were finished, Dotensk patted them on their backs.

"I don't want you to tell any of the other men about this . . . at least, not until after I tell General Komulakov."

Before he left, he would have to dispose of these two men who had just helped him carry out this conspiracy.

That will be a shame. We have been friends for nearly twenty years.

Syrian Border Crossing
23 km East of At Tanf
Monday, 23 March 1998
2220 Hours, Local

Newman breathed a sigh of relief as they passed through the Iraqi border crossing. Additional Iraqi soldiers were on duty, but even though the curfew had gone into effect at 2100, the Iraqi border guards had allowed vehicles already in line to proceed through. He and Samir had arrived at the dusty desert outpost just as the Iraqi customs officers, border patrol, and immigration police were changing the watch. In the confusion of the duty change, Samir's friend Nazir had seen them arrive, having been told by Eli Yusef to expect them just before ten o'clock.

Since his shift did not end until midnight, Nazir was still on duty and had made sure he was the one who checked the travelers' truck and identity documents. Two Iraqi soldiers accompanied Nazir and looked over his shoulder when he examined the Indian passport that identified Newman as Ram Fales.

"You are from India?" one of the soldiers asked him. "You do not look like an Indian."

"I am from the Portuguese section of Goa, on the west coast of India," Newman said, trying to speak with what he hoped sounded like an Indian accent. The soldiers found him plausible enough to shrug and move on to inspect the next vehicle.

As they walked away, Nazir said in a quiet voice, "You should not have any problems at the Syrian border crossing. If you run into any difficulties, ask for Captain Majhaar. He will let anyone cross into Syria for a small fee."

"How much will it take?" asked Newman.

Nazir shrugged and said, "I have never asked him, but I would suggest five hundred Swiss francs or English pound notes. I would not use American currency—although that is probably the favored one—since dollars will raise too many questions."

They had proceeded less than three hundred meters from the Iraqi border crossing to the Syrian checkpoint; Newman was immediately tagged as someone to check more carefully than most travelers.

After nearly ten minutes of questions and getting nowhere, Newman asked, "May I speak with Captain Majhaar?"

"He is not on duty tonight. I am the officer in charge," replied a surly fat man with very bad teeth, whose girth tested the limits of his uniform. "How do you know Captain Majhaar?" the officer asked.

Samir answered before Newman could make something up. He spoke in Arabic, and the words came out so quickly that Newman did not fully understand what he was saying. Samir gestured grandly and smiled as he spoke.

The fat officer blinked, then nodded, and finally he smiled. Then he held up the ten fingers of both beefy hands. The officer then looked at Newman and smiled, saying in English to Samir, "I will be back in a moment after you discuss it with your employer." After that, he gestured to the soldier next to him to follow him to the building where other travelers were being checked much more carefully. Newman had already decided he didn't want to be invited to leave the truck and go inside the building.

"What did you tell him?" Newman asked Samir after the two Syrians were out of earshot.

"I told him I was hired as a guide for the rich, Indian businessman. I told him you were unfamiliar with the customs here and would appreciate suggestions of how much of a gratuity you should give him."

"And he said ten," Newman said, holding up his own two hands. "Maybe I should give him fifteen hundred to make sure things go smoothly."

"No . . . I do not think that is wise. If you give him more than he asks, he will think he should have asked for more. The ways here are different. Take out five hundred-franc bills and offer them to him. If he doesn't like your offering, he will let you know. Then you can keep adding bills, one at a time, until he is pleased. Probably he will keep going until you pay him a thousand francs."

"This could go on all night. We need to get on our way. I want to find this place in Syria, not haggle over bribes all night."

"Please . . . do it my way, Peter. It will not take long."

Samir was right. The overweight officer pocketed the thousand in Swiss franc notes and let them through the checkpoint at the Syrian border.

As they drove away from the border checkpoint, Newman leaned back in the seat, closed his eyes, and uttered an audible sigh of relief.

TARGETS
AND SHOOTERS

C H A P T E R T W E N T Y - O N E

Damascus-to-Baghdad Highway
23 km West of Border
Monday, 23 March 1998
2250 Hours, Local

his is the place," said Samir, pointing to two large buildings on
the side of the road as he slowed the truck. It had been less than
half an hour since they had crossed into Syria. Ahead, several
kilometers down the highway, they could see the lights marking the
outskirts of At Tanf.

"Are you sure?" Newman peered at yellow, warehouse-like structures. Floodlights lit a truck parking area and loading docks in front of
the main building. A light glowed from one window on the ground
floor.

Samir pointed to a large sign next to a guarded gate between the two large buildings that fronted on the highway. "International Scientific Trading, Ltd."

Other than the single lighted office in one of the warehouses and another in the guard post, there was no sign of life. The truck crept past the complex at less than ten miles per hour.

Once they had passed the complex, Samir accelerated, pulling back onto the highway toward At Tanf. He glanced over at Newman. "You are worried about your wife, my friend."

"Yes. She's back there in that building somewhere, and—"

"She will be all right, Peter. I have been praying for her safe return to you since I learned of her capture. My father and all of our family have been praying as well. You must trust in the Lord. It is his nature to look after his children"

"Thank you, Samir. I hope so. But . . . I've done things that displease him."

"What do you mean?"

"I just can't help wondering . . . Does God answer the prayers of those who offend him?"

"We are all sinners, Peter. None of us is perfect."

"I know, but . . . my faith isn't as mature as yours, and especially your father's. I keep thinking maybe God won't answer our prayers when we do things wrong—like bribing that man when we crossed the border."

Samir pursed his lips and put his head back on the headrest of the seat as he drove through the darkness.

"Do you remember that passage in the Bible—in Hebrews—where Saint Paul writes about faith?" Samir said, finally. "He describes many people who were said to have great faith. He mentions Noah, Abraham, Joseph, Moses, and the other patriarchs . . . but he also mentions Rahab, a prostitute . . . and Samson, who sinned with Delilah . . . David, who committed adultery with Bathsheba and murdered her husband."

"Yes, but what does that have to do with what I did, Samir?"

"Sometimes we all do wrong things, but God forgives us and helps us to go on. He looks upon our hearts and sees our motivation. That is what counts in his sight."

"Do you mean the end justifies the means?"

"Oh no—not at all. But your intent back there at the border wasn't evil. The *baksheesh* you gave that border guard wasn't offered to smuggle goods or to enrich yourself. You did it with the intent of saving your wife—and perhaps preventing terrible weapons from being used against innocent people. I believe God takes all that into account. I am also confident that he will answer our prayers for your wife."

They had reached the outskirts of At Tanf. Samir pulled off the road into the empty parking lot of a petrol station, just inside the city limits. He turned off the lights.

"We will wait here for my father. He is driving here from his friend's house in town."

They sat silently for a few minutes. Headlights appeared in the distance, coming toward them from the west. While they watched and waited, a light-colored pickup truck pulled into the parking lot, stopped, backed up, and parked next to them. It was Eli Yusef. Samir and Newman climbed out of their vehicle and walked around the front of Yusef's truck.

"'As-salâmu shalaykhum . . . kayf hâluhk?" Samir said as he greeted his father.

The old man replied, *"Shukran. Al-hamdu li-lah."*

Newman smiled as the patriarch of the Habib clan climbed out of his truck and embraced his son, then extended his arms to the American. *"Shalaykhum,"* Newman said as he hugged the older man, who echoed the greeting to his friend.

Samir spoke in Arabic to his father. Newman was pleased that he understood most of it and could make educated guesses about the phrases that he didn't get.

"So what is your plan, my son?" Yusef asked the Marine.

"Well, sir . . . if Samir will take me back and drop me off near the place where they're holding my wife, I'll try to get some information to the commandos who are coming to help tomorrow night."

"And how will you pass the information to them?"

"With this," Newman replied, holding up one of the two Iridium sat phones.

"Ah yes." Eli Yusef smiled. "The marvels of modern electronics. It is too bad I did not have a device such as that when I was spying on Rommel for the British in North Africa . . . it would have made a great difference. Well now, how can we be of help to you?"

"It's important that neither of you be anywhere near that place tomorrow night, because when the commandos arrive, they might mistake you for one of the kidnappers, and your lives could be at great risk. But you *can* help me from a distance."

"How so?"

"We're going to need eyes and ears posted along this highway, both east and west of the warehouse complex," said Newman, pointing to the road in front of them. "It would be very helpful if tomorrow evening, Samir, just before dark, you could position yourself east of the IST complex—between it and the border. And Eli Yusef, if you would do the same, on the highway west of the target, perhaps even in At Tanf . . . ."

"And we would alert you to anything we see coming from our direction along the highway—especially the Syrian military?" Samir said.

The Marine nodded. "Yes, Samir. Your father raised you well." Newman turned to the old man. "Eli Yusef, this is simply more of the kind of thing that you did for the British in World War II, isn't it?"

"Yes. I would tell them the number and types of aircraft or vehicles, the size of troop units, how fast they were going, what direction, and how long before they were likely to get to the British lines. I assume that's what you want us to provide for you tomorrow?"

"It is indeed. But I'm hoping we don't have to contend with the sort of manpower and firepower that Rommel had with him."

Eli and Samir chuckled and nodded.

"All you have to do is use your cell phone to call me if you see any military or other hostile activity," Newman said. The two men nodded again.

"Were you able to obtain any of the things I called you about, Eli Yusef?"

"Yes . . . I have them in this knapsack." The old man reached into the cab and retrieved the pack. He took out a pair of binoculars and handed them to Newman. "I am sorry that I do not have a case for them. It was the best I could do on such short notice."

"These will do just fine."

"And here are four bottles of water, some bread, meat, and some boiled eggs."

"Well, thank you, my friend. I didn't even think about something to eat. Thank you."

"And I brought some other things that you did not ask for but which may be useful," Yusef said. He reached into the pack and took a bed sheet dyed in mottled khaki, light brown, and sandy gray. "You may find this helpful to keep you hidden during the daylight tomorrow. My friend's wife dyed it today. The colors are a close match to the terrain you will be in. Out here, there is so little vegetation. The soil is very hard—mostly ancient lava."

Next, the old man withdrew what appeared to be a bulky telescope.

"This belongs to my friend who owns the binoculars. He picked it up in his travels. It is a device for seeing in the dark."

Newman took it and held it in front of the headlights of the pickup. It was an older Soviet-made monocular military night-vision scope—he guessed it was made in the late '70s or early '80s. The stampings on it were Russian, but he recognized the word *Novosibirsk*, which he knew to be the third largest city in the Russian Republic, probably where it was manufactured. He looked it over, stepped away from the truck lights, and pointed it into the darkness to try it out. The new moon was just a sliver, but peering through the lens, Newman could clearly see scrub brush, rocks, and small details in the green-tinged, three-power magnification, all invisible to his naked eye.

"It is old," said Yusef, "but I put new batteries in so it should help."

"Well, I'm sure it'll help me a great deal in the darkness," Newman said. "Please thank your friend. I'll try to take good care of his things."

"There is one more thing that he provided that may be useful," Yusef said, reaching into the knapsack once more. He drew out an automatic pistol, an extra magazine, and a small cardboard box of ammunition.

Newman took the weapon and examined it. Holding it in the beam of the truck headlight, he recognized that it was a 9mm CZ 75B, made by the Czech manufacturer Ceská Zbrojovka. He remembered the unusual weapon because that model was available for .40 caliber Smith & Wesson ammunition or 9mm. Newman thought back to his days commanding 2nd Force Reconnaissance Company in 1990–91, when the instructors from Weapons Training Battalion at Quantico had brought weapons like this—and scores of others—to the range at Camp Lejeune so that his Marines could familiarize themselves with all the weapons that might be in the hands of their adversaries. Though old, the CZ 75B appeared to be well cared for and serviceable. He noticed that it was clean and oiled, with no apparent rust. He released the magazine and tried the slide action. It was quiet and smooth. He held it in his hand for balance and looked down the sights. The finish was a no-nonsense black military polymer, and the handgrip was a bit rough, but it was comfortable in his hand. Then he opened the box of ammunition that Yusef had given him, trying to guess its age. The gun was probably thirty years old, or more. He hoped the ammo was fresher than that. The glow of the truck's parking lights showed that the cartridges still had a brassy sheen, and they didn't have the dull patina of corrosion that would indicate that the bullets were unreliable. That reassured him greatly.

"Your friend seems to know how to take care of a firearm, Yusef."

The old man and his son watched as the Marine loaded fifteen rounds into each magazine, slid one into the weapon, pulled the slide to the rear, chambered a round, and engaged the safety.

"My friend does indeed know how to care for his weapons," Yusef said. "He was drafted into the Syrian Army many years ago. He fought in the 1948 war against Israel and was wounded on the Golan Heights in 1967. Ironically, as it turned out, he had more to fear from his fellow Syrians than the Israelis. His family—all Syrian Christians—were murdered by Syrian Muslims in Hims—I think you call it Homs—in 1968. It was during this terrible time that he bought and kept the weapon . . . just in case."

Newman put the weapon, the extra magazine, and the remaining ammo back in the knapsack. "This will do just fine. Yusef, thank you for helping me with these things," Newman continued. "They may help keep me alive. Now . . . I suppose we ought to get moving. I want to find a position where I can observe the IST facility before daylight."

Yusef put his hand on Newman's shoulder. "First, I must pray," he said. Samir nodded and put both hands on Newman's shoulders from behind, while the elder Habib did the same from the front. Newman bowed his head to honor his friends' benediction, but he was not quite prepared for the passionate petition that the old man presented to his God. Yusef poured out his heart in a plaintive cry for heaven's help and protection, and for God to safely reunite Peter Newman with his wife. Newman was touched by such devotion, and he hugged both men before they got into their vehicles.

The Marine was silent as he and Samir drove east, back toward the IST warehouse complex.

"Samir . . . turn off your headlights and pull over about a mile ahead. I'll get out and walk the rest of the way, just to make sure I'm not seen by anybody."

"Yes . . . all right."

Four minutes later, the Arab Christian pulled onto the shoulder of the highway and Newman jumped out, grabbing the knapsack.

"Masha salâma," Samir said, and then repeated the phrase in English: "Go now, without fear."

Newman nodded, turned, and disappeared into the darkness of the desert.

International Scientific Trading, Ltd.

At Tanf, Syria
Monday, 23 March 1998
2310 Hours, Local

Leonid Dotensk was on the phone with Qusay Hussein. There had been, as the arms merchant knew there would be, huge complications in the logistics of exchanging the nuclear weapons for two truckloads of gold.

"But when we discussed this sale, I explained to you that our terms were to be one hundred and fifty million Swiss francs wired to our bank. You insisted on making partial payment in gold—to which we have reluctantly agreed—but I cannot deliver the merchandise to you until we have had a chance to verify the weight of the gold in the two trucks. After that has been confirmed, we will send the truck with the merchandise that you want," Dotensk said.

His customer raised his voice in protest; Dotensk held the phone receiver away from his ear while the man screamed about the Ukrainian's lack of trust.

"I am sorry, my friend, but for people in my line of work, it is always a matter of trust. After you send us the gold and we verify the weight, I will release our truck to bring you the three machines you have ordered."

"Where are the machines now?" asked Qusay.

"They are in a safe place." Dotensk was instantly wary of the Iraqi. If Saddam's son knew how close they were to the border, he wouldn't send two truckloads of gold—he could instead dispatch several helicopter gunships and a team of commandos to take the weapons from Dotensk. Dotensk had no idea what mad scheme the Iraqi was planning, or why he seemed so insistent on having the weapons immediately—but it didn't matter. What mattered was getting paid in full—and being alive to spend the money.

There was a moment of silence and then Qusay said, "I will have two trucks loaded with the gold and brought to you. You said you wanted the gold delivered near a border crossing in Syria. Will you want the trucks sent to Qusaybah or Abjub?"

Dotensk had already thought through this option. If he had control over things, he would have had the gold delivered to Qusaybah, the border crossing further north, on the Aleppo-to-Baghdad Highway, to divert attention from the At Tanf facilities. But the Ukrainian arms merchant knew that if the Israelis really were preparing for war, such a delivery scheme would only delay the transaction further, as well as delay his departure from this region of the world at such an unsafe time. Dotensk was also concerned about transporting a hundred million dollars worth of gold bars across hundreds of miles of Syrian geography, rife with robbers and hijackers.

"Bring the trucks to the border crossing on the Damascus-to-Baghdad highway," he said. "I will have some of my men meet them at the Syrian side of the checkpoint. My people will take care of all of the 'paperwork' with the Syrian customs officers, so there will not be any delay.

"Please make sure you use commercial lorries, no military or government markings. I believe if you will do these things, you can have your three machines within twenty-four hours."

"It will be done."

"What time will they be at the border?"

"I have already ordered the Director of the Treasury to supervise an after-hours release of the gold. They will work all night. It will be packed on skids and stamped with the inspection and inventory numbers of the Iraqi National Treasury. You will know then that I have not shortchanged you when you weigh the gold in the trucks."

Dotensk ignored the sarcasm in Qusay's voice. "The time?"

"The trucks will be at the border no later than noon. They will come from Baghdad, after all. As you know, that can take seven hours."

"My men will be at the Syrian border checkpoint at eleven o'clock."

"Very well. And I am counting on you to have my merchandise back at the border no later than six tomorrow evening."

"That will be impossible," Dotensk said. "We will have a long drive as well. Damascus is four or five hours by truck. We cannot be in Baghdad until midnight."

Dotensk smiled at his own cleverness. Let Qusay think they had to drive to Damascus; the less anyone thought about At Tanf, the better. "We cannot deliver to you by six."

After a pause, Qusay said, "I am trusting you with one hundred million in gold. I had hoped you would at least send the truck on ahead with my merchandise. You can contact them once you have weighed the gold. Surely that way you can get the truck here by, say, nine?"

"I will do my best," Dotensk said, and hung up the phone, satisfied that he had outfoxed the Iraqi. These were the kind of details at which he had excelled during his career in the KGB. The Ukrainian arms merchant's lips turned up in a satisfied smile as he contemplated the arrival of the trucks laden with gold, and the return of Komulakov from Damascus. *And the general didn't think I deserved 50 percent!*

✪

Peter Newman was hidden in scarce cover some three hundred meters from the southeast corner of the IST complex. He had come in behind the big facility, crossed what he realized was a runway—a feature he hadn't been able to see when they had driven by on the road—and crawled up as close to the buildings as he thought was safe.

The Marine was somewhat surprised. It had taken him less than an hour to negotiate the distance from the highway, where Samir dropped him off, about a kilometer west of where he was now. His reconnaissance skills, unused for three years, came back as if by instinct. From his vantage point beside a cluster of rocks and scrub brush on a small elevation only thirty meters south of the east-west runway, he now had a clear view of the entire complex.

Newman lay down and began a detailed visual recon of everything inside the complex. Alternately using the binoculars and the night-vision device, he committed the particulars to memory. As he focused on the lighted hangar at the west end of the runway, the runway lights suddenly came on.

Interesting. A late night visitor?

While he waited for the aircraft to approach, the hangar door opened and he switched to the binoculars. Newman made mental notes of the interior of that building.

An office area, a workshop on the far end of the building, and space for at least two or three aircraft. Just outside . . . let's see, a fuel truck, and what appears to be a several-thousand-gallon above-ground fuel storage tank inside a berm.

He then tried to determine what the other various buildings were for and how many people occupied each one. He could make things out fairly clearly in the glow of the sodium vapor lights ringing the buildings in orange-tinged pools. One of the structures had two stories and numerous windows, and he could see men entering and leaving by a centrally located doorway. He assumed it served as some kind of dormitory for Komulakov's soldiers and workers.

A concrete, one-story blockhouse in the middle of the grounds, topped by a large satellite antenna and three smaller dishes, had to be a communications facility. Peering through the binoculars, Newman figured that the large utility building at least four meters high, without windows, was likely some kind of vehicle shed. Next to it, completing the quadrangle, was the large building that faced toward the highway. He had seen the loading docks on the opposite side of the structure and assumed it was the warehouse.

Across a courtyard from that building and also facing the highway, a large complex sprawled out in an L-shaped configuration. *Probably their offices.*

On the southwest corner of the property, adjacent to the runway, was a smaller, separate building. It was obviously constructed with more refinements than the other buildings. He made a mental note that this was either the headquarters for the facility or the residence for the on-site commander, or both.

Now, where is Rachel? If she's being held here, in which building? He used the night-vision device and binoculars, checking each of the buildings and areas once more, very carefully.

His heart pounded. He wished he could go in there and take the two women away with him into the night and let the commandos finish the job the following night. But he knew he had to stay with the plan that he had given General Grisham, Skillings, and Rotem. They needed him on the ground to make the raid successful. So he tried to put thoughts of Rachel out of his mind for the time being.

As he lay on the ground peering into the optics of the night-vision device and binoculars, he committed every detail of what he had seen to memory. He would recite what he had seen, detail by detail, to Skillings when he checked in with him at 2400 hours.

As he was looking through the lens of the night-vision scope, an enormous flare of light momentarily blinded his right eye. He reacted quickly and looked away, but he had to close that eye in order to see with his unaffected left eye. Then he heard the noise of the jet whose landing lights must have flared into the lens. The sleek Learjet touched down at the east end of the runway and immediately began braking, its engines roaring. It coasted to a stop and parked not far from the hangar. After a moment, the door was opened. One of the pilots jumped down and lowered the exit stairs that were built into the lower half of the clamshell door.

Fortunately, the door was on the left side of the aircraft, directly in Newman's line of vision. The effects of the sudden flare in the binoculars were wearing off. The person deboarding was Komulakov; once again, Newman's heart raced in anticipation of confronting the man.

✪

When he disembarked, General Komulakov ordered the two Swiss pilots to refuel the Lear and to pull it into the hangar. He then strode into the compound and directly to the guest house where Dotensk was waiting. Without speaking, he strode into a small office off of the living room and poured himself a glass of vodka.

The Ukrainian arms merchant waited until Komulakov took a second deep draught.

"Qusay is sending a shipment of two trucks filled with gold bars. They will arrive by noon tomorrow or so," the Ukrainian reported. "Can you imagine, General? Two huge trucks filled with gold bars!"

Komulakov just sipped his vodka. *Why doesn't he at least offer me a drink?* Dotensk thought. Dotensk was handing him a hundred million dollars in gold. *It is time for this partnership to end.* "Did you have a good trip to Damascus?"

"No!" Komulakov said. "It was a terrible trip."

"Uh . . . I am sorry to hear that." Dotensk walked to the credenza and poured himself a drink.

"I went to Damascus to receive an urgent message from the spy Morales," Komulakov said. "Apparently, he found something so important he was willing to risk being found out. Morales must work at the U.S. State Department; none of the other intelligence agencies would have such direct access to the material he sent. So there was some good news, at least—I can find him on my own, now that I know where he is."

"What did he want to tell you?"

"He said that Newman is not back in the United States, as I had ordered. He is still over here. In fact, he is in Iraq—looking for Saddam's nukes! I can't believe it. Why would he take such risks? Doesn't he know that I promised to kill his wife and her friend if he didn't do exactly as I instructed?"

"But how did this Morales fellow find out?" Dotensk asked. "Perhaps he is misinformed. I cannot believe Newman would put his wife in obvious jeopardy like that."

"Neither can I. I can only assume it has something to do with that general who was supposedly helping him get back into the States to find Morales."

"Weren't you using Newman to track down this spy because you felt Morales might compromise you if he was caught?"

"Yes. But now Morales himself has opened the door for me to find him. I don't need Colonel Newman to kill Morales now. And Newman knows too much. He'll put two and two together and figure out our role in providing those nuclear weapons to Saddam. He must be silenced before he can lead the Americans to us."

"How will you do that?"

"Go get his wife. Bring her over here. We'll have her call him on his satellite phone. I have the number. We'll have him go to a location that we can control—and then we'll kill him."

"Where, Dimitri? You cannot tell him to come here. His phone is surely monitored—by the Jews, the Americans, or both. If they know where we are sending him, they will meet us there with one of their commando units—like they did when they tried to kill you at the safe house."

"Yes, yes . . . you're right, Leonid. We need a place where they can't get to us but he can. How about if we tell him to go to the VIP lounge at the airport in Damascus, just as we did when we arranged for him to come in? It's too dangerous for the Duvdevan or Mossad to stage a confrontation, and the Americans can't get there either. We can have a couple of our PFLP men meet him at the VIP lounge as before, and they can drive him to our hangar over at the other side of the airport. Tell them to kill him there. Oh, and have him strangled—I don't want any blood in the hangar. Put his corpse in one of those body bags and we'll have it flown out and dumped in the desert the next time they are flying one of the MI-8s."

"Yes . . . that sounds like it will work. And what about the women?"

"Take them out into the desert and kill them both as soon as Mrs. Newman calls her husband. Have her tell him he'll be met at the VIP lounge by someone who will take him to where the women are. Tell him that in exchange for any information he has about Morales, I will release the women and he can take them with him from Damascus."

"Do you think he will believe her?"

"Of course he will. He *wants* to believe it. He'll be there."

Dotensk took the last swallow from his glass and stood up. "I will convince Mrs. Newman that they will be released, and that she must convince her husband to meet her in Damascus."

"Yes . . . good. But add this incentive: tell her that if he does not come to Damascus to give me information on Morales, they will never see each other again and that their child will grow up without her. That should make her a very convincing interlocutor."

NSA Collection and Analysis Center
Fort Meade, Maryland
Monday, 23 March 1998
1725 Hours, Local

"What's going on?" asked Roy Schumaker as he rushed into the watch center at the heart of the supersecret intelligence agency. He stared at one of the computer screens arrayed in the console in front of his subordinate, thirty-one-year-old Intercept Analyst Dale Morse. "Is this why the computer paged me?"

"Yes, sir," said Morse. "It's not the text of the intercept—but it's a 'Red Rocket' from GCHQ, and the SOP says we're supposed to disseminate this info immediately by Flash precedence even if we don't yet have the full intercept in from the field."

"Well, did you disseminate it?"

"Yes, sir," replied Morse, checking the electronic transmission log on another of the computer screens. He ran his finger down the list on the screen. "It's gone to the White House, the VEEP, the DCI, State, Defense, NORAD, all the military CINCs, and NRO. I called the old man, and a courier has been dispatched with a copy for him."

"Don't you generally clear that kind of thing with your superior *first?*" asked Schumaker, his voice revealing his irritation.

"Yes, sir. When I found out you weren't here yet, I tried calling your cell phone, but it wasn't turned on. I left you a message that we had an urgent matter. This seemed too important to wait."

"Uh-huh."

Schumaker picked up the printed advisory.

RED ROCKET / RED ROCKET / RED ROCKET
NUCLEAR ATTACK WARNING

UK MOST SECRET / URGENT / EYES ONLY BIGOT LIST ALPHA
U.S. TOP SECRET / FLASH / EYES ONLY NSC PRINCIPALS ONLY
23 2315:43 MAR 98 MAL LLT QX
   1. GCHQ STATION JULIET HAS PARTIALLY DECRYPTED AN
INTERCEPTED ISRAELI DEFENSE FORCES GENERAL STAFF
WARNING ORDER ALERTING ROCKET FORCES TO PREPARE TO
EXECUTE QUOTE JERICHO SANCTION UNQUOTE AGAINST IRAQ.
   2. ANALYSIS:
      A. JERICHO SANCTION IS ISRAELI CODE PHRASE FOR
NUCLEAR STRIKE USING CBM WEAPONS.
      B. SPECIFIC TARGETS: UNK.
      C. TIME OF ISRAELI MISSILE STRIKE: UNK
      D. MAY BE ISRAELI PREEMPTIVE ATTACK TO ELIMINATE
NUCLEAR WEAPONS ACQUIRED BY IRAQ.
      E. RELIABLE INTELLIGENCE INDICATES IRAQ IS ACQUIR-
ING OR HAS ACQUIRED AT LEAST THREE NUCLEAR
WEAPONS FROM UNK SOURCES.

"This is not good," Schumaker muttered. "What's happened since this went out?"

"The President and Prime Minister have already talked about this. The Pentagon wanted to go to DEFCON One, but the White House nixed it because they think it will scare the public."

"Uh-huh. Well, what now? Who's driving this runaway train?"

"I'm not sure. The Secretary of State, the DCI, and SECDEF are meeting with the President and the National Security Advisor," Morse said.

"Do we have anyone from NSA at the White House?"

"Not that I know of."

"Why not? I should have been called in."

"I guess everything was happening so fast, they didn't think of it. The President is on the phone with the UNSG to get ahold of Iraq right away, and the Secretary of State is calling the PM of Israel. They're trying to cool things off, threatening them with the worst possible sanctions if either of them tries to use their nukes."

"Yeah, well . . . I doubt if the Israelis will back down now. They've been making it pretty clear for some time that if Israel is hit with a weapon of mass destruction, they will—how do they put it?—'respond the only way they can.' I guess nobody ever expected Saddam to get a nuke. And unless somebody does something pretty quick, it looks like the Iraqis are all set to kick-start Armageddon."

NATO HQ, Incirlik Air Base
Adana, Turkey
Tuesday, 24 March 1998
0025 Hours, Local

Blackman and Thomas of MI6 were two very busy men as they prepared an operation to recover the nuclear weapons that Qusay Hussein was preparing to use. Blackman was on a sat phone to the commander of Four-Two Commando, Royal Marines Detachment in Saudi Arabia. Thomas, as the senior, was dealing with London while he waited for a call from this fellow Newman, who supposedly was to provide a reconnaissance report of what he found at the objective.

Blackman had already asked Gunnery Sergeant Skillings to find as many maps as possible of the area around At Tanf, Syria; Skillings also provided the imagery and details of the last two satellite passes over the objective.

Skillings came through the door into the little office adjacent to the NATO Operation Center that the two Brits were using as their temporary command post. "Excuse me, gentlemen; I have Lieutenant Colonel Newman calling on a sat phone. Would you care to accompany me into the Ops Center so you can talk to him yourselves?"

Thomas jumped up from the table and followed the Marine out the door while Blackman continued his coordination with the Royal Marines. In less than ten minutes, Newman was able to provide a detailed description of all he had observed of the IST facility. At Thomas's suggestion, they agreed that Newman would call again on his Iridium phone in an hour and attempt to conference in the Four-Two Commando leader and Major Rotem in Israel. As soon as Newman and Thomas terminated their call, Gunnery Sergeant Skillings set out to find the HQ signals officer to ensure their ability to connect and encrypt all the calls and record what was said.

"Well then," said Thomas as he and Skillings re-entered the office where Blackman had just finished his conversation with the CO of Four-Two Commando in Saudi Arabia, "thanks to Lieutenant Colonel Newman, we now have a very good idea of what's going on at the objective. So why the long face, Blackman? "

"Well sir, Colonel Banks says that even if they relocate our Royal Marines up to Turayf, the U.S. Marine CH-53 helos and the AH-1 Cobras that escort them can't carry enough fuel to make the round trip to At Tanf and back. One of the American Marine pilots said that he had signed for his helicopter and was loath to park it in Syria and walk home. He's asked if we know of any petrol stations on the way they could use to top off their tanks."

"Midair refueling isn't an option?" asked Thomas.

"Asked that myself. Apparently the Marines don't have one of their KC-130 tankers out here, and all the American Air Force tanker assets are tied up refueling the aircraft doing the no-fly zone surveillance flights."

"How about using the fuel at the airfield Lieutenant Colonel Newman just told us about?" asked Skillings.

The two Brits blinked at each other, then nodded. "Brilliant, Gunnery Sergeant, just brilliant," Thomas said with a wide grin. "Colonel Banks will be glad to know we've found him a petrol station."

"The Marines will want to know how much fuel there is," said Blackman. "Did Colonel Newman give quantity estimates, Gunnery Sergeant?"

"Yes, sir." Skillings checked his notes from the satellite phone call. "He says that the place has a mile-long runway, a tanker truck with jet fuel aboard, and he counted at least two above-ground storage tanks that he estimated to be of 20,000-gallon capacity each—though he doesn't know how much fuel is left in them. But assuming all that's accurate—and knowing Colonel Newman as I do—I'd say that there should be enough fuel for all our aircraft and the Israelis as well."

"Blackman," said Thomas, "be a good chap and ring up Colonel Banks at Four-Two Commando on his sat phone. Encourage him to tell his lads not to damage the fuel truck or the tank farm when they get to the objective. He should be able to see both on the satellite imagery we're sending him. Tell him that's our petrol for getting them back home."

"Right, sir," Blackman replied.

"And then, Gunnery Sergeant Skillings, would you be so kind as to get on the phone with Colonel Banks and bring him up to speed on the rest of your conversation with Colonel Newman? Let's see if we can work out a way for him to communicate with your Israeli friends so that we won't all be going bump in the night and running over each other."

"Aye, aye, sir."

It took less than a minute for Blackman to connect with Colonel Banks's encrypted sat phone and only a minute more for him to complete his business with the Royal Marine. The MI6 officer then handed the telephone to Gunnery Sergeant Skillings.

"Good morning, sir," Skillings said. "Lieutenant Colonel Newman asked me to confirm that you have received the overhead imagery of the objective from NRO."

"It's being downloaded now," said Banks.

"Sir, Colonel Newman suggests that the runway serve as the boundary between your unit and the Israelis—with Four-Two Commando taking the terrain and buildings on the north side of the runway."

"Quite clear on that, Gunnery Sergeant. And the Israelis are going in on the south side of the runway—is that right?"

"Yes, sir, that's right."

"I see . . . and just how many Israeli commandos are coming to this little party and what toys are they bringing?"

"Actually sir, no toys—just themselves—no aircraft even. They'll make a HALO drop just to the north of the target and then glide in to an LZ south of the runway. Colonel Newman will advise when they move up to within a hundred meters or so from the south entrance to the place. They will have a force of nine men, led by Major Ze'ev Rotem of the Sayeret Duvdevan. His wife is one of the hostages, and his team will lead the rescue while your Royal Marines come in from the other end and concentrate on the other targets."

"I think that will work. By the way, since we've been on this call, your NRO has sent us the latest overhead imagery of the place. This gives us a good picture of the whole area. Next time you talk with Colonel Newman, tell him we're going to designate north as twelve o'clock and number the buildings on the objective based on where they are around the clock. That way, we will take the buildings from nine to three, and the Israelis will take the buildings from three to nine."

"Aye, aye, sir," said Skillings. "I'll pass that to Colonel Newman and Major Rotem so that we're all in the same playbook. And as Colonel Newman sends reports in here, I will see to it that it's all relayed directly to you and Major Rotem."

"Well done, Gunnery Sergeant. Now, a few questions—and pass these along to those nice chaps from MI6 you have sitting there beside you, because I'm about to put my lads in harm's way and I want some answers: What time does this raid go down? Who is in command on the ground? Who is in overall control? Who makes the final go/no-go decision? My Marines can talk to your Marines in the helicopters, because we've been doing it all week out here in training. But what's the overall communications plan? How are my Marines to coordinate with the Israelis, and what arrangements are being made so that we can all talk to Lieutenant Colonel Newman on the ground? No offense, Gunnery Sergeant, but I sort of expected an officer to be running the show on your end."

"Sir, the chain of command is clear. Lieutenant General George Grisham, Commander in Chief of the United States Central Command, is the overall commander. Lieutenant Colonel Peter Newman, USMC, is the overall ground commander. General Grisham is more involved in this mission than you know, sir. He is monitoring every aspect. And Colonel Newman is running the show, sir . . . from the front door of the target. I'm just the ears and voice for them. And I will get a communications frequency and encryption assignment out to everyone well before you or the Israelis launch so that everyone can talk to one another directly."

"I see . . . very well, Sergeant. It sounds like everything is under control. Keep me informed via this secure sat phone in the interim."

"Yes, sir . . . you can count on it."

"By the way . . . just to confirm what Mr. Thomas of MI6 said about fuel. You're quite certain that your Colonel Newman believes that there is sufficient aviation fuel at the objective?"

"Yes, sir. There should be enough in the fuel truck and the tank farm for the Marine 53s and the Cobras, as well as the birds taking the Israelis back to their recovery bases—and all of them with plenty of fuel to spare."

"I see. And do you have a backup plan for refueling?"

"No, sir. Gassing up at the target—that's the plan."

"And what time is H-hour on the objective?" asked Banks.

Skillings checked his notes and responded, "As of right now, sir, it is set for 0300, Wednesday, 25 March for the Israeli HALO drop. Your Marines of Four-Two Commando are to land north of the airstrip at 0315."

"Roger. The Royal Marines will be there at 0315 tomorrow night. I hope the fuel is there as well. I'd hate to have my lads walk all the way home."

RENDEZVOUS WITH DEATH

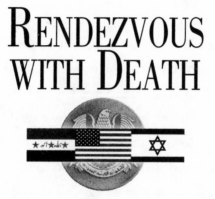

C H A P T E R   T W E N T Y - T W O

Al Thawrah Market
4 km East of At Tanf, Syria
Tuesday, 24 March 1998
0615 Hours, Local

The sound of a roll-up metal gate being thrown open awakened Samir Habib with a start. He had been dozing in the cab of his truck, parked at the eastern end of the dusty little town's market area. When he had pulled in last night, the place had been empty. Now, the tiny *souk* was awakening, with shopkeepers opening their storefronts and others placing their wares and produce in streetside booths.

Throughout the night he had tried to stay awake, serving as a lookout between the Syria-Iraq border and the site where Peter Newman lay hidden, waiting for British and Israeli commandos to arrive. Samir chastised himself for dozing off. *What if a Syrian military unit went by while I was asleep?*

Newman had told him that the place he was reconnoitering held three nuclear weapons—perhaps more. The Marine also believed that his wife was being held hostage there. Samir devoutly hoped that what Newman was planning to do would succeed because the prospect of nuclear weapons making their way into the hands of Saddam Hussein or his sons terrified the Christian Arab. So, too, did the thought of such weapons being used against Israel. Several hours earlier Samir had heard on his truck's radio that the Israeli military was calling up their reserves, and the BBC had carried a terse statement by Israel's Prime Minister stating that if Israel were attacked with a weapon of mass destruction, "We will respond the only way we can." Even the relatively apolitical Samir understood what this meant—that the Jewish state would counter-attack with nuclear weapons.

The young man climbed out of the pickup and shifted his weight a little unsteadily as he stood on the ground. He looked at the glowing light of the sunrise and stretched his stiff and tired frame.

The rumors of war had left Samir uneasy, and the long night in the truck had left him groggy as well. The cool morning air and slight breeze, however, helped to clear his mind, and he decided to follow the smell of fresh coffee from somewhere to his left. When he got to the coffee vendor's tent-like stall, he was the only customer. He asked for a strong Turkish-blend coffee, poured some milk into the steaming black liquid, and put his hands around the glass for warmth. Samir also bought a few sweet, fragrant rolls with almond-paste filling and cinnamon, and he ate them with great enjoyment. It had been nearly twenty-four hours since he had last eaten.

After getting some food into his stomach, Samir returned to the truck, turned on the radio, and tuned it to the Radio Damascus news broadcast just in time to hear the announcement that the Syrian dictator, Hafez al-Assad, had called up the country's reservists and was mobilizing "the valiant Syrian Army to defend the country from attack by the Jews." He turned off the radio, picked up the satellite telephone beside him on the seat, and called his father.

"Yes, my son," said Eli Yusef.

"Father, have you been listening to the radio?"

"No, why?"

"There is talk of war," said Samir, his voice reflecting his anxiety.

"Yes, there is often talk of war in this part of the world. It is a condition of the human race."

"Father, they are talking about a *nuclear* war. It sounds as if Israel will use its nuclear weapons against Syria or Iraq," said Samir, seeking some kind of reassurance.

"Well, that is what we are helping our friend Peter to prevent."

"But . . . I am afraid that the American may not be able to find those devices. If he does not succeed, Saddam may get them and use them against the Jews. It might bring about the Apocalypse here in the Middle East."

There was a long pause during which neither man said anything. Finally, Yusef spoke to his son, "We must pray even harder for Peter Newman. He *must* be successful."

Samir responded as though he had not heard. "But I just heard Israel's Prime Minister on the radio, and he was talking about what can only mean nuclear war. Who are we? We are nobodies. We cannot stop such terrible destruction. Peter said that if he fails in this effort, we should immediately get away from here and try to get into Turkey. I was thinking . . . from our home in Anah we can go to your friends in Cizre, Turkey—it is not much more than three hundred kilometers. I think that if we can get our family there we should be safe from the nuclear bombs."

"The Lord will keep our loved ones safe in Anah," the older man answered simply. "It would take us too long to drive that distance. If the bombs and missiles come, they will not wait while we drive across Iraq. No . . . we must stay with Peter Newman. I believe God wants us to help him."

The son was unable to accept his father's statement. It was hopelessly illogical, and so he tried a different tack. "What does God tell you to do concerning Mother, who is at our home in Anah? And what about my wife Hamilah and our children? Are we to abandon them while we stay with the American?"

"We will leave them in the care of their *heavenly* Father. Even if we were able to drive back to Anah, there is no assurance that we could bring everyone to safety in Cizre before the missiles come. I believe that God will watch over them all. There isn't enough time for us to drive all the way back to Anah and then leave on a three-hundred-kilometer journey to Turkey—before the missiles come. No . . . we will *call* them and tell them to take shelter. You must have more faith, my son. And please, call me again if you are anxious, but be more circumspect. We cannot know who else may be able to hear these conversations, and we do not wish to place our friend Peter in further jeopardy."

Samir concluded the call feeling somewhat chastised by his father's simple, unwavering faith. He set the phone beside him on the bench seat of the truck and reviewed the logistics of the situation in his mind.

His father was right about one thing: there was no way they could drive to Anah and then, after getting the family together, leave for Turkey and get there in less than twenty-four hours. He picked up the phone again and checked for any voice mail messages from Peter Newman. When he saw none, he called his wife. Samir explained to Hamilah what he had heard on the radio about the likelihood of war and what his father had suggested about seeking shelter. He urged her to depart immediately with their children and wait out the terrible possibilities.

His wife made no complaint and replied matter-of-factly that she would see to what he had asked her to do. She concluded the conversation with a simple comment: "Your mother and I will be praying for your father and you until God brings you both back to us. Be careful." Strangely, she then repeated what Samir had said to Peter Newman just hours ago—"*Masha salâma.*"

International Scientific Trading, Ltd.
At Tanf, Syria
Tuesday, 24 March 1998
0640 Hours, Local

The Marine was cold. Peter Newman had wrapped himself in the heavy, desert-camouflaged sheet that Eli Yusef had given him, but the air temperature on the desert floor had plunged with the sun, and the chill had kept him awake and shivering throughout the night. Newman lay without moving on the lip of an irrigation ditch south of the runway. Once, shortly after midnight, he had been startled by a small herd of camels grazing on scrub brush nearby. He watched through the night-vision device as a dozen or more of the ungainly beasts munched their way past, seemingly oblivious to him or to the possibility of encountering aircraft on the nearby runway.

Now the sun was finally warming his stiff joints and aching muscles. Newman wanted badly to stand up and stretch, but he knew that could instantly give away his position. Instead, he performed some isometric resistance exercises—a technique he used to teach his Recon Marines for dealing with the long hours on an ambush or OP.

At 0600, Newman had turned on one of the two Iridium phones and dialed the number for Gunnery Sergeant Skillings. In order to save the sat-phone batteries, he had established a schedule for reporting—on even-numbered hours he contacted Skillings at NATO headquarters at Incirlik, and on odd-numbered hours he called Major Ze'ev Rotem, his contact with the Israelis. But this time when he dialed the number for Skillings, he heard it automatically switch over to a call-forwarding protocol. On the fifth ring the gunnery sergeant answered, "Skillings."

Newman, crouching beneath the desert-dyed sheet, said quietly, "Thought I'd lost you, Gunny."

"Can't lose me, Colonel, but I've relocated to the Saudi Air Force base at Badanah. I just arrived here with Mr. Thomas and Mr. Blackman, the two gentlemen from London who have been helping us. Here's my phone number so you can dial me directly. . . ." Skillings gave Newman the number and continued, "General Grisham thought one less loop in this thing would be helpful, so he scared up a USAF C-17 to bring us here, along with some Sat-Com gear so he could stay on top of what's going on."

"Good. Have you linked up with the U.S. and Royal Marines yet?"

"Yes, sir, I'm at the Four-Two Commando CP right now. I've already been to the helo squadron, and there has been a change, sir."

"A change? What kind of change, Gunny?"

"It's not two CH-53s that will be inserting the Royal Marines. It's four CH-46s from HMM 268 that will do the work."

Newman pondered this information. It meant more birds in the air but greater redundancy. And though the CH-46s were slower than the 53s, they presented a smaller radar profile and would be flying lower— a hundred knots at twenty-five feet above the ground—with the pilots and air crew all wearing NVGs. "Can't complain about that, but it will increase the travel time from where you are to here and the length of time to refuel the birds because there will be four of them."

"Roger that. We'll plan accordingly. And there's some other good news. General Grisham has arranged with NRO for a satellite pass over the objective every 128 minutes. Be sure to wave when you see it go by so the Royal Marines know where you are when they come in with their guns blazing."

Skillings had made the comment in jest, but it reminded Newman of just how vulnerable he was, not only to being spotted by whomever Komulakov had inside the IST compound, but to the possibility of being mistaken for one of the bad guys when the Brits and Israelis arrived on the scene. He recalled some of the disasters he had seen in the Gulf War of '90–'91 when U.S. troops were hit by "friendly" fire.

"You've just pointed out one of the soft spots in this whole thing, Gunny. Let me think that part over and come up with something so the good guys don't take me out by mistake."

"Do you have an infrared strobe?"

"Nope. That would have been too easy. But hey, I've got a whole day to come up with something."

"Roger that. I'll noodle it here, too, and see if anyone has a bright idea on some IFF method for you."

"Many thanks. I'll be back up on this net at 0800. Out here." As Newman turned off the phone, he noted that the battery indicator showed he was down to one-half the maximum battery charge. He checked his watch. It was almost time for a call to Major Rotem. Using the second satellite phone, he dialed the Israeli. The IDF officer answered on the first ring.

"Colonel Newman, I have some news."

"What is it?"

"I just received a message from the National Police who are monitoring the phones at your apartment and my home. Have you checked the messages on your home phone recently?"

"No . . . I've been busy here. Why?"

"Rachel called."

"Rachel? How? When?"

"The call came in about two hours ago. It was from a cell phone somewhere in Syria. Our Telecommunications Intelligence and Security Service has been trying to pinpoint where, but that may take longer than we have. Your NSA may be able to find out faster."

"If you know the exact time the call was placed and any source identifier codes from the originating phone, NSA or GCHQ should be able to nail it down fairly quickly," the Marine said. "It would also help if we can tell them any specific words or phrases used in the call."

There was a pause, and Newman could hear Rotem talking to someone else. The Israeli then came back on the line, "Our service just delivered a tape of the message that was left on your voice mail. The call came in on your phone at 0508 local. They don't have a source ID code, and they still don't know where the call originated. Shall I play it for you?"

"Yes," Newman replied, his heartbeat quickening at the realization that the tape recording probably meant that Rachel was still alive as of two hours ago.

He pressed the sat phone closer to his ear to hear the sound of his wife's voice over the pounding of his pulse. "Peter . . . it's me. I tried your satellite phone but it didn't answer. They are making me read you this message. But before I read it, I want you to know that I love you and am praying for you. Here is the message: You are to go to the Assad International Airport in Damascus, to the VIP Lounge at the international terminal by 8:00 tonight, Tuesday, March 24. You are to wait there for two men who will ask at the reception desk for Mr. White. These men will escort you to a private area at the airport and take you to meet the man who has been holding us. He wants the following information: First, have you found the real identity of Morales? Second, what does the U.S. government know about Morales? And third, are any U.S. intelligence or law enforcement agencies on the lookout for the man who is holding us? He has instructed me to tell you that if he is satisfied with your answers, he will allow Dyan and me to leave with you. If you do not do as he instructs in this message, you will never see me again. And I will never see our little boy ag—" Peter could hear his wife suppress a sob. "Oh Peter . . . please do as they say. They told me to tell you that we're being held outside of Damascus and they'll release us when you provide that infor—"

There was a sudden click and then a dial tone. Newman's heart was racing at what he had just heard, and he tried to think what all of this meant.

"Are you still there?" Major Rotem asked.

"Yeah . . . is that all there was?"

"Yes. Do you think it is genuine?"

"Genuine?" Newman replied. "Who knows with this guy, but it's pretty clear from Rachel's voice that *she* believes it's true and that Komulakov means what he says."

"You believe it's some kind of a trap?" Rotem inquired.

"I don't think so. But who knows? And that last part—about being near Damascus—that's strange. I've got to get NSA to see if they can find out where this call came from. Until now, our people monitoring their radio chatter have been telling me that the women were being kept *here*—not Damascus. And I know that Komulakov is here. I saw him get off his jet last night."

"Yes, but Mossad has been keeping track of his aircraft. They reported last night that he flew to Assad International Airport and was there for a couple hours and flew back to At Tanf. You saw him land—but you didn't see him take off. It's *possible* that he took our wives with him to Damascus and left them there."

"Maybe he did take them. You're right, I didn't see the plane take off; I only saw it return. And except for the pilots, Komulakov was alone. On the tape Rachel says they told her to say that she and Dyan were being held near Damascus. Could he have taken them to Hims or Hamah?"

"It's possible, I suppose. But that poses another dilemma."

"What's that?" asked the Marine.

"If the only way for us to get our wives back is for you to go to Damascus, you'll have to leave where you are and get there as soon as possible. Do you still have access to your friends with the pickup trucks? It's less than 150 miles, so you should be able to drive that distance and arrive by 2000 hours."

"But if I'm in Damascus at 2000, there is no way I can get back here in time to give you a report on what's happening before you and the British arrive. You'll be coming in without any eyes or ears on the ground."

There was a pause while Rotem quickly contemplated the consequences of Newman heading to Damascus and leaving the IST site "uncovered" for more than twelve hours before the British and Israeli commando assault. "You're right. Your being there in At Tanf is critical. The satellites can only tell us so much. Without someone on the ground, a night parachute jump and a helicopter insert become much more dangerous. How quickly can your NSA tell where Rachel's call originated? That may be the only way we can figure out where our wives are being held."

"I don't know. I'll call right now and get them started. I'll call you back in two hours."

Newman terminated the call, picked up the other sat phone, extended the antenna, and dialed the number Gunnery Sergeant Skillings had given him only minutes before.

"Skillings."

"Gunny, I need General Grisham to get us some fast service from NSA."

"Yes, sir, here's his direct number. . . ."

Newman memorized the number then said, "Thanks, Guns. Out here." He terminated the call, waited for the satellite reception to recycle, and immediately dialed the number he'd just been given.

He heard the phone ring and then the no-nonsense voice of General George Grisham was in his ear. "Grisham."

Without preamble or pleasantries Newman quickly described Rachel's phone call to their apartment at the Hospice of Saint Patrick and concluded with, "Major Rotem has a tape of the call. As of a few minutes ago, the Israeli service confirmed that the call was received at 0508 local; they do not, however, have a source ID code for the originating phone, and all they know is that it came through a Syrian exchange. We've got to find out where the phone is that Rachel used. It's the only way we'll know where she and Dyan are being held."

Grisham had been silent, taking notes, but now he replied, "This Morales person must be terribly important to Komulakov. Here's the Russian dealing with weapons that can start a regional nuclear exchange and he's still playing spymaster. I'll get NSA working on this right away, but you need to consider the possibility that the message is a set-up or even that it was a tape recorded earlier and only *played* over the originating phone. It may be impossible in the next few hours for NSA to determine where the call came from. You also need to know that if you do go to Damascus, I can't get you any backup. The CIA hasn't had anyone on the ground in there for years. What time would you have to depart where you are in order to be at the Damascus airport by 2000 hours?"

"I figure I'd have to be on the way by 1500."

"And if you go to Damascus, is there a way for you to get back to the objective area before the British-Israeli attack?"

"No, sir."

There was a moment of silence, and when General Grisham spoke, his voice was tinged with emotion, "I can't order you to stay there, son. You have already gone above and beyond the call of duty. You know how important you being there is to the success of this mission and to preventing a nuclear holocaust. But I understand that your going to

Damascus could also make the difference between life and death for Rachel. I'll immediately pass on to you and Skillings what, if anything, NSA can tell us—but I'm going to leave it up to you as to whether you stay where you are or head to Damascus."

"But what do you think is the *right* thing to do?"

Once again there was a moment of silence as General George Grisham considered his response. His words came softly across the satellite link: "Only you and God know the answer to that, Pete. And no one can make the choice but you."

Sand Dollar Team HQ
Ar'ar Air Base
10 km East of Badahah, Saudi Arabia
Tuesday, 24 March 1998
1000 Hours, Local

"Colonel, your timing is perfect," Skillings said into the sat phone cradled by his ear. He was sitting on the hood of a Humvee parked near the refueling station at the Saudi air base. "Any word yet from NSA on where that call from your wife originated?"

"Not yet, Gunny," Newman answered. He had skipped his 0800 call to Skillings to save his battery, hoping that by now NSA would have been able to verify where the call to the Clancy apartment in Jerusalem had been initiated. Now, three hours later, Skillings's question was an answer—NSA had nothing.

"What are you going to do, sir?"

"I don't know yet. I've talked to General Grisham and Major Rotem, and they've both left it up to me. I've got to make a go/no-go decision here in the next hour because if I'm going to get out of here and back to the highway without being spotted, it will take me quite awhile. What's your status?"

"Quite a few changes since we last talked. General Grisham has added four Cobras to the mission. They are coming in with the four CH-46s to provide escort and suppression at the objective. They will be armed with TOWs, Hellfire, 2.75-inch rockets, and AS-2 missiles for some air-to-air protection. We're pulling out of Badanah as soon as we top off our tanks. We'll head about 150 miles west-northwest to Turayf, another Saudi air base, and top off again there. General Grisham also got the Jordanians to allow us to set up a FARP on the Amman-to-Baghdad highway just west of the Iraqi border post at Tirbil. Four CH-53s are already headed up there with fuel and ordnance to set up the FARP. The Air Wing guys figure that should give us all the extra margin we need in case something happens to the fuel at the objective. After the mission, we're to bring everyone back to the FARP for retrograde by C-130. He's having one flown in from Incirlik."

"That's good, Gunny." Newman muttered the right words, but he sounded distracted, and Skillings understood why.

"Look, sir, if you gotta go to Damascus, nobody here is going to second-guess you. There isn't anyone who would want to be faced with that choice right now. In fact, if we took a poll, I think everybody here would consider it a no-brainer—they'd go to Damascus if it were their wives. If you aren't there tonight, everyone here will understand, sir. We'll pull this thing off one way or the other."

"What do you mean 'we'? You're not planning on coming on this mission, are you?"

"Yes, sir, I am. These Royal Marines may be tough and these rotor heads may be brave, but they need a good grunt along with 'em to keep 'em straight. Besides," Skillings said with a chuckle, "they need someone along who knows what a gunfight looks like, in order to write 'em up for their air medals."

Newman, huddled beneath the camouflage-colored fabric, shook his head and said, "I don't like the idea of you guys coming in without me being here for last-minute intel—especially since the Israelis will already be on the ground. The potential for an intramural firefight is enormous."

When Skillings said nothing, Newman concluded, "I'll call again at 1200 to see if NSA has anything about where Rachel's call came from."

"Roger that, sir. And by the way . . . Mr. Blackman, the British gentleman, says that according to GCHQ the signals intercepted from those NATO-issued Marconi hand-held radios haven't changed. The chatter for the past several days has been about the women being at that place in At Tanf, where you are. For what it's worth, he thinks the message left on your phone in Jerusalem is bogus."

"Good grief, Gunny, does everyone in the world know about my personal situation?"

"Pretty much, sir. There are a lot of people aware of your predicament. And as I said before, nobody wants to be in your shoes right now."

"What do you think, Guns? What would you do?"

"Me? I wouldn't trust this guy Komulakov any farther than I could throw him. I figure he's an evil no-good who's probably trying to set you up for a hit in Damascus."

"But I don't want to take that chance if he *is* telling the truth."

"Sir, what would make this guy suddenly come on so friendly? You know him better than I do, but I can't picture him going out of his way to give you his hostages just for whatever you might have heard about his spy buddy in the States. It doesn't ring sincere to me, sir."

Newman considered the Gunnery Sergeant's words for a few seconds and said, "Thanks, Gunny. I've always been able to count on you to shoot straight. I'll run this by Major Rotem and get his assessment because it affects his wife as well. Please ask the Brits to keep on those guys who are monitoring the Marconis. I need to have some kind of confirmation, and fast—before it's too late to get to Damascus in time for Komulakov's deadline. I'll call you again in two hours."

Sayeret Duvdevan HQ
Tel-Nof, Israel
Tuesday, 24 March 1998
1100 Hours, Local

Major Ze'ev Rotem watched as the new shift of headquarters watch officers and NCOs came on duty and were briefed by their comrades finishing their shifts. The strike team that would go with him on the raid into Syria later that night was down the corridor in one of the billets. He knew that most of them would be asleep. Rotem also had tried to rest after Newman's last call, but sleep had eluded him.

The Israeli officer was feeling the effects of adrenaline-induced insomnia. He had considered taking one of the sleeping pills that the IDF medical officers prescribed but had not done so because he didn't want to miss any of the calls from Newman's lonely outpost. Rotem's brief catnaps at a command-center console left his eyes burning and his throat raw.

Things were much busier than usual in the command bunker, and he was aware that many of the duty personnel had not left when their watch ended because they knew how critical tonight's operation into

Syria was going to be, and they wanted to be there to see their comrades off on the mission.

Rotem took a long drink of cold coffee. It was bitter and unpleasant, but he needed the caffeine. As he put the Styrofoam cup down, his cell phone buzzed in his shirt pocket. He looked at his watch, withdrew the phone, flipped open the cover, and said, "Rotem."

It was Newman with his "odd hour" sit rep from the harbor site near the IST facility outside of At Tanf. The IDF major pictured Newman laying hidden in the area. Rotem himself had been near there as part of Duvdevan extrajudicial execution teams hunting for Abu Nidal and Abul Abbas. Now he wondered how the vaunted Mossad had missed the IST site all these years.

Newman got right to the point and told Rotem what Skillings thought about Komulakov's guile and the message that Rachel had left on their home phone in Jerusalem.

"Yes, I have been having second thoughts too. He would not ordinarily be so charitable as to release the women only for some information of questionable quality. *But* . . . can we take the chance?"

"I was thinking that maybe I could stretch this out," Newman said. "I have his number. I'll call him and tell him that I can't make it by 2000 hours and that I can give him the information he wants by phone, and then he can release the women near the American embassy in Damascus."

"Interesting idea," Rotem said. "Even if he says no, you can still tell him you need more time to get to Damascus."

"All right. We're agreed. I'll call you back."

Major Rotem pushed the button to end the call and turned his attention back to the operations plan on his desk. But first, he decided to get some fresh coffee.

International Scientific Trading, Ltd.
At Tanf, Syria
Tuesday, 24 March 1998
1125 Hours, Local

General Dimitri Komulakov and Leonid Dotensk were seated at the dining room table in the IST guest house reviewing the arrangements for the transfer of the nuclear weapons to Qusay Hussein when the satellite phone on the table began to buzz. Both men looked at the phone and then at each other. Even though the device was hooked to an external antenna cable that ran out the window, this phone rarely received calls.

Komulakov picked up the phone and was stunned to hear the voice of Lieutenant Colonel Peter Newman. "Colonel," he said with feigned delight, "so good to hear your voice. Are you calling me from Damascus?"

"No, I can't get there by your deadline. I just got the message. I need proof that Rachel is all right, and then I need time to get to Syria."

"Colonel, surely you heard her voice on your voice message machine. I can't let you talk to her now. She's in Damascus, just as she said. I am in another part of the country. I'm sure that you can have your CIA check with Assad International Airport. They will verify that I was there last night and then departed. I regret that we did not file a flight plan, but the tower will, I am sure, confirm my aircraft's arrival and departure times. I brought the women to Damascus, and as your wife told you on the phone message, I will give them their freedom in exchange for the information you have on my elusive Mr. Morales. Doesn't that seem fair?"

Newman didn't answer him directly. Instead, he tried to buy some time, to figure out what was really happening. Komulakov got up from his desk and moved absently to the window of his office and stared out at the runway. There, beneath the camouflaged sheet, baking in the sun less than a thousand meters from Komulakov's window, the American Marine he was talking to lay hidden.

"I said, doesn't that seem fair, Colonel Newman—to get your wife back for what you know about Morales?"

"What I know about Morales I can tell you on the phone. I'll do that and you can give me your word that you'll release my wife and her friend—you can have them dropped off at the American or British embassy in Damascus. I can't get to Damascus by your deadline."

"Hm-m . . . my word? Well, let's hear what you have to say first."

"Well, I thought that if this Morales fella is giving you the kind of secrets that he's sending you he has to be pretty well placed. That means *he'll know* if someone starts looking for him. He's smart and is able to cover his tracks. There's no way that I could have even gotten close to him. As I told you before, I've got someone working with me. We think we know who your man is. He's either in the FBI or CIA because of the stuff he's sent you. We're working on narrowing it down to those with clearances for the specific information you say he provided you—but it gives clues to where he works. My contact is working right now to set up lie detector sessions with those six or eight possibilities within the FBI and CIA. I ought to know by the end of the week."

Komulakov laughed. "I can see that U.S. intelligence has not improved. In fact, thanks to your president, I think your CIA is now in worse shape than the Russian intelligence agencies. He has gutted the CIA, and it is even more worthless than ever."

"You doubt what I'm telling you?"

"Yes, of course I do. You are completely off base, Colonel. *I* have made more progress than you have," Komulakov boasted. He had already concluded that the mole who called himself Morales was a senior official at the State Department, based on the data Morales had sent from the Secretary of State's computer. And while the former KGB spymaster still didn't know *who* Morales was, knowing *where* the spy worked was a major breakthrough in tracking him down and eliminating him.

"I have narrowed down where Morales works, and it isn't with the FBI or CIA . . . or one of the other agencies that you think. And I have to give him credit. He is in a place to give me the best possible information and never be caught."

"Well, where does that leave us?"

"I no longer need you to pursue this matter," Komulakov said curtly. He had concluded that when it came to threats Newman posed a more immediate risk than Morales, and he decided to apply one of the axioms of the KGB: *When dealing with multiple threats, eliminate the most proximate ones first.* "How soon can you get to Damascus?"

This was not going at all as Newman had hoped, but now that he was committed, he had no choice. "I can probably get there by tomorrow noon."

"Very well, at noon tomorrow go to the VIP Lounge at the airport and page Mr. Gray. You will receive a message for Mr. White with instructions for what to do next."

"And you'll release our wives to one of the embassies?"

"No, I have already made the other arrangements. It will have to be done my way. " And with that, he terminated the call and turned off the sat phone.

As Komulakov strode back to his desk, Dotensk was looking up at him expectantly. But instead of filling his deputy in on what he had decided, Komulakov went back to the topic they had been discussing before Newman's call. "So, Leonid, tell me more about the payment procedures for these devices we are to deliver tonight."

The Ukrainian arms merchant shook his head at how quickly his superior could change direction, sighed, and replied, "If all goes according to plan, three trucks carrying the gold will arrive at the border checkpoint at 1600 our time. We will put nine of our most trusted men—three on each truck—as soon as they cross into Syria. The appropriate Syrian officials have already been compensated so that there will be no problem on this side of the border. Qusay tells me that he has made similar arrangements on the Iraqi side. That means the trucks should be here by 1700. Qusay Hussein must have really been cracking the whip during the night. To get all that gold loaded and shipped from the treasury in Baghdad was quite an accomplishment in itself."

"Yes, yes, I'm sure," Komulakov interrupted impatiently. He then continued, "I've been thinking about how risky it is to keep the gold here. Our security isn't really set up for guarding such a treasure. Word is certain to leak. There are also hijackers and robbers who make the Baghdad-to-Damascus highway their own shopping mall. I think we should charter a cargo aircraft and transport the gold to Kiev before it becomes the property of some greedy band of thieves."

"Can we get a cargo plane on such short notice that will carry that much weight?" Dotensk asked.

"Let's find out. Call Romalyinov at the Damascus *Rezidentura*. He's the logistics officer, and he has good contacts for that kind of thing. I know you had planned to truck the gold to Latakia and ship it by sea to Odessa, but I prefer to get it out by air if we can. Who knows what our customer is liable to do with the weapons we're providing once he has them in hand. He might even decide to come here and reclaim his gold. While we're waiting to find out about the aircraft, keep guards posted around the clock. Beef up our security around the perimeter, and be on the lookout for intruders. Also make sure that no trucks can break through the front gates."

Dotensk nodded his acknowledgment of the orders as Komulakov continued, "How are you going to verify that we have received all that we are owed?"

"The gold is to be shipped as numbered ingots on pallets. The trucks will pull directly into the warehouse. I have arranged for the same nine men who accompany the trucks from the border to off-load the cargo inside the locked warehouse. They will inventory and weigh the shipment to verify we have received full payment. I estimate that will take no more than three or four hours. While that task is being completed, the Iraqi trucks will be loaded with the three nuclear warheads. As soon as we confirm that the gold is all here, they will be allowed to leave for Iraq."

"That means it will be well after midnight before the weapons are in Baghdad—if that's where our customer actually takes them."

"Yes, I think that is right."

"Well then, we should plan to be on our way by air to Kiev by midnight," said Komulakov, hoisting himself out of his chair. "We need to be gone, along with the gold, when Qusay gets his weapons."

Once again Dotensk nodded his head, sighed, and, taking his cue, rose to leave. But before he reached the door, Komulakov said, almost as a second thought, "Oh, and Leonid . . . there are two more things I'd like you to take care of."

"Yes?"

"As I'm sure you heard a few minutes ago, that was Lieutenant Colonel Newman who telephoned me. He is supposed to be arriving at the VIP Lounge at Assad airport tomorrow at noon. If he actually does as he was instructed, he's to page Mr. Gray from the lounge. Have two of our men meet him there and escort him to our hangar at the far end of the airport. Tell them to kill the American—slowly—and then dump his body somewhere in the desert."

Dotensk swallowed hard, nodded, and asked, "And the second thing?"

Komulakov turned toward the window and spoke with his back to the Ukrainian. "Tonight, after the gold has been delivered and it turns dark, take the women out there—" at this he gestured toward the desert—"and kill them both."

Residence of the Prime Minister
Jerusalem, Israel
Tuesday, 24 March 1998
1230 Hours, Local

"I'm sorry to interrupt your lunch, Mr. Prime Minister," the voice on the secure telephone line apologized.

"What is it, Madam Secretary?"

"Our intelligence directorates have reported to me that Israel has a number of its Jericho-2 missiles on full alert and ready to launch. When I asked your ambassador about this serious change in readiness, I was assured that the actions were merely part of a training exercise and nothing to worry about," the U.S. Secretary of State told her listener. "However, our CIA and Defense Intelligence Agency are telling me that this is more than a training exercise. We are concerned about what seems to be preparations for a nuclear attack, Mr. Prime Minister. And it must be stopped at once."

The Prime Minister was irritated at the imperious tone of her voice, and it made him testy. "Madam Secretary, we are simply taking a proactive stance in regard to our potential enemies. If our adversaries—who have promised to destroy the State of Israel—interpret this as aggressive, then that cannot be helped. But until we are able to discern a reduced threat to Israel, we shall continue to stand on full alert."

"Mr. Prime Minister," the chief American diplomat said, trying unsuccessfully to backpedal from her strident approach and muster a little sweetness into her voice, "three countries have already proposed resolutions to the United Nations to condemn Israel for its military aggressiveness. There is absolutely no proof whatsoever that Iraq is about to obtain weapons of mass destruction or that they are even attempting to do so. Don't you see? The United States will have to abstain if these resolutions are brought to a vote. Though we are Israel's staunchest ally, you won't have our support at a time when you will need it most."

"Madam Secretary, please permit me to remind you that neither the United States nor the United Nations makes national security policy for the State of Israel. As your intelligence will also point out, Israel is being threatened by one of our sworn enemies. It is a near certainty, as I am sure you know but are not telling me, that Iraq is *very* near to acquiring a number of nuclear weapons. The regime in Baghdad has made it clear that they intend to use those weapons against Israel as soon as they have them. It is *they* to whom you should be talking, Madam Secretary, although I understand the difficulty of having such a conversation. Nevertheless, you need to find a way to get word to Saddam Hussein or his sons or the Baath Party—or whatever madman is presently in charge in Baghdad—that Israel will not stand for these threats. In fact, Madam Secretary, unless the United States or the UN can locate these threatening nuclear weapons and neutralize them within the next eighteen hours, Israel will have no choice but to act preemptively in its own self-defense."

"Are you making a threat or a speech, Mr. Prime Minister?"

"You know that I don't make threats or speeches. I don't waste time with political platitudes and words that have no meaning—I speak my mind, plainly. That is what I am telling you now. If those weapons are not found within the next seventeen hours and fifty-eight minutes, it will be too late for threats, UN resolutions, warnings, or speeches. It will be a time for us to act in self-defense. Now, please permit me to go back to my lunch. I missed breakfast, and if the rest of today is as busy as my morning, I'll probably miss dinner too. Good-bye, Madam Secretary."

The Prime Minister hung up the phone but did not go back to his meal. In truth, he had just finished when the Secretary of State called. Instead, he walked from his office, where he had taken the phone call, into his study. Strolling over to the huge bookcase that took up most of two walls, he picked out a volume to read. The book was one of his favorites—a Hebrew translation of a collection of speeches by Winston Churchill. He browsed through its well-worn pages to a familiar passage. It was a speech that Churchill had given to inspire the British people during World War II, and he read it again because it always lifted his spirits.

He avoided thinking of tomorrow and its potential consequences. The Prime Minister did not want to be the first leader since Harry Truman to use a nuclear weapon against another nation, but he felt his tiny nation being pushed into a corner. He had tried all of the diplomatic channels. None had offered any progress. The Mossad reports from Baghdad and other Arab capitals provided little hope for any outcome other than the use of force. Now Israel had been reduced to only two options: a preemptive nuclear strike on Baghdad in hopes of preventing a nuclear attack from Saddam Hussein *or* the faint possibility that a raid tonight by a small team of commandos might be able to prevent the nuclear weapons from being delivered to Baghdad.

The PM shuddered at the prospect of what could happen if the raid failed. Most of Israel's nuclear arsenal was sequestered in the valley of ancient Megiddo—the place prophesied for a future battle of ultimate destruction—Armageddon.

For the third time since dawn, he opened the red folder on his desk bearing the legend in Hebrew: "HQ SAYERET DUVDEVAN— MOST SECRET" and below that, "EYES ONLY FOR THE PRIME MINISTER." Inside was a single sheet of paper that outlined the plan for an audacious raid against an installation in Syria, believed to hold three nuclear weapons destined for delivery to Baghdad.

He scanned the document again, picked up the secure phone on his desk, and when the operator came on, said, "Get me the Chief of Staff."

There was a momentary delay as the operator connected the call. After hearing the electronic *ping* as the Israeli version of the STU III encryption engaged, the Prime Minister spoke, "I know you are busy, but I have some more questions about the operation in Syria tonight. How certain are we that three nuclear weapons are at this International Scientific Trading site near At Tanf?"

"We cannot be completely certain. But the report you have in your hand is based on reliable signals intelligence and some equally reliable information that we have received from the Americans," the general replied.

"The Americans? I just got off the phone with the Secretary of State, and she wants me removed from office for putting the Jericho missiles on alert. She acted as if the nuclear weapons do not even exist and says the Iraqis are nowhere near to acquiring a nuclear capability."

"We believe she is wrong. I'm afraid that the American State Department and Pentagon are not always on the same page. In this case, we believe the State Department does not have the best intelligence."

"Who is 'we,' and who are the Americans who say that the weapons are there? Not the CIA, I hope."

"Israeli military intelligence on our side. And the American who also believes it to be so is General George Grisham."

"*One* American general?"

"Yes, but Mr. Prime Minister, he is not just 'one American general'—he is the Commander in Chief of the U.S. Central Command, a Marine. And he has a man on the ground at the site providing intel. The British also believe it to be so, as you can see from the Operations Plan."

"Who is this man on the ground?"

"His name is Peter Newman. He's a U.S. Marine lieutenant colonel. It's a long story, but he was the American who headed up the UN assassination team that was exterminated in Iraq three years ago. "

"I thought he was killed."

"We all did, Mr. Prime Minister. But he wasn't. And now his wife is being held hostage—probably by the same people who are attempting to deliver the nuclear weapons to Iraq, according to our intelligence services and the Sayeret officer commanding our unit in the operation."

"And the IDF officer you have leading our part in this raid—it's his wife who is also being held hostage?"

"That is correct."

"Are you sure that these two men aren't simply trying to get their wives freed—rather than focusing on the nuclear weapons problem?"

It occurred to the Chief of Staff to tell the Prime Minister that he was thinking like a politician and not like the general he had once been, but, instead, the weary IDF chief simply said, "I have no doubt about the loyalty and attention to the mission on the part of Major Rotem. He is one of our best and bravest officers. As for Lieutenant Colonel Newman, he has been in Iraq for several days now, and it is thanks to him that we have found this facility. He has provided much of the intel. And as for his commitment—a few hours ago he was told that if he ever wanted to see his wife alive again he would have to go to Damascus. But instead of heading to the Syrian capital, he's still at his post—maintaining surveillance over the At Tanf site where we believe the weapons are hidden."

The Prime Minister mulled this over for several seconds and then said, "One last question: "Why don't we just launch our Air Force and eliminate this site with conventional weapons?"

The Chief of Staff hesitated for a moment and then answered directly, "Because the whole Arab world will immediately go to war against us when our Air Force launches. Second, if the nuclear weapons are there, their destruction will release nuclear material—the so-called 'dirty bomb' effect. And third, because we believe that Newman's and Rotem's wives are probably being held hostage there."

"So we do care about the wives, eh?"

Once again there was a pause before the Chief of Staff spoke. When he did his voice was low, "The planned raid *is* worth trying, sir. If it fails, we can still go forward with the Jericho Sanction."

International Scientific Trading, Ltd.
At Tanf, Syria
Tuesday, 24 March 1998
1710 Hours, Local

"We've got trucks arriving at the site." Newman was cradling the sat phone between his shoulder and his chin as he peered through the binoculars at the IST complex. Lying prone beneath the desert-colored sheet at his OP south of the runway, Newman watched as three trucks wheeled around the north end of the compound and headed for the large steel gate that faced the runway.

Skillings replied, "Those must be the trucks that GCHQ has been picking up chatter about. They apparently crossed the border about an hour ago. Can you tell what's in the trucks?"

"Not yet, but they don't have license plates and none seem to have markings of any kind. And an hour ago, I got a report from Samir, who is east of here by the border. He reported a convoy of three black Mercedes, full of men heading east to the border. Then, three Mercedes *with drivers only* came barreling in *here* a few minutes ago, just before the trucks arrived. My guess is that they're Komulakov's men. The Mercedes took them to the border, and now they are driving the trucks, which are carrying the payment for the weapons. Wasn't it supposed to be in gold?"

"That's what GCHQ and NSA have been saying. They also said that Komulakov and his cronies had arranged for his own security people to accompany the trucks from the Syrian border. That kinda verifies your guess."

Newman watched the three trucks roll through the gate, the sound of their rough-running diesel engines reverberating across the desert. He provided a running commentary to Skillings as the trucks pulled inside a hangar-sized warehouse where several men jumped out as each vehicle stopped inside the cavernous facility. He counted a total of a dozen men who looked to be drivers, guards, and workers swarming over the trucks.

Then, as Newman peered through the powerful lenses, Komulakov appeared inside the structure, along with another shorter, fatter man. Newman didn't recognize the man with Komulakov, but he guessed that he must be the Ukrainian arms merchant that the NSA intercepts had described so well. The two men walked up to the back of the truck nearest the open door, and Newman watched as the canvas was thrown back. The scene took his breath away. Beneath the tarpaulin he could see pallets of gold bars, gleaming in the late afternoon sunlight.

Newman pursed his lips in an inaudible whistle and whispered into the sat phone, "Gold bars . . . somebody just paid for something that is very expensive."

"Bingo," said Skillings. "I'll ask our Brit friends if GCHQ is picking up any chatter."

"Speaking of chatter, Gunny, have the guys with the earphones picked up anything else?" Newman asked, hoping for some word about the whereabouts of his wife.

"Yes, sir. Komulakov sent an encrypted message to the Russian embassy in Damascus. NSA has only been able to get part of it decoded. He's asking them to inquire about the urgent availability of a Russian charter transport aircraft to be brought to At Tanf before midnight. He specified that he needed a heavy-lift plane, capable of hauling ten tons and a few passengers. Any ideas about what he wants to take out of there, Colonel?"

"Probably the gold from these three trucks that just pulled up. Anymore transmissions from the Marconi radios?"

"Yes, sir, I was just coming to that. Mr. Thomas says that GCHQ picked up a call about an hour ago from the site, and they think the voice was Komulakov's partner, the Ukrainian guy—calling one of the others and telling him to make plans to take the guests for a ride into the desert."

"Did he say when?"

"Sometime after dark. It was to be after the shipment arrived, according to GCHQ."

"Look, taking the guests for a ride into the desert sure sounds to me like they are planning to take Rachel and Dyan out and kill them after dark. And dark is only a few hours away. Can we push up the H-hour for the raid?"

"I don't see how, sir. The Royal Marines and the helo pilots all agree 0300 is best—probably everyone but a handful guards will be asleep. I'll push 'em on moving it up, but they aren't going to like it."

"Well, Gunny . . . let's push 'em. If those three trucks really are carrying the payment for the warheads, then they are probably planning to send the weapons out of here pretty soon. I say we push for the Israelis to make their jump shortly after dark, let's say about 2030 hours and get them into position just north of the runway and wait for the British. And I think the Royal Marines ought to plan to be here no later than 2100. Run that by your guys and let me know what they say. I'll ring you back in half an hour—sooner if anything else happens here. Out."

With that, Newman returned to watching the objective through the binoculars. He spent several minutes looking at the building where he thought Komulakov was keeping the women as prisoners, but he could tell nothing from the mute facade of the yellow stone-and-brick building. Most of the windows had their blinds drawn, preventing anyone outside from seeing in.

A guard patrolled the outer areas of the structure, occasionally entering for brief periods and then reappearing. Newman could see another man on the roof, carrying a rifle. But little else was visible. As he stared at the building through the binoculars, Newman had no way of knowing whether his wife was there. And for the hundredth time that day, the Marine wished that he had a longer-range weapon than the ancient 9mm pistol tucked into his belt.

Sayeret Duvdevan C-135

2,550 ft over Adana, Turkey
Tuesday, 24 March 1998
1930 Hours, Local

Major Ze'ev Rotem signaled to the crew chief of the aging 707 that despite the turbulence he and his nine-man team of commandos were still doing fine. The aircraft, bearing Gulf Air Cargo markings, was disguised to look like a freighter. It had taken off from Tel-Nof, Israel, at 1810 and headed for Turkey to pick up the commercial flyway from Adana to Riyadh, Saudi Arabia. The flight path would take them almost directly over At Tanf an hour from now.

Peter Newman's 1700 call informing Skillings that three truckloads of gold had appeared at the IST facility had set things in motion. Skillings had advised General George Grisham of the developments, and he immediately convened a secure conference call among the Israelis and the British. Everyone agreed that the arrival of what appeared to be Iraqi gold at the IST site and Komulakov's request for a charter plane mandated moving up the start of the operation. There was no point in waiting until 0300 in the morning if the weapons and gold were going to be moved out beforehand.

It had taken almost an hour to get the Turkish Ministry of Defense to go along with the overflight, but once approval had been granted, H-hour for the Israeli paradrop was set for 2030. The British would now arrive at 2100—giving the Israeli paratroopers time to descend and assemble north of the IST runway.

Rotem looked around. There was plenty of room in the aircraft. He had trained for parachute drops from this very aircraft with as many as sixty paratroopers jumping from the specially configured exit doors on each side of the fuselage. It required the pilot to shut down the two inboard engines and to lower the flaps fifteen degrees. Even then the big plane would be traveling at better than 150 knots. Tonight, there would be only nine jumpers. Rotem hoped that the air over the drop zone wasn't as turbulent as it was where they were now.

The four turbo-fan engines screamed as the venerable plane climbed over the ancient Turkish city and headed southeast. Below, Rotem could see the sun setting as the plane approached the dark blue water of Iskenderun Korfezi, the easternmost point of the Mediterranean Sea. He checked his watch. It would be dark in a matter of minutes. He also knew it would be very cold at thirty thousand feet when he and his team exited the bird for their HAHO parachute jump.

He was pleased to note that newer bluish-green lights had replaced the old red "night lights" in the aging aircraft's overhead space. These lights allowed the crew and passengers to use night-vision goggles and were easier on the eyes.

As the aircraft climbed through ten thousand feet, the crew chief signaled everyone to don oxygen masks because the plane could not be pressurized when rigged for paradrops. Rotem noted that several of his most experienced sergeants were already napping. They knew that the hour they had left before propelling themselves out the door into the night sky might well be the last good rest they'd get for awhile.

Unlike a commercial aircraft, the commandos were seated facing one another on nylon web seats. They leaned back against the fuselage, parachutes cushioning their backs, weapons strapped to their legs, equipment bags lashed to their bellies, beneath reserve chutes. At a station just forward of Rotem was the Sayeret EWO, tasked with the responsibility of staying in radio contact with the command center at Tel-Nof, with Peter Newman at At Tanf, and with Gunnery Sergeant

Skillings, who had launched from the Saudi air base at Turayf with the Royal Marine commandos as soon as the 707 reached Adana.

Major Rotem handed the EWO a handwritten page, from a note pad that he carried, asking the officer to confirm their ETA at the drop zone. Rotem estimated it to be right at 2030, but the final call would be by the EWO, who was also acting as navigator and calculating the effects of weather, wind, and altitude. Rotem wanted to ensure that his people were going to be on the ground, not descending, when the CH-46s and their Cobra escorts arrived over the objective area. The idea of parachuting through rotor blades had no appeal for him whatsoever. The EWO handed the note back. Below Rotem's inquiry was scrawled: "ETA DZ-2029." The major sighed, crumpled the note, and put it in his pocket. He turned to making a final check of his weapon and equipment. It was preferable to pondering where his wife might be at this moment.

International Scientific Trading, Ltd.
At Tanf, Syria
Tuesday, 23 March 1998
2025 Hours, Local

It had taken Peter Newman more than an hour and a half to crawl up next to the fuel truck parked on the apron beside the runway, about fifty yards from the back gate of the IST compound. He had started inching toward it from his hiding place as soon as it got dark, and despite the half moon, he'd had to summon every bit of the skill he retained from his days with Force Recon to cover the five hundred meters across open terrain to the truck.

Once General Grisham had made the decision to change H-hour from 0300 to 2030, Newman had begun to earnestly consider how he could identify himself to the incoming commandos, so that neither the Israelis nor the Royal Marines would mistake him for the enemy. The thought of being taken out by a Cobra gunner who spotted his silhouette on his FLIR was particularly alarming. Lacking an infrared strobe or any other kind of signaling device, he hit on the one place where he could hide that was to be avoided at all costs by the commandos—the fuel truck. They needed the fuel inside it to get home—so, he reasoned, it should be a safe haven from fire by all sides. He had made his last call on his Iridium phones to Gunnery Sergeant Skillings and Major Rotem to inform them where he would be when they arrived.

The truck had been parked with its rear toward the fuel storage tanks and a single gasoline pump. The passenger-side door faced toward the compound. Newman covered the last few meters to the driver's side door, inching himself along on his stomach, keeping the body of the truck between himself and the compound. He figured that if he couldn't see them they couldn't see him. When he finally got to the left front wheel of the truck, he carefully raised himself, first to his knees, then to a crouch so that the hood of the truck masked his silhouette.

When Newman was on his feet, he placed the night-vision device up to his eye and examined the vehicle. He thought about checking the door to see if it had been left unlocked but then decided not to risk the possibility that a light would go on if he opened the door. That's when he noticed that the driver had left the window down.

It took him another ten minutes to pull his body up over the door and to quietly lower himself down inside the cab. Despite the usual nighttime drop in temperature, he was bathed in sweat and out of breath once he got inside. Fearing that the security people inside the compound might have night-vision devices of their own, he tried to keep his body below the edge of the passenger-side window and the windshield. The inside of the cab was filthy. Food wrappers and empty cans littered the floor of the vehicle, and it smelled of old leather, grease, jet fuel, and sun-baked plastic. He had just stretched his arm out and checked his watch to gauge how much longer before the Israelis arrived when he heard the sound of the back gate of the IST compound opening. He could hear men's voices, speaking in Arabic, and then the headlights of a truck or car played across the windshield and the roof of the fuel truck's cab as a vehicle pulled out of the gate and started down the runway—directly toward him.

Newman rolled over on his side and pulled the pistol out of his belt in the small of his back, wishing it had a silencer. Clutching the weapon in his right hand, he waited, lying prone on the bench seat for the vehicle to pass. But instead of heading down the runway, the car pulled up and stopped next to the fuel truck. He heard the sound of a smooth-running, powerful engine just outside the fuel truck's window.

Suddenly the engine stopped, and he heard a door open and then close. Holding perfectly still, he waited on his back, his neck craned backward, the pistol on his chest pointed toward the door.

But instead of opening the door next to Newman's head, the driver of the vehicle walked to the rear of the fuel truck. Newman heard what sounded like a gasoline pump being turned on and then the sound of a hose nozzle being inserted into a gas tank.

Newman lay there frozen for what seemed an eternity. Then the gas pump was turned off. He heard the hose being put away, and there was silence while the driver of the vehicle replaced the fuel cap.

Suddenly, there was another sound—a muffled series of thumps— like someone repeatedly striking the inside of a large cardboard box. He was trying to determine the cause of the noise when he heard another sound, a muffled voice shouting, "Let us out of here! The fumes are killing us!"

The words seemed to be coming from inside the vehicle that had parked right beside him. Newman propped himself up on his left elbow and peered warily over the edge of the truck's driver-side door. There, with his back to him, was a large man with broad shoulders and blond hair—clearly not an Arab. Judging by his clothing in the dim moonlight, he appeared to be wearing some kind of desert khaki uniform.

As the Marine watched, the uniformed man took out a set of keys, pulled a pistol out of the holster on his right hip, and opened the trunk of the black Mercedes sedan. When the trunk light came on, Newman's heart seemed to stop. There, with hands bound and ankles wrapped in what appeared to be duct tape, was his wife, *Rachel.* She was staring at the man with the gun and absolutely terrified.

ENDGAME

C H A P T E R   T W E N T Y - T H R E E

International Scientific Trading, Ltd., Warehouse B
At Tanf, Syria
Tuesday, 24 March 1998
2025 Hours, Local

Did you take care of our house guests, Leonid?" asked General Komulakov as the pair walked out of the warehouse personnel door. They were instantly bathed in the orange glow of the sodium vapor security lights that illuminated the IST perimeter.

"Yes, I have seen to it," Dotensk replied, not bothering to disguise his distaste for this part of his job. The loyal Ukrainian had always done his share of "wet work" with KGB Department V—but his targets had all been men. It wasn't that Dotensk was suddenly becoming a kinder and gentler killer. He simply believed that killing women was beneath his dignity.

"Leonid, Leonid," chided Komulakov, "this is why you were not selected for colonel in the KGB. You must not allow these minor, unpleasant tasks to distract you from the requirements and benefits of our current endeavor. Now tell me the truth. You did not see to this yourself. You didn't have time. Who took care of this for you?"

"It is all being handled by our people. And before you ask, yes, it is being done 'the right way,' with all the appropriate protocols. I had Sedov and Babin bind the women upstairs and bring them down, one at a time, and put them into the 'boot' of one of the cars. Once Sedov and Babin departed, I had Pavel drive the women out there," Dotensk replied, gesturing in the darkness toward the runway.

"Is Pavel alone?"

"Yes, of course."

"Good. The fewer witnesses the better. It's not like the old days, Leonid, when there was a real code of silence. Nowadays it's hard to tell who can be trusted."

Dotensk looked up sharply at his superior, wondering if this comment was aimed at him. "Do you trust the men I have selected to inventory the gold?"

"To a point. That is why I told you to contact the *Rezidentura* at the Damascus embassy regarding a cargo aircraft. Did Romalyinov ever get back to you?"

"No."

"Then we have no other choice but to move it overland to the port at Latakia?"

"We could wait a day or two until I can locate an aircraft and make the charter arrangements to have it flown from here."

Komulakov pondered this for a moment and then said, "We are not likely to have that much time, Leonid. Our customer clearly intends to use the three devices we are sending him as soon as he gets them. It is also clear that the Israelis are going to strike first to prevent that—probably in the next twenty-four hours. Our gold probably won't even be loaded at the port by then. When is your friend Qusay supposed to wire transfer the balance owed?"

"After he gets the weapons."

Komulakov shook his head. "If the Israelis attack, we will never receive that money. He won't be alive to send it. And unless we get out of here quickly, we won't be around to spend any of it. We must change our plan. I want you to very quickly but quietly move a thousand pounds of the gold into the Lear. Spread-load the ingots on the floor of the aircraft so that they're evenly distributed, first in the aisle and then on the floor beneath the seats. Have the pilots help you so that the others do not know. After the gold is loaded, cover it with cardboard or something. As soon as you are finished, send the rest of the gold to Latakia on our trucks. Don't even bother to weigh the remainder. If we move it immediately, it may be possible to get it aboard your ship before the Israelis strike. While the gold is being taken care of, have Sedov and Babin load the three weapons on Qusay's trucks, one per truck, and send them on their way. Do you understand?"

Dotensk understood. He also realized that given how quickly things were changing he had better tell Komulakov what he had done with one of the nuclear artillery rounds. "There is something else that we need to take with us, General. I expected that Qusay would double cross us. So I . . . uh . . . took the initiative to hold back one of the nuclear weapons for just such a case. I had it removed from its shipping container, wrapped it in lead foil, and inserted it inside PVC pipe. It's in the van parked in the hangar. We should take it with us. We can always find another customer."

Komulakov didn't know whether to rebuke Dotensk or congratulate him. "Just when were you going to tell me about this, Leonid?"

"In the rush, there was no time, General."

"How much does it weigh?"

"As it is, about three hundred pounds. Can the aircraft take a thousand pounds of gold, the weapon, and both of us?"

"Don't worry, Leonid. I'll tell the pilots to dump some fuel. We need only enough to get to Diyabakir, Turkey. From there we can refuel again at Ankara, then across the Black Sea to Sebastopol. Even with all those stops we can be in Kiev before noon tomorrow. Now, see to all this while I go and pick up my briefcase and satellite phone in my quarters. I want to be ready to leave by 2100."

Relieved at the solution his superior had devised, Dotensk turned to re-enter the warehouse where the gold and the weapons were. As he did so, two shots rang out from the darkness, in the direction of the fuel tanks. The two men paused and Komulakov said, "Pavel?"

"Yes. He has disposed of the women."

"Good," replied Komulakov, turning toward the guest house. "Now, before we leave, kill him."

Hatzerim Tracking Center
Beer-Sheva, Israel
Tuesday, 24 March 1998
2026 Hours, Local

Duvdevan Senior Watch Officer Lieutenant Colonel David Hatzor was staring at a computer screen. Before him was displayed everything the Israeli Defense Forces knew about the situation on the ground in the vicinity of the International Scientific Trading complex east of At Tanf, Syria. Hatzor clicked on an icon, and a live satellite image appeared on the screen. He zoomed in on the specks that appeared on the screen. He smiled and said to himself, *Awesome!* He shook his head, marveling at the clarity of the image being down-linked in real time from the Indian Defense Forces satellite high above Syria to the dish on top of his bunker. Clearly visible on the screen were nine rectangular parachutes. As the satellite image tracked across the screen, he watched as one by one the parachutes billowed and then disappeared. Now he could make out the images of nine men—Major Ze'ev Rotem's commando team— as they moved quickly from their drop zone toward the runway of the complex. The IDF lieutenant colonel looked at his watch: 2026. *Four minutes early. Not bad,* he said to himself.

He adjusted the image to take in the rest of the area. There was the runway, less than five hundred meters south of where Rotem and his men had landed from their HAHO jump. Rotem had called the Command Center thirty-six minutes earlier to report that his team was exiting the 707 at twenty-nine thousand feet, ten miles northwest of the DZ. Wearing infrared strobes on top of their helmets, Rotem and his commandos had rendezvoused in the air and "flown" for more than a half hour in their specially configured parachutes to arrive silently, and just a few meters apart, almost dead-on their DZ. As soon as each man hit the ground, they had rolled up their gray camouflage chutes, stowed them beneath rocks and sand, put on their night-vision goggles, and headed for their tactical assembly area adjacent to the runway, near the fuel tanks, to await the arrival of the American helicopters and the Royal Marines.

Now, as Hatzor impatiently waited for Rotem to call in on his encrypted satellite radio, the watch officer scanned the area so that he could provide an enemy situation update for the IDF field commander when he made contact. Initially, the complex appeared unchanged from the last satellite pass. Hatzor could see no unusual activity around any of the buildings of the IST site—indicating that the parachute insertion had gone undetected. But then, as Hatzor made one last scan down the runway, he saw a vehicle parked next to the fuel truck that had not been there on the last satellite pass. Suddenly, as he tried to zoom in, the image on the screen froze—indicating that the satellite had reached its maximum slant range and was speeding over the horizon. It would be another two hours before he had another clear shot of the objective area from the Indian satellite. He checked the clock on the wall. The next American satellite pass wouldn't be until 2055—timed for five minutes before the U.S. Marine helos arrived with the detachment of Four-Two Commando.

At that moment, the speaker on the console next to the computer screen squawked with the sound of an encrypted transmission synchronizing in the radio receiver mounted on the rack above Hatzor's head. Then he heard Rotem's voice, speaking slowly, barely above a whisper: "Samuel, this is Joshua, over."

Hatzor instantly grabbed the handset, keyed the microphone, and replied, "Joshua, this is Samuel. I have you loud and clear. Any casualties?"

"Negative, all up and ready. We'll be in position by the fuel tank farm in five minutes. Request you advise Gibraltar that we will be in our planned location," Rotem replied, using the call sign for the Royal Marines.

"Will do."

"Anything happening at the objective that I need to know about?"

"Nothing that I can see at any of the buildings, but there appears to be a vehicle beside the fuel truck that wasn't there the last time we had sat coverage. I can't tell what that means for Papa November," Hatzor said, using the call sign they had created for Peter Newman. "It appears that this new vehicle is very close, about two meters, from where Papa November is supposed to be hiding. It's possible that he has been discovered."

"Any personnel visible?" Rotem inquired, still speaking just above a whisper, though Hatzor could hear the commando leader's heavy breathing over the helmet-mounted microphone as he dogtrotted toward the runway.

"It looks as if one person is standing between the vehicle and the fuel truck. That's all I can see."

"Can you tell where Papa November is from the transponder?"

"Negative. The battery must have died because he hasn't been showing up for the last four hours. Just be careful on your approach to the fuel truck because I don't have live coverage anymore."

"Roger that. I'll call again as soon as we're at the fuel truck."

Hatzor placed the handset back in its receptacle, picked up an identical one next to it, and keyed the transmission switch. After waiting for the electronic *ping* of the encryption, he said, "Gibraltar, Gibraltar, this is Samuel."

After a few seconds, the voice of U.S. Marine Gunnery Sergeant Amos Skillings came blaring through the speaker—along with the whine of CH-46 engines and the "slap" of the helicopter's twin rotors. "Samuel, this is Gibraltar, go ahead, over."

"Gibraltar, be advised that Joshua is safely at the objective. He will have his entire unit at the assigned location in less than five minutes.

I'm calling up your GPS plot right now," Hatzor said as he switched his screen to a map display. The 1:100,000-scale map showed the area around At Tanf, Syria. In the far lower left-hand corner of the screen, eight blue helicopter icons were blinking. A thin blue line—representing the flight path that the helicopters had taken—connected the icons and the Jordanian-Iraqi border post at Tirbil, the FARP from which they had launched.

"Roger, Samuel," Skillings replied. "We've got a bit of a tail wind and an ETA about 2055. Any word from Papa November? I think his sat phone batteries may be dead."

Hatzor repeated to Skillings the information about the vehicle parked next to the fuel truck. "As soon as I hear anything about Papa November, I'll pass it on to you."

"Roger, Samuel. Papa November has two sat phones—one of ours and one of yours. You try him on yours; I'll try him on ours."

"Will do. If you get through, let me know as soon as possible and I'll pass it on to Joshua. You and Joshua won't be able to talk directly to each other until you are on the ground."

"Aye, Aye," Skillings answered in the vernacular of the Corps as he picked up his Iridium phone and punched in the number he had already loaded for Newman.

International Scientific Trading, Ltd., Fuel Tank Farm
At Tanf, Syria
Tuesday, 24 March 1998
2031 Hours, Local

"You idiot!" Rachel Newman shouted angrily at the large blond man as the Mercedes' trunk lid sprang open. "Are you trying to kill us? We can't breathe with those gasoline fumes. Dyan has passed out!"

"Shut up!" the man shouted back at the American woman, pointing his pistol at her head.

Peter Newman, his heart racing, peered over the edge of the fuel truck door into his wife's eyes. She was on her back in the trunk of the Mercedes. Her hands were apparently bound behind her back and her legs were drawn back. *She must have been kicking the trunk lid,* Newman thought. He could plainly see the silver-colored tape wrapped tightly around her ankles and the light inside the trunk reflecting off her honey-colored hair. Beneath Rachel and farther inside the trunk he could see another pair of legs—also wrapped with wide tape. *That must be Dyan,* he thought.

Suddenly the Iridium phone he had plugged into the truck's cigarette lighter began to vibrate on the metal floorboard beneath him—making a buzzing sound. Newman's gut constricted, and he immediately ducked below the edge of the door window, holding the ancient Zbrojovka 9mm CZ 75B pistol on his chest as he reached vainly for the phone. Suddenly, he heard the door handle being grabbed, and the door sprang open.

The light inside the cab didn't come on, but Newman was plainly visible to the stunned blond mercenary standing only two feet away outside the door. The gunman reacted, but he was too slow. If he had simply slammed the door with his left hand, the outcome for him might well have been different. Instead, he muttered what sounded like, "What the—?" as he raised the automatic in his right hand toward Newman's head.

The Marine responded instinctively and squeezed off two 9mm rounds. The bullets hit the blond man in the face, and his lifeless body fell backward into the trunk of the car, the gun clattering onto the tarmac, his dead weight landing on Rachel. Newman bounded out of the fuel truck, jammed his pistol into his belt, reached into the trunk, grabbed the killer's lifeless body and pulled it off his wife. Rachel was covered with blood and crying near-hysterically in choked, terrified sobs. For an instant, Newman thought that she had been shot—but then he realized that the gore was from the dead gunman.

Newman gently lifted Rachel out of the trunk and held her against him. Knowing that the fuel truck obscured them from the IST facility, he simply held his wife in his arms, her head resting on his shoulder while she softly repeated over and over, "Oh Peter, thank God, thank God!"

Finally, the Iridium phone, persistently vibrating on the metal floor of the truck, interrupted their reunion. Peter gently turned Rachel around, sat her down on the running board of the truck, reached through the open driver-side door, and grabbed the phone. He punched the OK button and said, "Newman."

The voice of Gunnery Sergeant Skillings—accompanied by the noise of the helicopter he was riding in—came from the earpiece. "Colonel, just checking in. We're inbound in about twenty minutes. Major Rotem is already on the ground. Are you in position?"

"Yes," Newman replied quietly—suddenly fearing that the two shots may have alerted someone at the IST facility—or that the Israelis might have mistaken the shots for enemy activity and open fire on the Mercedes. "Are you in contact with Major Rotem?"

"Not directly, until we get into the area. But I can pass word to him through his Command Center."

"That'll work. Tell him that I have Rachel and his wife! In two minutes we'll all be inside the cab of the fuel truck. Tell him that the vehicle next to the truck is not a threat. Repeat, *not* a threat. Got it?"

"Aye aye, sir."

"Good, call him now. I'll call you back in five minutes," Newman added. He terminated the call, set the phone on the seat, and reached into a pocket for his Swiss Army knife.

Gently, he sliced the duct tape bindings on his wife's ankles. Then he turned her around and cut through the nylon wire-strap tie. Finally freed, she stood, somewhat unsteadily, and again embraced her husband.

"We've got to get Dyan out of the car and into the truck," he whispered in his wife's ear. "Is she OK?"

"I think so. I hope she only passed out from the gasoline fumes." Rachel started to move toward the car trunk, but her legs, tingling from restored circulation, wouldn't support her, and she grabbed Peter's arm to steady herself.

He picked her up and placed her on the seat of the fuel truck, behind the wheel. "Wait in here. Slide over toward the passenger side and stay low. If you see anyone coming, alert me. I'll get Dyan."

In less than two minutes Newman cut Dyan from her bindings, revived her, and carried her to the cab of the fuel truck. He then hoisted the body of the dead gunman into the trunk and closed the lid. Finally, Newman crawled under the automobile and retrieved the weapon the gunman had dropped. He was surprised to see that it was a 9mm SIG Sauer P226, a favorite of his old Force Recon unit. He checked the magazine, pulled the slide back to confirm a round in the chamber, put the weapon on "Safe," and jammed it down into his belt in the small of his back.

Making a final check of the area, Newman climbed back into the cab of the fuel truck to await the arrival of the combined British/Israeli raid force. The women were hunched down on the floor, whispering joyfully to each other as he quietly pulled the driver-side door closed.

With his right hand, he reached out and touched his wife's hair, and she looked up at him in the dim light. He smiled at her and, pointing toward the IST buildings, asked in a whisper, "How many of them are in there?"

Rachel and Dyan looked at each other and shrugged. Dyan said, "It is hard to tell. We only saw the Russian, his friend, a few guards—and that one," she gestured toward the Mercedes. "I'm sure now that he was going to kill us. The ones who tied us up and brought us down to the car said that they were taking us to you—but I think he was going to take us out in the desert to shoot us."

Newman nodded and said, "Maybe that's why no one came out after the two shots. They *expected* to hear two shots. But still, I wouldn't be surprised if someone comes looking for him."

"I would guess that given all the different men we saw there are probably thirty, maybe thirty-five, in there," said Dyan. "Probably half of them are Europeans—Russians, I think. The rest seem to be from somewhere around here—Iraqis, Syrians, Saudis—from the way they were talking outside the room where they kept us. I know one was from Egypt. I think they are here for some kind of terrorist training. All of them have guns."

"That's good intelligence," said Newman, picking up the phone.

"Peter, what are you doing?" Rachel said plaintively. "Let's get out of here. That Mercedes is full of gas; the man you shot just filled it up. Let's get back home. I want to see James."

"We can't, Rachel. I'm sorry, but we've another job to finish first." Then seeing tears beginning to well up in his wife's eyes again, he quickly continued. "Look, James is safe with my sister back in the States. But we're nowhere near Jerusalem. The Iraqi border is only a few kilometers over there," he said gesturing with his head to the east, out the left side of the truck. "There are others coming to help us—and to recover the weapons being hidden in the buildings where you were being held."

"What weapons?" asked Rachel.

"Nuclear weapons," her husband answered, picking up the Iridium phone and turning it on. The two women stared at him in stunned silence as he hit the autodial button for Skillings. When the Marine gunnery sergeant answered, Newman relayed the information Dyan had given to him and then asked, "How far out are you?"

"About ten minutes. Your Israeli friend should be there by now. I just finished talking to his command center."

As Newman ended the call, he caught a shadow of movement in the mirror mounted on the driver's door. Adrenaline spiked through his gut, and he went for his gun. But before he could react, he heard Rotem's voice, barely above a whisper, "In the truck, show your hands!"

Newman dropped the gun into his lap and held his empty hands out the window. Suddenly, the masked face of an Israeli commando was at the door, an Uzi with a silencer pointed inside. He lowered the weapon and motioned for them to come out, and the three slipped out of the truck cab. Dyan stumbled into her husband's arms.

The rest of the IDF commandos deployed around the tank farm and the two vehicles, ignoring the reunion embrace as they continued their vigilance. Newman could see one of them examining the

Mercedes, while several others set up a machine gun on the berm surrounding the two fuel tanks.

After waiting a minute or two, Newman, who was standing beside the truck with his arm around Rachel's waist, said, "Ze'ev, the British are coming."

Rotem looked up, smiled, and said, "I think I've heard that line before. Anyway, how close are they?"

"About five minutes," replied Newman. He then repeated what Dyan and Rachel had told him about the number of enemy and what little the women knew of the layout inside the IST compound.

Suddenly the IDF officer was all business again. "All right, Peter, you and the women get back into the cab of the truck. Since you do not have strobes, the British might mistake you for the enemy if you are out in the open. Everyone has been instructed to avoid any fire at this truck and the fuel tanks because we will need the fuel to get home. "Here," said the IDF major, handing Newman a handheld Motorola radio, "use this to stay in touch with us. It's encrypted and it has been preset to the frequency your Gunnery Sergeant Skillings and I are both using. My call sign is Joshua. His is Samuel. Yours is Papa November."

As Rotem turned to give final instructions to his men for laying down a base of fire to protect the Royal Marine Commando assault force, they heard the faint sound of helicopters approaching from the west.

International Scientific Trading, Ltd.
At Tanf, Syria
Tuesday, 24 March 1998
2050 Hours, Local

The assault force swooped in ten minutes early, so low and so fast out of the southeast that even Newman, holding his night-vision device, didn't see them until they opened fire. The Cobras came in first; four of them, without lights—at twenty-five feet, traveling at 125 knots, their 20mm M-197 three-barreled Gatling guns taking out targets inside the compound that appeared on the Cobra gunners' FLIRs. The five lookouts on the rooftops never knew what hit them. None of them even got off a shot. Nor did any of them have a chance to alert those in the courtyard or inside the buildings as to what was happening.

Then, as the Cobras wheeled around to make another pass, this time with TOW and Hellfire missiles, out of nowhere four CH-46s landed on the runway—two of them almost directly in front of Newman and in full view of the walled compound—to disgorge their Royal Marine commandos. The .50-caliber machine guns mounted on the aging birds opened fire at the compound to pin down anyone who might have survived the Cobra runs, assuring that no one inside could return fire. And no one did. The Royal Marines on the ground raced for the back gate of the IST compound.

As they deployed in the attack, Newman came up on the handheld radio that Rotem had given him and announced, "All Gibraltar and Joshua units, this is Papa November. The hostages are no longer on the premises. They are with me in the fuel truck. They do not—repeat, do not—know which building the nuclear weapons are in. Recommend that you avoid damage to building 3. That's my best guess where the weapons might be."

He received brief acknowledgments from both Skillings and Rotem, and now Newman could see the Royal Marines forming to assault the compound itself as the now empty CH-46s "Frogs" lifted and relocated to the east end of the runway, awaiting fuel. To his right, Newman watched as a squad of British commandos deployed along the back wall of the compound. There was a brief huddle, then the squad leader tossed a hand grenade, and he and his men rushed the first building. They immediately took fire from the second story of the barracks building.

Skillings came back up on the radio. "Papa November, I'm headed your way with two men. We need to move the fuel truck down to the far end of the runway and start refueling the 'Frogs.'"

"Roger that," Newman replied into the radio. "Take Rachel and Dyan with you and put them on the lead bird. Did you bring me the extra set of NVGs and the strobe?"

"Affirmative."

"Peter, what are you doing? Where are you going?" cried Rachel.

"I've got one more thing to do. We need to find Komulakov and bring him in. It's the only way we'll ever get our lives back, Rachel. I want him, and I'm going to go get him."

As he spoke, one of the Cobras swept overhead, and there was an ear-splitting roar as it unleashed a volley of five-inch rockets at one of the buildings in the complex. Off to their right, a series of bright flashes and crashes confirmed that the missiles found their mark.

Suddenly, Skillings was beside the truck with a Royal Marine—and another Brit, one Newman suddenly recognized. Bruno Macklin had come with them on the raid. The SAS captain was thinner than Newman remembered him from three years earlier, but he still had the same irrepressible smile. "Hey Colonel," Macklin shouted over the din of small arms fire and exploding grenades, "here's a flak and helmet. The strobe is on top. The NVGs are already on. I'm going with you to get Komulakov. I don't want anything to happen to him. He owes me too!"

Newman shook his head in amazement, and then he turned, reached inside the cab of the truck, touched his wife's face, and said, "I love you, sweetheart. Now go with Gunny Skillings to the helos. I'll meet you there in a few minutes." He quickly jumped from the cab of the truck and put on the armored vest and helmet, stuffing the sat phone into one of the front pockets of the vest and the Motorola radio into the other. Then, grabbing an M-4 carbine from Skillings, the Marine lieutenant colonel and the SAS captain jogged off toward the compound. Newman's leg muscles, cramped from two days of sedentary hiding, almost failed him. But by the time they arrived at the breached gate, the adrenaline coursing through his body had driven away the stiffness.

Newman and Macklin flattened themselves against the wall beside the breached portal. The once formidable steel gate was now a tangle of bent metal hanging by one hinge, apparently hit by a high-explosive rocket from one of the Cobras. Inside, they could hear the crack of rifles and automatic weapons as the Marines of Four-Two Commando poured well-aimed small arms fire into the windows of the two-story barracks building.

Pointing his M-4 at the guest house, Newman shouted to Macklin, "We've got to get over there. I watched Komulakov coming and going from that building for the last two days. I think that's where the snake is hiding."

Macklin cautiously peeked around the wall, taking note of the building Newman had identified—as well as the fact that there was still a heavy volume of fire coming from the barracks. Both men could see Royal Marines pinned down inside the courtyard. Some appeared to be wounded. "We'll need some covering fire or we'll never make it," Macklin shouted over the din.

Newman pulled the Motorola radio out and said, "Any Gibraltar or Joshua unit, this is Papa November. If anyone has comms with the Cobras, request covering fire on the south face of the barracks building!"

Immediately, a voice came over the net, "Papa, this is Snake Leader. Stand by. In fifteen seconds, Snake Two-Zero and Snake Two-One will do a pop-up from outside the south wall and work over the south face of the target building with overhead rocket and cannon fire. Make sure everyone stays down."

Newman replied, "Roger." He shoved the radio back into the pocket of his vest and shouted to Macklin, "Get ready!"

Moments later, two Cobras popped up over the wall and, from a hover, opened fire with their Gatling guns and rockets. The noise was horrific as tracer rounds and 2.75-inch rockets poured into the windows of the barracks. Pieces of brick, mortar, and wooden window casing flew in every direction. With the rounds spewing only a few feet over their heads, Newman and Macklin, bent almost double, raced the fifty meters to the "guest house" where Newman suspected Komulakov to be hiding.

As the Marine and the SAS officer crouched by the front door of their objective, catching their breath, behind them the steel door of the nearby concrete communications blockhouse opened a crack, revealing the ugly snout of an AK-47. The gunman had a clear shot at both Newman's and Macklin's backs. Neither man was aware that they had suddenly become targets. But in all the noise and combat, the gunman hadn't noticed the two Cobras hovering just beyond the south wall of the compound. The gunner of the left-hand Cobra, seeing the flare of heat from the doorway on his FLIR, reacted immediately. Placing the crosshairs of his cursor on the crack in the door, he toggled the switch on his stick to "Hellfire" and squeezed the trigger. The missile had barely armed when it hit the door. Newman and Macklin were knocked to the ground by the concussion as the blockhouse erupted in a fireball. As they huddled against the wall of the guest house, debris from the satellite dish that had been atop the communications structure rained down around them. Newman struggled to his feet, his ears ringing from the explosion, and he felt, rather than heard, the Iridium satellite phone buzzing in the pocket of his armored vest. As he took out the phone to answer, he noticed the time: 2105. The attack had been underway for only a quarter of an hour. It seemed like much longer.

Damascus-to-Baghdad Highway
8 km West of At Tanf, Syria
Tuesday, 24 March 1998
2105 Hours, Local

For nearly fifteen minutes Eli Yusef Habib had been watching the fireworks off to the east from the cab of his truck. First there would be a flash of an explosion, then five or six seconds later would come the muffled *crump* as the sound reached him. Several times he had seen streams of tracers coming down like a red hose from the sky—and then the *brrrrrrrt* of the weapon that spewed much fire. He assumed that these flashes and noises were from the helicopters. Peter Newman had said that there would be "gunships," and the old man guessed that these were similar to the MI-24s and MI-27s he had occasionally seen in the Iraqi Air Force. As Eli Yusef watched the flashes against the dark horizon, he prayed for Peter Newman and his allies.

Suddenly, Eli Yusef heard a different sound—the noise of armored vehicles approaching from behind him on the road from At Tanf. The old man looked over at the highway, less than fifty meters from where he was parked—and his breath caught in his throat. There, on the road, headed toward the fireworks display, was a column of Syrian tanks and armored personnel carriers.

The fighting at the IST compound must have gotten the attention of the local Syrian Army commander and he is responding with his entire contingent, he said to himself. Eli Yusef counted sixteen Soviet-built T-72 tanks and twice as many BMP armored vehicles and wheeled BTR-60 armored personnel carriers headed at high speed toward the IST complex. He reached for his satellite phone and dialed the number for Peter Newman.

The phone rang several times before Eli heard a familiar voice but an unfamiliar greeting. The voice was accompanied by the sound of gunfire and explosions: "Papa November. Go ahead."

"Papa?" responded the old man.

"Eli, is that you? This is Peter Newman."

"Yes, Peter, this is Eli Yusef. I must tell you with some urgency that sixteen Syrian Army T-72 tanks and thirty-three armored vehicles, BMPs and BTRs, have just passed me heading in your direction." The old man had a sudden sense of déjà vu, for he had performed this very service as a boy for the British Army in North Africa more than fifty-six years ago during their desperate battles against Rommel and his Afrika Corps. The experience was fresh in his mind even now. "I estimate that at the speed they are traveling they will be at the IST compound in less than one-half hour."

"That's not good," said Newman, as much to himself as to Eli, marveling at the old man's knowledge of military hardware.

"How can I help you?" asked the old man.

"First, alert Samir so that he won't get caught in any roundup. There's bound to be one. Second, as soon as you can, get out of there yourself. You both need to leave the area. The Syrian authorities will start blocking all the roads into and out of this province as soon as they figure out what's going on. And third, keep praying, Eli, keep praying."

"Yes, I will do that anyway. But precisely what do you want me to pray for. I like to be specific with God. I have been praying for your safety and that you would find your wife."

"Well, those prayers have been answered. I'm still safe, and Rachel is aboard one of the helicopters."

"God is good. I will continue to pray for your safety. What else?"

"Well, you might pray that we can locate the three weapons and the Russian who is behind all this. He's here somewhere."

The sound of firing died down suddenly in the vicinity of the barracks building. The Cobras had done their job. The Royal Marines who had been pinned down in the courtyard only moments ago were now poking through the wreckage of the barracks and heading for the warehouse and hangar complex. Newman could still hear sporadic firing from the warehouses a hundred meters to the north where the Israelis were hunting for the nukes.

There was a brief pause and the old man asked, "And when you find this Russian, what will you do with him?"

"We're going to bring him to justice."

"Yes, justice is good. But vengeance is not yours. Be sure that you know the difference, Peter."

Newman was growing impatient. While he owed his life to this old man, the information he'd just received about the column of Syrian armor alarmed him. In an effort to end the conversation, Newman said, "Thank you, Eli. I'll keep that in mind."

"I know you have much to do. Where are you searching for this man?"

"I'm standing at the front door of his quarters," Newman replied, wondering why Eli Yusef was asking these questions when so much needed to be done so quickly.

"But doesn't he have an airplane?"

"Yes, why?"

"Isn't that how he would try to escape?"

"Eli, that's what we're trying to prevent."

Undeterred, the old man continued. "Well, he must surely be at his plane by now."

"How can you know that? How would he have gotten there?"

"I don't know how I know. I just do."

Newman looked at Macklin and said, "The hangar. C'mon. We've got to get to the hangar." The two men headed back across the now silent courtyard toward the hangar two hundred meters away. As they ran, Newman handed Macklin the Motorola radio and said, "Alert Gibraltar and Joshua that there's a column of Syrian armor headed this way from At Tanf. Have the Cobras head that way to slow them down." Then, remembering that the satellite circuit was still open, he said into the phone, "Thank you, Eli. Be careful. Tell Samir to be safe . . . and hurry now. Get out of this area right now. I'll look forward to seeing you again soon. You guys will be in my prayers."

"As you and yours shall be in mine," replied the old man.

International Scientific Trading, Ltd., Hangar
At Tanf, Syria
Tuesday, 24 March 1998
2115 Hours, Local

The pilots were strapped into their seats in the Lear's cockpit, ready to start the two Garrett TFE 731 engines as soon as the hangar doors opened. The inside of the hangar was bathed in red emergency lights, to preserve their night vision. Though the gunfire and explosions outside had died down, both men were more than a little frightened. They had just finished loading the thousand pounds of gold when the attack began—and they were very anxious to get out of there.

For several days the pilots had been listening to BBC news reports about the likelihood of another Mideast war, and they both assumed that what was going on outside meant it had begun. Now, thoroughly alarmed, all they wanted was to be on their way to Turkey. The copilot had been filing a flight plan to Kiev, Ukraine, with intermediate stops in Diyabakir, Ankara, and Sebastopol, when the phone line went dead. The lights flickered and went out, the red emergency lights came on, and the sounds of heavy explosions echoed through the large, open hangar bay.

When the attack had begun twenty minutes earlier, Komulakov had been in his private office at the guest house. Dotensk had been in the warehouse supervising the loading of the nuclear weapons onto the three Iraqi trucks and the remaining gold ingots onto IST lorries for shipment to Latakia. Komulakov's first thought when the attack had started was that Qusay Hussein had dispatched a contingent of Iraqi troops to take possession of the nuclear weapons while reclaiming his gold. Dotensk, on the other hand, thought it might be the Syrians. Neither considered who it really was—and both thought of nothing but escape.

When the lights in the guest house went out, Komulakov grabbed three items from his desk drawer: a flashlight, one of the small Marconi handheld radios Dotensk had purchased from a stolen NATO shipment, and his 9mm Makarov pistol. Without waiting to find out whether his men were winning or losing the battle outside, he went to the center of the room, threw back a rug, grabbed an indented metal handle in the floor, and lifted a trap door.

Ten wooden steps led down to a concrete tunnel—an escape route constructed in the '70s to connect the guest house to the hangar at the opposite end of the complex. Komulakov switched on his flashlight, pulled the trap door closed behind him, and headed for the hangar, hurrying behind a cone of yellow light. Above he could hear and feel the concussions of explosions.

When he arrived at the end of the tunnel, another set of stairs led up to a second trap door—this one concealed in a tiny clothes closet within the hangar's small office. When he opened the closet door and stepped into the dimly lit office, Dotensk was standing at the desk, shouting into the dead telephone. The Ukrainian was so surprised he almost shot his boss.

"General!" he shrieked. "We are being attacked!"

"Yes, Leonid, I noticed."

"We must get out of here right away. The pilots are already in the aircraft going through the preflight checklist. The gold is loaded. We need only get the weapon we are taking with us," the Ukrainian shouted over the din of nearby battle, sounding ever closer.

"Yes, let's get that done."

The two men walked through the red light to a van parked about fifteen feet from the left wing tip of the jet. Dotensk opened the back door of the van and, pointing to a four-foot-long length of black, ten-inch PVC pipe that was sealed at both ends, said, "Here it is."

The Ukrainian, displaying considerable agility, leapt into the van and began sliding the pipe toward the back of the vehicle. Komulakov put his hands around the free end and pulled until Dotensk was able to jump out of the van and grab the other end. Together, they crab-walked toward the open hatch, just behind the cockpit on the left side of the air-craft. "How much did you say this weighs, Leonid?" asked Komulakov.

"A little more than three hundred pounds," Dotensk replied as they manhandled the bulky cargo into the aircraft and then slid it down the center aisle, atop the cardboard-covered gold ingots.

When the task was completed, the Ukrainian said to the general, "I'll move the van and then open the door and we can get out of here."

"Very well, Leonid. I'll tell the pilots to be ready to go."

Dotensk had just climbed into the van and was fumbling in his pock-ets looking for the keys when the small personnel hatch built into the fold-ing hangar door was thrown open and in rushed Peter Newman and Bruno Macklin. The two men paused for a second to flip back their NVGs, which had flared in the red light. As their eyes adjusted, they saw Komulakov's head and shoulders leaning into the cockpit inside the jet. He was talking to the pilots. Neither Newman nor Macklin noticed Dotensk inside the van. They ran to the open hatch on the left side of the Lear, leaving the Ukrainian behind them, hiding in the driver's seat as he watched the American and the Brit through the rearview mirror.

"Get out of the airplane, General," shouted Newman, standing at the bottom of the folding stairs of the jet. He aimed his M-4 at Komulakov's backside to make the point.

The Russian slowly backed out of the cockpit and climbed down the stairs, fully expecting Newman to shoot him and wondering where Dotensk had gone.

So far, Newman's wrath had been contained. But now, as he watched the Russian, the Marine's rage became overpowering. He released the safety on the M-4, almost as a reflex action—as he thought about the past three years of hiding, of the terror and grief that Komulakov had poured upon so many. Newman's lips curled into a snarl, and he took aim at Komulakov's left eye, lining up the barrel sight with the cold, blue iris of the man before him. Ridding the world of this cruel and merciless demon would be easy. All he had to do was squeeze off a single burst.

Newman's finger took up the tension on the trigger, and his eyes narrowed. Then, unexplainably, he blinked.

Komulakov noticed it. "You can't do it, can you, Colonel? Something has happened to you. You've become soft. You no longer have the stomach for killing me, do you?" Showing none of the anxiety he actually felt, the "retired" KGB general tried to change the subject. He said calmly, "So, Colonel Newman, this 'war' is your doing?"

"Yes, Komulakov," the Marine said, lowering his carbine but keeping it pointed at the Russian. "And you're our POW. You're coming with us—you *and* your weapons."

"My weapons?"

"Yes, your weapons. In the building next door, an Israeli commando team has found three shipping containers holding nuclear artillery rounds. We're taking them—and you—with us."

"Oh you are? And, then what?

"A trial, General. In a U.S. court."

"A trial, eh? You're a fugitive, a terrorist. And you're the only witness. It'll be your word against mine."

"Not so, mate," said Macklin, speaking for the first time. "*I* was on that mission you compromised in Iraq. And it's high time you paid for what you did to me and those other lads."

The Russian decided to try another tack. "If you do this, Newman, you'll never see your wife alive again. You know that, don't you?"

"I'm sure that's what you intended, General, but Rachel is at this minute sitting on a U.S. Marine helicopter. Your paid killer is dead."

For the first time, a flicker of fear crossed the face of Dimitri Komulakov. But it only lasted a second, for he suddenly caught sight of Dotensk inside the van. "And so, what is it you want me to do?"

"Get in the van, General. We're going to take a little ride out to the end of the runway. But first, put your hands up and lean against the van. Spread your legs. You know the drill. Search him, Bruno."

Komulakov did as ordered, and Macklin set his H&K MP5 out of reach on the hangar floor and stepped forward to perform the search while Newman covered the Russian. The British SAS officer instantly found Komulakov's Makarov pistol and shoved it in his own waistband. Newman was watching him pat the Russian down when the bullet from Dotensk's 9mm hit the Marine square between the shoulder blades. The second bullet struck his helmet, snapping his head forward and dropping him to the floor in a heap. Macklin reached for the Makarov in his belt, but he was too late. The third bullet from Dotensk's weapon hit him in the chest, and he dropped to his knees. As he fell, Komulakov spun and kicked him in the face. The SAS officer fell backward and collapsed.

"Well done, Leonid," said Komulakov, surveying the bodies. "Now, quickly, open the hangar door and we'll get underway." The general bent and retrieved his weapon from beside Macklin's belt and climbed into the Lear. Dotensk ran to the switch on the wall that controlled the hangar door, hoping that the backup power supply he'd installed for this purpose would work. As the large hangar door began to fold, the jet's two engines began spooling up to generate thirty-five hundred pounds of thrust each.

Dotensk ran back to the left side of the Lear, but instead of being welcomed aboard the aircraft, he was greeted by the sight of Komulakov standing at the top of the stairs pointing the Makarov at his partner in crime.

Dotensk looked up at the Russian in disbelief and screamed over the whine of the jet engines, "What are you doing? I just saved you!"

"I'm sorry, Leonid. But the pilots tell me that the jet would be dangerously overloaded if we tried to take off with the gold, the weapon, and both of us aboard."

"Well, we can remove the weapon!"

"But I need *it*. I don't need you." These were the last words that Leonid Dotensk heard. Komulakov's two bullets to the chest left Dotensk sprawled beside the bodies of Peter Newman and Bruno Macklin.

The Russian pulled up the stairs into the Lear and sealed the hatch. Then the jet, at full throttle, shot from the hangar, turned right, then left, and screamed down the runway. A hundred and fifty meters before it reached the end of the tarmac where the tank truck was fueling a CH-46, the Lear's nose came up and the heavily laden aircraft shrieked into the night sky, barely clearing the helo's rotor blades.

International Scientific Trading, Ltd., Hangar

At Tanf, Syria
Tuesday, 24 March 1998
2120 Hours, Local

Lieutenant Colonel Peter Newman heard ringing in his ears, his head was throbbing with pain, and he could barely breathe. But he was alive—and he knew it. He was aware of a face close to his, but it was hazy through his blurred vision. And then the face spoke, "Colonel? Can you hear me? Can you speak?" asked the muscular African American Marine kneeling beside him.

"W-what about . . . Komulakov?" Newman whispered.

"Gone. Got away in his jet."

"Cobras? Shoot him down?"

"They've been busy working over a Syrian armor column about six klicks west of here."

Newman slowly turned his head and saw two Royal Marines attending to Captain Macklin on the floor beside him. One of them, a medic, was clearing the wounded soldier's mouth and making sure his air passage was clear. The other was checking his pulse.

A figure appeared above them and asked, "Can we move them? We need to get out of here." It was Major Rotem.

"Yes, sir," answered the Marine gunnery sergeant. "I think Colonel Newman's got a couple of broken ribs and probably a concussion. Thank God he was wearing that flak jacket and helmet. The vest slowed the bullet, and the entry wound is shallow. The second round lodged in the helmet. I think we can get going. If you can pass the word to move the birds back here from the other end of the runway, we'll load him up, along with Captain Macklin and the other wounded men. We ought to spread-load your unit, the Royal Marines, and the nuclear weapons on the other three helos."

The major gave the order to one of his men and turned back to Skillings. "How is the captain?" asked Rotem, pointing to Macklin.

"Not too bad. Same story. The vest stopped the round. But someone did a job on his face. It looks like he's got a broken jaw. And with that smashed nose, he's not going to win any beauty contests. In any event, they are both a whole lot better off than that guy," the gunnery sergeant added, nodding toward the body of Leonid Dotensk.

Newman grabbed Skillings's right hand and tried to pull himself to his feet. "I'm OK," he muttered, feeling angry because Komulakov had escaped. But the effort proved too painful, and he sank back onto the floor, his head still spinning as he fought to remain conscious.

Outside on the tarmac, eight IDF operators were opening the shipping containers to remove the three nuclear weapons so they could be quickly loaded aboard the helicopters. As the Israelis did this, a Royal Marine captain came trotting in out of the darkness and approached Rotem. He shouted to be heard over the noise of the four CH-46s as they repositioned outside the structure, "Sir, Major Chilton asks that you come outside for a moment. One of our lads has made an interesting discovery."

The IDF officer and the British commando walked quickly to where four Royal Marines were standing in a semicircle. As the officers approached, one of them took out a flashlight and shined it on a pallet containing twenty gold ingots.

"We were wondering what to do with the gold when one of our troopers discovered just what all these folks were fighting and dying for," said Major Chilton over the roar of the rotors. "It looks as if these guys were robbed."

"How so?" asked Rotem.

The British officer held up one of the heavy bars that had been part of Qusay Hussein's gold shipment from Baghdad. The seal of the Iraqi National Bank was clearly evident. The Royal Marine unsheathed his combat knife and gouged a chunk out of the ingot and showed the gash to Rotem. To the IDF major's surprise, the bar was solid lead, gilded with a gold finish of some kind.

"Saddam wouldn't have had the time to do this just for Komulakov," Rotem observed. "This must mean that the entire Iraqi treasury is filled with bars of gilded lead! So much for the UN Oil for Food program. No wonder Saddam can afford to buy all that military hardware."

A Royal Marine captain ran up and interrupted them. "Major Rotem, shall we depart? I've been advised by base that there are two C-130s waiting at the Tirbil FARP for our arrival. Will you be riding on the lead helo out of here with your wife?"

The IDF officer looked around the devastated complex. A pall of acrid, black smoke hung over the warehouses and billeting areas. The barracks were still smoldering, as were several smaller structures. Overhead, the four Cobras, having refueled after attacking the Syrian armor column, were circling like angry wasps.

Rotem looked over at Newman, who was on his feet with his arm over Skillings's shoulder. The Israeli officer nodded his head and said, "Let's go."

"Yeah . . . let's do that. Rachel has already told me that she's ready to go home," Newman added.

Another British NCO approached the group and shouted, "Sir, both units have their musters complete, and the wounded are being loaded aboard now. Shall I signal base that we're prepared to lift?"

Before he could reply, one of Rotem's IDF sergeants called out to him as they headed toward the helicopters. "Sir, we've got a huge problem," he said as he caught up with them. "I thought I'd better let you and Colonel Newman know right away."

"What kind of a problem?" Rotem asked.

Two Royal Marines continued toward the helicopter, carrying Macklin, who was beginning to regain consciousness. Only Newman, Skillings, and Rotem heard what the sergeant had to say.

"We were taking the nuclear weapons out of the shipping containers in order to fit them onto the choppers," the Israeli sergeant began. "We have two of the three nuclear weapons aboard and tied down."

"And what's the problem?" Major Rotem repeated.

"Well, sir, when we opened the other shipping crate, we found nothing but sand. Sir, . . . one of the nukes is missing!"

EPILOGUE

P *eter Newman* was treated in Israel for the wounds he received during the At Tanf raid. On 30 March 1998, he and his wife *Rachel,* using the passports of John and Sarah Clancy, returned to the United States aboard a USAF C-17. When they arrived at MacDill Air Force Base, they were met by General George Grisham, CinC CENTCOM, and Florida Congressman "Sonny" Hester of the House Armed Services Committee. The Newmans were reunited with their son James that afternoon when he and Peter's sister Nancy arrived. On 5 April 1998, Peter J. Newman was reinstated in the USMC with the rank of lieutenant colonel and assigned to the staff of U.S. Central Command. In January 1999 Rachel gave birth to a daughter, Elizabeth Anne. Peter Newman was promoted to colonel in July 2000, and in February 2001 he was ordered to HQMC for duty as staff secretary to the Commandant of the Marine Corps. On 24 March 2001, at a White House ceremony, the President belatedly presented Colonel Peter J. Newman, USMC, with a second Purple Heart Medal and a second Navy Cross for the action in Iraq three years before. The citations are classified.

General George Grisham "respectfully declined" a presidential request in April 1998 for his resignation and retirement. Subsequently, he was summoned to testify before closed sessions of the House and Senate Armed Services Committees investigating what the press dubbed the "March Mideast Missile Emergency." Both congressional committees unanimously determined that General Grisham had committed no wrongdoing and privately commended him for his actions in preventing a nuclear war. In February 2001, the new President appointed him Commandant of the Marine Corps.

William Goode replaced "John Clancy" as the director of the Hospice of Saint Patrick in Jerusalem. He continued to serve in this capacity, working closely and quietly with the "Fellowship of Believers" in the Community of Saint Patrick until May 2001, when the new President asked him to return to the U.S. to serve as Deputy Director for Operations of the Central Intelligence Agency. In June 2001 the Senate quietly confirmed his appointment and he became, at sixty-seven, the oldest head of the CIA's Clandestine Service. He now keeps the *Pescador II* berthed in Annapolis, Maryland, and sails regularly on the Chesapeake Bay. He remains in close contact with the members of the Fellowship around the world.

Gunnery Sergeant Amos Skillings was awarded the Bronze Star with Combat "V" for his actions during the At Tanf raid. The citation reads in part, "for heroic action on the night of 24–25 March 1998 during a classified operation essential to the national security of the United States. After repeatedly exposing himself to enemy fire, Gunnery Sergeant Skillings skillfully organized the retrograde of U.S. and allied forces from the objective area to a clandestine FARP established in a neighboring country and, from there, onward to allied territory via USMC C-130." The pilots and aircrews of the USMC helicopter squadrons that participated in the At Tanf raid and the U.S. Marine C-130 crew that lifted the British commandos from the FARP at Tirbil, Jordan, were subsequently recognized with Air Medals and a Navy Unit Citation. None of the certificates mention Iraq, Jordan, Saudi Arabia, Israel, or nuclear weapons. Skillings was promoted to first sergeant in 1999 and was assigned to Second Force Reconnaissance Company at Camp Lejeune, North Carolina, in 2001.

Major Ze'ev Rotem was cited for his heroism during the At Tanf operation, and the Prime Minister presented him with the *Itur Hagvura,* Israel's highest military decoration at a secret ceremony in June 1998. In October of that same year, his wife *Dyan* gave birth to a boy, Joshua Peter. Promoted to lieutenant colonel in November, Ze'ev Rotem served as military aide to the Prime Minister from December 1998 until January 2001, at which time he was assigned as the assistant military attaché at the Israeli embassy in Washington, D.C. Although Lieutenant Colonel Rotem wears the gold and silver *Itur Hagvura* medal on his uniform, he is not permitted to display or reveal the text of the citation that is classified "Most Secret."

Robert Hallstrom, aka Julio Morales, continued to spy for the Russian Intelligence Service until he was seized by the FBI on 18 February 2001. When he was apprehended, Hallstrom was in the process of making a "dead drop" at Foxstone Park, less than a mile from his home in Fairfax

County, Virginia. Though he subsequently made a plea agreement to avoid trial for capital espionage, he never revealed his relationship with his original "handler" from the Washington, D.C., *Rezidentura,* General Dimitri Komulakov.

Dimitri Komulakov remained in Kiev, Ukraine, pursuing "business interests" until October 2000 when he returned to Moscow as a consultant to the SVR on "matters in Chechnya." The nuclear artillery round removed from At Tanf on 24 March 1998 was never recovered. No charges were ever filed against General Komulakov, and no warrant for his arrest was ever issued. In August 2001, a Top Secret CIA report entitled "Proliferation of Weapons of Mass Destruction" charged "individuals in the Russian Federation appear to have established contact with elements in the Islamic Republic of Iran for the purpose of selling Soviet-era nuclear weapons and/or fissile material to the Iranians."

Qusay Hussein blamed "dissident elements and traitors" for his failure to acquire nuclear weapons in March 1998. In December 2001, Qusay was given command of the Special Republican Guards Division in Baghdad. On 21 March 2003, when U.S. and coalition forces launched *Operation Iraqi Freedom,* he fled Iraq with more than $500 million in gold from the Iraqi National Bank.

Dr. Hiran Aranul, the head of Iraq's nuclear weapons program, was executed by firing squad on the orders of Qusay Hussein on 28 March 1998.

Captain Bruno Macklin was treated in Israel for the wounds he incurred during the At Tanf raid. He returned to London on 15 April 1998 and was awarded three and one half years' back pay and promoted to major. In a private ceremony at 10 Downing Street, he was decorated with the George Cross for "heroic action during a prolonged, sensitive assignment of vital interest to Her Majesty's government." Major Macklin's citation is classified "Secret." He has petitioned his SAS Regiment for permission to write a book about his experiences.

MI6 Officers Blackman and Thomas were both awarded the Distinguished Intelligence Medal by Queen Elizabeth II on 30 April 1998. They continue to serve in MI6.

Eli Yusef Habib and his son *Samir* successfully eluded the Syrian Army dragnet on the night of 24–25 March 1998 by driving to Damascus. They returned to their homes and families in Anah, Iraq, along the banks of the Euphrates, a week later by driving through Jordan—after picking up two truckloads of hard-to-get consumer goods at the port of Latakia. Both men remain active in the "Fellowship of Believers" and continue to ply their trade from the Mediterranean to Iran. In the spring of 2003, Eli Yusef and Samir assisted U.S. intelligence agencies in efforts to locate weapons of mass destruction in Iraq. It was Samir who subsequently contributed the information that appeared in the CIA's National Intelligence Daily: ". . . foreign intelligence sources report that Iran has recently obtained a Soviet-era nuclear artillery round and is attempting to reverse-engineer the device in an effort to build their own. North Korean scientists are said to be assisting in this effort. The CIA is unable to verify or confirm these reports."

MISSION COMPROMISED

OLIVER NORTH

with JOE MUSSER

"Oliver North's own life reads like a novel, and now he and collaborator Joe Musser have concocted with exquisite timing a sly thriller about terrorism."

—James Brady, author of *WARNING OF WAR*

ON SALE: 8/26/03

0-06-055584-X • $7.99/ $10.99 CAN.

HarperTorch
www.harpercollins.com

www.olivernorth.com